For Thérèse. Have fun. Love Beti

LORD HATHERTON'S PENNY

a novel by

Beti Hand

ISBN 9780955722141

Cover design and artwork by the author.

Dedications and Credits

Dedicated to the pottery workers whose toil made the pottery industry of the nineteenth century the source of much of the United Kingdom's wealth, but they themselves were rewarded with poverty, hardship, ill health, and lack of recognition.

Thanks are due to Paul Howard who helped me with the difficult task of revised publication, and with technical help concerning the cover as well as taking the photo on the back cover. Also thanks to Pam Sinclair who helped with the text correction.

I also recognise my debt to local friends and neighbours in North Staffordshire who have inspired me to look into the social history of this unique part of the English Midlands and its special ambience.

As always a big thank you to my family for their continuing support of my literary dreams.

Description

This is the story of the family of a pottery master in the context of the late nineteenth century. He is a rich, successful man living in a prestigious house near Stoke. His only child is a girl. He decides to train her to be the next manager of the factory to take over when he dies. This action flouts the conventional practice of local society. His wife becomes involved in the action, and a strike by the potters causes chaos which may turn into disaster. How will the family survive, and what of the future of the pottery industry, and the wealth of the master potters?

The story was the basis of a play produced in Staffordshire at several venues, and as a novel it was originally published under the title of "Hear the Pennies Fall". It has been completely revised and this edition reverts to the original name of the play.

Table of Contents

1

Cramp. Another second and it would sear through his calf muscle. Enoch stretched his leg gingerly down to the cool recesses of the bed. The eiderdown had slipped, as usual, towards his wife's side. She stirred, turned away from him, and slid back into slumber. Enoch felt her round bottom pressing into his groin, and put his hand tentatively on her right hip, gently feeling over the vastness of her curves, towards her breast. He was always amazed at how large she seemed, lying next to him. In the daytime, coming towards him, or sitting, unaware of his presence, she seemed so small and unassuming, a doll of a woman. But here, in bed, she was huge. His hand was like a little animal, a mouse, creeping over her.

Edna felt his hand, and moved. At last, he thought, at last. But nothing happened. She'd moved, but she'd said nothing. Her flesh suddenly seemed just that, flesh, not the embraceable substance of a woman.

Enoch took his arm away. That was it, wasn't it? Without speaking, Edna had made her wishes clear. He opened his eyes again, and was fully awakened by the first small promise of light through the curtains. He knew Edna would sleep for another hour, but he couldn't wait that long. What would be the point anyway?

There was a gentle thud outside in the passage, and a light rattle, then soft footsteps departing. The coal scuttle had arrived.

Why hadn't they brought it up last night? It was unbelievably bad service to be woken like this with rattling coal. It was probably that new maid. Enoch sat up, taking the bedclothes with him, and peered down at his wife's face. Still, her eyes were shut, but her gentle breathing had stopped. In fact she didn't seem to be breathing at all.

"Good morning, my wife. Will you tell the wench to bring the coal the night before, not morning time."

Edna opened her eyes to see Enoch glaring down at her. "Jeannie? It won't happen again. Did it wake you?"

"It did. And you too."

Edna kept her eyes tight shut. She realised she would have to explain to her housekeeper that the new girl wasn't learning quickly enough. She dreaded facing Deaker with anything. Since her old nanny, had become housekeeper, Edna had become less and less able to face her with any kind of criticism.

"I assure you, I had a good night's sleep."

"And would have gone on for an hour or more." Enoch rested back on his pillow. There was the familiar ache at the base of his spine. He was getting older. At the same time, he was still man enough. But it was no use. He swing his legs out of bed. "I'll be the one who decides when I wake up, in future. Not the maids, if you don't mind."

"Is it late, Enoch?"

"Of course it isn't. It's only just light now. Can't you see it? You would if you was to keep your eyes open. Open them up now, and see for yourself."

Edna's eyes fluttered open, and she made a conscious effort to wake up. The dream that she had been trying to retain, disappeared. She was aware suddenly, of the despondency with which she had gone to bed.

"Will Tilly be going with you to the factory today?"

"I told you, Edna. Do not keep on so. She'll come with me every day, unless I say otherwise."

Edna felt a lump somewhere about her midriff. She swallowed. He wasn't going to change his mind. He never did. Why had she ever hoped he would? Why did she care so much? She wouldn't care. He wouldn't see her fretting. She hunched her legs up.

"Don't speak about it again." Enoch rumbled on.

Edna put her hands over her ears, hidden by the eiderdown. She could scream, go out onto the landing, and scream. She could go on and on, like Enoch with his perpetual criticism. Perhaps she would break the glass in the belvedere, with her screaming, like that soprano woman, what was her name? Apparently she could break crystal with her high notes. So Dorothy Dawkins said. Dot had heard the singer once, at Covent Garden. How wonderful to be there, in her most beautiful dress, with a velvet cloak. At least Dorothy had had a life, before she'd had all those children. Edna had only the one child, but she hadn't had a life, not a life like Dot, holidays in London, mixing with society. The way Edna had lived, she might just as well have been a Persian lady. And now Enoch was determined to deprive her of her only source of happiness, her daughter, to learn about their business in that dreadful place, the pot bank, in Saghead. Why would Enoch never listen?

The bell was jangling down in the servants' corridor. Almost immediately there was a tap on the door. Jeannie came in.

"Good morning, sir, morning ma'am," she said, bobbing. She went straight to the grate. She built a tiny wigwam with sticks on top of the embers, still glowing from the night before, and was down on her knees, blowing. Next, she went back into the corridor, to bring in the coal.

"Bring that of a night, not in the morning." Enoch watched as she lugged the heavy scuttle. His voice was soft. "Hasn't nobody telled thee? Hasn't Deaker?"

"No sir. Yessir."

"Well, do it then."

He watched her take the tongs and carefully pile little lumps of coal. Her cheeks were glowing. "That'll do," he said, abruptly. "Get my water," he ordered, to her departing rump.

Two doors down the corridor, under the belvedere, was Tilly's bedroom. She'd been awake for ages, and by the time her hot water arrived she was already up, looking out of her window. It was a bright morning, birds were fluttering among the hawthorn trees, where the branches were already heavy with red berries. Across the meadow, down by the stream, a few tardy rabbits were still up, nibbling grass. Tilly stretched and twisted her body this way and that, looking at her reflection in the cheval mirror. Her silk robe parted to show full breasts, a small waist, then a bush of dark hair. She studied her face, peering at her nose, pressing her fingertips into her cheeks, smoothing down her eyebrows. If only she had blonde hair, and thin bones. How she envied her friend, Ros! But then, Ros would never dare to do what she was doing, going to work as her father's assistant. She wouldn't even think about it. Ros only had one aim in life to be married. At the sound of a knock Tilly hurriedly tied up her dressing gown.

"Deaker!"

A short, plump woman entered, carrying clothes over her arm.

"Mistress says you're to wear this. For the office."

"I'm wearing the black skirt. I told her. It's all pressed up ready. Jeannie did it."

"Your mama says this is more fitting. You're going with her to Mrs. Dawkins, when your Pa has finished with you."

"I see." Tilly took the clothes, and the jug of hot water, which Deaker had deposited "You should get Jeannie to bring those jugs," she said. It was getting too much for the old woman. She often heard her panting up the stairs. As she turned again towards the window, it occurred to her that things were changing. Deaker seemed suddenly to be older. And she herself was an adult. From today, she was a grown woman.

Suddenly Tilly realised why her mother wanted her to dress up. She wished the whole episode at the factory to be ignored. Really, mother was just taking her with her to pay calls, as she usually did. The short morning in the office would not be mentioned to her friends. Obviously Mother did not think they would consider it seemly for her to be working. Well, she was not ashamed of it. On the contrary, she was proud of her father, and of what he did. She'd promised to do what he wanted and she would do the best she could. For the time being anyway, until she had decided what she did want to do with her future. Her future. The words sang to her. Her future, her future. She couldn't think of a rhyme for that, future, future. Suture.....was there such a word? It sounded medical. Perhaps she would be a doctor. There were women now, who had qualified to be doctors. She left the velvet dress on the bed, and put on her black skirt.

In the morning room Enoch was breakfasting. This was the day he had been awaiting for so long, a full nine months in fact. He smiled as he wiped his moustache with a napkin. That was the time a woman took, for a baby. Of course it was. If Edna had shaped up, and given him a son, they wouldn't be going through all this. Sending a girl to the Works, indeed. It wasn't fitting, according to his wife, and all the old biddies. But he wasn't changing his mind, for all their gossip. Where he came from, girls and women, they all worked, and nothing wrong in that. His mother had been the best woman in the world, and had known all about the pottery works his own father had run. Only a few workers, true, but she'd not been too proud to get her fingers into the clay. That was the way it was.

He poured another cup out of the heavy silver tea pot, specially ordered from Sheffield. Enoch had always done the best he could for his wife. Now, she'd have to put up with the neighbours' gossip about Tilly. Besides, he'd decided, after reading about that Tay Bridge disaster, last year, he'd have to take a hold on life. We're all mortals, and no-one know what was round the corner. Here one minute, gone the next. If you yourself didn't make provision for the future, who'd would? It wasn't so much that he'd felt for the victims of the disaster, in the way that Edna had. It wasn't sorrow for them, but despair for himself. He'd realised that his future, which he'd worked so hard for, could suddenly vanish, like it had for the people drowned in the Tay. He'd made a decision that he must take his fate into his own hands, not wait for it to shake him by the scruff of the neck. Now, he would never have a son. So, his daughter would have to be a son to him. He would take her education in hand.

That was why, nine months after the railway train plunged into the Tay River, Tilly was on her way to spend a morning at her father's factory, to begin learning the business.

There was a sound of a shot from outside. Enoch went to the window. It was old Sacks from the bone mill further downstream, shooting rats. The bones brought to the mill for processing be be used in the china industry, still had flesh on them when they arrived. This attracted vermin. Enoch vowed that he would solve this problem. Fortunately, in the other direction the house looked over a wide terrace to the wood beyond.. Today there was a slight mist over the water meadow, and the tall beech trees on the opposite bank were like phantoms. Enoch felt as if he were in the middle of a secret oasis, he was the centre, and everything in the world outside was turning about this room, with its gleaming silver, and brilliant firelight. Nothing else was real but this.

An hour later, Enoch and Tilly were stepping off the tram that had brought them from the station to Manstone's Works. When they had left home, it had been a fine morning, with shafts of sunlight sprinkling leaf shadows across the gravel drive. On the journey into town every golden, brown or russet tone had hinted that autumn was here. But now, in Manstone's yard, it was winter, foggy, damp, dreary, endless, depressing. Tilly felt the sulphurous smoke at the back of her throat. She coughed a little.

"We'll get inside," Enoch said. They set off to the office steps, past three bottle kilns, which, high above the yard, and scarved in smoke, effectively blocked out all signs of daylight and morning. The driver of a dray that was being unloaded, tipped his cap to the Master, and one of the labourers, with a heavy load on his back, stood aside for Tilly. A wooden stairway led up the far wall to the outer office.

Once inside, there was a small fire burning in the grate, and Tilly extricating her hands from her muff, warmed them at the flames. Here, in this tiny room, full of dusty account books, she could feel the deep pulse of the engine which was driving the pot making machinery. She suddenly felt a flicker of excitement. This was a new world.

Enoch took Tilly's arm, and guided her in front of him, along a narrow passage. At the end was a panelled door, leading into his office. It was a small, dark room, with a window, high up. It contained a large table, a leather chair, and a glass case, in which were various highly decorated ceramic vases, dishes and plates. A swivelling bookcase held leather bound volumes, and on a lectern was an open folder of meticulously drawn patterns. Seeing all this comfort and style, Tilly felt shy, as if she was in the presence of a stranger.

"It's very fine, your office, father."

"Well, that's as may be. It's not for show. Come and see these." He took one of the leather bound volumes down. It was the latest edition of the Pottery Gazette. "I always save those. You must read them carefully, every month, young lady. All that goes on in the Potteries is set down here. You must know it all. You should make it your business to get this by heart as soon as you can. You have to know all there is, about glazes and clays, and who makes what and so on, and what the latest designs are, and what the fashions are turning to." He flicked through the pages of advertisements, articles and drawings. It all looked immensely complicated to Tilly.

"I'll do my best, Papa."

"Aye, that you will, if you're to succeed. It's no job for a simpleton. And I know you're not that. You've got to be a chemist, and an artist, and you've got to know how to manage your workers and all. And most of all, you've got to be ahead of the others. You've got to have the will to be ahead. Have you got it, my lass?" He shut the book up with a bang, and set it on the shelf, turning to her. "What do you think? Hast?"

Tilly was tongue tied for a moment, but there came a knock on the door. Almost immediately a man entered. He stopped short, startled when he saw the young lady.

"Beg pardon, Mr. Manstone. I didn't know you had company." The man was tall, thin and angular, with deep set eyes, his shoulders slightly bowed. Tilly could hardly hear what he was saying, he spoke so softly. His voice was deep. He would make a baritone, she thought, and wondered if he sang in a choir.

"Come in, Robert. I wish to introduce you to Miss Manstone. She will be learning the business. Matilda, this is Mr. Willoughby, our chief clerk. He has the running of the place, if I'm away, or out. If you're to see what we're about, there's nothing better than to start off in the office. Robert, if Miss asks any questions I can't answer, then it's up to you to put her right."

"Very good, sir," Robert nodded, looking directly at Enoch, but avoiding Tilly's eyes. "I'll do my best."

"I shall go round the works now, with Miss. There's that pattern to attend to for the Duke of Sutherland service. Take it down to Porter and see what he makes of it."

"Sir. Miss." Robert went out, closing the door quietly behind him.

Enoch began going through some papers on his desk, and Tilly remained standing beside the fire. The clerk had somehow made her feel uncomfortable. Perhaps she should have held out her hand, for him to shake. But she hadn't felt she should do that. And he hadn't appeared to be pleased to see her. Quite the opposite. She couldn't find anything to say, nothing was what she expected. Grime, and work, and dozens of people, yes, she'd imagined that, but not this, this amazing comfort and, what was it.....? Bustle and cheer, a bright glowing heart in the middle of this dreary factory. But there was something else, more subtle. She felt an energy surrounding her. She thought of her father, now, as the source of that energy. But the clerk, also, she knew he had a kind of presence too. She felt he was someone she would have to reckon with. As she stood there, in silence, watching her father, she tried to describe the feeling she had about Robert. It was as if he had been sizing her up. That was it. She did not quite like him. Well, it was too soon to decide on that. She shook herself and looked around. She'd never thought of the ordinary details of her father's life, how or where he ate, and with whom, nor indeed what he did all those hours that he was away from home. It never occurred to her that he might have a little cosy parlour of his own, for that was what this was, this office of his. His life suddenly became real to her. The sight of the big desk, the little bell on it, the people surrounding it, all served to delineate her father and bring to reality the shadowy person that he had seemed to be.

"Now then. We'll take you round. And show how it's all done."

"Will I be seeing the workers, Father?"

"Oh aye. You've got to. And listen to all their mithering."

"What mithering?"

"Oh it's nowt. There's always summat. It's to do with the penny."

"The penny?"

"Come on," Enoch said, rising from his desk and clapping his hat on again. "There's no time to waste. Your mother will be coming at lunch time sharp, so we'd best get on. We'll start off with the engine room, where it all begins." Down the stairs they went, into the yard.

For the first time in her life, Tilly beheld, close up, a steam engine at full throttle.

Raising his voice above the racket, Enoch said, "This is where it all starts. Understand this, and you're half way a potter." He pointed out the shafting and belts, which connected to the machinery in the grinding loft, and the slip house.

Tilly could hardly hear Enoch, let alone understand the mechanism, but she felt a thrill, deep down, to see the piston rod going to and fro, and to hear the thin whistle of escaping steam. Enoch explained to her how the raw materials were processed. She glanced up into the grinding loft, then they emerged into the slip house itself. The combination of filters, arks and mills produced, at the end, pure and malleable clay. There was plenty of dust, the noise was intense, and the workers dirty and often ragged, especially the youngsters, boys and girls, but Tilly felt a kind of awe, similar to what she had felt once before, when she'd heard the Ceramic Male Voice Choir in full throat. There was a force here, expertise, virile excitement. Afterwards, when they visited the other workshops, where the clay was worked, and then decorated, the magic stayed with her. This was what it was all about, the creation of beautiful and useful things. Last of all, they went past the kilns, and Tilly felt the warm bricks of the bottle ovens with her hands and watched the ovenmen shovelling coal, their backs muscly and slick with sweat.

Mrs. Manstone came early to collect Tilly. She was with Enoch in the decorating shop, and when Tilly left with her mother the girls went on with their work in silence. They had an order to get through before knocking off time, dinner plates, and it took all their concentration.

Mrs. Manstone told Tom to drive the carriage straight to Leason's and the two women entered the emporium, the most modern and largest establishment in Saghead. A uniformed assistant took Mrs. Manstone's cloak, and Tilly's mantle.

"May I know your pleasure, Ma'am?"

"I wish to see some good Scottish tweed, suitable for a walking coat for my daughter, and some silks, for blouses."

The ladies were ushered to a long mahogany counter, behind which stood two more servants of the drapery, wearing frock coats.

Tilly stood for a while, taking in the costly and lavish accoutrements of the shop. There were two more counters stretching along the other walls, and behind all of them were shelves, laden with bales of cloth. Above were two gas chandeliers, both fully lit although it was still daylight outside. In one corner was a small glazed booth, within which, on a high stool, sat a young woman. Her eyes caught Tilly's momentarily, but she then averted them to the ledger in front of her. Another working woman, as well as the paintresses, Tilly thought. It wasn't just servants' jobs or factory work which were available for women, that was obvious. Why was Mother making such a fuss about her working?

In the far corner was a staircase, with a highly polished, turned, balustrade, leading to a narrow gallery. The walls up there were fitted out with yet more shelves full of material.

There was so much, almost too much. Tilly had never been into such a shop before. Previously her dresses had been made by Mrs. Manstone's dressmaker, and she herself had never been expected to choose the cloth. Now, her mother was treating her like an adult, and giving her some choice.

The assistant gave an order to one of the other attendants, who brought over three huge bales of material, and deposited them onto the counter. Mrs. Manstone fingered each bale in turn, rubbing the cloth between her forefinger and thumb, and stroking the hairy surface of the tweed. "We'll try this," she said, at last. The man immediately unwound several yards from the bale. There was a muffled thud as it was bumped over to unwind the cloth, which then slid in a slippery stream along the counter. Mrs. Manstone took hold of one end, and held it between her two hands.

"Now, let me see." Edna held some material under Tilly's chin. "Turn round. "As Tilly swivelled, her mother wrapped the cloth length round her. "Quite nice. Yes, quite good. What do you think, dear?"

Tilly said nothing. She felt the eyes of the young man on her, and she realised the cashier was also looking. "I don't know, Mama. It might be too....."

"Too what? Bright?"

"Yes. I don't know. More..."

"Something a little more subfusc, ma'am?" the assistant interposed.

"That's it," said Tilly. How had he known, just like that, and Mama hadn't realised what she wanted?

"Would Madam like to try this?" With a series of deft flicks of his wrist, the salesman had another few yards of a different tweed unrolled on top of the first. In a moment, Tilly was unwound, then shawled again with the replacement.

"Now then, what do you think?" Edna was beginning to feel tired. A pain was starting over her right eye, as it did, often, nowadays. Sitting on this stool was not at all comfortable. She had looked forward to this expedition, it had made the day seem less awful. Why could not Tilly enjoy it? It had been a complete mistake to bring the girl. Tilly was always setting herself up like this. She hadn't even worn the velvet dress which had been suggested for today. No, she had to have her own way, just like her papa. She was becoming more and more like him. Not long ago she would have been quite satisfied to have her clothes chosen for her, as was customary. Why, in fact, had she decided to give Tilly her head? Was she being swayed by Enoch's strange idea, that Tilly was a grown woman now? What nonsense.

"I don't know, Mama. I can't see. You choose. As long as it isn't..."

"A little darker, Miss? I have just the thing." Once more the young man addressed Tilly directly. Without waiting for an answer, he went straight to the end of the counter, and hauled down a fresh bale of cloth. He was back at the point of departure before Tilly had been able to utter a word. Again, she was divested and invested with the flowing material.

She stood for a moment, gazing at herself. Whatever she had, she knew it wouldn't make any lasting difference to her look. She'd still have that dark, bushy hair, which she hated, and the heavy brows.

"Perfect, Mama. it's perfect." She flung the length of cloth back on the counter, and moved abruptly aside.

"But it's very dark, dear. I preferred the first."

"This will do very well indeed. It's just what I want." Tilly heard herself saying these words. The young man was looking at her, and she smiled. "In fact it's exactly what I had in mind." She stressed the word 'exactly', glancing at her mother, and began to smooth out the wrinkles in her gloves.

"Really?" Mrs. Manstone stifled a small sigh. "Well, if you're sure." It was obvious Tilly did not know how to go shopping. She hadn't even looked properly at the pattern, and fancy being foisted off with that dull colour. Well, at least, she herself wouldn't have to see it, if the girl was to wear it at the office.

"It'll be just perfect for the Works," Tilly said.

Edna began to blush. She could feel it coming up, and spreading all over her cheeks and neck. The assistant, and that woman in the cash desk, must surely have seen it. The more she tried to control her feelings, the more the rosy flush would be obvious. It suddenly seemed unbearably hot in the shop. She would have to give in to Tilly, and get out into the fresh air. "Six yards," she said. "And we'll need some lining." How could Tilly reveal to all and sundry the secret of where she would be wearing the coat? All the assistants would think she was just a little clerk somewhere. No better than them, really. Well, it was done now. Edna looked straight at the young assistant.

"Of course, Ma'am. If I may send for the cutter. We can perhaps take the measurements." The man glided away.

There were no other customers in the shop. Mrs. Manstone reflected with relief that Tilly's remarks about the office might not go further than these four walls. Then she realised that everyone would soon know about Tilly's forthcoming employment at the factory, because she, Tilly, had no intention of keeping it a secret. Really, Enoch and the girl were a strange pair. They just seemed to go their own way. How was it that Tilly had grown up like that, when she had never given any trouble, as a young girl?

"Your father wouldn't mind, you know, if you didn't go. He wouldn't, and we could have a riding coat made from the cloth." Edna's voice was low and urgent, as she stretched out her hand to Tilly. "Then we could have lots of time together.... shopping....and other things."

Tilly sat still, unable to speak. "He would," she managed to say.

"You could do your painting, and walking...and everything." Edna's voice faded.

"It's no good, Mama. I am doing it. And father would mind, you know he would. In any case, I don't like shopping. You know, don't you?"

Edna sighed and accepted Tilly's choice. All the arrangements were made for the new clothes.

By the time Tom returned to Leason's with the carriage, there was a miasma hanging over the pot bank chimneys, turned sickly yellow from the glaring gaslights which had already been lit. At half-past two, it seemed evening was coming on already. Mr. Manstone would take the train home later.

"Straight back, Tom." Edna ordered. Turning to Tilly she added. "We'll leave the call to till another day."

The horses set off at a spanking trot, no doubt aware in of the chopped carrots, oats, and bran already ladled into the mangers by George. At Terrilea, Jean was lighting fires, and Pedley, the daily cook, was overseeing vegetable preparation for the evening dinner. Deaker, in the garden, was gathering a few late roses for Mrs. Manstone's dressing table. "No point in saving any," she told herself. "They won't last now." She reached to cut the highest flowers. One of these nights, very soon, there would be a frost. And then, they'd all die. She looked up at the sky. No sign of fog here, but it was colder. She shivered and went inside.

To come home, Tom took a short cut through back streets. Both women held handkerchiefs over their mouths and noses to protect them from the acrid smoke in the atmosphere. The factories were interspersed with low, red brick terraces of houses, where the fires had already been lit, adding to the pollution from the factories. The horses had to slow down on account of the ruts in the road, the press of wheeled vehicles, and the pedestrians pushing loads. Tilly caught a glimpse of an open market, where lanterns hung over stalls of vegetables, bread, pastries, and cheese. It was slow progress through the throngs of people, and it wasn't until they reached a main street again that the surface was cobbled and there were pavements. But here, tramlines went down on one side, and Tom checked the horses, to slow them down. A bare-foot boy with a basket of apples on his head, gestured to them to buy some from him.

"Shouldn't we have some, Mama?"

"Certainly not. We've plenty of our own."

The boy gave them a sullen look, and Tom turned off the main road again. Once more they were in narrow streets of terraced houses. Shawled women, some with babies on their backs, were hurrying along, carrying jugs and baskets, evidently from the market. Tilly huddled up closer to her mother, and Edna tucked the rug tightly round their knees. Peering into the kitchens of little houses, Tilly could see lamps lit in the shadowy rooms, and in one, racks of ghostly washing put to dry. In another, a woman was standing by a coal range, rocking a baby. Tilly shuddered.

"Cold, dear? We'll soon be home. Father shouldn't have kept you so long."

"I'm not tired, Mama." It was the sight of that woman's face, the one with the baby. Her skin was yellow, and round her thin face, her greasy hair, wispy. Tilly had a feeling she had never had before. It was in her stomach, but it wasn't like a sickness. She felt empty and slightly nauseous. Now, she shut her eyes and swallowed hard.

By the time Edna came back from Saghead, she had a bad headache, and Deaker advised her to have hot milk and go to bed early. She felt a sore throat coming on, and was only too glad to miss dinner and lie in bed watching the firelight flicker on the ceiling.

"It's that time of year," Deaker had said. "It's no good thinking to stay out late, getting cold and shivery. I'll see Miss Tilda don't stay up late, neither. You've both had a long day."

"I wish Mr. Manstone didn't have this notion about Tilly, Deaker."

"It do seem strange, though I say it." The old nurse shrugged her shoulders. "But there, they've got to have their way."

"If I'd had a boy, none of this would be happening." Edna's face was pale. Her head was aching. Why did she have to suffer so? Everything was going wrong. She huddled in bed, drawing the cover up over her ears. She didn't want to listen to the old woman. She always went on so. Edna knew just what she would say.

"Can't be helped now. Don't dwell on it, it's God's will, and there's an end of it." Deaker went out. It was pointless the Missus moithering like this. The Doctor had made it clear that she was to have no more babies, after Tilly was born. That was the way it was, and it wasn't a bad thing, for a woman. One child....Miss Tilly. And she'd brought her up properly, a good girl, though she'd always shown a will of her own. Downstairs, she paused a moment outside the dining room door. She could hear Mr. Manstone's voice.

"Your mother's not well, but I trust your day at the Works hasn't put you out of sorts."

"I enjoyed it Papa. It's good to understand, a little, about what you do." Tilly watched her father's face light up. This surprised her. After all, he'd never apparently wanted to divulge anything about his life at work. She couldn't remember her parents ever discussing anything about the factory.

Deaker moved along the passage. It didn't seem right for Tilly to be going into the business. Poor treasure, it wasn't the life for a young lady. The potters were a rough lot, she'd heard tales of them working late, and then staying on, sleeping on the factory floor, young lads and lasses all together. Surely that couldn't be happening in Mr. Manstone's works, but she had heard tell. It wasn't fitting for a young lady. There was only one thing for it, she'd have to marry someone who understood the business, and then he'd run it for her. The old housekeeper went off up the backstairs, to her own room.

In the dining room, Enoch went on with his conversation. "You'll find Willoughby a good worker. He's learned the business quickly and he'll tell you anything. If I don't have time. They taught him a lot, in his previous position.

"Where was he before, Father? "Tilly was tired and only half interested in what her father was saying about Robert Willoughby.

"In a law office. Don't know why he came up to the Potteries. Perhaps he didn't...."

Enoch was just about to explain something about Robert's past, which was common knowledge, but he stopped.

Tilly noticed his hesitation. It seemed he didn't want to talk about the clerk. Perhaps he found him as disagreeable as she did. She changed the subject.

"Shall you be going to the Dickens lecture, father? On the 24th. Mama wishes to reserve some tickets."

"Where? Your mother omitted to tell me."

"The Town Hall. Reverend Francis Morgan, from Australia, is giving it. Mr. Wiseman is in the chair."

"Wiseman, eh?" Enoch had seen Wiseman the day before, when he had been on the train coming home. Wiseman was a magistrate, and they had been commiserating with each other about the increase in the incidence of poaching now that the winter was coming on.

"Will you come? Mama would like it, I know."

Enoch frowned, put down his napkin, and pushed away his plate. "I don't know, Dickens, he's not my.......well I don't have so much patience with all that."

"But it's interesting, isn't it, an Australian? To read one of our famous authors. Why do you think that is?"

"He's a cleric, isn't he? I suppose he's one of those philanthropists. Don't know which side his bread is buttered."

"Yes." Tilly gave up. Her father wasn't going to agree to go to the lecture, she could see. He'd probably already decided what he was going to do on that night, and it didn't include Dickens. But she would go with her mother. Seeing those dismal streets and gloomy houses this morning had made her think of what Dickens had described. Of course London was no longer like that, she supposed. But from what she'd seen today, nothing much had changed in this part of the country. She put her table napkin in its silver ring. "I'll go upstairs, father, if you don't mind."

"You go, go on. Don't forget, you're coming again with me, Friday."

"Certainly, father." She went round to his chair, bent down, and he kissed her on the forehead.

Enoch took a cigar out of his waistcoat and lit up. Good girl, Tilda was, if she didn't get spoiled with any new-fangled ideas. Do-gooders, they were, reformers in general. They didn't know anything about trade and economics. If they had, they wouldn't talk rubbish. No doubt this cleric from Australia would have some nonsense to say on the subject. But Tilly was level-headed. She wouldn't be taken in by a lot of sentimentality. She was sharp too. Or she would have been, if she'd been a boy. He got up, and stared into the fire.

Later that same evening, while Enoch was dozing in his study, Robert, in the Manstone pot bank at Saghead, was just making ready to leave the factory. He's worked late, to finish a register he was making of spoiled ware, and the reasons for it. Out of a certain amount of clay, one should expect a certain number of finished articles. In that way, by adding on labour costs, the wholesale price of ware could be ascertained. That would help him in the current debate about wages. However, the amount of spoiled ware seemed to vary from time to time and he was trying to understand why. By keeping better records he hoped he could solve the mystery. Was it wholly due to variations in clay quality, or was it the fault of one of the processes, and the workers engaged in that? Also, he needed to be sure that goods classed as seconds, really were seconds. What was the specific fault, which condemned them? By rights all seconds should be broken. But he knew that a lot of them were sold on, by the very managers who had found fault in them. Even Mr. Manstone had had some of them, although the workers would not be paid. If there was any flaw, when a piece came out of the kiln, no-one, all along the line, would get their money. It was a wicked tradition that only ware "good-from-oven" was paid for. That was the sort of anomaly the Union was trying to sort out. "It's not paid for, because it's not been passed as 'good-from-oven.' But it's good enough for him to put on his mantel piece." Rob said to himself, as he went through the figures again and again.

It would soon be Saturday. In the evening he was going to meet his friend Dick Chambers, and they'd do some singing together. Then they were going down to the Union meeting at Drury House. They'd have another thrash at this 'good-from-oven' racket.

Robert wiped his pen and blotted his figures. He stretched and looked out over the yard. Gas lamps shone onto the wet cobbles, and there was an orange glow through the mist, where the smoke was still pouring out from one of the kilns. He ran his fingers through his thick hair, then sniffed at them. There was a faint smell, the result of Manstone smoking cigars all day long. He hated the man for that, each cigar costing as much as Enoch paid him for half a day's work. He went into Manstone's office, straightening his tie in the mirror over the fireplace. His collar, clean on this morning, was now soiled. He took it off, loosening it from the collar stud at back and front, put it in his pocket, then wrapped his muffler tight round his throat. He didn't want to emphasise his rank when he met his friends later on. In front of the mirror, he sang a note, then the scale. He came down the scale, then sang fifths and thirds.

Robert locked up the offices, then clattered down the stairs, to inspect each of the different workshops in turn. The engine that drove the blunger and pugmill had been stopped. He had to make sure everyone had gone home. Now, there was no more noise of grinding, no more banging of clay being wedged, no more shouts for moulds. The women's work was finished too, they'd gone to catch the late markets, though by this time in the week there was precious little money left in their purses. The decorating shop was empty. Rob's candle lit up the rows of chimney pieces ready for the glost firing.

No-one was about, until Robert went outside again into the yard. At last he came to the shed by the biscuit kiln. Two ovenmen were sitting smoking.

Rob went in. “What time is it out, Dan?” He asked a little bent man, with a lined face and sparse hair.

The old man took his long clay pipe out of his mouth. “Why dost ask? Tha knows ‘tis ten.”

“I want you to come to Union meeting Saturday.”

“Master’s in favour of Arbitration, I heerd. That’ll get us no road.”

“Beeston’s reet. Arbitration will get us nowhere. They plan to take us, like they said.” Dan’s son chimed in.

“Owen’s not in favour, but he sees there’s no other way. They’ll do what they want, and we won’t have a say, otherwise.”

Silence greeted this remark. Robert pressed on. “We have to show strength. They’ll lower the wages again, if we don’t. Come Martinmas, they’ll put ‘em down. It’s not just we won’t get that penny back “

“That penny Lord Aitch took off us! That should never have been taken off in the first place! Arbitration, my foot!” Dan flared up.

“It’ll be worse. I want you to come.” Robert put his hand in his pocket and extricated the great key for the main doors to the tunnel, which connected the yard to the road outside. Handing it to Dan, he momentarily pressed his hand. “Be there.”

Rob walked off down the road, his eyes on the ground. Sometimes he felt his ideas were floundering in a sea of mud and he would be pulled down into the sludge himself. It was anger which kept him going. Through the circumstances of his birth, not knowing who his father was, he felt himself to be between two worlds, not a Master, but not a lowly paid clerk either. Working in the Potteries, and seeing the poverty, ignorance, and ill health of the workers, he burned with a determination to better their lot, and in the process, to bring the Masters down. The particular master in question was Enoch Manstone.

Hurrying through the market, where there were still folk waiting about for bargains as the stall holders shut up for the night. Robert spotted the hanging lantern of a pie seller. “My usual, Amos,” he said. He stood for a moment surveying the busy scene. Gas lamps were flaring on the main road at the end of the street. Oil lamps were swinging off the stalls. There was a smell of vegetable refuse, mixed with drains, and coal fires. The air was clearer than it had been earlier on as some of the bottle kilns had been damped off.

Looking up, he could see a few dim stars. He thought about the visit paid to the Works by young Miss Manstone. A well-built girl, but not pretty, in the normal way. Still, there was something about her. A bright eye. He sensed she had a mind of her own. She’d kept looking at him. More like her Dad, than her Ma. These dark ones, there was something about them. Her mother though, she had been a beauty, still was, in spite of her age. Probably in her late thirties.... Manstone didn’t deserve a woman like that. But she seemed twittery and nervous, the way she kept smoothing her dress, and fiddling with her bonnet. Probably she got all her comforts from religion, he couldn't imagine old Manstone doing much good for her.

As Robert munched his pie, he thought about the day. He hadn't seen Gertie in the decorating shop when he'd been up there earlier on. If she didn't come tomorrow, he'd have to go round and see what was up. Maybe her mother had had a turn for the worse. Also he could confirm they'd be meeting as usual, on Sunday. Perhaps that Miss Matilda, Tilly as old Manstone called her, would keep coming to the office. Manstone had set his mind on it. Robert was whistling as he put the key in the door of his lodgings. The walk home had lifted his spirits. He'd sit down for a while, and read before going to bed. He began to feel, maybe he was getting somewhere at last.

2

By Saturday, Edna's cold was better. Before going to work Enoch told her he would not be going to the Dickens's lecture the following month.

"But Mrs. Dawkins, and Rosalind, are going, I suppose?"

Edna peered out of the bedclothes at him putting on his jacket. She closed her eyes, murmuring "Perhaps." She didn't care if Enoch came or not. She'd got used to him not coming to things with her. She watched his muscular back as he lifted his arms, brushing his hair, first on one side, and then on the other But when he came to give her a good-bye kiss, she pretended to be asleep. When his soft beard tickled her cheek it smelled stale. She closed her eyes more tightly and he was gone.

Edna's friend, Mrs. Dawkins, and Rosalind came to tea. Tilly had a chance for a short walk with her friend. They went along the path by the walled garden, and then through the wood until they came to some stone steps that led into a wild valley. Rhododendrons and other shrubs had been planted along the edge of the path, but otherwise nature had been allowed to run riot. The path itself had been swept clear of leaves, but it was slippery. After a short way, the path climbed again, up a flight of stone steps to a steep knoll, where Enoch had planted young beech trees when he had bought the house. Their foliage was now Autumnal shades and interspersed were young holly and yew bushes. Through the gaps in the trees could be seen, on one side, open fields, and on the other, the house, surrounded by neat lawns and gravel paths.

It was sunny and warm. The girls sat down on a cast iron bench, which had been placed at the vantage point.

"Now, tell me about your visit to the Works."

"I suppose it was all right. You know, Ros, Papa is funny."

"Funny?"

"I didn't realise. But he's so strange in the factory. He seems somehow involved, in a way he isn't when he's at home. It's as if he's really interested."

"I've never been to my Father's office. Well, I did, once, when Cousin Richard was starting."

"It's different in a lawyer's office. All the people... well, you know..."

"More like us, you mean?"

"That's just it. But, going to the Works. All those women. And the men too. They don't look at you, you know. They just look at what they're doing. And if anyone says anything to them, like Father, they still don't look. There was just one of them, different. He's the clerk.

He looks at father. He watches him. But he doesn't look at me. It's very curious, though because I feel as if he's watching."

"He doesn't sound nice. My father doesn't seem different in his office. But, anyway, there are common people, workmen, in the office sometimes. So Richard says, he's a poor cousin of mine. Fancy, even in their best rig, they, well, they need a wash. I couldn't stand what he does, talking to all those criminals, the ones he sees anyway."

"I don't see how you can say that, Ros. I thought he was involved in civil disputes. Masters and men, and such like."

"That's what I mean. They shouldn't be making a fuss. They contract to work, don't they? Then they try to get out of it. That's not honest, is it?"

Tilly said nothing but gazed into the canopy of bright colours, which was penetrated by broad shafts of sunshine.

"Have you ever thought about things, Ros? You know, why we're here, and all that?"

"No, probably not," Ros said, stretching out her muddy boot. "I think that things are as they are, for a reason. We can't understand what that reason is, but if you believe in God, you know it's all right." Ros was surprised at herself. She turned towards her friend, then smiled and stretched out both her arms, arching her back. "Anyway, I'm not going to worry about any of that till I'm married. Then I'm going to have lots of children, like Mama."

"That's right." Then you won't have any time to think about anything, Tilly added silently to herself. Not that Ros ever thought serious thoughts, as far as she knew. "I wish I was like you,"

"You're better than me. You've got lots of brains, and you like reading, and discussing and all those things."

"I would like to be like you, just the same. Who wants to be brainy and all that, when they could be beautiful, and jolly?"

There was the sound of a bell being rung, and, looking towards the house, they could see Jeannie on the terrace.

"Don't be silly, Til. You are beautiful. Everyone is beautiful in their own way. Anyway we're all different. That's the point." They stood up and waved, and the maid went in again, with the bell. "I don't want you ever to say that again. Comparing us." Ros put her arms round her friend and they stood like that for a moment. Then she turned down the path. Tilly lagged behind her, scuffing up the leaves with her buttoned boots. Ros always had an answer, and it was always 'God.' She was a bit like Deaker. What did they know, what did anyone know, what it was all about? Besides she was prettier. What was the point of denying it? That wasn't honest.

"We won't go through the kitchen, so we can change our boots before Deaker sees them."

They crept in by the side door, and took their places, in clean shoes, at the dining room table. Tilly was silent. She was still pondering about their conversation in the beech wood. Why wasn't she like Ros? As sure of her future as she was? What had made her different? Was it the visit to the factory? And why hadn't she been able to tell Ros about all those work people, and the poor people in the streets, and in those tiny houses?

Edna noticed her daughter's abstracted air. There she was, off in one of her daydreams, and frowning. That was the way to get lines on her forehead. She clapped her hands suddenly. "Eat up, before they get cold."

Tilly turned her attention to her muffin and jam.

A few days later, Tilly had been asked by her mother to help with a household job. Deaker and Jeannie were to bring all the linen to the sewing room, sort and count it. Tilly was to inspect it all and enter up the revised list into the linen register. She had helped her mother with this task last year, and Mrs. Manstone said at breakfast that if Tilly was old enough to help her father at the Works, then she was old enough to learn about housekeeping.

Accordingly, Tilly was sitting at the sewing table with notebook and pencil, while Deaker stood by the growing pile of linen on the chest. Jeannie kept on coming in with more piles of sheets, pillowcases, napkins, and towels.

"There's six of these swan towels, the big ones, and there's those four of the face, to match," said Deaker.

"Why's that not six of each?"

"Well, you know how it is with face towels, Miss Tilly, as well as I do."

"So we've lost two this year, since January, I mean?"

"Yes."

Tilly wrote down the revised figure. What was it all about, all this counting and checking? She might as well be in the factory. Yesterday Robert had been showing her how to enter up the register of seconds he'd just instituted.

"Is there much more, Deaker?"

"Bless you, Miss. Not so much now. There's just the sheets to go through. And Jeannie and me will have to fold them again."

"Why can't it be done at the time? Why do we have to do it like this? All at one go?"

"This is the way it always is done. Has been since your Mama was a tiny babe, at Longacre."

Deaker stooped to the chest again.

"So you've done this twice a year, since then. Thirty-five years?"

"No, no, not at all. I was Nanny to madam. It was her mother and the housekeeper that counted the linen." Deaker went on unfolding and inspecting bath towels.

"I wonder what it's like going on doing all the same things year after year. Don't you get bored with it, ever, Deaker?" Tilly tried to think of the old woman as a plump young girl, a nurse, with Mama as a tiny baby in a shawl. It was impossible. She must always have looked as she did now.

"Nothing's boring if it's a good, worthwhile job. That's what life is, doing a good job, well."

"Papa has told me I have to learn the business. That's so I can take over, or at least know what's involved, if I marry a man who'll take Papa's place. What do you think, Deaker, do you think it's strange? No other girls like me do it, do they?"

"It's all according, Miss."

"According to what?"

"According to God's will, Miss Tilly. If he's called your Papa to treat you like a son, well, it must be right. You're to accept it and do your best. Have you said your prayers about it?"

"Of course I have. Every night." Tilly was silent for a while, waiting for Deaker to give her another number. She watched the old woman carefully, stretching the towels out, and matching the corners exactly. "And do you know what I say?"

"No. I don't, Miss. Now don't be fired up."

"I say thank you. Thank you, Lord, because I really, really want to do it. I really do want to work for Father. In fact, if you really want to know....." Tilly threw down the pencil and pad and walked over to the window.

Deaker put the last towel on the pile. "I don't know whether I do. You sound as if you might not like to tell me - do you?" There was no answer. Deaker sighed and went up to the girl. She grimaced at Jeannie, who went out of the door to collect more piles. Deaker put out her hand towards Tilly. "Tell your old nurse. You're still my baby. Just as much as your dear Ma is."

"I'm not. I'm not your baby." Tilly shook off the old woman's hand, and pressed her mouth and nose hard against the window pane. "I'm me. And I want to be me. Not anybody's baby." Tilly stopped short.

"What is it, my lamb? Can't you tell me? I want to know if you want to tell me. What is it?"

"I want to go to the factory, not just because of Papa. It's because I really want to learn something. Does that surprise you?"

"No. I knew from the start, when you were just a tot, that you'd have your own ideas about things. But it won't make you happy. However much you learn, you'll never find it's enough. You can look in books, and go to talks, and in the end, you still won't know why we're here, and what we're supposed to be doing. You've just got to make the best of it, in the long run. And have faith. Faith. That's all there is."

"You are just like Ros. I knew you'd say that. I want to do things, because I believe in them for myself. Not just accept what other people have told me."

"But that's what reading does for you, in the long run. It just tells you what other people think. In the end, you have to make up your own mind. You will go to the factory, if you've a mind to. But you may find there's not so much very different. It's as much checking and re-checking, I'll be bound, with them scoundrels. That's what some of they potters are. But that won't change your mind, I doubt. You'll have your way." Deaker went back to the chest.

"I want to find out. I just want to find out. Is that such a crime?" Tilly's voice was so low that Deaker could hardly hear her.

At that moment, Jeannie came in with another huge armful of linen. In a muffled voice from behind the wobbly pile, she said,

"That's it, Mrs. Deaker. Shall I start taking them back?"

"You may as well. Miss Tilly and I will soon have these finished." The old woman glared in Tilly's direction, then took the linen off Jeannie, and placed it carefully on the few remaining flat surfaces in the room. All the flowery coverings of the chairs, and the chest, were hidden under starched white mountains like fruit cakes under icing.

Tilly dragged herself despondently away from the window. She put her arm round Deaker's waist, and hugged her. "I suppose I'd better help you finish." She sat down on the stool, and retrieved her book and pencil. "999 sheets, 2000 pillowcases. Is that what you said?"

"Get on with you! Such nonsense."

Half an hour later, the notebook was up to date, and Tilly was free to go out at last. She hurried to put on her boots, and in a few moments was running down the steps into the field. She stood on the little brick bridge over the stream and watched the water swirling and eddying. She took in deep breaths, and flung her arms sideways. She was free, free. She smiled, and shouted, hearing her voice echoing off the wooded bank beyond the water. She shouted again, listening to the answering whoops. It was as if someone else was there. But it was all right. No-one would hear her.

Then she stopped shouting and began wandering along the margin of the stream. She wasn't free. Not really. In a few weeks' time she would be at the factory nearly every morning. And even when she was at home, she wouldn't be free. There would always be things, things, things, like the sheets, to be looked after, counted, and worried about.

Clothes, sheets, things. Was that all there was...things, things, and more things?

Suddenly she was aware of an amazing flash of colour, which came, and went, almost like an explosion, blue, blue, brilliant blue, dipping and darting along the water. A kingfisher! It must be.

Thrilled, Tilly ran to the point where the bird had disappeared. But there was no sign of it.

As a result of choosing the cloth and pattern for Tilly's new costume, Edna wished for a new winter coat for herself. She had brought a swatch of samples back with her from the drapers, and had laid them on the dining room table. Deaker, who had on her afternoon apron, was leaning over Edna's shoulder.

"What do you think of this?" Edna asked, "Feel it." She passed a square of heavy cloth to the housekeeper, who took it between her thumb and index finger.

"That's nice, that is. Mr. Manstone would be ever so pleased. It's your colour."

"Or this?" Edna passed another sample.

"He'll have to make it up to you. Now he's taking Miss Tilly away. He'll agree, I'll be bound."

Edna sprang up, and walked to the window. "I wish I was so sure, Deaker. " She turned. "I never do know."

"Of course he will. He knows he owes you. Trust your old nurse. For sure, he'll want to treat you, he will."

"I wish I didn't have to ask him. I wish he would...just suggest something. Sometimes. I honestly don't think he notices at all, what I'm wearing."

"Of course he does notice. He just don't say it. Your Ma, now, she had a knack. She could get anything she wanted, didn't have so much as to look at it, and it was there. Wonderful, she was."

"Perhaps it was my Pa himself who was so different."

"No, he wasn't. No man is different. True, I've not been married, but I know it, only too well. They're all of a piece. They need handling. Your man, God bless him, he is a good one. You just got to make him think it was his idea first." Deaker sighed, smoothing the piece of cloth. "Not that I haven't told you that often enough."

"Well, it was his idea, about Matilda. I can't even consider it without trembling. Look." Edna held her hand out, and stretched the fingers. True enough, her hand was shaking. "What am I going to do?" She began gathering all the samples from the slippery polished table. "I can't bear to talk to Mrs. Dawkins now. She thinks we're doing something terrible."

"She shouldn't be the judge. It's the Lord above us, who should be the judge. Come now, you sit here, while I go and see if Jeannie's put the kettle on." She held the chair for Edna, who sat down on it, resting her head on her hand.

Deaker put her arm lightly round her Mistress' shoulder. She couldn't abide seeing her poor lady like this. "It's decided now. It doesn't bear fretting about. Happen Mr. Manstone will come to his senses soon enough. We canna tell what there is in the future, nor should we try." She went out of the door, and after a moment, Edna began fingering the piece of cloth, again. She felt slightly sick. She'd been out of sorts, this last week or two. She'd been expecting her period, she recognised the signals. But it hadn't come. A few times recently, it had been late, and once, she'd missed altogether. Perhaps it wouldn't come again, ever. That would mean she wasn't a woman any more. She'd be old, finished, just waiting to die, and be gathered to her ancestors, as they said. Sometimes, she thought she wouldn't mind that. Life seemed interminable and empty, now Tilly was gone. Virtually gone.

The mantel clock was ticking, there was a slight murmur from the fire burning in the grate. A figure passed by the window. It was a tall, strong looking man, wearing a waistcoat over his shirt, and pushing a barrow full of bricks along the gravel path outside. His brown arms were muscular, and his short blond hair was stuck to his forehead with sweat.

When Jeannie came in, with the tea things, her mistress was standing by the window, looking at the builder, and his labourer, who were working on a large hole that had been made in the lawn. The older man was beginning to arrange bricks in a circle in the hole, while the man with the barrow repeatedly emptied more bricks into a pile, and disappeared round the house, to collect another load.

"Put it on the table, Jeannie," Edna said. When the maid withdrew, she filled her cup with tea, then drank it, watching the labourers. The older man was silent, completely absorbed in his work, choosing bricks, and placing them in a long curve. The young man was whistling as he went back for more supplies, but on the return journey, his mouth was slightly open, and his tongue protruded a little between his teeth.

Edna suddenly became aware that the men had realised that she was watching them. The old man had glanced in her direction, and then touched his cap, saying something to his assistant. He, too, then glanced momentarily at Edna, and caught her eye.

She felt herself blushing. A flush was creeping all over her body. The young man had looked at her, and she had responded in a way that she hardly ever did nowadays, with Enoch.

Understanding all this, she now experienced a shock so strong, it made her short of breath. She put the cup down, and it rattled in the saucer. She must turn away, leave the room at once. Then she thought of Enoch. Why had he decided to have her precious lawn dug up for the purpose of making that grotesque fountain? She remembered his saying something about this plan a few weeks ago. She had opted to stay silent. There was little point in arguing. He was always spending money on these grandiose schemes. Why didn't he spend the money on hiring a manager for the Works, instead of stealing away their only child away to do such unsuitable work?

Looking in the mirror above the fireplace, Edna could still see the men at work, and she bent her forehead on the marble mantelpiece. "He's nobody," she said to herself, but she could feel her heart beating. "He's just a hired man," she said, and she was the mistress. Indeed, she was the mistress. He was in her domain, and she could do anything. She could stop his work, order him to do anything, and he would do it. If she wanted to, she could watch him.

She went back to the window.

Both men were now down in the hole, with their backs to her. The barrow had been propped neatly against the trunk of the cedar tree. The brick circle was growing fast, perfectly formed, as the old man measured, and set the bricks. The young man was watching intently. One day, he would be in charge. He would be the master, with an apprentice. Edna watched, too, as the circle grew. They were clever, these men, and they had a skill, and an interest.

The sick feeling in her stomach was worse. She envied the men. They were out there, doing their job, and doing it well. She was in here, lonely and bereft. Yes, she was bereft. The tears came into her eyes as she thought of herself, standing in the huge room, in this vast house, with no-one at all, in the whole world, who loved her, properly, as she deserved to be loved.

3

The sunset that evening at Terrilea heralded several days of fine weather. But October came in with rain, and by November winter had truly arrived. In the Potteries it began to get dark at two-thirty, and by three-thirty all the gaslights were on, and a second scuttle of coal had been brought in to make up the fire in Enoch's office at the Works. It was two months since Tilly had begun work at the office though she was still only expected to come for half days. Manstone's gig collected her at twelve-thirty, and she either joined her mother to make a few calls in Saghead, followed by a little desultory shopping, or she was taken straight home to take luncheon in the morning room at Terrilea.

So by half-past three Rob was alone in the anteroom to Enoch's office The connecting door between master and clerk was open, but there was no fireplace in Rob's domain, and draughts whistled round his ankles and knees as he sat on his high stool, hunched up over the ledger. However he seemed oblivious to the cold, frowning as he concentrated on some spidery notes which Miss Tilly had written in the margin, beside various entries. Next to "paint for window frames" she had pencilled 'Which' with a question mark beside the amount 'three shillings.' Then further down, on the credit side of the account, was the entry 'two seconds candlesticks... 5/– each.' Tilly had pencilled 'Where to? No trace in sales ledger.'

This was Rob's Day Book, and was supposed to be a record of petty cash amounts. Obviously Tilly had been going through it with a fine tooth comb, checking on every transaction. He pulled out a new sheet of paper, and proceeded to make a list of all these queries, and of his answers to them. It irked Robert to have to do this. No doubt the young madam would have made a copy of her queries to present to her father. She was treating him like a junior clerk, when it was she who should be treated thus. Well, he would play her at her own game, spoiled young wench. He could make a list of all the contraventions of the law which Enoch allowed to exist at the Works. The Master was, after all, responsible for any malpractices. For instance, how many of the workmen still employed young children as runners?

Rob sat and thought for a moment, then began compiling his list. In it were the names of Seth, Bartholomy, and Ned, all saggar makers. Then there were Elias, John, Barnabas and Paul, all mould makers. Each of these men had young children running from shop to shop, sweating hot, near the kilns, freezing cold, as they raced back through the yards. The Master turned a blind eye to this, in the interests of getting the work done cheap. Then there were other malpractices. The dangers of using lead based glazes were recognised and the women in the glazing shop were suffering. The workers were supposed to wash, and use special aprons, for this work, but the Master didn't care about enforcing these safety precautions. Everywhere the factory was filthy with dust getting into every corner, especially in the grinding loft, where bone and flint was milled. Manstone had no idea how to enforce precautions against the noxious effects of these processes. Gertie herself, bless her, had worked in the dipping shop till Rob had managed to get her into the decorating shop as a paintress.

Even this job was dangerous, if the women didn't wash themselves regularly. But what provision was made for washing? None. Manstone's daughter would do better to oversee basic hygiene rules, than fussing about a shilling here or there, on candle sticks. He'd have to open her eyes to the matter.

Rob must see Gertie. He bent his head to one side, so that he could catch a glimpse of Enoch seated at his huge desk in front of the fire. Manstone was leafing through a book of patterns, designs to be used for a forthcoming run of plates, ordered by Messrs Armitage, of Regent Street, London. He seemed to be completely involved in what he was doing.

Rob stood up, then, without raising his head, Enoch spoke to him in a low voice.

"Come here, and take a letter for me, if you've no work to do."

"Excuse me Mr. Manstone. I wished to check on old Elias. I have to ask him something in particular."

"What might that be, that's more important than my letter?"

"It's this, sir." Rob stood in the doorway, tall and erect, looking down at his master. "It seems he still has young Ben, and Isaac, doing the running for him. And as you know, sir, that's not in keeping with our duty, sir, as the law now is."

"It's the man I employ. Not his runner. How Elias takes the moulds about is his own responsibility. So long as he gets paid for what he does, then it behoves us to mind our own business.

"With respect, sir, the law being as it is, it is our business if young persons under eight years of age are in employment here. My information is that the governor of all is responsible."

"Oho. And your informant? Who might that be, may I ask?"

"Mr. Fortescue, sir. I went to an explanatory lecture. At the Union House. On the law as it now stands."

"Did you indeed? Pray ask Mr. Fortescue to convey his information to me, or keep it to himself."

"Yes, sir." Rob spoke softly.

"Take this letter."

Rob took his stool beside Enoch's desk.

"Dear Sir," Enoch began to drone, "with regard to your esteemed order of the 6th inst., we have pleasure in noting for your consideration the following points in connection with patterns nos. 401B and 403C, for which you have shown a preference in your order."

Rob continued committing the dreary jargon to paper, realising that he would later have to copy the whole out again in fair copper plate script. Then there would be several other equally dull letters. At the same time, bored though he was, half of his mind was conscious that he was in the presence of a master of business, who could haggle over prices, to the suppliers of the raw materials, or simplify the finished design to save a few coppers, while charging the client not a penny less. That was how he'd built up his business, that and his scant regard of the new laws about conditions for the workers. Enoch had always gone ahead, whatever the laws were, with the excuse that he had to keep the Pot Bank open, if anyone was to remain in work, and to do that, it was up to him to make the operation profitable. That was Enoch's attitude. But everyone knew that in this day of intense competition, with upstarts in the pottery business cutting selling prices every day, the masters just put down the wages, and kept as much profit for themselves, whatever price they charged for their products.

Rob's mind turned to what he would say at the union meeting. He could think of this, while he was seemingly concentrating on taking down Epoch's words.

Later, the clerk managed to slip down to the decorating shop. Inside, it was a little warmer. A pot-bellied iron stove in the middle of the exterior wall was piled up with coal, and the tables were pulled up as near to it as possible. The women looked up as Rob came in, but only momentarily. Gertie was sitting at the far end, her shawl round her shoulders, and a man's felt cap on her head. From under the cap her long hair reached down to her shoulders. She had mittens on, and was carefully applying a thin gold line to a plate which she was revolving slowly on her turn table.

Rob went along the line of women, peering at what they were doing. Then he addressed an older woman, sitting on her own, who was painting delicate colour on a plate. Once she had filled in all the leaf patterns, she passed it down the line to the next woman who then filled in some of the petals with a different glaze.

"Alice, you've to finish these tonight. The orders for Stintons is ready and must be done for the glost by Wednesday." he said.

The supervisor turned to Robert. "It's always the same, Meester Robert. Theer's no sense in tell us agin We canna werk more'n we're doin. See 'ere if you can do better nor us." She passed him the brush and put her head down on her left hand.

"If I tell the master you're not half way through, maybe he'll get you some help?" he said, raising his eyebrows.

"Maybe he won't. And if he do, there's no way they can do more'n us." She took the brush off him with a weary gesture. "You go on up there to your wench. She'll likely tell you something as will make you smile. Even if she hasn't finished yet, no more than the rest of us."

Some of the women looked up at Rob as he went down the line. When he came to Gertie's table she half turned to him, then looked quickly away.

"You should not come here. I told you."

"I can come where I wish. The master asked me. Besides, I've something for you." He perched on the edge of the table, and produced out of his pocket, a small twist of paper. He put it in front of Gertie. The girl's eyes lit up, and she laid down her brush. She took the small packet, and unwrapped it on her lap. Inside there were five humbugs.

"Keep them for yourself, my wench," Robert admonished.

"Will you be at chapel on Sunday?" Gertie asked.

"I will. We'll go for that walk after. Mind you remember, now." He was speaking very low, but all the women were silent and it appeared to him they were listening intently.

"Depending on how Mother be," Gertie said as he rose to go.

Robert walked quickly to the end of the shop, nodding briefly at the supervisor. His feet rang out smartly on the wooden boards. Apart from that there was the hacking sound of one of the women who seemed to be coughing continuously, and the low throb of the machinery in the engine shed across the courtyard.

Why had Gertie said that about her mother? As if he could forget the conditions at Gertie's home. There was a younger brother, as well as the ailing mother. He knew for a fact that the lad, only eight years old, had work at one of the other pot banks. He hardly ever saw the boy, as he usually slept over at the pot-bank, in one of the workshops. It wasn't allowed, but it happened. He knew the lad's wages were essential to the family. And yet he, Robert, realised he had to persuade Enoch to put pressure on his adult workers not to employ their own under age runners. The law had been passed, and it was in the workers' interest, in the long run, that it should not be flouted. If Manstone did not enforce it, Robert would make sure the facts came to the notice of the Inspectors. Yet this would rebound indirectly on Gertie's family. Something must be done for her, and soon.

At that moment Enoch came striding across the courtyard. "Just inspecting the painting of those Stinton plates, sir," Robert said.

"Will they be ready?"

"They will, sir, they will."

Enoch nodded and left the Works to catch his train.

When Robert himself left, he bought the late edition of the Signal. In it was the announcement about a forthcoming lecture about Dickens, to be given in the Town Hall, at Epsilon.

"Aye, I'll go," Rob murmured, fairly running up the hill, to his lodgings.

The following week Edna fetched Tilly from the factory a little later than usual. They had been invited by Mrs. Dawkins for tea, and it wasn't worth the girl going home first. It was several weeks since Tilly had seen Ros and she was looking forward to hearing the latest news.

Mr. and Mrs. Dawkins lived at "The Cedars," a large double fronted brick house, which was now about thirty years old. It had been built in the grounds of an old mansion, now demolished, and the trees in the original garden gave the new houses their names. There were four other houses, which had been constructed at the same time, "The Chestnuts,", "The Beeches,", "The Hollies," and "The Lawns."

Edna and Tilly walked down the gravel drive, flanked by laurel and rhododendron bushes, to the carriage sweep. This was a smaller house than Terrilea, neater and cosier, and Mrs. Manstone rather envied her friend. She sometimes wished that Enoch hadn't elected to live so far out in the country. Dorothy had close neighbours, and she was so convenient for town. In fact it would be quite a good idea for the Manstones to swap houses with the Dawkins. All the Dawkins children would fill up the big rooms and rambling corridors of Terrilea, and the youngsters would be able to run wild in the extensive woods and grounds. However, Edna knew it would be pointless suggesting such a thing to Enoch, even in jest, or, indeed, to suggest any move nearer to town. He wouldn't hear of it. He loved his long grey house, with stuccoed walls, and low pitched roof. Tilly matched her father in her passion for the fields and woods surrounding Terrilea, which were also part of Enoch's estate.

Before Edna had time to pull the bell, the maid had opened the heavy front door, and was bobbing a curtsy.

"Now, don't mention the factory, Tilda," Edna whispered, as they were ushered in.

They entered the drawing room. Dark red wall paper covered the walls, which were hung with portraits of ladies and gentlemen in formal attire, looking superior and bored. Ros had often pointed out to Tilly the picture of her mother, painted about thirty years previously. She had been wearing a huge crinoline. At least, Tilly reflected, the clothes women were expected to wear weren't quite so outrageous nowadays. It was quite acceptable, now, for young women to dress as she did, with just the slightest hint of bustle, unlike those great skirts.

Dorothy Dawkins presided over the tea table. "My dear," she said, holding out her hand to her friend. "It's seems to have been so long. Matilda, dear child."

Edna sat down on the opposite side of the fire and Ros and Tilly perched primly, holding their cups, while little plates of sandwiches were passed round by the maid.

There seemed to be a great deal of catching up to do, they didn't know where to start.

"Do you like your new occupation, my dear?" Mrs. Dawkins addressed Tilly.

Well, there it was, out in the open. What could Tilly say? She would tell the truth.

"It's very interesting, thank you. Much more so than I would have thought" She glanced at her mother, whose face was blank.

"Just so, my dear. Just so. Well, times are changing. We must all do the best we can, to make the world a better place."

Edna sighed. What could Tilly do to better the world, by working for Enoch? In fact, her own world was worse since Tilly had been going out every day. Tilly frowned. She couldn't follow Mrs. Dawkin's train of thought, but it seemed that she was making some kind of excuse to explain why Tilly was doing what she was.

"And you, my dear? I expect you enjoy having a little free time and some rest to yourself?" Dorothy had turned to Edna and they began talking, leaving the girls to chat to each other.

"Not really. Enoch is always so busy and full of ideas.He's been putting in the new fountain. The men were working on it recently. It's finished."

"How lovely! You must have us to view it."

"Of course. But I don't know...." Edna's voice trailed off and she looked at the two girls, who had finished their tea, and were looking through a book of drawings together. She lowered her voice. "I find it quite tiring, really. All this coming and going, and new projects."

"But they are all so fine, his ideas. The new Church! That must be nearly completed."

"Yes, it is. But it's taken up so much of his time. And now, there are the decorations for it. Enoch wants me to approve them, and then put in hand the fund-raising."

"Yourself? I thought the Committee would see to that."

"It's always chopping and changing. The architect this, and the architect that. Enoch and the others decide something, then it's all got to change because of the architect."

"Well I shouldn't have that. He must be firm, and I am sure he is. You mustn't let it worry you my dear. Is there anything else, anything I can do? It is sad to see you worried."

Tilly and Ros had moved to the window seat, in order to get a better light. After a moment, Tilly turned to look at her mother. Edna was frowning and appeared to be discussing something quite sad.

Ros put the book down. "Enough of art for now. I've got something splendid to tell you," she said. "Mama is arranging a party to go to the New Year Ball."

"At the Town Hall? Honestly?"

"Yes. You must try and come. There'll be about ten of us. Richard is inviting some friends, and I've got something else to tell you...." The doorbell jangled.

"What, what?" Tilly whispered.

"Later," Ros said, holding her finger to her lips.

Enoch was ushered in.

Tilly rose to her feet. "Papa!" She was astonished that he had left the factory in mid-afternoon.

"Dear Mr. Manstone. How pleased and glad to see you here so soon." Dorothy put out her hand to Enoch without rising.

Enoch made a small bow and touched her fingertips.

"I see you've been keeping a good fire burning, Mrs. Dawkins. I trust you'll allow me to stay long enough to warm my hands?"

"Please. My dear friend." Dorothy smiled and signalled a chair.

"Have you walked?" Edna enquired.

"Of course. It's a fine sunny day. Why shouldn't a man walk? A man may use his legs, I suppose, if he has a mind to."

Fresh tea was ordered. "I suppose you will take a cup after that long walk, Mr. Manstone? The nights are drawing in, are they not?"

"Yes, ma'am. The days are getting shorter, and we'll have to be burning the gas at midday soon enough. That's the way of it."

"You must be very occupied at the moment. They say Trade is good. So I believe from what I see in the Signal."

"Fair."

Tilly wondered why her father was always so abrupt with anyone when they wanted to talk about the business with him. Anyone, that is, who wasn't in the business. After all Mrs. Dawkins was only being polite.

"Yes, indeed." Enoch added, as if he had read Tilly's thoughts. This woman Dawkins obviously took an interest in her husband's work. Mr. Dawkins was senior partner in a local law firm "Yes. But we have to work hard to stay where we are. It's always a hard struggle. No doubt you are aware of that. Every foreign upstart, they've tried to copy our techniques, but it's not a knowledge you can get overnight."

Enoch was sitting with his knees apart, and his feet flat on the floor. He had put the cup down on the carpet between his feet, and taking a proffered biscuit, put it whole, into his mouth. "Those Germans, and our American brethren, they're all taking our trade. Not to mention all the ones hereabouts, they'll use any means to get a cheaper way to produce ware."

Tilly, watching her father, quickly averted her eyes, and gazed out into the darkening garden. He never disclosed his worries to her. Besides, she saw no lack of orders, all seemed to be going normally.

"We've got these new regulations, what we must do and mustn't. No one can just get on and do a good job, without every Tom, Dick and Harry poking his nose in"

"I was only just saying, to your dear wife, times are changing."

"Mr. Dawkins knows what it's like these days. Men not honouring their contracts, all this talk about changing the contract date and such. Well, I won't be burdening you ladies with all this. But we have the law on our side, as you must know, well enough."

The mantel piece clock struck four. "We'll be catching the half past back, Enoch. I think we should be taking our leave." Edna rose to her feet.

"Aye. Wife's right, Mrs. Dawkins. Must catch that train if we're to beat the night air. Wouldn't do for my lass to be out in the damp air. Nor Missus neither." He picked up his cup, rose to his feet, brushing the front of his trousers, and drained the last dregs from the fine china cup in his hand. He held it up to the light, and then inspected the bottom. "Thowt it were one of old Adam's cups. That's a nice line he's got there. You've good taste, Missus. But you should look at what we're doing now. We're doing all sizes now. I'll gladly take you round our showroom if you've a mind to it. Very good value for money they are too, and we only make a limited run of this latest design. You tell Mr. Dawkins now, and see if ye won't both come round. It'd be a pleasure, that it would."

The two girls had left the room, and Ros was helping Tilly put on her coat and hat. "I can't tell you any more now. When you get our invitation, we must meet." Ros said. "We must make a plan." Before Tilly could find out what this momentous news was, her mother spoke.

"We really must be on our way. I do not wish to have to wait for the next train. It's becoming foggy. Please come, Enoch. Goodnight, my dear, and thank you." She kissed her friend, smiled at Ros, and went out of the door, held open by the maid.

"Mr. Dawkins and yourself, ye must both come to the factory. You've never been, I fancy?" Enoch bowed to the ladies, stood on the step to put on his top hat, and marched off down the path, with Edna and Tilly close behind. The two women linked arms, and Enoch strode ahead along the road." We must move along now. It's not ten minutes to get there, but we mustn't dawdle." They all began hurrying. As they came back into the city, a nearby pot bank was sending out sulphurous fumes to mingle with the damp mist which was settling as the evening became cooler.

"Mebbe a frost tonight," Enoch said, stamping his feet as he clumped along. Edna began to be breathless

"You should have come away before, Enoch, we shall all have bad throats after this."

"Well, I won't. I always have this every night. I don't fuss. Tis what you get used to." Enoch was still marching along in front of the women.

Edna wished to remind Enoch of his words to Mrs. Dawkins, but she said nothing. He had told Dorothy he was thinking of his wife and daughter in the cold night air. That was what he had said. But no matter. Did he ever think of them? She couldn't think of an occasion when he had put her first. At last they reached the station waiting room, where a coke stove was creating comparative comfort. A minute later, the train puffed in and they climbed aboard. Tilly wondered why they'd had to rush off so quickly. She watched her father gazing out of the window, his face reflected in the glass. She could see his face, without him seeing hers. She felt she loved him, with his direct manner, his keen eyes, his heavy brows. She used to be a little afraid of him. But not now. Somehow she was now able to look at both of her parents, as an outsider would. She loved her mother too, of course. Sometimes she felt impatient with her, she didn't know why. She wished, in a way, that what was inside her mother, an inner something, which she knew was there, would be revealed, and come out into the open.

4

It was the evening of the annual Dickens lecture, held in the Town Hall at Epsilon and given by the Reverend Francis Morgan. Enoch had declined to come as he said he had other urgent matters to attend to that evening. Three business friends were calling after dinner, and they would play billiards afterwards.

The hall was already nearly full when Mrs. Manstone and Tilly arrived. At the door two gentlemen in frock-coats were taking tickets. "Good evening, ladies," Silas Lockhart said. "So good of you to come on such a night. "I trust Mr. Manstone is quite well," he continued, helping Edna off with her coat.

"Quite well, indeed, thank you," she replied, pursing her lips together. Silas exchanged glances with his companion, and Edna felt herself beginning to blush. She was sure that in some way the two men understood how she felt about not having her husband along with her.

"We're only just in time, mother. Let's secure a seat." Tilly was peering through the door. "We'll have to go right down to the front."

They made their way down the middle aisle, to some vacant places just below the stage. Tilly turned round to see if there was anyone she knew. At that moment, a tall, portly man, wearing a long gold chain, came towards them from a door leading up behind the stage. With him was a stout lady dressed in dark purple with a large feather hat.

"It's the Mayor, and Mrs. Scott," Edna said, bowing slightly to the lady as the couple came along the row past them. "Mr. Mayor," she said, "Mayoress."

"My dear Mrs. Manstone. How delightful to have your company. And Mr. Manstone? I'm sure he will be with us directly?"

"I'm afraid not, Mrs. Scott. But may I present my daughter, Matilda? I'm sure my husband has spoken of her." Indeed Enoch had met the Mayor on several occasions.

"Delighted, Miss Manstone. To be sure, your worthy father has spoken often of his lovely daughter." He gave both the Manstone ladies a deep bow. "So nice for you to have your grown daughter with you. Such a comfort, Mrs. Manstone, Girls are such a blessing. We must thank God for his bounty. I have five daughters, so we should know."

"And three sons, my dear. Just as important. We are blessed indeed," the Mayoress pointed out. "Perhaps you will call on us, Mrs. Manstone. "

At that moment, to Tilly's relief, the curtains parted, and the chairman of Epsilon Literary Circle, came through and bowed. "It is indeed a pleasure to see such a large gathering to welcome our speaker tonight. I can see by your faces that some of you are strangers in this town, and have made great efforts to join us on this prestigious occasion. But how much more of an effort has our renowned speaker made? He has come from the Antipodes to expound to us from the depth of his great learning on a subject which is very dear to our hearts. The subject is 'Dickens as an Educator.' Reverend Francis Morgan. Let us show our appreciation in the usual way."

There was a burst of clapping, and the curtains withdrew to the full extent, revealing a lectern, and beside it, the tall, thin, bearded figure of a clergyman. He put his hand up to secure silence, and began to speak. "Ladies and Gentlemen. It is my pleasure to speak to you, on a subject you really know very much about already. A thing that is familiar to all as sits here, or they wouldn't be 'ere. Education."

Tilly was surprised at the man's voice. He sounded as if he came from the South of England, perhaps, London. She didn't know if he sounded like an Australian. She had never met anyone from the colonies before. She began wondering what he was doing here, telling them about an English author. It hadn't occurred to her that in the colonies there were people who read books, and argued about them, as they did here at home. She hadn't really thought about those places before, or the people who lived there. In history lessons, she had learned about Captain Cook, and the penal settlements. But she hadn't much knowledge, or interest in the Empire. What she did know, she found vaguely unsettling.

"To make my point clearer, Ladies and Gentlemen, I must ask you to listen carefully how Mr. Dickens describes Pip's friend, Abel Magwitch, in "Great Expectations."

Edna recognised the quotation, smiled at Tilly, settled herself more comfortably, and relaxed. Her composure had been ruffled by the remarks made by the Mayor and his lady.. In some way, it seemed to be a criticism of her that her husband had found some important business to do on the evening of the lecture. She knew that anybody who was anybody would be here tonight. Enoch really have could have come, for her sake. She had noticed the looks the Mayor and his wife had given each other, especially when talking about their children. She felt the usual pang when she thought about this. She glanced sideways at Tilly, then pressed her hand. Tilly appeared riveted on what the speaker was saying.

The Reverend was becoming more and more excited as he got into the flow of his argument. He was showing that Dickens did not believe in child depravity. For Dickens, children were innocent creatures, who needed praise and support to enable them to achieve their rightful purpose in life. "Education," he was declaiming, "must reinforce the self-confidence of the little ones. It should not be founded on the theory that children are wicked. The old discipline and training take as a premise that children like to do wrong, better than to do right...."

There was a loud noise at the back of the hall, followed by a cry. The clergyman stopped in mid flow, peering towards the back. A young man had come in through the entrance, tripped up on something, and was now sprawled on the floor behind the last row of seats. Everyone was looking backwards, staring, some getting up out of their seats for a better view. Tilly turned round immediately, and whispered to her mother. "It's Robert Willoughby."

"How extremely unfortunate," Edna said.

The Reverend nodded to the audience. "Let's hope our new friend will be able to pick up from where I have got to, as well as pick himself up... We will continue." There was a slight laugh at these words, then the lecturer continued. "We now come to the question of community. Mr. Dickens' dearest and most cherished belief is that the duty of every individual in this world is to add something by his life to the general good. Everyman has something of worth in him, every man and every woman too. Listen to some lines from 'Hard Times' ....'Not all the calculators of the National Debt can tell me the capacity for good or evil, for love or hatred, for patriotism or discontent, for the decomposition of virtue into vice, or the reverse, at any single moment, in the soul of any one of these its quiet servants. There is an unfathomable mystery in the meanest of them, forever.' We all have a responsibility to every other person, to our fellow humans. Listen and hear. Read this passage, my dear friends, for yourselves."

Tilly's concentration, in danger of straying, after the spectacle of Mr. Willoughby overturned on the floor, now began to wander off, in earnest. On and on went the diatribe about Dickens as a reforming educationalist. From time to time the words, "training"," nutrition", "minor schools", impinged on her consciousness, but mainly, she was on a different plane. The image of the women whom she had seen in the street when she had come home from the factory after her very first visit, flashed before her eyes. The sulphurous fog, the ceaseless throb which pulsated round her in the office every day, were now more real to her than the rows of well-dressed men and women sitting solidly about her. Edna too had lost the thread of the lecture, partly because she felt that it was becoming more and more like a sermon, and she couldn't quite see why she should be listening to a sermon on Saturday night. Her mind was elsewhere; there was some puzzle she could not resolve. Then she realized what it was. Why had Enoch's clerk come all this way for this lecture? Perhaps he had a special interest in Dickens. That seemed unlikely. Enoch had spoken of him sometimes, but she had not taken much notice, and she had only met him once, on the occasion that she had fetched Matilda back, after her first tour of the Works. He hadn't been Enoch's clerk for long, and in any case, she was not in the habit of calling at the Works. She decided that she did not want to meet him at the end of the talk. It would be better if she and Tilly were to be among the last to leave, thus, no doubt, she could avoid him. Then Edna wondered why she did not want to meet him. She had to admit that she hadn't expected anyone of his class to be present. But things were different nowadays. All sorts of people were rising in the world, or trying to do so. Education for all was having this effect. Enoch's father himself, she thought ruefully, had been a working potter, perhaps he had even been as poor at one time as this clerk. Life was curious. Perhaps she should try to be kind to those people who weren't as fortunate as herself. After all, that is what this clergyman was saying, really, wasn't he? The lecture was all about Dickens and his concern for poor people. But when you came to consider it, why should she help people? Surely they should help themselves. Probably it was all beyond her anyway.

"Ladies and Gentlemen. After such an interesting talk, I am sure many of the audience will wish to ask questions. So I open the floor to them. Please let us begin the discussion." The chairman was standing up, to field the questions. Tilly realised, with relief that the greater part of the lecture was now over. Nevertheless, she might have another look at the Dickens novels which were in Papa's library. After reading them with her governess, she'd not gone back to them. They seemed to be left over from another generation.

After a moment an old gentleman rose to his feet.

"Would Reverend Morgan agree that a little knowledge is a dangerous thing, and that a little education is worse than none at all?"

"An interesting point, I assure you. But we must remember the date at which Mr. Dickens wrote. Some of the anomalies to which he drew our attention have since disappeared. But we must not become complacent. Many injustices still remain, and it is only when all our young people can have good, free education, that our society as a whole will be the example to the world which we wish it to be."

At this a young man rose to his feet at the back of the hall. As soon as he began talking, Tilly recognised his voice. She turned round to confirm her suspicion.

It was Robert, of course. He was speaking confidently, and with clarity. "We would agree, sir, that the education now provided in this country will enlighten our ignorant population, if they are able to profit by it. Unfortunately, sir, the provision of free education, presupposes that young people are free to receive it. But I put it to you, sir, that too many of our young people are still clandestinely involved in work which will help to keep their families from starvation. How can such young people profit from our educational reform? They have not the time or energy to go to school. Such education is not free. To go to school means that their families may starve. Is the true price of schooling, the starvation of one's brothers and sisters, even of one's parents? This is a blot on our civilisation, especially here, in the Potteries, a blot which has not yet been removed. It is a blot which was apparent to Mr. Dickens. I put it to you, sir, that Charles Dickens, if he were to be among us today, would still find sufficient anomalies in our society to describe which would fill another fifty novels."

Edna became tense as she listened to Robert. Somehow, she felt he was criticising herself, her way of life, and everything she knew. Could her way of life be criticised? She thought about Enoch, and her marriage. How he had loved her when they were first married! And she had loved him so much too. She still did. Of course she did. But it was no use. As she sat there, she began to think how she would describe her feelings, if she had to, perhaps to her friend, Dorothy Dawkins...God forbid that she would ever wish to describe her innermost feelings in this way. In any case, she felt she really could not do so. She just felt a kind of aching hollowness, and emptiness, when she thought about herself. It appeared to her that Enoch did not love her any more. That was one thing which she had always assumed would go on for ever. She was so sure that he loved her, from the very first time he had met her. She knew he did then, and he had wanted her so much, and she had been so sure of him, that he would always love her, that she had gone against her mother's wish, she knew, to marry him. She had found him exciting, and different from all the suitors whom her parents approved of. It was true, he did not come from an established, landed family. His riches were formed by his own father, and his own success, in the manufacture of pottery. But he was a real man, successful by his own unaided efforts. She admired him, became dependent on him, and eventually she knew, she had fallen in love with him. He had seemed to love her so much, he would do anything for her, would allow her anything she wanted, for so many years. But now, she realised, things must be different. Else why did he never spend time with her, why would he go against her wishes over Tilly working, why was he so uncommunicative? Suddenly she wished the lecture would finish, so she could get back to her warm bedroom. The fire would be lit, and she could curl up, under her eiderdown. Jeannie would be putting the warming pan in soon, and when she and Tilly had eaten their supper, she would go straight to bed.

A few people had risen from their seats to get a better view as Robert held forth. One or two began muttering, and there were a few low murmurs of "shame." Some people began to wrap scarves round their necks or adjusted shawls and coats preparatory to making an exit.

The chairman rose to speak, holding up his hand for silence. "The young man has asked a pertinent and grave question. However I do not feel our speaker is in a position to ...." He was interrupted by the Reverend himself.

"A moment, if you please. I am not here to make hypotheses about the nature of Mr. Dickens' testimony, as it would apply to our enlightened times. I merely wish to show how much of our advanced thinking is based on Mr. Dickens' ideas. The actual application of his ideas in modern society is the domain of your statesmen, Sir."

The meeting was wound up with a burst of clapping and people on every side began to make their way out of the hall. Tilly began to do the same, but Edna remained seated.

"Aren't we going, Mama?"

"We'll wait until the Mayor and his lady have gone," Edna whispered. In a moment the mayoral couple bowed to Mrs. Manstone and went up the steps to have a word with Reverend Morgan and the chairman on the platform.

"Shall we?" asked Tilly.

Edna looked round. There was a busy throng of people trying to get through the back exit. Everyone was turned away from her, and the hall was gradually emptying.

"Another moment, dear, we don't wish to be jostled." There was no sign of Robert. He must have gone out with the first to leave. Edna picked up her mantle and gloves.

Suddenly there was a shout. "Mrs. Manstone, Miss Manstone." Robert was squeezing his way along the row of chairs towards them. Mrs. Manstone realised that she could not avoid speaking to him.

"Mr. Willoughby!" Edna said. She wished she had hurried to the exit along with everyone else. By hesitating she had made her whereabouts even more obvious.

"Did you enjoy the lecture, Ma'am? And what of you, Miss Manstone? Didn't you think it was powerful and... energising?"

"Energising?" What a strange word. "What exactly do you mean," Tilly asked.

"Dickens' themes spelled out so well, only the most obtuse would not take them to heart."

"But do you believe he was right. About education? In all respects?" Tilly found it strange to be talking to the clerk in this way. They had only exchanged a few words, apart from business matters, in all the time she had been at the Works.

"Of course, of course. I have always respected his ideas on the subject. And you, Mrs. Manstone. Were you completely converted?"

"I don't know, Mr. Willoughby. Perhaps not quite converted. I haven't given it much thought." Edna felt her colour rising.

"These notions should be put before the governors of all the schools. The truth of natural innocence is still not accepted in its entirety. We are trying to stamp out an evil in young people, which would not be there if the conditions they were raised in were suitable for humans, rather than animals. It is the conditions which make them criminals, rather than their own sinful natures." Robert's voice was ringing out in the nearly deserted hall. His face, usually quite pale, was flushed and animated.

Tilly looked round to see if anyone was listening......

"I'm sure you would understand, if I had a chance to make myself clearer." Robert was bending towards her, his eyes gleaming.

"Perhaps some time..." Edna said gripping Tilly's arm. "Come along, Matilda, Tom will be waiting with the carriage." They hurried to the door. In the vestibule there was a small knot of people peering out into the street. Rain was deluging down in torrents. Tilly could just see the carriage drawn up a few feet up the street, and Tom was coming towards them with an umbrella.

"Oh Mr. Willoughby," Tilly turned towards him, "have you come all the way from Saghead for the lecture? How will you return?"

"On the train, of course."

"But it's pouring. Mama, couldn't Tom go back by way of the station, then we could set Mr. Willoughby on the train?"

Robert's jacket collar was turned up, but he had no overcoat. Already, he looked pale again, and his long fingers were gripping the edges of his lapels to draw his jacket tightly round his chest. "Come with us. Do." Edna said. She couldn't leave him to get all wet. That wouldn't be the act of a Christian. Even though his ideas were strange, to say the least. "Of course, you must. What time is the train?"

"I've time to walk, Mrs. Manstone."

"Nonsense. I know quite well Mr. Manstone would wish me to give you a lift. Think nothing of it." She climbed aboard the carriage, sheltering under the umbrella.

"Very well, Ma'am. Very much obliged I'm sure." Robert knew the carriage ride was only a respite, because the walk from Saghead station to his lodgings would be another mile through the rain. He'd be thoroughly soaked by the time he got home. And the fire would most certainly be out.

"I'm sure you wouldn't have come all this way, if you had foreseen the rain."

"I should indeed, ma'am. I always achieve what I've a mind to. I make that my rule."

"And is that your great interest? Reading the works of our prominent authors?" The horses were trotting along at a good pace. It was damp, but warm, inside the carriage.

"In a manner of speaking, Mrs. Manstone. But especially the reformers. Reading, yes, that is a great interest to me. But singing is my first interest, apart from my work, of course."

"Singing? The choir, I take it."

"No, Ma'am. Part singing. There is a group of us do it. I would have gone tonight for our practice. But I wished to hear this lecture."

"So you've had to leave your friends to manage as best they can without you tonight?"

Robert smiled. Tilly, sitting in her dark corner, noticed that his face was transformed, in a way she had not seen it before. He seemed quite human, suddenly. "Tonight, we couldn't meet," Robert continued. "One of our members, he has to be with his wife tonight.... She..." Robert's voice trailed away.

At that moment the carriage rolled into the gas lit station yard. A high, thin whistle announced the arrival of the train. Rob flung himself out of the carriage. "Thank you, Mrs. Manstone, you're very kind.

"Hurry, or you'll miss it," Tilly shouted.

He raced through the gate and onto the platform as the engine came roaring in, making much smoke, and with a squealing of brakes.

"Poor man, I fear he'll be drowned before he gets home," Edna said, signalling Tom to be off again.

"It was his choice to come, Mama."

"I expect he's trying to better himself. Lectures, and music with his friends. Very laudable. Papa chose him wisely." Edna sighed, and tucked the rug in round her knees. "Did you know he could sing, Tilly?"

"I certainly did not. We're far too busy in the office to gossip about that sort of thing." Did Mama really think her work at the office left time for social relations of any kind, let alone with Mr. Willoughby? In any case, she wasn't particularly interested in Robert. Whether he could sing or not, was of no importance to her, at all. She realised she had a duty to learn what she could from him, and eventually to supervise him. She didn't particularly want to know him as a person. Besides, he was so old, thirty, at least, she supposed.

"He certainly seems to be an ardent admirer of Mr. Dickens, his ideals, that is. I've never really thought about Dickens in that sense. I was always more interested in his stories, I'm afraid..." Edna broke off. Tilly wasn't listening to her. "You seem tired. A little hot bread and milk, and off to bed with you, straight away. I don't want you coming down with a cold."

"Mama! Really! I hardly got wet at all." Why did Mama fuss over her? "No bread and milk, thank you." Tilly relaxed against the cushions. It had been an interesting evening, but now, she didn't want to talk. There was so much to think about. She would sit by the fire for a while, and read, when she got home.

Edna fell silent. She too was thinking about her bedroom. Would Enoch be upstairs yet? When the carriage arrived at Terrilea, lighted oil lamps had been put along the edges of the drive way, and candles in the hall shone through the stained glass windows of the front door. For a moment Edna thought of Robert, making his way home on the sooty little train. She suddenly had the idea that she wished he had come with them, and seen their luxurious house. She stifled the thought at once. What would Enoch have said if she had produced his clerk at this hour, into their home? It was nonsensical.

Jeannie was at the door to open it for them.

"Is Mr. Manstone still with his visitors?" Edna enquired, as the maid took her mantle.

"Yes, Ma'am. They're in the billiard room."

"Well, we won't need anything but a hot drink. Bring me some tea, upstairs. And for you, my dear?"

"Nothing at all, thank you Mama."

Edna went down the passage, to the door of the billiard room. She could hear the click of balls, and detected the whiff of cigars. There was no point in waiting for Enoch. He would be late to bed.

Edna turned round and went up the stone staircase to her room. Now she felt very tired; she would have her tea beside her fire. She wasn't hungry. She wished to be alone. Her long dress, wet round the hem, swished up the steps behind her. The candle on the window sill of the staircase window flickered in the draught. She shivered, and thought about the little train again, going towards Saghead. She imagined she could hear it whistling, far away, the sound of its whistle seemed to be echoing up the valley towards her. She pressed her face close to the window for a moment, looking out at the trees, which were shaking in the pale light reflected on them from the billiard room windows. It was windy out, and the rain was still blowing across. Down there, the stream must be high. She thought she could hear that too, making a rushing, gurgling roar. Even though she felt so tired, Edna was sure she wouldn't go quickly to sleep. Probably she would still be awake when Enoch finished his game. He would creep in, trying not to disturb her, on the way to his dressing room.

Tilly went into the library. She looked along the shelves for 'Great Expectations.' There it was. She was just reached the door to go upstairs, when Deaker come in with a candle.

"You're late back. I expect Miss Edna is tired."

"We had to come back by way of the station. Mr. Willoughby was there, and Mama decided we must give him a lift to the station."

"Your papa's clerk?"

"Yes. He was there. Mama says he's trying to better himself."

"I suppose he must be. Though I don't know what good that's doing for him."

"It was interesting, Deaker. You should have been there. It was all about education." Tilly was resting on the arm of Papa's chair.

"I thought Mr. Dickens wrote storybooks. I remember your grandmother, weeping she was, at some of those stories. Every week I think it was. She'd go mad for them. I never did know what she saw in them, getting so sad." Deaker bent to put a shovel full of coal on the fire.

"Well, it's all told in a story, or stories. But it's what he believed, that's the point."

"I'm still not sure what good it all is. Or why that clerk should take it into his head to go to the talk."

"I suppose he has a right to."

"They have classes for workmen, for all sorts of things. Night classes. Things to do with their work. But the Literary Society, I don't know."

"I'm glad to think anyone can come. Workmen could come too, I've no doubt. After all, they're not barred from Church and Chapel."

"Of course they must attend the Church services. It's not my place to say they mustn't. But lectures now, that's different. I don't think it's right to go above your station."

"Oh, Deaker, sometimes I think..."

"What do you think, Miss Tilly? That this old woman has some funny old fashioned notions?" Deaker perched on a chair. "Old fashioned they may be. But they've stood the test of time. It's like this. We've all got our place God gave us, and who's to argue with the Lord's plan. To alter it would bring heartache and sorrow."

"Oh, you're all for ever going on, like that. About what's lasted, and the test of time. But that means nothing will ever change. Not get better."

"Better? If it's stood the test of time, it can't be bettered."

Tilly put her book on the table, and bent down to hug Deaker quickly round the shoulder; "What have you done tonight? Crochet? Something for the bazaar?"

"I've promised a dozen table mats for your Mama's stall."

"You never fail, do you? What's the money to be used for?"

"The Christmas Meal for the Workhouse children"

"That's good. But it's the system which needs changing."

"And what does that mean, Miss Tilly?"

"Oh, I don't know. I really don't. But I do know something has got to happen. Do you know there's talk of a strike, if Arbitration doesn't work. What'll that mean to everyone? It'll be terrible for some of them."

"Don't you go worrying. That's for your Papa, and all of them."

Tilly looked as if she was going to say something, but held her tongue. What was the point? "I'm going up. Goodnight, Deaker." She put her arms round the old woman, then went into the cool hall. As she went upstairs she realised with a pang that her mother had not insisted, this year, on her embroidering some napkins for the Christmas Church Bazaar. She wouldn't have time now that she was going to the Works every day. But still, she wished she had been asked. For a moment she considered going into her mother's room, to give her another goodnight. Then she pictured her own little fire, crackling and glowing in her bedroom. She tiptoed past her parents' bedroom to the candle lit seclusion of her own.

5

The following Monday morning, Tilly was in the office casting up some figures relating to sales of chimney ornaments. She totalled up, and put a line under her addition. She wriggled for a minute on her stool, then peeped round the door to her father's office. He wasn't there. She remembered he had called for Robert a few minutes before. Probably they had both gone out without her noticing. She walked back into the ante room, uncertain of what she should do next.

On Robert's desk was a sheaf of papers, showing the figures for total sales of china for the last month. In another pile were the invoices for materials for the month in question. She still didn't understand how these two amounts related to each other. How much clay, bone, and so forth, would be needed to make one cup, or a plate, or an ornament? How much would the labour cost? How could her father, or Rob, calculate their needs in raw material? How much was wasted through bad workmanship or accidents? After working in the office for several weeks, she still didn't really know much about the business which gave her father and all his workers, a living. It seemed strange to her that something was deducted from their wages for candles, coal, and even for use of the machinery. She understood that this was something to do with the industry as it was in the old days, when all the journey men were working for themselves. But why did it apply nowadays? She'd managed to have a talk with her father about the coal needed for the fires, but as for the other matters, she couldn't piece it all together. Some factories had better systems, but her father wished to stick to the old ways.

Tilly sighed. She now understood what a saggar was and the names of the different occupations of all the workers in the pot bank. There were flat pressers, dippers, glost placers, paintresses, ground layers, colour dusters, leith and transfer dusters, dish makers, hollow ware pressers, mould makers, throwers, handlers, oven men, jiggerers, cup and saucer makers, and basin makers. She could recite these names like a litany, she had learned them through studying the wages book. But that didn't mean she had really got to grips with what was happening.

She sat down in Enoch's chair, her elbows on his desk. She couldn't imagine ever taking his place. She frowned and drummed her fingers on the table as her father often did. It would be another hour and a half till Tom would come with the gig to take her home. The fire was low, and she decided to make it up. This wasn't her job, but there was no sign of Willoughby. She decided that she might as well bring a book to read, if they were going to leave her alone, and not even bother to tell her what to do.

Suddenly there came the sound of shouting and clatter of hooves on the cobbles in the yard. Tilly went to the window, and peered down. A large dray pulled by four horses had come in, and was being manoeuvred into position, to be unloaded by the open door of the clay house. Two men were waiting to take the heavy clay onto their backs to stack it inside the store. If only the doorway was a bit bigger, the dray could be backed right in, relieving the men of half their task. She would speak to her father about it. She was surprised that he hadn't already thought of that. Perhaps he had, but had decided to do nothing. She wondered if he would be pleased to have her suggestions.

A young woman came down the exterior stairs from the upper floor of the building opposite. She had a shawl over her head, bare arms, and a long apron. Tilly recognised her immediately as Gertie, a paintress. She saw her speak to one of the labourers, and he gestured with his head towards the engine shop. At that moment she saw her father coming out of the doorway opposite, to go towards the clay store. Both labourers, by this time, were busy unloading and he went behind the dray and was lost to view.

Tilly decided to go and find him. There must be something she could be doing. It was quite boring to be unoccupied. She went down the external stairs to the yard door, and opened it.

Standing in the open doorway to the engine room, with her back to Tilly, was Gertie, evidently talking to someone inside. As Tilly came across the yard, the door was suddenly closed, and Gertie turned to the right, presumably to go towards the stairs to the painting shop.

"Gertie," Tilly said. "Is Mr. Willoughby in the engine shed? I need him."

Gertie did not immediately reply. She had taken off her shawl, and was now rewinding it more tightly round her head and shoulders

"Oh, Miss Manstone. You did give me a start," she said.

"Well, is he? I mean, did you see him?"

"I don't know Miss. It's just that...."

"What's the matter? I thought he was in there."

"Well perhaps he was, Miss. It's just that Mr. Seth said as he'd gone."

"Oh, I see." It seemed to Tilly that Gertie was waiting to speak again, but she didn't. "Did you want to see him? Has he been sent for? If so, I'll request him to go to the paint shop the minute he comes back to the office. Or perhaps it's something I can deal with." Tilly paused. "Now what is it? Tell me what's the matter?"

Gertie seemed to recover herself. "Happen Alice will show you, Miss. If you'll please to come up."

They went up the wooden staircase opposite. In the long painting shop all the women were busily at work. When Gertie re-entered, Tilly, who was just behind her, heard one of the girls cry out, "Was 'e there then?" Then, as she herself went in, there were startled glances, and the chattering stopped.

"What seems to be the problem, Alice?" Tilly asked, going straight to the supervisor's desk.

"Oh, Miss. Nothing at all. Just a query 'bout these figurines. Mr. Robert, he telled us what to do, but Gertie here, she wasna really sure."

"Oh, I see," Tilly said. But she didn't. If Alice knew the solution to the problem, why had she sent Gertie to find out? If she didn't send her, why was she wandering around the yard, out of her rightful place in the factory? It was true that the women were paid piece work, but if they weren't all working together, then the others wouldn't achieve their wages, everyone would slow down, and the work wouldn't be done. She would have to mention to father what was happening. She could understand that it would be impossible for one person to be responsible for all the painting on any object. That would take far too long. But to pay them like this, for each completed object, wasn't really fair on the quick and conscientious. At least there should be a rule that no-one was to wander off from her work place to the detriment of the others. Why had Gertie been down the steps in the engine shed? Had she gone there to meet someone?

As Tilly went down the wooden stairs back to the office, she pondered on the unfairness of things. Here was she, enabled to take a few minutes off without jeopardising the well-being and wages of anyone. But for the factory girls, that couldn't be the case. Unless of course, everyone were to get their basic wages, whatever they produced. Could that be done? There seemed to be so many different kinds of goods made, and so many different operations, how would it be possible to give any kind of basic standard wage? Perhaps Father could explain. If he indeed wanted to.

Enoch was still not in the office when Tilly returned, but Robert was.

"Miss Manstone, if you would, please see to these figures for me." He handed her a sheaf of invoices. "You've been shown how to enter them. From last month. They have to be done by next Thursday."

"I've been waiting for something to do," she said, obediently sitting down on her stool. As she dipped her pen into the inkwell, she wondered what Ros was doing at that moment. Probably shopping, or taking some of her younger brothers and sisters out to play. They did have a nursery and nursery maids of course, but Ros always liked taking a turn at playing ball, or turning the rope for the children. They had a big garden, and Ros was often outside with the little ones.

Tilly didn't envy her. She'd rather be here, helping her father, even though the work could be boring at times. At least she felt grown up, doing something, and not still half in and half out of the nursery. If only Father would see her point of view. She wanted a proper training, in a skill. What was the good of all her hours in the schoolroom, learning to draw and sing, if she couldn't do something which really meant something? All the girls she knew could draw and sing, but how many of them could do something to do with real life? She'd like to learn to type, and perhaps do shorthand. She could get a paid job, with her own money. But then, even typing and shorthand might become boring in the end. She realised that what she wanted was some occupation that would take her whole mind. She'd learn a skill which not many people had, and things which other people didn't know. But how could she do that, if she didn't even yet understand the chemistry of making glazes and pots? Her mind was wandering. All this seemed to her more important than adding up and copying. She'd never told anyone her thoughts about this. It was too secret. Even to mention it might make the dream go away, like waking up.

Tilly started copying out figures into the ledger, very neatly, with each number accurately and exactly beneath the one above. This made it much easier to cast up at the end. She'd learned that at lessons, of course, but here, in this office, she really understood the importance of accuracy, and neatness.

Robert was sitting at his desk, with his back to Tilly. The door was open into Mr. Manstone's office. The clerk's shoulders were hunched up over a sheaf of papers which he was sorting through. There was something, something about his back, Tilly thought. She suddenly felt she wanted him to approve of what she was doing. He never told her if she had done a good job or not. All at once Tilly became conscious of the fact that Rob was aware of her gaze. She glared at the back of his head, his short hair, his bent neck pushed forward from his stiff collar, his long, slightly stooping, back. She noticed, for the first time, that his hair was becoming thinner on top. The scalp was just beginning to show. Her breathing became shallower and shorter. The clock ticking, the tiny sounds of the fire burning next door came through. Why wouldn't he say anything? He must know she wished to speak to him.

Tilly felt she had to move. She was in the grip of some kind of spell, as if the moment was caught in time, as if she was a tiny insect, for ever paralysed in amber. She must do something.

She rose from her chair, quietly, to go next door. Now, she didn't want Robert to turn round. In Enoch's office the desk was just as it had been, half an hour before.

"Where is my father, Mr. Willoughby?" Robert couldn't see her in here, and she was able to speak.

Robert voice was low and precise. He sounded irritated. "Mr. Ashkin. Those new glazes."

"Oh." She went back to the doorway. The clerk was still bent over the figures. "Will he be back before I leave?"

"Couldn't say. I expect he'd have let you know." He still did not look up.

"Well, he didn't. I went to look for both of you just now. It's not right to leave me without any instructions."

At this, Robert laid down his pen, and turned round. "What's to do? I gave you the figures to cast up."

"Please do not speak to me like that, Mr. Willoughby. Remember your place is to teach me, and that means in all aspects. If you want to know, I've had enough of entering and casting up figures. I'm meant to learn all branches of the business."

"Well, I suggest, Miss Manstone, you speak to Mr. Manstone about that. I'm only doing what I've been told to do. Teaching you the office side."

Tilly turned back into her father's office, picked up the poker, and began prodding the glowing coals into flame.

"I quite understand that. I shall speak to Papa. I'm not going to learn much like this. I could have gone down to the colour mill with him."

"Yes, you could have, Miss. Perhaps next time, he'll have a mind to take you, no doubt."

There was silence for a moment. Tilly looked at the clock. It was still half an hour before the gig would arrive to take her home. There was nothing to do but get on with her work. But not in there, with Robert.

"Mr. Willoughby," Tilly raised her voice. "I've decided to work in Mr. Manstone's office. It's not so draughty, and I can see better, by the window. Help me move the desk and stool."

"Move the desk? I doubt Mr. Manstone would want that."

"Of course he will, if I ask him. Just do what I wish."

Robert again put his pen down, this time wiping it carefully first. He went over to the little table which Tilly had been using. "Here you are, then." He picked up the table quite effortlessly, and carried it into Mr. Manstone's office.

"And the stool. There's just nice room."

The stool was soon arranged to Tilly's satisfaction. She sat down to get on with her work. That was better, she thought, dipping her pen again into the inkwell. Why hadn't Father realised from the beginning that she couldn't work properly in that dreary outer office? She realised that her position as trainee manager was now established, by the simple device of moving the desk and stool alongside her father's table and chair. So it should have been, from the beginning, she decided. Robert had gone back to his work.

It seemed no time till Tilly heard the gig come into the yard. As she got up to get her coat and hat, she handed Robert the completed figures.

"I think you'll find they're all as they should be," she said.

"Thank you. I am sure they will be."

Tilly was surprised at his tone. It seemed as if he was trying to be friendly, which was strange, after his obvious reluctance to move the furniture for her.

"Did you enjoy the talk the other night?" she asked. "I hope you didn't get too wet on the journey home."

"I did and I didn't," he said.

There came a knock on the door and Tilly had to go. As she hurried down the stairs after Tom, she pondered over Robert's ambiguous reply. As usual, she was never quite sure what he meant.

In the event, Enoch did not return to the factory until after lunch, by which time Tilly had already been collected, to go home. He had lunched with Hatch, the newspaper editor. As soon as he saw Robert, the Master came straight to the point.

"Mr. Hatch tells me there was advertisements this Monday, for a meeting Saturday, about Arbitration. Not in the Advertiser, of course, he won't take them. But he's seen it in the Signal."

"That's right, Mr. Manstone. It's Frank Borthing, and some of them. They're not convinced this Arbitration's going to bring any good. If there's a settlement they doubt it'll stick."

"So that's it. They're not convinced they can bring the men with them? Or they won't bring the men? Can't, or won't, which is it?"

"I'm speaking for our men, sir. Dan and the others'll go along with what I tell 'em. Definite." Of course they would. Rob knew he could persuade them to accept or not to.

Enoch sat down heavily at his desk and burped. He'd had a good lunch and two glasses of claret. It was not his custom to indulge at lunchtime, but Hatch had been persuasive and the matter in hand seemed more important than returning to the office in this instance.

"Is it about this good-from-oven?"

Robert hesitated before answering. The old man was all about, he knew very well what the gripes were for. "They want a basic wage for each job, sir. They don't see why, if they've each done their best, then the ware is spoiled in the oven, sometimes from being bad clay in the first place, why it is none of them get paid, all along the line."

"It cannot be the clay. It's all been through the mill, and you know that as well as I do."

"Of course, sir."

"They're half-drunk better part of the time. And why is there this absenteeism, if it weren't they're too drunk to work Mondays? I thought you had that in hand?"

"I'm doing my best, Mr. Manstone. I've instituted a system to check who are the persistent drinkers. When the time is ripe, I'll let you have it."

"When the time is ripe...oh yes. Well it should be obvious to any fool who the drinkers are. And let them know, I won't tolerate it. You'd best come up with that list, or I'll have the lot of them. They've to mend their ways. Times are hard now. We've stiff competition now from abroad, they should know that. The Krauts in particular, they're ready to take us, if we don't watch it. Now isn't the time to be changing a system which has served us since I was a boy, and my father before me. Basic wage!" Enoch spat into the fire.

"Quite right, sir. But....."

Before he had time to explain, Enoch interrupted. "And what will you tell 'em, Willoughby?"

"I'll tell 'em they've a good master, sir."

"Get me those orders from Dales of Bond Street. We need to do some figures. I've no costs yet for those new glazes. And the price of gold has gone up. It was bound to, with trouble down in Johannesburg."

"The Kaffirs sir? They don't know they're well off, do they?"

"No more do ours. No more do ours. But it seems we'll sort 'em out, the natives, I mean. I fancy we'll mek 'em toe the line." It was trade which would make them toe the line. It all came down to that.

"Yes, sir." Robert went into the back office and returned with the letter and specification from Dales. The order was a big one, for a 100 piece dinner service with intricate pattern and gold border. Manstone had done well to get that order, from a new customer. He couldn't fault the Master as a salesman. He knew how to pitch the price just under his rivals and still return with a profit. Unfortunately this meant economies; there was no doubt piece rates would be cut, and there was also no doubt the arbitrators would find on the side of the masters, as usual. "Miss Manstone had me move her table, sir," he said, putting the pile of papers in front of Enoch.

"I can see that. I didn't suppose she had moved it on her own."

"No, sir."

"If that's what she wants, in this case, I'll allow it."

"There's another thing, sir. She's not too happy about how things are going."

"What's that? Not happy?"

"She wishes to learn all aspects of the business. More than what she's doing now."

Enoch gave no reply. He was offended that this news had come to him through Willoughby. He expected Matilda to trust him enough to speak to him directly.

"Will there be anything else, Sir?"

"No. Get on with your work." Enoch began to leaf through the papers which Robert had presented to him. He felt tired and despondent. It was as if Tilly had somehow criticised him. Then it occurred to him that there might be another reason why she did not want to be working in the same office as Willoughby. An hour later Enoch was pacing towards the station, to catch his train home. He still felt ill at ease. His conversation with Robert hadn't convinced him that the clerk would back him up against the workers. He wasn't sure about the man, there had been some rumours going round about him. But on the whole, he was excellent at his work. He knew he could trust him, if he were to be away from the office for a few days, and it did seem likely that he would be away more and more, if he were to chase up contacts, and monitor the work of the salesmen, in their areas. And he would like to get to London, sometimes. Now, it seemed, too, that Tilly was taking to acting without his permission. Moving her desk, indeed. But he couldn't reverse her order to the clerk. That would only make him seem a complete fool in Robert's eyes. He'd have to put her right when he arrived home.

It was Tuesday, and being so, the factory closed late. There was no chance of Robert going home for hours yet. Absenteeism, after heavy drinking over the weekend, was the norm on Monday, and this left the men short of time, on the last five days of the week. So they had the habit of working extra-long hours, to make up their money. Piece work rates meant late night working was necessary, to make a living wage.

Robert stayed late. He was trying to weed out persistent drinkers. He hated the habit. It meant the works being open till ten or later. It was part of a vicious circle caused by, and causing, poverty, ill health and degradation. Still, he understood why the potters took to drink. Some of them were highly intelligent, many of them were highly skilled, and a few of them were even his friends. He hated the conditions they lived in, as much as the drink itself. He was watching for the notorious offenders, making mental notes about who would not be employed again, when it came to the next hiring day, which would be at Martinmas. He didn't discuss the matter with Mr. Manstone, but there were a lot of things which he didn't discuss with the Master. He knew that some of the children employed by the moulders as runners to keep them in a supply of empty moulds, or as dippers, to dip the ware into glazes, were under age. They should be at school, now the new Education Law was in force. Enoch was closing his eyes to this fact, but

Robert foresaw the day when a nosy factory inspector would sniff out those children, and then there would be all hell let loose.

Dire poverty was the reason why the children had to work. But in the long run it would serve the working community best if the men were to take home enough money for all the family, so the women could mind the infants, and the young children could go to school. The only way to combat disease and bad conditions at work, was if the working people themselves realised what was right and proper. All the grumbling in the world wouldn't make any changes. It was the workers themselves, the 'little maisters', in charge of each workshop, who would have to get things going, and have the vision of what could be achieved. Education, of everyone, that's what would make for a better life. It was as a committed Union man that Robert saw that unjust practices, by masters and men, must be stamped out. If the men wished to get better conditions, they must improve their own side of things, not turn up to work late, or not turn up at all.

Robert was hungry. His snapping, put up by his landlady, was long since finished. He wished he was homeward bound as he should be, by now. He was also despondent after his conversation with Enoch. It would be a nearly impossible task to get the two sides in the dispute to understand they would both have to make changes, to profit the industry as a whole, and their own livelihoods.

6

The weather turned really wintry, with low fog. Enoch gave Tilly the day off, as she was speaking with a hoarse voice. She must stay indoors, and not risk a bad cold. She was late getting up and Deaker was helping her.

"What do you think of a musical evening? Mama and I were talking about the new church last night."

"Oh yes, I know, your dear Mama, she do have that very close to her heart. It's like another child to her, that new church."

"She wants to raise some money for the furnishings. She thought we might have a party, a concert really. So that people could come with their music, and we'd have a collection."

"Well, I never. That is a good idea, I do think. That will give the dear soul something to occupy her. That will certainly...."

Tilly cut her short. "I don't think she needs anything really, Deaker. She's always fully occupied. Pass me my petticoat." She got out of bed. Tilly raised her arms and Deaker slipped a long white silk chemise over her head. The girl wriggled in, letting the shawl fall on the floor. Deaker lifted out Tilly's long hair which was trapped inside the chemise. Standing in front of the fire, Tilly began the complicated process of dressing.

"One thing I do say, Miss Tilly, working dunna harm your looks. You're as bonny as ever, in spite of the grime up there. Oh, we do have to scrub those silk blouses of yours, yes we do."

"What do you think, Deaker? They call it 'soiree' in London. 'A musical soiree at Terrilea." Tilly danced a few steps holding an imaginary violin and bow.

"It'll be good for her, like I said. We did use to have those sort of things, before you was born, and I remember at your Grandma's. But they times is over, since then, well...." She knelt down to put a lump of coal on the fire.

"'Well', Well, what?"

"Nothing really, Miss Tilly. Nothing you don't know already."

"You mean about Mama?"

"That's it, Miss. It dunna do to talk on it. After you was born, it took her strength, and then, there wasn't to be any more little ones. It saddened her." Deaker was poking the fire. "But she's got you, and you're everything to her, I have to say."

"I suppose it is hard for her, me going out to the business every day."

Deaker did not reply, and Tilly sat down at the dressing table. Deaker came up and took the silver brush off her. She took long hard strokes, but she couldn't smooth down the wiry curls. "You're not like your Ma, Miss Tilly. You favour your Pa. The hair. Everything. You're the spit of Mr. Manstone, bless you." She began trying to twist the thick bunches of Tilly's hair round and round into a rope.

"If only I didn't have all this hair. I would like to have it all off, I would. It's nothing but a nuisance. I could wear a wig, for best, and the rest of the time, I'd just stuff it into a cap."

"You are a caution, you are. You shouldn't make mock of the Lord, giving you such lovely hair. I don't know."

"One day, I will do what I like with it. It's nothing but washing and brushing all the time. I takes me half the day."

"Stop talking nonsense now. You won't do no such thing." Deaker had a mouthful of hairpins in her mouth and began stabbing them furiously into Tilly's bun. "There now. That looks lovely."

When it was done, Tilly poked a few strands out from the sides, so they hung down in front of her cheeks. Well, she supposed it didn't look too bad. But now it was all scrunched up into a bun, it might just as well be cut short, for all you could see of it.

"A party would be nice, Miss Tilly. We must live in hopes, mustn't we?" She gazed at the girl's reflection. She stood back, her head on one side, and her arms folded. "A few flowers in your hair, and you'd be like a bride. You'll make a lovely bride. Perhaps that won't be too long."

"Don't say that. You know I don't think of marriage yet. It's just a party, we're organising. Nothing grand, you know, a musical party." Tilly rose from the dressing table stool, and spun round on her toe, examining as well as she could, the back of her head.

Deaker followed her round, holding the little silver hand mirror this way and that, to give the girl a better view.

"I don't know, you've put me all about, now." The old woman sank down on the foot of the bed. "What would your dear mother say if she knew what you just told me? You are a strange one. I don't know."

"I don't know either, Deaker. It was different in your day, and her day, come to that. Did the girls have any choices then?"

"Young ladies," Deaker stressed the last word, "they were happy with what they got. And if you talk about choice - to have to go and work for a living, if you call that choice, well I don't think much on it."

"I suppose it depends." Tilly sat down again on the stool. She sighed. There was some truth in what Deaker had said. After all, Gertie and the other paintresses weren't working from choice. But she was. She was. Even if it had been Papa's wish in the first place.

A bell jangled.

"There now, your Mama's set down and she'll be asking for her egg. Your porridge won't be kept hot for ever, Miss Tilly. Come along now."

Tilly swished out of the bedroom, leaving Deaker to put the fireguard up.

In the morning room, candles had been lit on the table, the morning was so dark. Edna was seated at one end, delicately prising the last of the egg white from the crown of her egg.

"Well. Tilly!"

"Didn't Papa tell you? I've the day off." She kissed her mother on the cheek, then went over to the bay window. "It's the weather." She couldn't imagine how anyone could go anywhere, with the fog like it was. The trees on the other side of the valley were hardly visible, just menacing, gloomy shapes. She had always thought that about those trees. She didn't know why father had planted that barrier on the ridge opposite the house. It would have been nice to see through to the green fields and the cattle. The trees were an obstruction between Terrilea and the town, the rest of the world, in fact. Tilly felt enclosed, they enclosed her, as if she were hemmed in to this little spot on the universe.

Jeannie came in with the porridge.

"Come and eat up, before it gets cold," said Edna.

Tilly sat down, took her table napkin out of its ring, and helped herself from the porringer.

"You seem put out, my dear. Are you sickening for a cold?"

Mother hadn't noticed her sneezing. Father had. "I'm all right, Mama." Tilly ate her porridge in silence. It was silly to be sulky. The fact that her mother had thought she was out of sorts made her feel like that.

"I'm sorry, Mama." She scraped the last of the porridge of of her bowl. Making a big effort, she smiled at her mother. "It's just, I was put out, a little, Father suddenly deciding not to let me go to the Works today. I know I should be glad really, but it's not like that. If he wants me to do a proper job, he should take me seriously, you know. If he can do without me one day, without warning, then he could do without me any day."

Of course he could, Edna thought. "It's early days yet." She poured another cup of tea. "I know he's pleased with you. He's told me how well you're doing. Even that clerk of his, the one who came to the lecture."

"Mr. Willoughby?"

"Yes. Him. According to father, even he doesn't find fault with your work. And you know, father speaks quite highly of him."

"It's for father I'm doing it." Silently Tilly added, "and myself." She wanted to go to the office to be somebody, to do something. Perhaps working at Manstone's might even lead to something else. This was her secret thought. She couldn't tell it to anyone. But, - she didn't really see herself as taking over the Works, eventually. Also another reason, perhaps the main reason why she wanted to learn all about the business, was that her work there was teaching her another side of life. The more she saw, the more involved she had become in the lives of these people, whose destiny was so different from her own. She had begun to recognise she had strange ambivalent feelings towards the other people with whom she was coming into contact; Gertie, the other paintresses, the labourers in the yard, even Robert Willoughby. In one way, she disliked them all. Everyone treated her with respect, but underneath, she felt they resented her. She felt they watched her from the corner of their eyes, as she went about her duties. She was sure they gossiped about her, perhaps even laughed at her. But, she pitied them. She feared them, but, in a way, she wished to help them, to make life better for them.

Edna was speaking again. "I'm so pleased that Father let you stay at home today. It's very fortunate. It's the meeting of the ladies connected with the New Church Foundation. You'll be able to come and help me."

"I can't come, Mama, they wouldn't like that."

"Of course they will. They're full of interest. It's not at all how I thought it would be. They actually want to see you, and talk all about it."

"I'm just the same as I was. Just because I'm working, it's not as if I have a contagious disease."

Edna ignored this remark. Tilly often seemed so sharp and prickly. The best thing was to pretend she hadn't heard.

"We're all very proud of you. Doing your duty as Father wants you to. Anyway, I think you can help me too. We have to have a fund raising event for the church furnishings. Your ideas will be useful."

"Oh, mama. You're always doing that. Raising money, and then raising money again. It's so time consuming. Why can't the church benefactors just give a little extra money, and all that would be covered? Father and the others, who gave the money for the building. They could all just give a little more. Otherwise it's all crochet work and sewing, and in the end you'll only collect a little bit, and you'll have to do it all again."

"Tilly! You know the ladies wish to do their bit. This is their chance to show how involved they are. They're so proud to be doing it."

"That's all very fine, Mama. But it's such a little bit. It's the men really, with their enterprises and businesses, who've really made it possible."

Edna did not reply. It was best to say nothing when Tilly was in this humour. She was so like her father. Where did her own wishes come in? Enoch had told her he might be going on some trips to London, to do with business, but when she'd suggested she might go with him, he'd dismissed the idea out of hand.

"Anyway, I am glad to be home for once." Tilly drank another cup of tea, which made her throat feel a little better. "What about that idea we were talking about a week ago. The musical evening. Don't say you've forgotten. I mean it seriously Mama. If you think it would be possible to have one of those musical evenings here, we could collect then for the church furnishings. Why not get the Committee involved?"

Edna struggled to think about what Tilly had said. She sighed. "It seems like a great effort."

"The others would help."

"No. I think not. It is my house. It is your father's house. We should see to it ourselves. But I would prefer that, without the committee ladies having to be involved."

"I see. You hadn't forgotten then?"

"Of course not. I'm not quite stupid, whatever you and Father may think." Edna said this with a smile. But the remark went home to Tilly.

"We don't think that at all. You must know that."

"As a matter of fact, your father and I both used to go to musical parties, when we were very young. That was how we met."

"Really, Mama?" Tilly had never heard this before. She had never really understood how her parents had ever become friends, and then, husband and wife. She'd just taken it all for granted. But recently, she had begun to wonder how two people so different should ever have decided to spend their lives together. Perhaps they were the same, when they married, and had changed since. Or perhaps it didn't matter if people were entirely different. Marriage must somehow work a spell on them. However, that seemed to be taking a big risk. Supposing the spell didn't work?

"But then he became so busy, after we were married. It's like that. Sometimes." Edna rose to ring the bell by the fireplace. "I'm sure he would be very content with the idea, if it's in aid of the new church."

"I'll help you, Mama. I could ask Ros to play, and her brother plays the violin, they could do a little sonata. And then singing too."

"I think we need the highest standard. It has to be something different. It won't do to just ask friends and relatives. Not if we are going to raise money. Do you know any singers?"

Tilly was surprised at her mother's tone. She suddenly seemed....energised. "Only the clerk. Don't you remember, he mentioned it? Part-singing, with a group."

"Of course. Robert Willoughby?" Robert's face came into her mind, as it had been when he'd been talking to them in the carriage, thin, pale, but animated. "I don't know. They may be Chapel. That would put it out of the question for our church funds."

"Why? If they would do it, I can't see why it should matter. Surely true religion doesn't see any obstacle to people joining together for a good cause, whether they're Church or Chapel, or Hindu or Hottentot."

"Don't be ridiculous. People might talk. We shall have to be very careful."

"Mama. I am sure we could arrange it, and not upset anyone. Write a letter for me to take to Willoughby, and ask him if he'll sing at your party."

The fog grew thicker as the morning progressed. All the gas lights were on in Manstone's yard.

"If it don't lift soon, we shall have to send for more candles," Gertie's neighbour croaked. Her chest, always painful, was worse. Even in the summer, she had difficulty breathing and today, with the chimney fumes unable to rise, she could hardly speak.

"I dunna have money for more." Gertie replied. "Robert says we shouldn'a be paying for candles 'ere"

"He may say so. He may." An older woman spoke up. "But that wanna help us. It's allus bin the case we have to pay for our own candles. Nowt's going to change that."

"He vows he'll bring it up at the meeting, Saturday."

"It'll be last thing the masters will do, give us money for our own candles. They'd rather see us blind."

"Then we'd be no good for nothing."

There was silence for a while, as the women peered at their work. Even inside the fog had penetrated. The air was damp and cold, the little stove which had been lit only dispelling the chill in the area immediately adjacent to it. Every now and then one of other of the women would come and warm her fingers, or put her mittens on the stove itself, where they would immediately begin to steam.

"We wunna' finish these in time if you wenches keep warming yourselves. You're nesh, that's what. I've worked in this shop when there'd be no fire at all."

"It's that Miss Manstone, she's the one what persuaded her Da to give us some coal, on top of what we've paid for out of the wages. No more having to sneak off down to scrape together a shovelful from the yard. We've something to be thankful for at least." It was Gertie's turn to warm herself. She squatted on her haunches for a few minutes, rubbing her hands. On her way back to her stool, she looked out of the window. Robert was just coming out of the office door, and automatically glanced up at the decorating shop. He saw Gertie and smiled. "There he is now, I shall tell 'im to make sure he brings up about candles at the meeting. Can I go, Alice?"

"Make sure Abraham don't see thee, wench. We know it's not about candles tha'rt going." There was general laughter, and Sophie began to cough. Gertie pulled another shawl over her head, wrapping it tightly so that little was visible of her face, except for the eyes. At the bottom of the wooden steps she could just see as far as the yard gates. Robert, his back to her, was hurrying down the tunnel, towards the street doors. Gertie put on a burst of speed, and as he went into the road, she caught up with him. There was no sign of the entry clerk anywhere.

"Rob."

"Oh. There. I wish you would not come up to me like that."

"I had to see you."

"What is it? I thought we'd agreed not to be seen together in work time."

"Why not, Robert? We're walking out, ain't we? What's the harm?"

"You know full well, Gertie. It's in Mr. Manstone's time. He's paying you and me, to be working. It's not right to have time out,"

"Well, I like that. Who's talking, pray? I suppose you'll say Mr. Manstone's paying you to have a walk down the street, is he?"

"He is. That's just it. I'm ....." Robert stopped. There was no reason why he should explain to Gertie where he was going.

"Why cannot he send that wench of his to do the errands, or go with her if he's learning her the job?"

"You don't understand anything. Anyway, she's not in today."

"Oh, is she not? I suppose the weather's too inclement, that's it. And does that please you, Robert Willoughby, to have the office to yourself?"

"Gertie. Don't use that tone to me. I don't think about what Mr. Manstone and the girl do. It's nothing to me, so long as I get my week's money. Which I won't do, if they see us gossiping here."

"That's not so at all, Robert. You do mind what Manstone does. What about the meeting you was going to Saturday? That's what I come to tell you about."

"Oh, yes. I thought you didn't wish me to go to the meeting."

"I don't. I'd rather be walking down the river, on a Sunday afternoon, I would. But it ain't Sunday, and if it were, I doubt you'd be too busy, what with your singing and all, and besides, I know you've set your heart on this meeting, and so it should be, and you might as well know what the paintresses want, and see if you can do something for us. We want coal and candles that's what."

"So, it wasn't to see me, you came running up." Robert was standing in the entrance to a narrow alleyway. "If I bring it up in the meeting, will that satisfy you, my wench?" He seized her by the waist, and pulled her close. "You do know I'll help you all I can, and the other girls too."

"Yes, I know, especially the other girls." She began to push him away.

"Since you've come, you may as well give me a kiss?" He would not let her bend away from him.

She felt his thin body against her, and suddenly relaxed. After all, he had said they were to be married, hadn't he? "Just the one." He kissed her gently, on the mouth. His soft lips were wet, and he felt her responding. Delicious warmth flowed through her as his hands squeezed her breasts.

"You're a beauty, you are my wench. You know when you're best off. I'll look after you, come now, come now. You'll see, you will," he murmured. There was the sound of clogs, coming up the alley, but no-one was to be seen.

Gertie pulled away quickly, and peered over her shoulder.

"I'll come round Saturday, after meeting," Rob said.

Gertie fled back up the street, and slipped into the factory, pulling her shawl even tighter so that the women wouldn't see her red cheeks.

Next day before breakfast, at Terrilea, Enoch was in his study, looking at drawings delivered by the first post. These showed detailed plans of the pews to be constructed for the new Church of St. Bartholomew.

There was a tap on the door.

"Come in." Enoch grunted, without looking up. It was Tilly, dressed in her work costume. "Did I say you were to go in today?"

"No father. I dressed like this to be ready, in case."

"Well, you're not going. Nor me neither. If you're well enough to get up and get dressed, you can come with me to see to the Architect. See here. He's put in for all this carving on the bench ends. That won't do." Enoch stabbed at the drawing with his fat, blunt finger. "We don't want oak leaves and the like. Whoever heard of such a thing? He's trying to bleed me for money, that's what it is. Well, I'm not having it. We'll see who's calling the tunes here. I'm not made of money."

"I came to ask you to come for breakfast. Mama is waiting to pour."

"I'm coming, I'm coming. Why is there such a hurry for me to have breakfast? Are you and she planning anything?"

"Not that I know of, Papa."

"Just as well. You're to accompany me to the site where they're building that new papist church. We'll see Mr. Lugando ourselves. I want to make sure he's not neglecting us in favour of that Duke, who's putting up the money for that. Might have got the drawings muddled up."

Tilly raised her eyebrows. Hardly likely, she thought, but kept silent. Over the porridge, Enoch told Edna he would be out all morning with Edna.

"She should have had another day's rest. I trust your expedition isn't to be tiring."

"Don't fuss yourself. We shall take the carriage, and there's no need for her to be outside.

After a long drive, with Enoch barking directions every so often, the carriage pulled up. A large stone edifice, newly built, stood in the middle of a patch of ground covered with piles of sand, and rough-hewn stones. Lengths of wood lay in untidy heaps.

"Goodness, Papa," Tilly said.

Enoch took her arm, and they picked their way over rough ground towards the structure.

"Look at what they're doing." Tilly pointed to where workmen were balanced far up on what appeared to be the base of the spire. So high up, they looked like large young birds, which, unable to fly properly, had landed awkwardly on the jutting masonry.

"That is a fine sight," said Tilly. "I should think it must be fearful up there."

"I expect they're used to it." To Enoch, the whole building seemed unnecessarily gaudy. There were several different kinds and shades of stone, giving varied colours to the façade, and carvings adorned the spire, as well as the window embrasures and door frames.

The doors were already in place.

Two men came through the main door, one tall, with a full head of silvery grey hair, and a small beard, over which protruded a curving, bulbous nose. He was conventionally dressed in smart frock coat, with high collar and cravat. The other man, hardly more than a youth, had on an informal suit, with cravat, and a silk handkerchief in his breast pocket. His hair, brushed down very flat, was pale brown, and his eyes, rather deep set, were hazel. "Mr. Manstone, sir, the older man said. "To what do I owe this unexpected pleasure? And Miss Manstone, I presume?"

"I've come to say what I think about these drawings. For our new church, Saint Bart's." Enoch flourished the roll of paper. "We've got to get this sorted out. Time's going on."

"Of course, Sir. I welcome you to my other project. Alphonse Lugando, at your service." The man bowed to Tilly. "And this is my assistant, Mr. Lockyard."

"How do you do.

The assistant spoke up. "Please come inside."

"We can't be long, but since we're here..." Enoch followed Tilly inside.

Inside there were ladders everywhere, and on the ladders were painters. All the walls were completely covered with intricate designs of red, green, blue, and above all, gold.

There was silence in the building except for someone singing. Tilly looked up to see who was the owner of the voice. A young man, perched on top of a pair of long steps, was carefully applying gilding to the edge of a complicated pattern of green leaves. He had not noticed the visitors and continued to sing. The words were incomprehensible, they might be Italian, or French. Tilly could not guess which.

Tilly was amazed. She did not know what to think. She had never seen anything like this. The dazzling colours, and the singing, all came together in a crescendo, forcing itself upon her senses and attention. The young man, high up, was oblivious of his audience. This made it all the more unreal.

The architect and his assistant were silent, evidently aware of the impression the atmosphere of the place was making on the visitors. The song finished, and Enoch turned round. "We haven't much time. Let us look at these drawings at once."

He did not wish Lugando to think he was in over impressed. He was impressed, but that did not mean he wanted that sort of thing in the new St. Bartholomew. Of course he knew the man was famous for his decorations, but he could also get the better of the builders. That was why Enoch had engaged him.

Lugando turned to Lockyard. "Show Miss Manstone the pulpit." He took the drawings off Enoch and spread them out on top of the font.

Lockyard pointed towards stone pulpit.

"The alabaster carving, dates from the twelfth century. But I am sure you will find our own workmanship surpasses all that they could do in former times. Let us go and see it, then you can judge for yourself."

.....Tilly blushed. She felt that she was expected to make rapturous comments about the work the painters were doing. She followed Lockyard to the front of the church. As they went, she craned her neck at the vaulted ceiling and the men, lying on their backs painting it, in all colours of the palette. The pulpit itself was standing on a block of white stone, all carved with various figures, and swirls of leaves, fruit and flowers. Tilly stood in silence for a moment.

"They are lovely," she said. "Do they tell a story?"

"Of course. There is Eve, and there is Adam. And there is the serpent." He pointed out all of the images in the story of the Creation, running his fingers over the curves of the petals, and the little faces and limbs of the two humans.

Tilly noticed how slender his hands were, and pale. She couldn't think what to say. It didn't matter. The man continued holding forth.

"Some people think that the Art of the Middle Ages has never been bettered since." David Lockyard took the handkerchief out of his pocket, rubbed his hands on it, then, with a flourish replaced it.

Tilly tried to think of an intelligent response. "You don't believe that, do you? Surely modern Art must be better. We've got so many more....materials. And then, they didn't have photographs."

"Their art was based on strong convictions, faith, and I think that shows, in this work for instance. They also had great sense of humour. See." He indicated a lion, lying with his head on his paws, and a smile, yes, definitely a smile, on his face. He seemed to be gazing at a lamb, standing near him. "He looks as if he's just waiting for his chance. And he'll get it, any minute, when God turns the animals out of the Garden of Eden, to fend for themselves."

Tilly peered at the beast. There was something which could be interpreted as a smile. "You're right." She continued to gaze at the carving then felt herself blushing. She wasn't quite sure what more to say. She knew she was expected to comment on the work in progress. All the people were working so hard. This architect, if that was what he was, was so proud of it all. Yet somehow, she could hardly say in all truth, that she thought it beautiful. In fact, now she thought about it, it seemed ostentatious. All this gold, and richness, didn't suit the small grey town nearby, and the bleak landscape. Nevertheless, she had to be polite. "It's not what I'm used to. None of it. Do you like any other period? I think this is all very beautiful, but maybe..... "

"Perhaps you like the more austere style of a later period?"

"Perhaps. Are you an expert in all this?"

"No. Just a student. I shall be that all my life, I'm sure. I'm very lucky to have the opportunity to work with so renowned a man as Signor Lugando."

"You're not from Italy, then."

"I! No, I'm afraid not, Just Dulwich, a suburb of London."

To Tilly, this seemed equally exotic. "Well, you're lucky. You must be able to go to all the lectures, and, well, anything you want to, in London."

"I have been lucky, to have the chance to study there. But it also broadens the mind, to travel. Both are necessary. And I don't mean, just to travel to faraway places, but to travel into other people's worlds, as well. To meet many different people. That is necessary, to be an artist."

"I would like to have a chance like that, to meet lots and lots of people."

"You will. I am sure."

"I don't know. I'm busy, with my father's work."

Mr. Lockyard looked at her quizzically. Was she being facetious? Just then they heard a shout. Enoch was waving his hand.

"I must go. Father has finished his business."

"Would it possible for us to meet again? It has been so delightful talking to you. Perhaps you enjoy music. You looked captivated by the singing."

“I was. Your painter has fine voice. As a matter of fact, we may be having a concert at home, shortly. A soiree. I am sure my mother would be pleased to meet you. She is the artist in our family. Would you like an invitation? An invitation for both of you. And your ladies. We are actually raising money for our new church furnishings”

“I am quite certain that Signor Lugando would be more than pleased. Unfortunately, we could not bring ladies, as the Signor’s wife is in Florence, and I.....well....I am not so lucky as to be married yet.”

It was decided. The gentlemen would be sent formal invitations for the party. Tilly had the pleasant feeling, as they drove home, that she hadn’t made a complete fool of herself, in front of the stranger, and Enoch was quite satisfied that he had managed to persuade Lugando to make fresh drawings, for no extra charge.

7

On Saturday, Rob was late for the Union meeting. Mrs. Jakes had asked him to help move a heavy wardrobe downstairs, as she was to utilise her own bedroom for two more lodgers. "Mr. Willoughby," she had announced that morning, "Breakfast will be taken in the kitchen and the evening meal will be in the front room as usual."

It seemed that Mrs. Jakes would be sleeping in the front room, on a couch, which would be pushed back for the meal to be served, when the table would be unfolded for the guests. After they had gone to bed, she would reinstate the couch for herself.

Since her husband, a flat presser, had died of potter's rot, a few months previously, Mrs. Jakes had had to make as much money as she could out of her house, so that she could help support her grandchildren. In some ways, her life had become easier. She could sleep at night, without the constant coughing of the sick man, and she wasn't trailing about nursing him, as well as all her other worries. Lodgers, God bless them, weren't near so demanding as an ailing husband. It was all for the best, and God would help those who helped themselves.

It was Rob himself who had suggested the new arrangement, when he found Mrs. Jakes sitting in front of the fire one night, with a handkerchief held to her nose, and wet cheeks. So when she at last made up her mind to take his advice, and put the plan into action, he did not feel he should put her off by suggesting another time for the move. In the event the wardrobe got stuck on the stairs, and the whole operation took much longer and a lot more sweat than he had anticipated. Also there was a broken stair rail to mend, but this would have to wait till tomorrow. He crammed his cap on his head, and his muffler round his neck and sprinted up the street towards the market square.

Frank was already holding forth by the time Rob arrived on the fringe of the crowd. Men and women packed the whole area, spilling down into adjacent streets. Frank's deep voice boomed out as effectively as any Shakespearean actor. He kept taking off his cap and readjusting it with a flourish.

"You know what this settlement means... you've all heard it, haven't you. The Arbitration says we'll have not a penny more; Lord Hatherton's penny stands. It's ours by rights, they took it off us, and now they won't reinstate it. And the contract stands. St. Martin's is still to be our contract day.

Whistles and boos came from the crowd and there were cries of "Shame," "Down with the Masters."

"Arbitration is just another word for surrender. That's what I have come to tell you. They dunna listen to what us workers tell 'em. We have men dying from silicosis, and women dying from the potters' droop, and what do we get for it? Starvation money, that's what, my friends. A pittance, what isn't enough to keep body and soul together. And our children. We're forced to bring them to work, to get bread to eat. Where's the free education we was promised? It's two years since the Education Act, and since then, what has been done for us? We shall be prosecuted ourselves for taking our children to help us make ends meet, to put bread in their mouths. It's not us who wish that on our children, creatures of our flesh and blood. It's our paymasters, the Pottery Masters. Do you see their children, starving, uneducated, in rags? Do you? Do you?"

"No, no, no!" shouted various people in the crowd. "We want fair pay. No more long dozens."

"That's right. We should be paid for twelve if we've done twelve, and thirteen, if we've done thirteen. No more calling thirteen, twelve. Where's the fairness of that, where's the end of it all? We're skilled. They couldn't do without us, for all their fine houses and carriages. They couldn't have any of it without us, without our hard graft. Our hard graft, my friends."

Rob waited for the shouts greeting this remark to die down.

"What have we to do, Mr. Frank?" someone shouted.

"That's what I'm coming to. I put it to you friends. We'll go on strike."

There was a momentary pause from the crowd, then fists were raised, and a voice shouted from the back.

"Aye, strike if we must. That's why we put money in the fund. We've done what we can."

"We have, we have, my friend. We sent our comrades to America, in hopes that would give us the answer. There's too many of us - that's what we thought. Our fathers saved up, in hopes of a better life. How many of our Dads gev sixpence every week? But where's the Emigration Society now, where's Pottersville? Did it help us? Not a bit. It's here, we want to live, here, this is our home. But how can it be called a home, when we haven't the money to feed our children? It's no good. We have to live. Your Dad gave to that fund, and my Dad gave to that fund, and they thought that would solve it. But it's no good. We've put our trust in the Arbitration Board, but what has it got for us? Nothing. It's all on the side of the Masters. We have to live, and we canna on that miserable pittance the masters pay us. How many of you have children to support?" Frank roared at the crowd.

Hundreds of hands went up.

"And how many take their children to work, to make ends meet?"

There was silence, broken after a few minutes by a raucous laugh.

"Dunna you ask, Frank, lad, tha' knowst it be agin the law."

"You cannot say it, but we all know it. A man's wages won't support a family unless the family work too. You know it, and I know it, but we cannot say it, for fear of the law. And what if the master will not pay your wages? If orders don't come, or buyers won't buy, what then? Can we go and get other employment?"

"No," shouted a voice.

"Right. We cannot. We're hired to the contract, and cannot leave it till the contract's fulfilled. Even without pay."

"You're right, Frank, remember Dick Worsley."

"That's right. Worsley. Remember Dick Worsley. Rotting in gaol for breaking his contract, and trying to work for wages at another Pot Bank. What then, my friends? Off to the magistrate, and a twelvemonths hard labour. His wife widowed, as good as, and six orphaned children, as good as."

"Shame, shame," came cries from the crowd.

"Slaves, English slaves, that's what the contract makes us."

"Strike, strike!" came a shout.

"Aye, that's what it has to be. We'll have it out with them, once and for all."

A huge roar went up from the crowd. Caps were tossed in the air, and the men were slapping each other on the back.

Robert was still standing silently, hand in pockets all this while, as Frank continued with his diatribe. He pushed his way over to the right, where there was a railing around the cellar steps to some houses. He climbed up on the bottom rail. He could see over the heads of the crowd, and peered around to see any faces he recognised. A light rain had begun to fall, and the dim light flaring from the gas lights hardly provided enough light to disperse the gloom. The men had their caps pulled down, and their collars turned up. Rob saw Dan standing not far away. He was excitedly yelling something at the speaker and had not noticed him. So that was it. Dan had decided to go along with the strike. Rob's heart sank. Everything was true that Frank had said, and he'd put it in such a way, there was no doubt what the men would vote for. But he knew that they would never succeed. There would only be enough in the Union funds to last a few weeks. The Masters could last much, much longer than that. Rob climbed down from the rail, skirted round the back of the crowd, and made his way to Tregarth Road, and then down in the direction of Lombardy Square. The thin rain was beginning to penetrate his coat at the shoulders. The cobbles were shiny with the damp, but greasy and slippery.

Away from the market square it was quiet. Houses and shops were shuttered, kitchens fires were smoking, and the only lights in the gloom came from the pie and chip shops now just opening up.

As Rob passed the turning which led down to Manstones, he glanced down the street, drawn by a strange magnetism, to look at the Pot Bank. The heavy metal doors to the yard were shut, and the kiln fires had been damped down several hours previously. The factory looked deserted, even dead.

Suddenly Rob had a vision of what it would be like if the men came out on strike, as was evidently their intention. Manstone's would look like this every day of the week, perhaps for months, perhaps for ever. He knew the Master would never go against Arbitration, and give the men what they required, in excess of the Arbitration award. The men had originally agreed to abide by Arbitration, and so had the masters, and Manstone would see that they kept to their bargain. There wouldn't be any deviation by Manstone, and Rob knew that if he himself were to support the strike, he'd be sacked immediately. Indeed, Manstone relied on him to support the management, and influence the men to take the sensible and rational course, that is, to accept the award. If Manstone had any cause to suspect Robert of disloyalty, he'd see the clerk should never got another job in the pottery industry. It would mean moving on again, for Rob. The men, poor devils, they couldn't move, no funds left to send them off to America, even if they had wanted to go. That experiment had not been a success.

Rob knew the men hadn't a chance. True, the masters would lose orders, if they couldn't fulfil their current promises to buyers. But there was every chance they'd be able to rebuild their sales network without much trouble when the strike ended, as they had such a dominant hold on the market.

Rob stood outside the locked gates of the factory. His place would be inside those gates, if it came to a strike.

Just at that moment, there came the sound of a horse's hooves on the cobbles. A man on horseback was coming down the hill.

"What the devil are you doing here, man?" It was Manstone. He reined in his horse. "I've got proper wet, looking for you in that crowd up yonder. I telled you to find out what was happening."

"I've been up there, sir. I don't need to wait longer, the crowd's behind that Frank Borthing, sir."

"I can see that. But I suppose we don't have to go just by that group of men. There's plenty have been to the football and they're not back yet. Do you think it will come to strike?"

"I cannot see it, Mr. Manstone. You don't have to fear that."

"I don't fear it, Willoughby." Manstone turned his horse round.

"It's they who encourage the men, they're the ones who have to be afeared. Nothing but sorrow and starvation will be the result. They cannot win, they've got a settlement, and should stand by that."

"Yes, sir."

"I'll see you in the office on Monday, as usual." Manstone touched the horse's flank with his whip, and off it trotted, with a quick bound. Manstone would have to hurry to be back in daylight.

Rob's fists were clenched inside his pocket, but he extricated one, to touch his cap. He watched the Master leaning back, and bumping heavily in the saddle, as the horse went down the hill. He pondered whether the horse would slip on the cobbles, and the master would, perhaps, break his neck, or his leg at least. Manstone didn't hunt, he called it a waste of time and money, and too dangerous, and yet he'd come here on horseback this afternoon, all the way in the drizzle. It was obvious he'd ridden over to see the fun, and brought the horse to lord it.

Robert marched off down the street, his boots clattering. He was warm, inside his damp jacket. The excitement of the meeting, and his confrontation with the Master had roused him. A few lads were beginning to trail up the hill from the football ground, and Rob had to dodge between them as he hurried down to the junction. He could hear the noise of the crowd let loose, from here, the sound of their tramping feet, and the low barrage of voices. Why hadn't they all gone to the meeting, instead of the football match? That would have given the Masters something to think about. As it was, if that was all the support they could get, the Potters Union might as well whistle for more money.

Gertie's house was the end of the terrace, and, as the next street went off at an angle, this resulted in the house standing in a small triangle of land, giving slightly more scope than the neighbours had, with their tiny back yards. Rob had managed to salvage some wood from the builders who had been working at Manstone's the previous year, and he had knocked together a low fence round the patch, to keep off scavenging dogs and the neighbourhood children. Inside was a rabbit hutch, and a small cage in which lived two chickens. Rob provided some food for them, and Gertie made up scraps from her household. Thus there were eggs in the summer, and, occasionally, rabbit stews.

Normally on a Saturday afternoon, Rob and Gertie would go along the canal, foraging green stuff for the rabbits. The rest of the tiny plot was taken up with potatoes in the summer, and these plants were dug up, one by one. By now, the plot was nearly all dug over. Rob went into the garden, squatted down in front of the cages, and poked his fingers into the rabbit, which was sitting there, nose twitching, half asleep.

"Has Missus fed you lass?" he asked. "See what I've got." He pulled a bag of crusts from his pocket, scavenged from Mrs. Jakes' kitchen. He switched round the wooden catch on the hutch door.

"I've already fed her, Rob. You dunna want to spoil her." Gertie had quietly come out of the door, and was bending down to him, her cheek towards his, her arm round his shoulder.

He stood up, and clasped her round the waist.

"Is Mother home?" he asked, feeling for her mouth with his.

She pulled herself away.

"She went out an hour since. To Aunt May. I telled her you was working this afternoon!"

"You didn't tell her of the meeting?"

"I didn't."

"Then we'll go inside, shall we, my lass?"

"She'll not be out long.

"Perhaps we'd better go down to the bridge, then?"

"Oh, stay here. It's too wet now, to go out. Besides, I'll make you your tea. She knows you're coming."

They went round to the back door, and into the kitchen. The range was alight, and well made up, with coal, the lamp on the table was lit, and the curtains closed. The cat was asleep on a cushion in the Windsor chair by the chimney corner.

Gertie began to remove skirts and petticoats which were hanging on the line in front of the range.

"Never mind that, Gert. I've seen your knickers before. Come on, now, my girl." He grasped her by the waist again, this time from behind, and began to draw her skirts out of the way.

She turned round, with the damp washing under one arm.

"Bolt the door."

"Aye." He got up, and fastened the bolt on the back door. "She knows what we're about, I'm sure."

"You won't have time for me, when you're rich."

He caught hold of the sheet she was folding, then pulled her towards him. "Don't be so sure," he said, bending her head back. He kissed her on the mouth. He felt her relaxing.

Gertie could smell the wet wool of his jacket,

"Oh, Rob. I wish we could be married. If we was married." She put her arms round his neck, pressing herself against him. It was always like this, she wanted him, so much. She wanted him with her, but he was always impatient.

"We can be married. We shall be." He was stroking her hair, touching her cheek.

Gertie brought her hand up, grasping his fingers. "Leave me be, Robert. She'll be back this instant." She was panting. Robert's other hand was round her waist, his fingers slid down, and was smoothing the skirt, down, down, across her buttocks. He kissed her, gently at first, then forcing her mouth open. She turned her head a little.

Robert felt his penis, hard against her. "Won't you hold me? It won't hurt you. I'll see nothing happens."

She pushed against his shoulders, pressing him away from her. "Don't you do it, Robert. Leave me be." She wrenched herself away. "You know we canna do it till we're married."

"What is the matter with you? Don't the other girls tell you? There's nothing wrong. It'll make you happy. Come on." He caught her round the waist again. "Come on, now then."

She caught his hand and held it. "Don't force me. Let me be. I love you Robert Willoughby," she said.

He let her go. What was the point? Love! She talked about that. But she would never do it. He was sure, now. He closed his eyes. She watched him, oblivious of her. He gave a low groan as if the life was coming out of him. She turned to the stone sink, supporting herself, her hands flat, on the cold brown glaze. After a moment, she pumped the water, and it splashed her hands. She turned her face up towards it, and let it drizzle into her mouth and over her cheeks..

Rob became aware of a cold draught, then a door banged. It must be the old woman returning from her visit. "It's her." He turned towards the fire, making it up with fresh coal. His back was towards the door. He didn't want the old woman to see him like that.

"Are you there, our Gertie?" It was Mrs. Lambert. A moment later she appeared in the doorway, still wearing her black bonnet and mantle she stared at Robert, then at Gertie. "Oh, you've come for your tea, my girl wasn't too sure."

"I've something for you, Mrs." Rob groped in his jacket pocket and brought out a small object wrapped in newspaper. He put it on the table.

The old lady balanced her stick against the wall, removed her bonnet and shawl, then hobbled to the wooden armchair. She sat down, heavily. "There now," she gasped. "That's it. Now then, what've you brought me?"

"Open it."

Gertie had gone into the yard.

"I'll wait till our lass is ready," said Mrs. Lambert, wiping her eyes on the corner of her handkerchief. "Hurry up now, girl."

Gertie came in and the old lady began to fumble with the wrapping.

"I'll manage it, Ma. Give it over here."

Inside was a small pottery figurine. It was that of a small child, leaning against a wall over which was growing a flowering plant.

"Oh, it is beautiful." Mrs. Lambert wheezed. She turned it over and looked at the bottom. "Leviathan pottery! Well. It's too good for the kitchen, we'll put it here, on the chimney piece. Here you are Gertie, take it now, dinna you break it." Her eyes were watering again. "You're good to me, young Robert Willoughby. Where's my tea, my lass, I'm all about with the walk back. I've been down to Cousin Arthur's. Their little one's poorly, I doubt they'll raise him. But that girl of theirs, Mavis, she's a good lass. She's a treasure to her mother."

Gertie went back into the kitchen, and Robert followed her,

"How did you get that?" she whispered to him.

"I got it. That's all you need to know. Make the tea now."

Gertie mashed the tea. Robert certainly knew how to behave to her mother. How did he get that figurine? Frank! It must be. Frank worked at the Leviathon. No doubt Rob had swapped it for something from Manstone's, something which had been rejected. There was plenty of that, which the potters had sweated over and then it was rejected, and they didn't get paid for it. Often times there didn't seem to be a thing wrong with it. Rob knew as well as she did that those things ought to be smashed, if the potters got nothing for them. But they weren't all smashed. Oh, no. Plenty of things slipped through, they did, and someone got the benefit. Well, this time, it was her Ma. She didn't want to know any more.

At the table, no one spoke. The sound of the rain, which had increased, was like a waterfall. Rob got up, to peer out of the back door. He could see the gutter over the window was blocked.

"It's getting worse, Mrs. I can't stop now. I'll be down tomorrow, to clear that gutter for you.

"Good lad."

"Afterwards, I'll take Gertie down the wood at Eatham. I know where there's a tree down. I'll take my saw, and bring you a bag of logs, if there's any left. We could manage it between us."

"You'd like that, wouldn't you, our Gertie?"

"Come early, if you're coming Rob. Me and Ma will go to chapel late. That's the best. Since we've got to do that errand."

"I'll be off, then," Rob said, standing up. "We've a practice. We're singing in Manstone's house in a week."

"Manstone's!" Gertie exclaimed. "You didn't tell me. How's that?"

"Mrs. Manstone's having a musical party, raising money for that new church, they've built in Epsilon. She's inviting a host of people. Old Manstone found out about our singing group and his wife asked me to go."

"I hope they'll pay."

"Of course. I wouldn't do it for nothing.

"Paid!" Mrs. Lambert chortled. "You're well in with Manstone's. Be off then, and practise your sol-fa, young man."

When he'd gone Mrs. Lambert raised her hands, warming them on the flames. "He's a proper one, my wench. Look after him, and he'll do you proud."

"I'll freshen the pot, Ma", she said, replacing the kettle on the range. Rob had this knack with her Ma. He knew how to get round her. And he had arranged their outing very nicely. But she knew what Rob wanted. He'd made that only too clear. But he must wait, least until they'd named the day. She wasn't about to be like those girls in the mould shop, with tiny youngsters dogging their heels all day.

"Here you are, dear." She handed her mother the fresh tea, and they sipped in silence. The water was still pouring from the leaky gutter. Gertie thought of Rob, getting wet, and then drying off, singing, with his friends.

Enoch was back just in time from his ride to Saghead to bath and get dressed for dinner at Shepperton's house. Edna had been sick with worry that he would be late. When he came back, wet through, but smiling, she was so relieved she could not scold.

"We got it, my dear," he said, as she looked up from her book. "The Arbitration, I mean."

"Good," she said. "Very well. You and Dudley will having nothing to grumble about, then. We have an hour, Enoch. It won't do to be late." She rose, her silk skirt, rustling. She had liberally used the scent spray.

Enoch stopped as he had his hand on the door knob.

"You're looking well, my dear. There's no-one to match you in the county. I'm a lucky man. They all tell me that. I am, that's true."

"You're wet through." Edna had her hand on the bell pull, and tugged it hard. "You'd best go up. I told Deaker to have the water ready for you."

"Don't you own, my lady, I am a lucky man?" He stood with his back to the door. "I have all this, and you too; and now," he came nearer to her, "a hot bath. Well, is that lucky, or what is it, Mrs?"

"Go up, please, Enoch. I do not wish to be late."

"They'll wait for us, my dear, to be sure. Still, I mustn't drip all over your fine turkey carpet. So, off I go."

In his bath, Enoch thought over the events of the day. He felt excited by what had happened. He wouldn't mind a fight if it came to it, but he didn't think it would. He lay full length in the long iron bath, dipping his sponge into the water, and squeezing warm rivulets over his soapy torso. He surveyed his body, still firm and strong looking. He fancied he could smell Edna's perfume. He closed his eyes, wishing her warm flesh could be near to him, now, this minute. His prick began to swell and harden as he swished the water to and fro. He grasped it. A picture flashed into his mind, Jeannie's rump presenting itself to him as, on her knees, she wiped down the bannisters that morning. He began to smile. He could give her such a thrapping, such a thrapping. Where was she now? Was she stretched out in her iron bed, her hair out of its cap, across the pillow, her soft arms over the sheet? Or was she coming along the corridor now? If only she would come to him, with warm towels in her arms. He would stand up in the bath, and and she would wrap them round him, one by one, and pat him all over. Why not? He was the Master here wasn't he? He could order her to do it. He could order her, and then that so-called wife of his, she would be happy, too. He'd not need to bother her no more. "Jeannie, Jeannie," he mouthed the word, his lips wet. He leaned back in the water, with a grunt, and gave himself up to the best moment of the day.

An hour later Mr. and Mrs. Manstone were announced by the butler at Lowenbar, the residence of the Master of Leviathon Ceramics, Mr. Dudley Shepperton.

"Edna, my dear, how delightful," murmured Mrs. Eliza Shepperton. "Come by the fire. You must be cold after the drive. I fancy it's really wet." She motioned Edna to a seat by the fire.

Enoch and Dudley stood near the door.

"I expect you know already, the Arbitration result?"

"Of course," said Dudley. "I had it at first hand, when it came out at twelve o'clock. The men are already talking about a strike."

"They had a meeting this dinnertime. Fools. There's no other word for it. We're striving to keep them in work, and all they can do is demand better money."

"They'll kill this industry."

"They cannot. They've more sense. Any road, they won't all come out. My clerk, he's got his ear to the ground. His opinion is there isn't much support."

"Robert Willoughby?"

"Yes. He's a sound man."

"He's on our side is he? You're sure? That's a strange business about him."

"About his father, you mean? No more strange than many a thing. He knows which way his bread is buttered that's all. I don't make much of gossip. There's nothing to say it's true."

Dudley nodded, turning down the corners of his mouth. "You may be right, my friend. What's his standing with the workers? He's more a manager than a clerk, so I understand."

"Well, you've heard wrong. I'm my own manager. And I'm training my lass up too. You've heard that, I don't doubt? ""

Dudley was about to reply when the butler came in to announce dinner. The Manstones had arrived last of the guests, and as Enoch had predicted, now they had come, the meal could be served.

Edna was at Mr. Shepperton's right hand.

"Will you be going to the Brahms at Skinner Hall next month, Mrs. Manstone?

"I think not, this time. I'm planning a little musical event myself, Mr. Shepperton. In aid of the new church which is completed now, just in need of furnishings."

"I hear it's going to be very grand. A credit to your husband." Dudley wiped his mouth on the napkin tucked into his collar, and beckoned to the maid. After helping himself to a liberal second helping of pheasant, he continued. "No doubt you've been the inspiration of that. You ladies won't be gainsaid, will they, Enoch?"

The butler went round refilling the glasses.

"Mrs. Manstone, Mr. Manstone," everyone murmured.

Enoch was rubbing his nose with his finger, and nodding vigorously in response to the toast. Edna stared at her plate. The blood was rising to her cheeks, and she smiled without raising her eyes. Of course she was pleased her husband was being congratulated. But it wasn't true that she had encouraged him. In fact the opposite was the case. She'd tried to dissuade him. What was the need for another church in the town? There were already two others. And she really liked the old one, at the bottom of the main street, with its box pews, all named, and its choir and small orchestra. Enoch would have done better to endow that church, to help with its restoration fund, even pay for an organ, if that's what he wished. But no, Enoch had to go for the whole works, a brand new church, to save people walking the extra mile to the old one. It had completely absorbed his attention those first few months of last year, when the plans were being drawn up. The work had at last started and he had been out most evenings, at meetings of one sort or another.

"Did you read the account of the meeting of that new Noxious Substances Committee? They were concerned with the smoke from the Brickworks. But it'll affect us all, if any new legislation is made." Dudley addressed his friend.

"They can't legislate for that. It'll be the end of the smaller pot banks. Everyone knows that." Enoch saw all this interference with the way industry conducted itself, as a colossal imposition, by people who knew nothing.

"Something will be done, make sure of that, if these fellows carry on. My belief is that some of us should join the Committee, so we've got a voice." Dudley went on.

Enoch said nothing. He'd got no time for such nonsense. Nothing would change in a hurry, that was for sure. With business as it was now, any more unforeseen expenditure might kill the trade altogether.

The talk passed to discussion of the plans for the new road which would take the same route as the railway, round the edge of the city limits. Edna lost concentration. Why was it that Enoch was for ever immersing himself in new projects? Always something to do with the town, or his estate, new plantations - the new water wheel, it was now. Yet to get him to take an interest in her own plans, well, she might as well admit defeat, and do what she wanted to do, without him. He'd just agree to her ideas, but take no action at all to further them himself. She'd thought of the soiree as a means to raise the money still needed to complete the furnishing of the church. But he hadn't even discussed the date with her. She had had to make the decision on her own in the end. He just seemed uninterested.

The ladies rose after the dessert, leaving the men to their port and cigars. Tea was handed round in the drawing room, and Edna sat next to her friend, Dorothy Dawkins.

"Now then, tell me. How is dear Matilda standing up to her father's plan?"

"Oh, that." Edna sipped gingerly as the tea was still very hot. "She seems quite well pleased. And so am I." She smiled. "We have no doubts we have done the right thing."

"But surely, my dear, can you seriously suppose it is to be her profession now? To run the business, as it were."

"As you know, my husband is far from retiring. And it will be many years, please God, before we need think of Matilda taking on the business. In fact I am sure she will not - although I am not inferring she could not."

"But times are changing." Young Mrs. Bond spoke up. "I admire you both, Mrs. Manstone. I would do the same, in the same circumstances. Of course we already have two healthy boys, so the need won't arise, God willing."

All the older ladies stared at the young woman for a moment. Mrs. Shepperton wondered suddenly why she had invited the new solicitor and his wife to the dinner party. She did not want her friend upset.

It was Edna who replied.

"I am aware of our special circumstances. But my husband, now, he is a man who will not be deflected.

"Of course, Mrs. Manstone." Mrs. Bond was blushing.

Mrs. Shepperton spoke. "If Mr. Manstone hasn't a son, I am sure he wishes to ensure his business will be well looked after on his retirement. We ladies can very well manage. Our own Queen is an inspiration to us."

Edna smiled. Eliza had shown the flag. Now, local society might realise that it was acceptable to educate their daughters as well as their sons, if necessary. Yes. Times were changing, would change.

8

The next day the fog disappeared, and the weather came in fine. Most of the trees round Terrilea had now turned flaming colours of yellow and scarlet, as if the woods were having a final burn up before the cold of winter. Martinmas was fast approaching and the men had failed to persuade the Masters to promise better wages to start on the new contract dates, now imminent. Talks of strike became more insistent. Suddenly, it was upon them. The pot-banks were closed. Men and women wandered the streets, excitedly, for the first few days, then with growing despondency. Enoch and Robert, with the gate man, still went to the factory as usual. Otherwise there was no-one there, no work for the engine, nor the engine man, none for the throwers, pressers and dippers, none for the jiggerers, paintresses, oven-men and all the others. Children were out in the streets, playing, foraging for late apples, and kindling, and picking waste coal off the colliery tips.

The strike was universal. Everyone was affected, the shop-keepers, the market stall-holders, even the canal people, who got no orders to transport clay and finished ware. There was no threat in the behaviour of the knot of men who stood at Manstone's great gates every day. In fact they were still polite and deferential. Nevertheless, Enoch did not wish his daughter to be involved in all this, and gave her a holiday.

A world away from the strike, enjoying the autumn sunshine, Tilly and Ros were sitting on the stone bench half way down the steps into the valley.

Tilly had a stick in her hand, and was carefully peeling away the bark. "Father says the natives in Africa clean their teeth with sticks."

"Don't fidget, Till. I want you to talk to me."

Tilly threw the stick down into the bushes at the bottom of the slope.

"Well?"

There was silence from Ros.

"Go on -"

"It's Cyril. You know, Cyril Arbuthnot. Well, he's been to call a few times. And he came to tea. Now they've asked us all to dinner. Next week."

"I see."

"What do you mean by that? 'I see. 'You must think...it's all..."

Tilly clasped her arms round her knees. "That was the secret was it? I thought you'd tell me, eventually."

"It wasn't that I didn't want you to know. I couldn't be sure."

"But now, you are sure."

"Well....."

"You're not sure?"

"I don't know what I think

"It's what you think that matters. I thought you didn't find him very nice."

"Oh, he's nice. Too nice, almost. He's so good to me, Tilly. Always asks my opinions, and then changes his, to suit. He's so... smooth."

"Smooth?"

"Well, everything about him, His voice – oh, it's quiet, and soft, I feel he's .... waiting."

"Possibly he is. For you."

"I know. That's the trouble. He's a bit like a... Just still and smooth.".....

"Like a pond? For goodness sakes. If that's what he's like, I don't know why we're discussing him. Just tell your Mama, and finish it off."

"I know, I know. That's what I want to do. But it's not so easy."

"I'm sure your mother doesn't want him to keep coming if you don't like him."

"He's a good match."

"Catch, you mean."

Ros laughed. "He has got piles of money. That's true. And, he's not in pots. Oh, sorry, I didn't mean that nastily. But you know what Mama is. They've got an estate, near Chesterton."

Tilly shook her head. "It's not complicated. If you don't like him you've got to tell him, now."

"It's all very easy to say that, but it's not you who has to do it."

"That's true." Privately Tilly thought she wouldn't have let things get to that stage.

"Isn't there anyone in your life, Til? Surely you must have had to deal with it. Do tell. I just feel you're so sure of yourself."

"Of course there isn't anyone. You'd be the first to know. Truly. No man at all, except Father. And that clerk at the office. I see plenty of him." Tilly had been going to tell of her visit to the half-built church, and the artistic assistant to Mr. Lugando. But she decided that Ros would put the wrong interpretation on this.

"The clerk. Is he abominable?"

"Well, I can't say anything horrid has happened. But he looks at me sometimes, as if I'm a mouse. He's going to pounce. I feel he's watching and waiting."

"You sound a bit afraid."

"Afraid! Certainly not. He's one of those people who....you forget they're there, and then you look up, and there he is, glaring at you."

"That makes me shiver."

"It's not so bad as all that. Now, tell me about the dance."

"Oh, the dance, the dance! What am I going to do, Tilly? I just want to know what to do. Supposing he proposes? I shan't know what to say."

"Don't worry, my darling. " Tilly put her arms round her. "If you don't know what to do, then it's a mistake to commit yourself."

"Suppose he asks me. He might."

"Just tell him. You're not ready for it. He's got to wait. Like that, you'll have a chance to make up your mind properly. After all, what's a six month wait, in a lifetime?"

"You're a brick, Til. I wish I had your sense, and your strength."

"You have, you have. You just don't know it. Have confidence. For goodness' sakes don't just throw yourself away. You're a real, strong person, of your own. Don't let anyone let you think otherwise."

Both girls began to make their way down the steep steps, holding their skirts out of the way. It had rained in the night, but now the sun was shining and the ground steaming.

"You'll just have to come out with it, to your mother. Just say you're not going to the dinner party. Or wait till the time, and then be ill, have a sore throat, or a headache, something. You've got to, Ros."

"He won't be put off by that. And I'm afraid of myself, really, Tilly. . . If he does propose, I have a horrid feeling I shall say yes. After all, it would be quite nice. All that money."

"Is he very rich?"

"I'll tell you better when we've been to his house. It's a great hall, bigger than your house, much bigger. And ancient. I think his uncle is a baronet somewhere."

"So you are going to the dinner?"

"I don't know, I don't know."

They stopped on the little wooden bridge over the stream. The water was flowing fast over the gravelly bottom, and tiny fish were darting about between the stones.

"I don't suppose it matters much what we do, Ros." Tilly had her arm round Ros' waist. "We do something, for lots of reasons, and we don't understand, and we marry and have babies, and then we die, and it's just nature, carrying on regardless. Like these fishes. Or birds."

"But shouldn't we be happy, Till? Shouldn't we strive for that? Otherwise what's the point?"

"I don't know where you got that from. I don't expect to be happy."

"What do you expect?"

"I'll just do what I have to do, and make the best of it, and I expect I'll survive. That's what it's all for. Just to keep going. Surviving."

There was silence. They stared at the water. The sun wasn't warm at this time of the year, and Ros shivered in the cool breeze.

"In that case, I might as well do what they expect, marry Cyril, and have children."

"I'm doing what father expects. But I might do something else as well."

"What's that?"

"I want to get a proper education. Away somewhere. A proper College. Maybe even University."

"Tilly! You've never said that before. When did you have that idea?"

"I don't know exactly. In fact I've only just decided. It's you talking about Cyril. It's made it all real for me. I do want to have my chance before I lock myself away, and all that. And now I've said it, it all becomes real."

"You mean, you won't ever get married? Be like those women who have to work? Why do that Til?"

"I didn't say that. What I said was, I need to know a lot of things, properly, before I get involved in all that." Also, Tilly had begun to realise, though she couldn't explain it to Ros, she wanted to prove to herself, and to everyone else, that she was someone in her own right, not just the appendage of someone else. She put her arm into Ros' and together they went down the path, towards the next set of steps, which went up the slope to the beech wood beyond.

Ros stayed the night, and the next morning came up clear and sunny. The girls went towards the walled garden at about eleven.

Tilly smelled baking as she went across the small yard, and decided to beg some tartlets or apple turnovers for a mid-morning treat for herself and Ros.

"Wait here," she said, at the door into the walled garden, "I want to show you the hyacinths. Father's found this early variety. We're bringing them on, for Christmas. I'll bring us some juice and cakes. We'll have it in the conservatory,"

No sooner was she gone, and Ros was standing by the door into the glass house, than Enoch appeared at the garden gate. He'd come round from the back, where he'd been inspecting the planting of some north-facing cherry trees.

"Well, Rosalind." he took off his cap. "I didn't know you were coming again this morning. No-one told me."

"I stayed, Mr. Manstone. Mama has some business in Epsilon, with regard to the church furnishings, and she said she'd come and fetch me if Tilly wished me to stop over. I didn't want to miss the chance. I'm sorry if I startled you."

"Not at all, my dear. It's a pleasure. I don't know what the ladies are doing half the time, I'm that busy."

Enoch stood in silence for a moment, staring at the neat garden, with its rows of winter cabbage, and well-trained and pruned espaliers of fruit trees along the walls.

"Your garden's looking very well, Mr. Manstone."

"Oh, I have a fair gardener – though it wouldn't do to let him know that. I took him on as a boy, and there's little he won't try, and usually makes a job of it."

"Papa would like a garden like this, sir. It's what he envies you for, this garden. And the fields and woods."

"Happen he could have it if he really wants it. But I suppose he's too busy with all his affairs as it is. It is a lot of work, even with the men to do the donkey part."

"I'm sure it is. And Father's a magistrate. That takes up a deal of time."

"It will do, it will do." Enoch said, thinking of the poachers, who had trebled in number since the strike. It would make more work for the magistrates, no doubt. There was another silence.

Ros had pulled up her collar, and now wrapped her arms round herself.

"There's a chill wind. Winter's coming. We'll do well to step into the conservatory." Enoch held the glass door open, and stood aside for Ros to go in first.

The long, low conservatory built along the length of the West wall of the garden, gleaned all the rays of the November sun.

"'Tis better in here, out of that wind."

Ros took a deep breath. "It's beautiful. The hyacinths. Tilly told me. It's so delicious." She let herself relax in the warmth and fragrance. She wandered off down the tiled path between the orange and bay trees, stooping to sniff the blue hyacinths.

Enoch was watching her, and suddenly felt himself stiffening, again. He had difficulty breathing. She was a woman, young, fragrant, vulnerable. He desired her.

Ros looked back. He felt the flush in his cheeks, and began to perspire

"When will these oranges be ripe, Mr. Manstone?" She was fingering one of the green orbs, twisting it this way and that."

Enoch managed to speak. "Won't be too long now, young lady. They'll ripen very soon. If we have some more sunshine." He turned away from her, unable to say more. He thought his voice was shaking. This was his daughter's friend, his friend's daughter. He had always thought of her as a young girl, a child. But now, suddenly, she was a woman. Soon, possibly, she would be a wife. He felt a stabbing pain. Was it jealousy? Or despair? He desired her, desired her. It was like a blow, which struck him in the chest. He could not have her, nor would he ever have a woman, like that, again. Not truly, not possess her. Even his own wife.

“Father, I didn’t know you were here. I would have brought some for you.” Tilly had come in, carrying a tray. On it were two large pieces of apple pie, and two glasses of milk.

“Hast been making up to Deaker, then? I doubt she’d have done that if she’d known I were out here.” His voice was gruff.

Tilly laughed. “Probably not, Papa. You’re always saying we shouldn’t have this eating between meals. I had to persuade her. You can have some of mine.”She kissed him tenderly on the ear, and set the tray down on the low wall surrounding the bank of hyacinths. “Come along, Ros, see what Deaker has given us.”

“You two enjoy yourselves now. But I’ll expect some help in my study, this afternoon, for overlooking this, my wench.” He turned to go to the door. She was a monkey, no doubt of it. So was Deaker, they all contrived to flout his orders. He did not agree with all this supping that went on. Folks did not need it, and it was all a waste of time and money, taking tea and cake, all the time. “Don’t forget now, Matilda. And I’ll say good day, to you Miss Rosalind. Give your father my regards.” He nodded to them both, and went out.

“Was he really annoyed, Till?” Ros asked.

“He’s such a dear. I take no notice. In fact he dare not say much. He wants my help. I’ve been a good help to him in the factory. And will be, there’ll be a lot of work, when this strike’s finished. He has to watch what he says.

“You’re lucky, Tilly, you seem so close to your father. Mine isn’t like that.”

Tilly said nothing, but reflected that her feelings for her father were very special. Something to do with her being an only child, perhaps.

Enoch, walking down the brick steps from the garden, felt like a man who has had sudden warning of an earthquake, and taken flight, just in time.

The next day, Edna, in the drawing room with Tilly, asked “Have you made sure Rosalind will come with her mama to our musical evening?”

“I didn’t ask. But I’m sure she will. Don’t fret, mama. I know it will be a success. I came to ask if there was anything to be done.”

“Nothing, I think. Deaker has it all in hand, and all the invitations are out. So far there’s only one refusal.”

“Who is that?”

“Dr. Makepiece. He is previously engaged.”

“I don’t know he’s any great loss. I don’t think he has any interest in music. Not that I’ve heard.”

“In fact, there isn’t much interest hereabouts. How many of our neighbours are to be seen at the concerts in Saghead? Most of the audience comes from Chesterton, and Parklea.”

"It's our duty to educate them, Mama."

"I don't know that I feel capable, Tilly. One has these dreams, and then, in the end, there are no thanks for it." Once more Edna had put down her embroidery and was gazing at the French doors. It was grey, the sun had gone, and the strike dragged on.

Tilly had never heard her mother speak in this way. She sat down beside her on the carpet, her arms round her knees. "I know it will be a success. Everyone I have spoken to is really looking forward to it. And I saw Willoughby discussing the programme with father. Two weeks ago, before the strike."

"What was he saying?"

"Just seeing if he had the approval for various songs they are going to sing."

"He should have approached me. I gave the programme to your father, of what I required. The actual songs were to be at Willoughby's discretion. If there was any doubt, it should have been referred to me."

"I'm sure Father didn't wish to delay matters by referring back again to you. No doubt they wish to rehearse them again."

Edna got up and went to the window. She was so looking forward to the soiree, but dreading the occasion as well

Tilly added. "It's not long now, then it will all be over."

Edna said nothing. Perhaps what Tilly said was true. She was putting great store by the evening. She felt a missionary zeal, almost, in introducing music to a wider circle of her friends. Most of them, of course, had learned to play and sing as children, but very many did it as a duty, not feeling, as she did, about music. When she'd been brought up, her siblings had formed a small band. She'd played the violin, her sister had played the piano, her mother, a harp, and her brothers, various wind instruments. Edna had tried to educate Tilly to her own standards, but the child had not responded. She would rather be outside, cultivating her little beds of bulbs in the rockery, or playing with the dogs. She had always wanted to be out in the open, doing, doing. Tilly was more like Enoch than herself. The girl had never once complained about the gloomy office, or the noisy factory. She'd gone every day, willingly, as if she was fulfilling a mission. Edna envied her. She felt her daughter growing away from her. Tilly seemed to be a person, in her own right. Even the work she was doing, at the business, seemed to be helping her, in a strange way. She was responding to it. She was defined by it. Edna, by contrast, felt herself to be an amorphous liquid, flowing round boulders, unable to make any difference to anything, just running round all the obstacles, going down, down.

One thing Edna knew about herself was her ability to respond to music. After Enoch had departed every morning, and Deaker and she had discussed the menu for the day, Edna would go up to her own quiet boudoir, and there she would practise scales on her violin, and eventually turn the pages of a Chopin waltz or a Mozart minuet. Two hours might pass like this; sometimes she would feel satisfied. But no one listened to her, she had no accompanist and none of her friends were sufficiently interested to make the journey over to play for her. In any case, most of the ladies of her age were still fully occupied with their large families and household. If only, if only she hadn't married out of her own county. Her acquaintances here had few of her own interests. She knew them only because their husbands were connected with Enoch. Apart from Mrs. Dawkins, Edna couldn't think of a single real friend within an hour's carriage drive.

But the soiree would change all that. Perhaps Mr. Willoughby and his friends' efforts would introduce some of her acquaintances to an unknown interest. Edna had discovered in the last few weeks that she was counting on the soiree in an inexplicable way. She was pining less over Tilly's departure, and thinking about the future, in a way she had not done for many years.

Some of these thoughts invaded Edna's consciousness, but of the others she was only vaguely aware. They presented themselves as dreams, or day dreams. She imagined her house as a centre of musical talent, a breeding ground for musicians. She would be a teacher, an apostle. She would reign as a queen. Enoch would lead her forth, as he had when she was a bride.

But this was all nonsense. Enoch didn't like music, he never had. He looked on her practising with patience, and amusement, but without understanding that for Edna it was as necessary to her as water. Edna was aware that Enoch still loved her, desired her. But she felt he did not desire her in the way she wished to be desired, for herself. He looked at her music askance, and at her childlike respect for Deaker, also with amused tolerance, but sometimes with impatience. Edna realised her character, her personality, was not what her husband desired. What he wanted was only her....well, she could not say that to herself, but without words, in her true heart, she knew. He desired her, but did not want her.....self.

"Mama, shall we ring for tea. I'm thirsty."

Edna immediately got to her feet, and flung her embroidery on a chair. "This silly wool work," she cried.

"It's not silly, it's pretty," Tilly was astounded, seeing this response. "And your soiree will be wonderful. We'll like the music those people make, and everyone will applaud."

"Maybe." Edna shook her head. Tilly rose and tugged the bell over the mantel. She was beginning to be anxious of the consequences to her mother, if the soiree were not a success.

The next day, Enoch too, had the day off. He asked Tilly to go for a ride with him, in the early afternoon.

Tilly pulled her snug fur hat, and set out for the stable. Inside it was warm and smelt of horses. Tilly felt a sneeze coming on.

Father was stroking Dimple on the nose, and talking to George, who was grooming.

"Hardly a grey hair. Not like us, eh?"

"Aye. She don't look bad for her age. For all she's gone eighteen."

"I mind the day we bought her. We've both gone on a bit since then, George. Ain't only the horse.

"That's right, master. Times have changed. Folk dunna know when they're well off. That's right."

They were both silent. George carried on with the curry comb. A cloud of dust was hanging round Dimple's hind quarters.

Tilly, by the door, sneezed four times.

"There you are, lass." Enoch turned towards Tilly, and moved to the next stall. Silver had her head over the half door.

Soon, the two horses were crunching down the drive, their riders bouncing eagerly on top. Tilly had put on her riding habit though she wished she could ride astride, like any farmers wife. She had done so, as a young girl, but now, it wasn't considered seemly. Really, she thought, current conventions were strange. Why, now, in the late nineteenth century, did it seem indecorous to ride astride? However, Tilly had a good seat, and was quite capable of riding well, side-saddle though it might be. They trotted off at a fast pace, because the days were drawing in fast and there was no time to be lost if they were to get all the way to Northedge and back before dusk.

Neither spoke much, until they came to a long incline. This would take them to the top of the ridge, then a short descent would bring them to the high valley where lay Dacre's Mill.

"Your Silver doesn't do too bad. He's not blown at all." Enoch had reined in Dimple, in deference to the rising ground. "I was thinking you might have growed out of her by now."

"I haven't grown any taller for the last twelve months, father."

"Happen you'd like a new mount, Tilda? I were thinking you'd happen like one now. You've been a good girl these last months. I'd like you to go about, if you wish to. Young Jim could go along with you, if your Mother don't wish to."

"Mother won't come. She doesn't wish to ride."

"She used to like it well enough." Enoch pulled his horse back to be alongside the pony. "She would ride everywhere with me, one time."

Tilly said nothing, but stared ahead between Silver's ears. Up here, now the pace had slackened, a sharp breeze was getting between her shoulder blades.

"Perhaps you weren't so occupied then, Papa." She paused. But she must speak her mind. "Perhaps you could ride with her in the afternoons sometimes."

"Of course. I were that busy. There's not a time when I haven't been busy making a shilling. But she would go with me often times in the summer, or of a Sunday. We went as far as Unction or Fairlea, many a fine evening. And I suppose we would ride out from their place in Cheshire. I do remember as we did that."

"I sometimes feel... you must forgive me father... but sometimes...I think she wishes you weren't so occupied even when you're at home. Little things she could enjoy with you, but work comes home too, and then there's so much to do with the new plans and so forth..." Tilly's voice faded away. She'd never spoken to her father like this before.

There was silence. Suddenly he kicked his heels into Dimple's flanks. The road had levelled out, and the horse went off at a quick trot. Silver jumped and set off too, causing Tilly to lose her seat for a moment. She grabbed the reins up short, clung to the saddle and quickly regained her balance. When she caught up with her father, he turned his head towards her.

"Ah well, so that's what you think. You're right to tell me, lass. I'm not one as can't face the truth.

"I'm sure you're not." Tilly said.

"Never be sorry at telling the truth. I dare say it has been a trial for your mother, she's so set on making you a lady. Well, you are one, just like she is. But, more'n that, you're doing a man's work. You'll find it good, my lass."

"I know, father. I don't complain." Tilly let Silver trot on. Had she ever complained? She had not. She had nothing to complain about, really, now that she was able to sit in the office, with her father, away from Robert, with his sideways glances at her. There was something else about him, she wasn't quite sure what. Indeed, she liked the factory and really missed the business, now that she was on an unlooked for holiday. The workers she knew by name always acknowledged her, and they didn't have to. She had noticed the look they gave father, or rather they didn't look at him, till after he'd gone, and the looks they gave about him, were to each other. But, she felt out of their lives. How could she possibly know how they felt or thought? How were they managing, these days? They must be suffering, how could it be otherwise? She knew the main reason for the strike, the reinstatement of the wages they'd had before Lord Hatherton's ruling that all of them should get a penny less. She understood now that even a penny meant a lot to them. She found it difficult to ask Robert about it. He seemed to be part of two worlds. She had seen him with Gertrude. And he would be coming to sing at the Soiree. She suddenly had the idea that he should tell her more about the life of the ordinary workers in the factory. If the works were to run properly, the ordinary folk should be thought about, their welfare considered.

"Father," Tilly said, as their mounts drew parallel again. "Mother asked me whether the clerk had sorted out the songs for the programme."

"Be a right pickle if he hadn't. What does she think? Of course he has. He's not stupid. He knows what to serve up. It does seem to me your Mama should stop fretting. She doesn't need to saddle herself with all this how-de-do if she don't want. Those guests of hers they'll be right pleased to come to Terrilea, whatever's served up. In fact, truth to tell, they'll not know if it's good or just fair. Or care for that matter."

"That may be so, Papa. But Mama is just like you. She wants to have everything just right."

Enoch looked hard at her, but he wasn't smiling. The road began to go sharply downhill, and it was rough underfoot. Both riders had to watch carefully where the horses were putting their hooves. Now and then Silver would slip a little as the loose stones skittered off down the path. Tilly could see the mill below them in the valley. A large white heap rose up beside it, along nearly the whole of its length. As they came nearer a sickly stench wafted along the road towards them.

Tilly struggled to pull her scarf up over her nose with one hand while holding the reins in the other.

Suddenly Dimple stopped, and Enoch jolted heavily in the saddle. Silver hesitated at once, and then she too would go no further.

"It's the bones, Tilda. They won't go near to that smell. It's worse now, there's no call for bone at the pot-bank. So the stock builds up." Enoch hit Dimple smartly on the withers with his crop. "Get up, there." She jerked her head up, and then was off again, plodding. Silver took the lead.

They drew alongside the pile of bones stacked for crushing for use in the pottery making. In spite of her scarf, Tilly could smell the putrefying flesh still on the bones, and she felt sick. As they came nearer, the crows and seagulls, swarming over the heap, took off in a great clattering cloud

Riding along behind her father, Tilly's mind went round and round. So much seemed to depend on the men working. When they weren't, so many others were affected. How could it possibly be right that so many people should be out of a livelihood because the men weren't getting their extra penny? It wasn't even an extra, it was what they'd had for ages before Lord Hatherton had knocked it off. How long would the Masters go on refusing to pay it? Tilly wished she understood all this better. When the strike was over, she would try to find out what was the real truth, about the whole matter. She would speak to Robert about it all. It was no good talking to her father. What was the law about it all? Could Ros find out anything, from her father? It was unlikely. Tilly felt as if she was sinking into a swampy pool, thrashing about among the reeds. She needed to understand, and she didn't know whom to turn to.

When Tilly came in from riding, she had a bath. She didn't have to wait for the water to be carried up, because Enoch had caused a big coal boiler to be installed in the cellar, and the water to be piped to the bathroom two floors up. Now, the whole family could bath every day, if they wished, and there was also hot water in the scullery for washing the dishes. There was no fear of it ever being already used up for other purposes, since the laundry was still done in the wash room in the yard, served by the large copper boiler which it was Jim's job to light and tend.

Coming along the lofty passage back to her bedroom, Tilly felt chilly, as the belvedere over the landing let in not only light but also draughts. Back in the bedroom there was a good fire, and she sank down to sit beside it for a while, before dressing. She wanted to read the latest novel by George Eliot, and there were two hours before the early dinner. But as soon as she opened her book, she began to think of the conversation she had had with her father. He hadn't really understood what she was trying to say. It was so difficult to talk to either her mother or her father. Was it true that nothing could be be perfect, and no-one? Probably it was. People had lots of different sides, different qualities, as well as things you didn't like about them. She'd never thought this way about anybody above her in authority. To her, they'd always appeared to be endowed with all the qualities to be expected. In fact, they were grown up. That was enough. But was being adult, enough? Sometimes, people appeared to have some characteristics, but then, you discovered, they had others, which were more important. Like Robert Willoughby, for example. In the office he was just a clerk, but now, she suspected he was more than that....

There came a tap on the door.

"Did you have a good ride, my dear?" It was Edna.

"Perfect, Mama. I'm a bit tired now, though. I've decided to have a rest. Do you need me for anything?

"It's all right. Deaker and I have all the arrangements sorted out. The main thing was the chairs, but I've ordered some."

"Very good. I'm sure it will all go without any hitches."

"I'll leave you. You're not to worry about me. Tomorrow, I'd like to have a treat. Will you come with me, for a drive?"

"Of course, Mama, I shan't be needed by Father. This strike seems to be going on and on."

"Yes, poor folk. I wish they would come to their senses." Edna went out, closing the door quietly. She stood in the passage, listening to the wind round the stained glass windows above her. It always howled up here. She was undecided what to do. She'd hoped to have an hour with Tilly, but obviously the child wished to rest. The wind ceased it's moaning for a moment, and there was a sudden quiet. Involuntarily, she shivered. It was so cold here. She pulled her shawl closer. She would go for a rest. There was a book in her boudoir which she would read for a while. As she went through the door, she saw Enoch, standing with his back to the fire.

Edna jumped.

"You startled me."

"You startle easy. I suppose I have a right in my wife's boudoir?"

"I thought you were bathing."

"So I was, my dear. But it don't do to linger too long, that little grate in the bathroom don't give out much heat. We'll have to do what I said, get those radiators."

"Oh. Not another of your plans, We're well enough, surely."

"We may not have them everywhere. But one in the hall, I'd like, and one in the billiard room, and perhaps the dining room." He waited for some comment. "It would save work for the servants."

Edna sat down by the fire. "How would that be?"

"They just light one fire, and it's lit any way for the bath water. Just keep it going, and you'll have four or five fires' heat from it. Four or five rooms hot all the time. For the price of one fire, you have near the whole house warmed up." Enoch started fishing around in his dressing gown pocket. He produced a small stub of pencil. "Will you give me some of your writing paper?"

Edna rose obediently, and took a sheet of embossed paper from her escritoire. "Will this serve?"

"Champion. Come here, lass." Enoch put the paper on his knee, and drew out a section of the house, showing heating plant and radiators. "Now then, ring for a whisky and soda, and we'll sit by the fire, while you think about it, my wench."

Edna pulled the bell, and when Jeannie came, she gave the order. Enoch, comfortably installed, glass in hand, watched her as she pondered over the plan. Finally she looked up.

"You must do what you wish, Enoch. You know I can't say 'no' to you. It's just that we always have a new plan, and a new plan. It's everything upside down. Can't we be settled?"

"Don't you wish to have the best, the most modern house, in the whole of the county? You must do, you deserve it. Come here." Enoch still had on only his dressing gown. There was something very attractive about his wife, fully clothed, while he, beneath the velvet gown, was naked. He took her hand, and pulled her towards him. "Come here," he said. His voice was soft, gentle, but not to be gainsaid. "Come here, you know you can trust me. I do what's right for thee."

It was the use of the second person singular, "thee". That was what had won Edna in the first place. Enoch spoke the dialect. When roused, he spoke the dialect.

Now, she was kneeling on the floor beside him, her arms round his waist, her head on his lap. He was gently undoing the buttons on the back of her dress. "Dost tha still love me, my wench? Dost tha?" He was kissing the back of her neck. He took the pin from her bun, and ran his fingers through her hair. "Come on now, come on now." He turned her face to him, put his hand to her head, and kissed her.

Suddenly Edna began to have feelings she had almost forgotten. She felt very hot, her heart was beating.

"Enoch, be careful, be careful."

"Be careful? Why? Tha' art my wife." He kissed her again, slipping his hand round her back, and onto to her breast. "Come on now, come on." He forced his leg between hers, pulling the dress off her shoulders. Now her breasts were exposed, she felt the cold air on them. Enoch took them in turn, in his teeth.

Edna realised that Enoch was asking more of her than he usually did. Why? Why was he crossing their unspoken but rigid agreement about what he expected from her? "No, Enoch. Let me be." For a moment, she thought she would give in. She was panting. He held her fast round the waist, and at the same time was pushing her back onto the bed. She saw the perspiration gleaming on his forehead. He was hurting her. Now, with him breathing on her, she didn't want him. She writhed and struggled. "No, Enoch, it isn't possible." He was on his knees in front of her. The lamplight shone through the hairs on his scalp which gleamed pink. "Leave me alone. You know it isn't possible." She wriggled, and pushed his hand off her. "Don't do it. We can't. You know it's not safe. Ever. Even when you...." She was forcing him away, pushing his hands off her. She grasped her dress to her, and rushed to the door connecting with her bedroom

Enoch fell forward on the floor, moaning. The pile of the thick turkey carpet was under his nose and cheeks. "What do you mean? Tha was all long ago. Listen to me! Come back, come here." He raised himself up. He was like a dog, four paws on the carpet. Why could he not get up, and chase her? He was aware of the door banging. He moaned. It wasn't fair. It wasn't fair. After a moment he lay full length, his panting breath grew more steady. He wouldn't follow her. He wouldn't beg. He knew where she would be now, curled up in bed, crying. He wouldn't comfort her. He needed comfort himself. How long could this go on? He rolled onto his back, and gazed at the high ceiling, the ornate plasterwork, the decorative gas lamps. She had everything... a beautiful house, an estate, a daughter, a husband. But she would not give to him what he desired most. He knew why. She was frightened, frightened to death of having more children, all because of what that fool of a doctor had said. Why had he listened to Tilly about giving her mother more of his attention? Of course she didn't want that... it was obvious. Hadn't he tried countless times in the past? And what good had it ever done?

There was no hope in it. His wife didn't want him. His chest felt heavy, as if he had a great bruise on it, as if he'd been kicked. He couldn't feel worse if Dimple had thrown him off, and he'd been winded. He lay, breathing heavily, his eyes closed tightly. He would not look at that cursed ceiling, or the lamps, or anything else in this mausoleum. It was nothing but a hollow sham.

Lying on the floor, Enoch could hear the wind roaring round the belvedere. It was a fair storm tonight. He suddenly thought of the tall chimneys at the pot bank. They would stand up to this, they were built strong, like his house. He would stand firm too, with the other Masters. He wasn't about to give in.

He sat up, then clambered to his feet. He would go to his dressing room, which could be reached from the passage without disturbing Edna. He picked up the piece of paper with the drawing on it, of the central heating plan. He would think about that for a moment, beside his own fire. He wished he could talk to someone. If only he could talk to Tilly, but that he couldn't do. She was only a child, but then too, she was a woman, and he couldn't explain his feelings to her. Any road, talking didn't do no good. It was up to yourself, what happened. Talking wouldn't mend it.

Back in his dressing room, he pulled the bell, and when Jeannie came in, he ordered another whisky. He watched her, she seemed to flounce out. What would she do, if he were to ask her which room was her bedroom? He smiled at the thought. He wasn't even sure she didn't share with Deaker. Surely not? He didn't know anything about them, the servants. No doubt, though, they would do as they were told. Anyway when the strike was over, he'd be off to London, to see how trade was down there. Maybe that chap Goodrich would know how to fix him up. Some circumstances, you couldn't change. Some you could.

Edna huddling in bed, had been crying, but when she heard the maid come and go, she began to relax. Probably Enoch had ordered whisky. He could always drown his sorrows. Perhaps she had been unkind to Enoch. Her period had still not come, and she was beginning to wonder if it would ever come again. Maybe she'd finished with it for ever. Would Enoch stop bothering her, when she became an old woman? If he did still want her, would there really be any reason why he shouldn't let him have his way? Was she an old woman already? The tears began to flow again. She didn't understand what was happening to her. Deaker might know. But then, Deaker had had no children. There was no-one she could talk to. She was so lonely. She pulled the pillow towards her, and hugging it, muffled her sobs in its soft downiness.

Downstairs Deaker was knitting by the fire as Jeannie came in to say Master was in a bait.

....."Happen they've had a how-d'ye-do. I thought I heard words, earlier." Jeannie added.

"You'd best keep your opinion to yourself, girl." Deaker frowned as she picked up a dropped stitch.

9

It was two weeks since the Arbitration found against the men, followed by the mens' decision to strike, in order to have their wages restored to the level previous to Lord Hatherton's decision. The Union funds were already beginning to run out. Even now, by the beginning of December, everyone was on short commons. Robert met Frank and Dick Chambers, and his other friends, in the upper room at the Swan, to remind them about the engagement to play at Manstone's soiree.

"How can we do that, when the Masters won't listen to our needs? It won't look good, taking owt off of them," Dick said.

"I've got an idea for that. We'll give the money into the Union funds. That'll stop any talk. And it'll put Manstone in his place. We'll not tell him before, but when it's done, he'll get to know." Robert had it all worked out.

"He'll blame you for it. Sure he will. Then he'll know for certain whose side you're on."

"I shall say it's the only way you'd all agreed to come. His Missus is so daft about this party, she'll make him do it."

"It's risky, Robert Willoughby."

"I know that. But they're not going to sack all the Union men, and that's what it would come to, if they sack any of us. "

"They might cave in before it comes to that," Frank said.

"If I could swim the channel."

"We need not give it all to the funds." Robert had already decided he would give most of his money from the soiree to Gertie and her mother. "I need some for my lass."

"And I do, and all, my Missus."

"We'll make a contribution any road."

"That's decided then. I'll treat you fellows," Robert said, clattering down the stairs to get them all pints. They must made a final decision on the programme, he thought, and begin to rehearse. For once, with the factories being shut, they'd be able to make a good job of it, could take their time. And, they wouldn't too tired to enjoy it. Having time off work wasn't so bad, as long as he kept getting paid. But he knew the men wouldn't last out much longer. Somebody should open the eyes of the Masters, as to where their true interests lay. But who could do it? Robert didn't think he had the wit or strength. They needed another Robert Owen. He was a wily one, but his ideas had been totally rejected, years ago. His idea of a co-operative of workers managing their own factory, had been tried and had failed. Then, there had been the fiasco about the settlement in America, in the fifties. Robert knew that this strike wasn't going anywhere, either. But still, most of the workers were in favour, though a few of the factories were already in the process of negotiating with their employees. Of course the Union was totally opposed to their returning to work. At this rate, the Union itself would go to the wall, and then they'd all have to start again, from scratch.

As usual, Robert was able to concentrate on the job in hand, and he put all these thoughts about the possible outcome of the strike out of his mind, and settled himself at the piano. "Let's be having you," he said, and gave them their notes.

The following Saturday, all the staff at Terrilea, had been working hard in preparation for the Soiree. Banks of chrysanthemums and hyacinths, against a back ground of bay trees, and yukkas, had been arranged in the hall, and up the marble stairs. Outside, paraffin lamps lined the drive, and a huge holly wreath, in anticipation of Christmas, hung on the front door. When the guests arrived, Edna and Enoch greeted them, and they were shown to their seats in the ball room, by Jeannie. At last, Edna thought, the house fulfilled its potential, though she did wish, for an occasion like this, they had a butler. It irked her that Enoch considered this an extravagance.

Robert and the rest of the group, were in the study. Lemonade and ginger beer were provided, but none of the young men wanted that. They were busy warming up, and the sound they made could be heard in the passage, under the belvedere.

At last it was time to begin. A hush fell on the audience, as Enoch introduced the performers.

"Now, Ladies' and Gentlemen, it's time we showed what we're made of. We're not about to let little upsets put us off enjoying some fine entertainment, whatever the tide of fortune brings us. We've got a grand country here, and neither Kaffirs, nor yet any misguided fellows in our own country, are going to get in the way of us having a grand time, this evening. I am sure any worries we have at the moment, will soon be resolved to everyone's satisfaction, given the fact of Good British Common Sense." Enoch emphasised the last four words. "We've got some talented folk here tonight to give us some songs, some of them you may know, and I ask you to put your hands together for these."

Robert could hardly believe what he was hearing. When had the Masters ever shown a bit of Good British Common Sense? If they had done, affairs would never have gone downhill to the complete confusion everyone was experiencing today. Obviously Manstone still thought he was right, and good British common sense, to him, meant getting exactly what he wanted. Robert, sitting at the piano, glared at the audience. Could he really bring himself to play tonight? He despised them all, all the Masters and their wives, and daughters, and all the other so-called gentry who were here tonight. They did not know anything. They'd never really lived, the way he had. They had no idea. He should take his chance now, and tell them exactly what was what. For a moment there was silence, his hands resting on the notes. Then he thought of Gertie, and Mrs. Lambert. They needed the money he could make tonight. He'd find some way of getting at Manstone, he would. But not now. He looked up at the fellows standing in line, ready to sing, and crashing down into the introductory chords, nodded at the singers, then, off they went into the first song.

Tilly, too, was puzzled by her father's introduction of the musicians. Why could he not have said something about the music and the good cause the money was to go to? Why bring in about the strike, and show so clearly what he thought about the strikers? Surely he must realise that they had some right to their cause, that only compromise would win the day. If he believed in common sense, why had he thought the Arbitration decision had been right? How could it be common sense to pay the men starvation wages, when the Masters lived in such luxury? Common sense would tell him that it was in the factory owners' interest to have a happy, healthy work force, not a work force which was half-starved, and discontented. Besides, reducing wages just meant that prices were reduced, and everyone was undercutting everyone. It was all so complicated, but she was sure she was on the right track. If only she could understand it all properly. When the music started, she realised the men were singing well, they were obviously enjoying themselves. She glanced around to see what other people were feeling. She hoped so much that the concert would be a success, not for the sake of raising money for the church furnishings, but because it was her mother's creation. At the end of the row in front, she spotted Mr Lugando, and Mr. Lockyard. They seemed to be completely absorbed by the singing. When the first song was over, they both clapped heartily.

"Bravo, bravo," came a shout. Both the strangers were showing their enthusiasm. Tilly wasn't surprised, she expected Italians to behave like that. Then she remembered that Mr. Lockyard said he was English, and lived in Dulwich. Suddenly he looked round, and smiled at her, nodding in the direction of the stage. Tilly felt herself blushing. She hoped that no-one had noticed. At the same time, she was pleased that he was enjoying himself. After all, if he liked it, and he must go to concerts all the time in London, then it must be good.

After the choral group had sung a few songs, an older man appeared on the stage, to play a sonata on his violin, accompanied by Robert. Tilly watched him in awe, as he tuned up, and put the violin to his chin. He seemed so wrapped up in what he was doing. The music started, and she concentrated, trying to follow the complicated repetitions and inversions of the melody. Suddenly she felt transported by the music.

The room, and the people in it, all seemed to be swept up into a bubble, which was floating away, over a glassy lake, up, up into a still blue sky. There were birds flying there, and stars, and a kind of brightness, over which the notes soared and fell, soared and fell. Tilly closed her eyes. She couldn't remember feeling this way before. There was a sadness mixed in with her feelings, as if all that beauty was just out of her reach, and it would disappear before she could experience it. This was the best moment of her life, she decided. It must be. Nothing could possibly equal this, this feeling of rapture. There was so much to know, and experience. How would she ever be satisfied?

As soon as Tilly stopped listening properly her awareness of some perfect reality, outside of herself, drawing herself into it, evaporated. As soon as she realised she was experiencing it, it was gone When would she find it again?

Just at that moment, Edna noticed her daughter's expression. She nudged her. "Are you all right?"

Tilly opened her eyes and shook her head. Why had Mother broken into her moment? She felt she had been under a spell. "I'm listening," she said. Why couldn't Mother listen, like she had listened? What was the point of music, if you didn't listen? She would never recapture the moment. She was right. All the rest of the sonata was played, not by two demi-gods, but by an old man, in a baggy, much-pressed tail coat, and Robert Willoughby, the clerk at the Works.

In the concert interval, Robert went for a breath of fresh air, into the front hall. No one was about. Evidently all the servants were serving refreshments to the guests who had gone into in the drawing room. He paused for a moment to look at the large brass candlesticks on the side-table. They were glinting in the light from the hallway fire, which was lit for this special occasion. There was a thick rug on the floor which covered the grey stone slabs. Ornaments and polished woodwork gleamed, and there was the scent of women's perfume, and hyacinths. The contents of the conservatory which had been brought in, made the air moist and heavy with transpiration.

Robert felt immersed in luxury. At the same time, he felt a kind of dread. Very soon he would have to face all the men in the Union Committee, and make them understand that there was no alternative but to go back to work. People like the Manstones, who lived in this luxury, could last out virtually for ever, against the men. How could he tell the fellows that they would have to go back to work? These 'Masters', so-called, with all their riches and style, would give nothing to the workers. Robert feared that the Union members would think he was a black-leg, pandering to such as Manstone, and playing at his concert. He knew they wouldn't just overlook the fact, just because he was donating the proceeds. Of course he'd had to tell the other singers that the workers would overlook that, but he knew it wouldn't work.

Mrs. Manstone was talking to Signor Lugando, and Mr. Lockyard had made his way, through the rows of chairs, to where Tilly was standing with Mrs. Dawkins and Ros.

When Lockyard came up, Tilly introduced him. "Father and I met Mr. Lockyard when we went to visit the new church being built for the Duke of Greatmarsh."

"We've heard all about it. It's been in the paper. My husband will be so sorry now, he missed seeing you both, Mr. Lockyard. He was unavoidably prevented from coming tonight. I expect you've heard, there was an ugly scene, in the centre of Saghead, and he thought best not to come in case he was needed by the Magistrates. "

"No. I didn't know."

"It was quite dreadful. Someone had put a barricade on the line. Everyone had to get off the train. It only just stopped in time. Then some fighting broke out, on the platform."

"Oh. It sounds awful." Lockyard didn't look all that shocked.

"It doesn't surprise me. People are starving," Tilly said.

Mrs. Dawkins looked at her in horror. "Violence. They should never resort to that. I'm surprised at you, Matilda."

"I feel very sad at what is happening to people, and at the need to use violence. What do you think, Mr. Lockyard?"

"These are difficult times. I am sure everyone will come to their sense, and a solution will be found." He was looking at Tilly, and his voice was grave. Turning to Mrs. Dawkins he said,"It will soon be over, I am sure. You must come and view the work Mr. Lugando is involved in, any time. I am sure he would be delighted."

Tilly thought about what he said, but stopped herself from pursuing the subject. Why did people always have to set aside the facts, or put some facile interpretation on them? Everyone should be involved.

Mrs. Dawkins thanked Lockyard for his invitation, and swished off to speak to Edna, fanning herself.

"Mr. Lockyard lives in London, Ros." Tilly explained to Ros.

"We shall visit there, sometime. Papa has promised. I've always wanted to visit. But I should not like to live there."

"Indeed! I suppose it would be hard to leave all your friends here. And you, Miss Manstone, would you like to live in the capital?"

"I've never thought much about it till quite recently."

"And now, what do you think."

"I think it might be interesting."

Ros intervened. "Excuse me. It has been pleasant to meet you. I need to ask my mother something." She hurried off.

Tilly continued. “Recently, I’ve been wondering whether I could improve my education. You see, what I said just now, I really believe. There is so much hardship in the world. My work at Father’s factory has allowed me to see a little of how poor people live. I believe that if I had more knowledge, I might be able to do some useful work in the world.” She was breathless when she was finished.

Lockyard was surprised to see her eyes shining as she said this. Her cheeks were flushed, and he realised her words came from the heart. Immediately, he wanted to put his arm round her. He could help her in her quest. He felt the life force in her, drawing out his own.

Tilly continued. “I do admire people who have found something they really want to do and then do it, very, very well. I envy them, in fact. Like the musicians tonight. It’s just that I don’t know yet, what it is for me, and I think if I had the space and time to just....be....I might find out what it is I want to do, really, really want.” Tilly rattled all this off so that she was quite breathless. She hadn’t meant to say so much, it had all just poured out, unbidden.

“Well, put that way, I can quite understand. In fact, I had the chance myself. In just the way you describe.”

“Tell me, please. I would so like to know.” Tilly gazed at him, hanging on his words.

“I became concerned at the way poorer people in London were living. My home is in Dulwich as I told you, and I had the opportunity to see many of John Ruskin’s beautiful work, in the gallery there. Then I took to reading some of his writing. Through this I became aware of the dreadful fact that so many ordinary folk nowadays have no chance of enjoying the beauty of nature, because towns are grown so large, and all the common land is disappearing. “

At that moment Mrs. Manstone clapped her hands. The chatter died down, and she said “We have five minutes to take our seats again, Ladies and Gentlemen, and then the second half of tonight’s programme will commence.”

“Please go on,” Tilly said earnestly, “what happened?”

“In short, I thought architecture should be my profession, perhaps to ameliorate the housing conditions of poorer folk. I shall be happy to tell you, but maybe some other time.”

“What about later on, after the music?”

“That would be a pleasure. But I wait on Signor for a lift in his carriage, so I’m not sure. May I call on you?”

“Of course. I am sure my mother would be very pleased.”

Lockyard bowed, and went off to the end of the line, back to his chair.

Jeannie, who had been collecting up the empty plates, went out of the drawing room to see Robert standing in the shadows.

"Oh." She started. "You made me jump."

"Are they ready to begin?"

"My word, they'll be in there all evening, if you don't watch out. They do like their victuals."

"Well, tell your mistress, we shall recommence at nine o'clock. There's some of us have other things to think about. The arrangement was until ten o'clock." Robert added the last few words under his breath. Business was business after all. Manstone knew all about that. He didn't work for charity either.

Most of the guests hurried back into the ball room when Mrs. Manstone gave the signal. Two gentlemen stayed in the corner talking to Enoch.

Edna turned back to look at them

"We'll be in directly, my dear," Enoch said, raising his hand. "Don't wait on us."

Both Isaac Jordan and Daventry Enruff were members of Saghead Scientific Society, which Enoch wished to join. He was canvassing them for admittance. "We'd best wait to go in till this is over. We won't be missed. They're happy enough. Best sit down. These weekly lectures, who's going to give them? Not the members, I suppose?"

"Oh no, my dear fellow"

"Do you think there'll be many coming forward to these public lectures?"

"We have to give them the opportunity, Manstone. With free education, we've got to face it, there's more and more want to improve themselves. Times are changing. We have to admit that. Our society has to encourage the dissemination of knowledge."

"Very good, very good." Enoch drew on his cigar.

A burst of clapping could be heard. "Your wife's soiree seems to be a great success."

"Aye. She's one for educating people as well. This is all her doing, her invention. I just do as I'm bid in these matters."

"Don't we all? Besides, general culture is a necessity as well as scientific knowledge. I understand one of the musicians is your clerk, Robert Willoughby?"

"He is that. Not a bad lad."

"I've heard he's an asset."

"He's coming on. But I've had work training him. The old saw's been proved to me many a time. If ye want something done proper, do it yourself. They're all the same, these workers."

There was a tap on the door, and in came Tilly. "Papa, excuse me please. Mama sent word...."

"Well, my dear, in a moment, in just a moment. I'm coming." Enoch stood up. As soon as Tilly had gone, he turned back to his two friends.

"You've heard of Royton Box, my engineer? He's installing my new Ram pump?"

"Tell us about that," Isaac said. Enoch sat down again.

Tilly slipped back to her seat in the ballroom when the next pause came, and smiled at Edna. "He's coming."

Edna looked round at the large mantel clock. There was no more time to waste. She couldn't wait for Enoch.

She looked in Robert's direction, caught his eye, and raised her eyebrows. He came to the front of the stage.

"We come to the final items, ladies and gentlemen." He announced the numbers, bowing low.

Edna forgot her annoyance with Enoch as she listened to the song which, this time, was unaccompanied, so Robert was singing. Robert's baritone stood out among the others, and she found herself watching and listening for his part. It was a lively melody, and she felt the appreciation of the crowd. At the end everyone was clapping whole heartedly.

"Encore, encore."

Once more the young men bowed, and they were off again, this time into Gilbert and Sullivan.

There was prolonged applause but nothing would shake Robert's decision that enough was enough. Suddenly Edna saw Enoch making his way along the side of the room to a point just below the platform. He held up his hand for silence.

"My dear guests. Thank you for your cordial interest in our little concert tonight. I'm sure we're all aware of the talents of these young men. And of course none of this would have happened without the efforts of my good lady herself. I'm no musician myself, but, as you can see, she is, and can pick winners. Edna, my dear, you'll be good enough to acknowledge our thanks." He went up to her, took her by the hand, and raised her to her feet. She blushed and bowed. All the performers, as well as the audience cheered and clapped.

Tilly went up to her mother, and put her arm round her shoulders. "It was lovely, Mama. A beautiful evening." It was true. Everyone was coming up to make their congratulations, and take their leave.

The musicians began to collect up their song sheets and Enoch turned towards them.

"There's some dinner for you lads. And I'll settle up with you."

Deaker came forward to lead the men into the servants' dining room where the meal was ready laid. Edna watched them file through the door nearest to the kitchen, then followed the last of her guests into the hall.

"A sensation, my dear." It was the Mayor's wife.

As Edna turned towards her, she noticed some cards which had been arranged on the table. She picked one up and realised they gave Robert's name, and that of his group. How was it that he had put the cards there without asking her permission? She swept them up into a pile. She would return them to him. He had no right to do this. But supposing Enoch had given him leave? She couldn't really blame the man for wanting to better himself. She put one of the cards into her reticule, then rearranged the rest. Upstairs, in her boudoir, she took out the card, and wrote on the back. "You may wish to see me about accompanying me on the pianoforte. Please let me know your terms." She put the card into an envelope, and addressed it. When Jeannie came she told her to take the card down to Mr. Willoughby.

10

After three weeks, everyone had had enough of the strike. Various factories opened their gates, one by one, and employed whoever would come in, for reduced wages. The sight of the Christmas poultry hanging up outside all the butchers' shops, broke the resolve of all but the most committed strikers. The weather worsened, Union funds were running low and there was no possible outcome but to accept the Arbitration decision.

Christmas at Terrilea, and all the other big houses, was celebrated in the usual style. In the Saghead terrace houses, it was enough to have a warm fire, and a leg of roast chicken, to feel human again. The Union and all its efforts were consigned to oblivion. No one ever criticised Robert for playing at Manstone's party. When all was said and done, it was every man for himself.

By the time Mrs. Dawkins and her party arrived at the Shire Hall for the New Year Charity Ball, there were already numerous carriages standing in the big cobbled square. The horses were happily munching from their nose-bags, steam rising off their haunches. Some of the coachmen were huddled up on their seats, others were standing in knots round a brazier and eating hot chestnuts and pies off the many little stalls erected round the square.

When wraps and overcoats had been deposited in the cloakroom, Dorothy led the party up the grand staircase to where the Lord Mayor and his Lady were welcoming guests. Each arrival was announced by a liveried footman, and the appropriate greetings were given.

"Good turnout, by the look of it, Samuel," Enoch said to his host.

"Indeed. It gets better every year. We should be able to top what we sent last year to the Fund."

The party arrived in the ballroom. Gilt chairs within recesses between pillars lined the floor, and Mr. Dawkins quickly appropriated one group.

Dot sank down thankfully, pointing to a neighbouring chair to Edna. But before the rest of the party had time to be seated, the Master of Ceremonies was announcing the first dance. It was a quadrille. Many sets were already complete, and soon there would be no more room on the floor.

"May I have the honour of a dance, Miss Manstone?" It was David Lockyard, who had been invited at the last minute, by Mrs. Dawkins.

Tilly had only two spaces left on her programme. The first was to be with Donald Westerham, Father had booked the second dance, and Cyril Arbuthnot was third.

"Mine is number four." It was Ros's father. Tilly realised that she could not politely refuse. She wrote the name in her programme, then turned to Lockyard. "The first dance after the interval," she said and rose to give her gloved hand to Donald. Gathering her train onto her left arm, she set out to make up the set with Ros and Cyril Arbuthnot, and four others.

After all the complicated gyrations, and to-ing and fro-ing, Tilly was relieved that the next dance was with Father.

"You looked very fine, with mama," she said, as as they glided out onto the floor.

"Are you proud of me, my lass? I thought you were too busy remembering all those steps to take note of me. "

"No-one could help taking note of you and Mama. You must have been the stars of the ballroom."

"Well, we did make a good couple, in our day. We'd have had the prize for dancing, if there had been one."

Nevertheless, Enoch did not dance again. He made sure that Ros' programme was full, before asking her for a dance. Having obeyed the conventions, he could now settle to talk to Westerham, and Mr. Dawkins. Edna, too, kept her seat most of the evening. She had felt a light headache coming on, since her turn round the floor with Enoch. She would relax as best she could on the straight backed chair. She would watch the young girls, flowers in their hair, swooping and swirling with their partners. Those tall and vibrant men! As the orchestra got under way, she felt her body responding. Enoch had never danced much, since their courtship. She'd become used to her role, sitting out, and gossiping.

At last the interval was called, and the guests filed in, by couples, to the refreshment room.

A loaded buffet provided every kind of cold meats and salads, and at the far end were various desserts.

"They won't make much money, if they're paying for all this, "Enoch remarked, to Westerham.

"I assume some of it's given. I can only think that. It's probably from some of the shop keepers and farmers. That's how they can get on the guest list," Dorothy Dawkins said.

"Well, it's a fine spread. And you're to be thanked for your part in arranging it."

"It's my pleasure," Dorothy said.

Edna gazed at her plate. Even if she had been feeling perfectly well, she knew it was unwise to eat this rich creamy food. She would only suffer for it later. She sat, stiffly, hardly aware of what everyone was saying. She longed for the dancing to begin again, so that she could lose herself in the music. Tilly too, wasn't enjoying the food. She wanted to be back on the dance floor, and in particular, she was looking forward to her dance with David Lockyard.

Suddenly the wine waiter came back to Mr. Dawkins, with a huge bottle of wine, in a silver bowl full of ice. Mr. Dawkins had a quick word with him and he proceeded to remove the cork, which was held on with a complicated contraption of wire. Suddenly there was a loud bang, much louder than Tilly had ever heard before when a bottle was opened.

Dawkins touched the rim of his glass, with a fork. At the high tinkle it let out, everyone at the table stopped talking. Mr. Dawkins rose.

"My dear friends, I am sure that you have guessed why we are all gathered here together." There were knowing glances between Mrs. Westerham, and Dorothy Dawkins.

"To get straight to the point, your glasses will be filled and I ask you please to drink a toast to my dear daughter Rosalind, and our good friend, Cyril Arbuthnot. They are engaged to be married."

"Well.....!"

"How wonderful!"

Gasps and cries of delight followed this announcement, and then everyone raised their flutes of champagne. The whole party rose to their feet. "To the betrothed couple."

"Cyril and Rosalind." Ros put her arms round her father, then looked towards Tilly, tears in her eyes. "Thank you, thank you all, so much."

Tilly raised her glass and took a tiny sip. The wine was so sour tasting, and bubbly, she could hardly swallow it. The whole room seemed to have shrunk to the little space round her, and the glass. She couldn't bear to look at Ros, standing over there. Had she just witnessed her friend throwing her life away? So, none of her words to Ros had had any effect.

David Lockyard moved towards her. She looked so pretty, in her yellow silk dress. Everyone was standing round Ros and Cyril, the men were shaking him by the hand, the ladies embracing her. Tilly felt paralysed. She knew Ros was waiting for her to come up and give her congratulations. But she couldn't move.

"Miss Manstone," David said, "please do not forget your promise of a dance."

"Oh. I haven't forgotten. But I prefer to sit for a moment. Will you sit with me?"

"Of course, please, whatever you wish. Should you wish to go to the fountain?"

"Yes."

Down the stairs, in the reception hall there was a small oval pool, and above it, built into the outside wall of the building, was a stone basin, shaped like a shell. A trickle of water was running through the mouth of a sea creature, carved into the stone, down into the shell, and from there into the pool. "Oh, this is so pretty. I didn't see it when we came in." On each side of the shell, were two stone benches, protruding from the wall. Tilly perched on one of them, resting her head on the wall behind. She closed her eyes. "That is better. I was too hot." She could just manage to get the words out. She was aware that they were coming out at intervals, and were slightly slurred. "Oh dear. Excuse me." She held out her hand. Was she going to be sick?

"Just rest," David said. He unfolded a white handkerchief, and dipped it into the pool. Wringing it out, he gave it to her. She put it to her forehead. Her head was slightly bowed.

"Thank you," she said. Gradually, the nausea was passing. She kept swallowing, and applying the damp cloth to her cheeks.

"Would you like me to fetch Mrs. Manstone?"

"That won't be necessary." Tilly sat up straight. "I'm spoiling your evening. Don't wait. I shall be better in a moment."

"Would you like a drink of water? Or anything else?"

I would like you to go away, Tilly thought. She was making a complete fool of herself. "There's nothing you can do. Nothing anyone can do."

"My dear Miss Manstone. Please tell me, if you can, what is the matter? Perhaps I can help?" He was down on his haunches beside her. Or was he on one knee? Whatever, his face was close to hers.

She couldn't bear it. She stood up abruptly. "This is too ridiculous. I am just making a fuss about nothing. Now, I must go and congratulate my friend. She is to be married." Tilly's voice trembled. She took a deep breath, and stood still, clenching her fists. "That's what's the matter. Now you know." She turned and darted to the stairs. "I'll see you for the dance," she called, without turning her head. "Excuse me."

David Lockyard made a step towards her, then stopped in his tracks. Dusting the knees of his trousers, he stood for a moment, listening to the dissonances of the orchestra as it tuned up for the second half. Then he shook his head, and went through the door, to the outside. It was fiercely cold, with a hard frost. The carriage horses, still waiting for their owners, appeared to be dozing, under their blankets, lifting first one hoof, then the next, to rest each leg in turn. The braziers were still burning, and the carriage drivers were huddled round it. David lit a cigarette. He would wait here, too, and cool off.

"Tilly, where have you been?" Mrs. Dawkins and Mrs. Westerham were back in their place in the ballroom. The rest of the party had vanished. A few bags and shawls were the only evidence of their existence.

"I was so hot. I went to have a breath of air." Why was it that it was her absence which was noted, Tilly wondered. "Are they all dancing?"

"Yes, yes. Except for the old gentlemen. As you can imagine. They're talking. All making merry. Cyril has appropriated all Ros' dances now, so everyone has to make new arrangements."

"I thought that would happen, that's why I didn't hurry too much."

"We're all so excited. Of course we've known for a little while now. We were saving up to tell you. Now tell me, my dear," Dorothy took Tilly's hand, "will you be Ros' chief bridesmaid? I know she's counting on you. Absolutely counting."

Tilly had known this was coming. But she couldn't answer. Her throat seemed to have closed up. Mrs. Dawkins was gazing at her with shining eyes. The words eventually came out. "Of course. Thank you."

"Good. That is so wonderful!"

The dance was ending, and in a moment, Tilly found herself hugging her old friend. "You did it then!" She squeezed her hard, trying to avert her face, to hide the tears.

"I couldn't help it! Dear Tilly!" Ros seemed radiantly happy, as she clung to Cyril's arm.

Edna recovered her spirits, and substituted herself for Ros, for any partner who had been supplanted by Cyril. When David Lockyard did not reappear, no-one seemed to notice, all the programmes were in such confusion. But at last, there he was, standing silently by Tilly's chair as she sat through the pause before the last dance.

"May I?" he said as the musicians struck up again.

Tilly said nothing, but allowed herself to be led onto the floor.

At the first chords from the musicians, as she made her curtsey, Tilly felt a sudden surge of life. She wouldn't let the news of Ros' engagement depress her, or affect her in any way. She had her life before her, her own choices to make. Probably what Ros was doing, was right for her. So be it. That was her affair. Meanwhile she felt a throbbing impulse of energy. The chandeliers glittered with thousands of sparks, the music flowed through her feet, carried her along, so that her skirt swayed, as she twirled and twirled again. She glowed all through. Through her arms and shoulders, through her flaming cheeks and shining eyes, she felt a force, which would take her up, and guide her, to her own special destination. She would skim with it like a seagull, banking on the wind, and be caught up by it, in heady spirals, till she could dive through it, and take her prey. She would go with life, use it, its power, this was what she wanted to do, for ever. She would fly her life till she dropped.

As the final notes were played, David Lockyard held onto her hand, pulling her gently towards him. "That was wonderful. You are a marvellous dancer. Please let me dance with you again"

"Perhaps. A dance. Yes..... sometime. Thank you.....we must talk. I'm sorry about this evening."

"It was wonderful. Of course we must talk."

Shortly everyone was waving to each other, and climbing into the carriages.

Edna and Tilly sat down on one side, while Jim arranged rugs. Enoch climbed onto the opposite seat, and sat down heavily. "I don't need that," he said, when Jim came to do the same for him. "I'm hot enough. Just get us home, and be quick about it." He knew he would be asleep in a moment.

The carriage rolled away. Tilly closed her eyes, and Edna gazed out of the window. Away from the centre of the city, there were no gas lamps. The dark streets were lit only by starlight, and the occasional candle in some windows. But as they came down the hill, towards the canal, the sky seemed to be getting lighter. In fact there was a pronounced glow under the clouds, which was becoming more and more obvious, the nearer they came to the canal bridge. Suddenly the carriage stopped with a jolt.

"What's happened?" Edna had her head out of the carriage window. "Enoch?" She turned round.

But Enoch was fast asleep, his head lolling against the cushioned head rest.

Tilly rose and went to the window. "I'll get out and see." Jim's face appeared at the window. "If you please, Ma'am, there's no going on this way. There's a fire down yonder, and all these carriages can't get on no further."

Sure enough, when Tilly looked she could see a long line of vehicles, in front, and more backing up behind. Horses were stamping and whinnying, and coachmen shouting at each other. All round the air was getting thicker and thicker. There was a pronounced smell of smoke. Tilly began coughing.

"It looks like there's a fire, ma'am. No going on this way."

"Or the other, I shouldn't think," Tilly said.

"Wake your father," Edna said. "He'll know what to do."

"Mama! What good is that going to do? We'll just have to wait. If there's any other solution, I'm sure we can think of it, as well as father."

"I think he should know."

"I think we should consider what is happening over there. Perhaps some help is needed. Let the steps down," Tilly ordered Jim.

At that moment, there was a noise of shouting, and a bell was ringing. On the road, coming down towards them from the other side of the bridge, was a fire engine, pulled by four horses. It was approaching at a snail's pace, owing to the press of carriages still trying to go on. Tilly saw it stop at last, on the bank of the canal, and the hose was let down into the water. Evidently they were going to pump water to replenish the tank, and then go back up the hill to the fire.

"You could go and help them," Tilly said to Jim. "George and I can manage the carriage. Off you go."

Jim ran off down the road to the bridge, and joined the little group of men round the fire engine.

"He's gone to help them, Mama. Why don't you come and see for yourself. It's interesting."

"Tilly! You never did such a thing! How could you, without asking father?"

"It's quite all right. I am sure father would have done the same."

Just then, one of the men detached himself from the group helping to pump the water, and appeared to be talking to Jim. Then he came up the road, towards the carriage. Tilly recognised him. It was Robert Willoughby.

"Is Mr. Manstone there?" he asked. "I need to see him urgently."

"Of course. What is it? Father!"

Enoch, opened his eyes, and immediately understood that there was some kind of crisis. Robert's white face peered at him through the smoky atmosphere.

....."It's one of the chimneys at Leviathon. Caught fire. Just out the back from us, sir."

Enoch climbed down. Without a word he set off down the hill with Robert. Tilly watched the two men, her father with his square frame and ponderous stomach, and Robert, lean and tall. Edna was peering through the carriage window, but all she could see was the black mass of the houses, silhouetted against an orange glow, out of which rolling fumes belched off into the sky.

"Come back inside. There's nothing we can do. We're stuck here."

Tilly did not move. "It looks as if it's got to some of the houses, Mama. If the wind changes, it may be up as far as the works."

Edna said nothing, just closed her eyes and laid her head against the back of the seat. "God preserve us," she murmured. "Do as I say, Tilly. Your father will know what to do. He must." The prospect of anything happening to the factory was too dreadful to contemplate. If anything really serious were to happen, she would suppose it was God punishing them all. Nothing ever happened just by chance. Everything was meant. Perhaps this was all a warning. "Come inside. We might die of cold." Edna's voice was plaintive.

Exactly, Tilly thought. And what of the people who had lost their homes this night? Tilly realised that what she wanted most of all, was to go down towards the fire herself. It was pulling her, like the red eye if a cobra, twisting, turning, flickering. Why could she not just run down there, and see for herself?

"There may be people hurt down there. And what about their houses? We might be able to help them."

"How, for goodness sake? Sometimes, you do talk nonsense, child."

"It is not nonsense, Mama. There must be something we could do." Tilly heard herself shouting. She thought of her father, and Robert. They were probably in the factory by now, maybe allowing the firemen in, to draw water from the Manstone supply. She supposed that was how her father could help. She tried to control her voice, speaking slowly and precisely. "We could go down to the factory, Mama. It would be more comfortable down there, in any case. We won't be able to get home with this crush. Besides you can't leave Father. There are no trains now."

"I am definitely not going down there, through these muddy lanes. Nor are you. We are going to turn round, and then George can drive us back."

Tilly said nothing, but continued to stand on the grass verge beside the road. From all the scattered streets higgledy-piggledy across the slope of the hill, hundreds of people were swarming down the muddy paths across the wasteland, towards the canal, then up the opposite bank to the fire. They formed black streams which were converging into a river, which flowed against gravity. How could mother possibly imagine that the carriage could turn round?

George, standing by the horses heads, suddenly raised his whip. An old man, in a nightcap and long coat, with a muffler round his neck, was making his way against the press of people, to speak to him. When he saw Tilly he snatched off his nightcap. She immediately recognised him. It was Silas Reith, the engineer.

"I've just come from the works. A message from Mr. Manstone, Miss. You're to make you way home, not to wait for him. He says there's no danger to your property, it's well under control, but he don't want you waiting about no more. They've got a chain going, passing the water. The Master has opened his pump as it's needed. You're not to worry."

"Mr. Reith, thank you. Could you help to get the carriage turned round, so that my mother can get home? Then I'll come down with you, to the factory. There may be something I can do."

"Certainly, ma'am. But it's not the place for a young lady. I don't know as what your father would say."

Tilly closed the door of the carriage. "I'm getting some help to turn the carriage, Mama," she said.

Edna's eyes opened. "I knew we could get back."

"You'd best get out, Mama. It will mean unharnessing the horses, then the men will push the carriage round. It'll be lighter for them. You'll be quite safe."

Holding her train as high as she could, Edna managed to come down the steps and stood out of the way, picking her path between broken shards scattered among the tussocky grass. She shivered as she gazed over towards the blaze, which seemed to her like the gates of hell, yawning wide, to swallow up all the ant-like creatures swarming towards it. She felt desperately tired, she could hardly take it all in. The news of Ros' engagement had filled her with a sense of gloom, which she knew was founded on jealousy of Dorothy, for her large family, who were all fulfilling their parents' wishes. How different and empty, her own life seemed to her. Always, as now, she felt she was a witness, looking at life, but not properly participating in it.

George and Silas had picked some volunteers from among the hurrying crowds, and were now directing operations. Two lads held the horses and they were led away onto the rough grass, which they immediately began to munch. Two or three others lifted each shaft of the carriage, while others pushed from the back. Nimbly, they negotiated the two verges, pushing the vehicle to and fro, until it was facing the opposite way. Tilly was standing by her mother, holding her arm. "Now then," she said, as the horses were re-harnessed. "I am going down with Silas, to see father. I can come home with him. I'm not in the least tired, and I wish to be of service." She tucked a second rug round her mother's knees. Before her mother had time to remonstrate, Tilly had closed the door, and told George to drive off. Quickly, she ran down the slope, to Silas, who was already striding back towards the fire. "I've come to help," she said.

"Aye," he said.

As soon as she had started to run, Tilly realised how stupid she was being. Her satin slippers were already letting in the cold and wet, even if she stuck to the cobbles. Holding her train up with one hand, it was all she could do to keep her balance. At any moment she might slip over, then she'd be another liability for people to attend to. She suddenly regretted her decision. How could she possibly be of assistance, with her silk dress and velvet mantle, and these shoes? She felt useless and stupid, amongst all the press of people. But it was too late to change her mind, her mother, the carriage and George were out of earshot. Probably her mother had decided to let her have her head, because she realised she would only learn if she had to live with her own foolhardiness. Well, that was true. She'd just have to make the best of it. Keeping as close as she could to the reassuring back of Silas, and clutching her cloak even more tightly round her, she made her way through the crowds. No-one was taking any notice of her, which was a relief. Everyone seemed intent on only one thing, to get as near to the fire as possible. No-one seemed to notice her stupid, impractical clothes.

As they crossed the canal bridge, the atmosphere changed. It was warmer. As they clambered up the hill, towards the factories, it was warmer still. The air was thicker, huge flakes of soot were wafting down, and great sparks were shooting up against the dark billows of smoke. The smell of burning, which Tilly had been able to perceive even when she was beside the carriage, intensified. Against the background of shouts and cries, came the noise of flames crackling, and every now and then, the roar of collapsing masonry.

Tilly felt Silas' hand on her elbow. "Come this way round, we munna get tangled up in that." Straight ahead, at the end of the street, Tilly could now see the actual centre of the fire. It was leaping upwards through windows and roofs of tiny terraced cottages, but the black bulbous kiln chimneys, shaped like upended wine goblets, seemed to stand resolute, against the scarlet, orange and yellow. For a moment, she could do nothing but watch, one of the massive crowd, mesmerised by the spectacle. She suddenly remembered that it was New Year's Eve. It was as if all the past was being obliterated in the conflagration. Perhaps this was what had made so many people turn out to watch. They were not here to help, but to wonder. Well, she would not be deviated from her purpose. She was here to help. She must go on. Silas was beckoning her.

The heavy metal doors of the factory were open, and a large pipe was snaking its way from the Manstone water supply out of the tunnel, and off down the street. Tilly was amazed. How had they managed to organise this in such a short time? "Did you do it? Did you get our engine rigged up, to pump our water over?"

"It was necessary." Silas said.

Skirting the group round the temporary water conduit, Tilly went to the stairway up into the office. She went up three steps, and looked round the crowd in the yard, to see her father. There he was, only a few feet away, talking to Robert. At the same moment that Tilly spotted him, he turned towards her, and Robert went off across the yard, to the gates.

"What are you doing here? I told you to go off home. Where is Mama?" Enoch's face was red, and perspiring.

"She's gone, Father. I came to help. You must let me do what I can."

"What dost think tha' can do? Tha'll just be in way."

Tilly noticed that her father was speaking in the dialect. This was a sign he was very angry. She'd only heard him speak this way when he was reprimanding a servant. "I won't be in the way. I want to help. Have many people lost their homes, father? What has anyone done about that?"

"Their homes? What art talking about? It's the factory which we're after saving. This is their livelihood, Miss. That's what matters. Their livelihood, and yours too, and mine, and your mother." He was shouting.

"I am aware of the need to save the factory. But obviously, that is not in danger now. If it were, I am sure you would not be letting Silas pump the water away. I mean to find out what is happening to the folk in those houses."

"Tha shall do what I tell thee."

"Of course, Father. But I mean to find out, all the same. There maybe people at risk. In any case, they will need shelter, and some food and drink, if they have lost everything." Tilly felt a sharp needle of ice in her chest as she said this to her father. She'd had never before confronted him like this. But she was driven to it, by this needle in her heart.

At that moment, two women carrying babies, and various other young children, came through the tunnel. Robert was behind him, supporting a bent old person, completely swathed in a tattered shawl. Tilly dashed towards them.

Robert's face was drawn and his coat had a light coating of ash on it, like snow. "The fire's taken their house, and I brought them here. Could we find shelter for them for the night?"

"Of course. Father will allow it." She ran back to her father. "There are some women who need our assistance, Papa. I know you will let them stay. Please."

Enoch was sitting on the bottom step of the wooden stairs, his head in his hands. He did not appear to hear her. He felt suddenly nauseous and his head was throbbing. "Don't you bother me." He regretted his harsh words, of a few moments since. "It seems you've already said they may. Just while morning now, then their relatives mun do it."

Tilly was about to ask what would happen if they had no relatives, but thought better of it. "They may use the decorating shop," she told Robert. "That is if we can get the old woman up there."

"I'll manage," he said. Within moments, the women and children were installed upstairs, a fire was lit in the stove, and a kettle was put to boil. Robert went off again, and after a short while came back again, with another group of destitute people. For the next two hours, until all the people who'd lost their homes, were accommodated, Tilly supervised the arrangements. During all this time, Tilly and Robert hardly exchanged a word. There was no need to. Each of them understood what the other was doing, and they acted in perfect harmony. There was no thought of what Enoch was thinking or doing. He had his priorities, they had theirs.

After speaking to Tilly, Enoch had managed to stagger upstairs to his office, and from the window, he was able to see that the blaze was gradually being contained, and presented no further danger to the Works.

A little before dawn, George came back with the carriage. Enoch and Tilly climbed thankfully aboard, she, with her dress and train dirty and torn, he, still suffering from the after effects of all the champagne and whisky.

The next day, Enoch told Tilly she was to stay at home, with her mother. Edna had not appeared for breakfast, due to a migraine headache. When Tilly tried to speak to her, in the darkened bedroom, she turned away, murmuring, "You will do what you will. It will have to be between yourself and your Father. I do not intend to be involved. That is my wish."

Tilly could think of no response. Shaking her head, she let herself out of the door quietly. She went to sit in her own room, but she could not concentrate on her book. She kept having to fight back the tears. No-one understood her, her father did not, nor did her mother. Did anyone at all, in the whole world? At the fire, last night, she hadn't needed to explain her actions to Robert. But her parents, especially her mother, did not appear to want to understand, or even to take her seriously. How could she prove herself, once and for all? It suddenly occurred to Tilly that she would never be able to fulfil her mother's expectations. She had been born a female. Nothing could change that.

Returning from the factory, that evening, Enoch found himself in the same carriage as the newspaper editor.

"My sincere congratulations, dear fellow. You did sterling work last night. It's all round the town."

Enoch frowned. He must be referring to his allowing the fire engine to use his water. "Aye," he said. "Well. It wasn't much."

"It seems your young clerk did a power of good there, but of course the credit has to rest with you. Helping all those folk."

"That. Yes. He worked hard."

"Indeed. A very laudable act on your part. I'll be writing an editorial now, this night, for tomorrow's Signal. I'll make sure everyone in the town has heard of Manstone's Ceramic Works."

"Indeed"

"What is the young man's name? Shall I refer to him? Or would you rather I didn't."

"To be frank, I'd rather not dwell on the whole matter. It's no good to let people think Manstone's is some kind of charity. I'll thank you to say nowt about it, any of it. Best thing is, to find out who started the fire. Make a story out of that, if you will."

When Tilly returned to work, she went straight up to the decorating shop. There was no sign of what had happened so recently. The long rows of tables were back in their places, the straw which had been put down for bedding for the homeless women, had been swept away, and the paintresses were all sitting in their usual places.

Alice looked up, and the low murmur of the women's voices ceased abruptly. "Can I be helping you, Miss?"

"I just wished to know whether everything was as usual."

"Of course, Miss. It was a dreadful shame for those who was in the fire. But they're all cared for now, so I believe. I don't know as how they are managing, but there....."

"Were you acquainted with any of them, Alice? I should like to know how they are managing."

"Well now!" For once, Alice seemed to be nonplussed. "These people, living down this way, we don't have none of them in this workshop."

"One of my cousins, as works in the clay shop, his wife's nephew, his sister was telling me, they've all been given blankets and such by the Ebenezer."

"Did you see it? We happened to be in this area, when it happened."

"I know someone as has lost their house." Tilly recognised Gertrude's voice.

"Oh! Could you tell me if she's is all right now?"

"It's true what Alice says. The Chapel has made them comfortable, as far as they can. But she's grateful, I know, for what you did, the night itself. Mr. Willoughby too. They're that pleased, I know she wouldna' mind me saying."

"It was nothing. My father was pleased they could use the room, and the water."

"Of course, Miss. No-one is forgetting the Master, he did famous."

"Thank you, Gertrude." Tilly felt uncomfortable by the attention she was getting. Anyone would have done what she had done. It was nothing. She nodded and went down the stairs, then ran up the other wooden steps opposite, to the office.

"The women are very pleased with the help we managed to give, father," she said, hanging up her long coat, and taking off her fur hat. "That's due to you, you must know that."

"That's as may be. Get on with your work now, I don't want anyone to think we're all put about."

Later on, Tilly went to speak to Robert.

"Apparently some of the people you brought in the other night, are known to the workers here. We must see what is to become of them. I was told they're still taking shelter in the Ebenezer. But that can't be the case for long."

"No. You're right. You aren't the first to have considered that."

Tilly said nothing for a moment. As usual with Robert, she felt put down. Why did he always have to put on this superior air? "What do you think would be the best thing to do?" She stressed the word 'you.'

"By rights, they should have new houses. Isn't that what you would like in the same circumstances?"

"Of course. But then, that is what we would have. We are insured, I am sure."

"Of course." He stared at her.

"You mean, they wouldn't be."

"So is their landlord, Shepperton. He owns most of the houses round here. What he'll do about re-building them, I don't know the cost of building these days, I doubt he'll bother. The rents aren't high enough to make it worthwhile, I suspect."

"Mr. Dudley Shepperton. Why, father was dining there recently!" Tilly waited for a comment from Robert, but none came. "What's to be done then?"

"It's all part and parcel of the ills of this society. The wages aren't high enough to allow people to pay decent rents which will allow the landlords to maintain their properties. And why aren't the wages high enough?"

Tilly couldn't reply. The answer seemed too obvious, and at the same time, too difficult. "I would like to visit that woman whom Gertrude mentioned. Would you arrange it for me? It is someone who is a distant relative of hers, I believe." Even if she could not understand or improve, the economic conditions of the country, Tilly thought that she might make a difference to the life of one person.

A few minutes later, Enoch came in.

"Father, I would like to make some errands in the town. May I take an hour off?"

"Errands? Your mama won't have you wandering about the streets on you own. No."

"The night of the fire...."

"I want to hear no more about the fire. You disobeyed me then. Let it be. I don't want to know anything more about that night. Control yourself."

"It is important to me that...." Tilly's voice was very soft, but she spoke slowly and clearly.

"Do not speak to me in that tone. What is important to me is that you should control your tongue and behave like a young lady and a dutiful daughter. Now, hear me."

"Yes father, I wish to please you, I do really, but there are people out there who have lost....."

"Silence."

Tilly stared at him, unwavering. She suddenly saw him, not as her father, but as a stout, red-faced old man, his fists clenched on the desk, the knuckles showing white. Quite coolly, she determined what she would do.

"Excuse me," she said. She went out of the door, along the corridor past Robert's office, and out onto the head of the wooden steps. Here it was chilly, but the sun was out and she stood for a moment, with her head turned up, her eyes closed. She was going to disobey her father. The only thing which he could possibly object to, reasonably, was the notion of her going about the town unattended. In that case, she would find herself a chaperone, and visit the homeless women, as she planned. She went back to her desk and silently carried on with her work.

Just before lunch, Enoch stood up. "I'm going up to printers. If you want to come." He spoke gruffly.

"Thank you, but no, papa. Jim will be here shortly. I promised Mama I would be back for luncheon."

....."Very well." He put on his overcoat, and was off. As soon as Tilly could no longer hear his heavy footsteps, she went in to see Robert.

"I wish to see the woman of whom you spoke, to see if we can be of assistance. However, I do not wish to go there alone, my father wishes me to have a companion. I wonder if your friend who works in the decorating shop, Gertrude, I think, would be able to accompany me. Just for an hour?

....."She couldn't take time off. They'd all stand to lose if she's not there. They have a complicated order to finish."

"I see." Tilly saw that her own concerns were of little importance in comparison to the women getting their wages at the end of the week. Of course! "It doesn't matter. I would like to go myself, but perhaps you could take an hour yourself, and assess what is best to be done. I am sure that my mother could arrange some help."

Robert looked at her. "I can tell you without meeting anyone." Why did the girl think it would help, to see for herself? She probably just wanted the honour and glory of showing everyone how concerned she was. "Food and shelter, that is what is needed. Can you provide either, Mr. Manstone, Mrs. Manstone or yourself? I wonder."

Tilly felt rebuffed. He was a monster, this man. How could he be so rude and unpleasant? "Food and shelter? What about friendship, Mr. Willoughby?"

"Friendship! Don't think they don't have friends. That is one thing the poor do have, though you wouldn't know that, Miss. However, I will do what I can. I'll make some enquiries about the people worst affected, and perhaps you may do something. Yes, I will." He nodded.

"When you have a list ready, and some proposals, we'll do something. I promise." Tilly swished out of the office, back to her desk. But her eyes would not see the pages of figures in front of her. She was smarting from Robert's remarks, and, at a deeper level, still angry with her father. But she would not be put down by either of them. The whole difficulty, the absolute heart of the matter, was that she was not allowed to go out alone. Why not? She would be going in broad daylight, in the centre of town? Inwardly, she raged, but still, she couldn't quite find the courage to do what she wanted to do, on her own. When she heard the gig come into the yard, she was relieved to be going home. She would persist in her aim to help the victims of the fire. Perhaps she could persuade Deaker to come with her. Tomorrow.

In the event it was Deaker who came up with an appropriate solution to solving the problems of at least one family affected by the fire.

Two days after the conversation between Tilly and her father, Deaker came into the morning room while Mrs. Manstone was having her mid-morning cup of tea. The painting of a vase of flowers, which she had begun the day before, was on the easel by the window. "That's a fair picture, you've made of that, Miss Edna," Deaker said. "It's nice to see you back with your paints. Now, if you got a moment to speak to your old nurse."

"Of course. Any time." Edna patted the chair beside her. "Sit down here, and we'll see what's to be done."

For once, Deaker thought, the Mistress was more like her old self.

"I do hear there's some hardship among those who lost their homes in the fire."

"Who's been worrying you about that? I heard myself that the Ebenezer people have it all settled."

"That is so. No-one can deny, they've done well. But it's only for a while. They all need new homes, even though for now they've shelter with friends and the congregation."

"Is there anyone in particular?"

"Yes, Miss Edna, there is. I have it from my sister, there is one. I don't know them, but it seems, there's too many of them to all stay together, with those that have put them up. It's a crowd of great girls, and one of them in particular....."

"What are you suggesting?"

"It's the youngest, Mavis, I think she is. She's just coming up to fourteen, now, and, well, being as I'm not so lively now, there's a deal for Jeannie to do. Would you think we could take her on, here? I'd train her. We have to think of the future, Miss Edna."

"Has she been in a situation?"

"Not as far as I know, she's been kept at home, to look after the young brother, but he's better now, so this is the time to get her something. But now, she needs to have the bed as well."

"Well, I am sure you are right. It seems as if it's something we can do to help. And you're right. You need to take it easier. I've thought you weren't looking so well yourself. Do you get tired now?"

"Of course, we're none of us so young now. In ourselves I mean." Deaker looked hard at Edna. She thought she would know she was referring to the Change. Edna registered nothing.

"We will give her a trial period. We don't usually have city girls. But I trust your judgement." At least, Edna thought, she would have something to tell Tilly, which she would surely approve of, for once. She picked up her paintbrush again.

11

In February, Ros was invited to stay at Terrilea for a few days. This was so that she could have a rest before having to start the serious business of wedding plans.

Tilly and her friend were sitting together on a fallen tree trunk in the beech wood. Although it was still wintry, there were signs of spring. Calls of birds bounced and rebounded across the valley, pigeons, blackbirds, thrushes and finches.

"I heard a nightingale here last year. Do you remember, I told you? It was the middle of the night, I woke up, and it was completely dark. I could hear this bird singing. It must have been a nightingale."

"How romantic. You did tell me, but I still find it romantic. Don't you, Ti1ly?"

"I don't know. Perhaps. It was beautiful. But I don't know about 'romantic.' Sometimes I think that's just in the mind. False in a way."

"But everything's in the mind, if you look at it that way. It's what we make of things. Anyway, what's wrong with romantic, if that pleases you?"

"I can't stand it, if it's false, superficial. Like those songs that group sang, Mr. Willoughby's group. Do you recall? Nice melodies, I'll grant, but...Didn't you think they were a bit false?"

Ros laughed. "Everyone liked them. Your tall thin Robert Willoughby, the way he did them, with his deep voice, everyone liked them. Even that one about the dove."

"I didn't. Not really. I just said so, for the sake of Mama. But I did like his playing."

"Oh. So he did strike a chord." Ros was peeling the bark off a twig she was holding, and she ran her finger down the sappy stem. "And what about David Lockyard? After the Ball, has he called again?"

Tilly looked cross. "I can't believe you. He was just a friend. Besides, he's always working."

Ros broke the stick in two, flinging down the pieces. "Well. I don't believe you. About romance, I mean. There must be something, somewhere inside of you, just a little bit of yearning for romance."

Tilly was silent for a while. She was looking at the trunk of an old yew, which had formed into a corkscrew shape, where the wind had been hammering it into submission for years. "There isn't really, Ros. Really not. I am glad for you and Cyril, of course, truly I am. And of course, you'll make a lovely bride. And I'm dying to be a bridesmaid, your bridesmaid, but..." she hesitated.

"But...what?"

"Perhaps you're right. We see people differently and things differently." Tilly didn't go on. She didn't wish to seem at all critical of Cyril, or Ros. They loved each other, and that was that. But she just couldn't see it happening to her."

"You don't like my Cyril?"

"Of course I do. He's a grand fellow. You'll be very happy, and I shall be a dutiful auntie to all your crowd of children. I couldn't wish for anything better than that, you know Ros." She put her arm round Ros. "I feel jealous, a bit, I suppose. He's got you now. And we won't have many more chances to be together like this."

"We shall, you'll see. We'll be bringing the babies here, and Deaker will pack us all up picnics, we'll let the children play tag round the trees. It'll be grand. You'll see. And you'll have a husband too. Our children will be like brothers and sisters."

Tilly tried to picture it. She could imagine Deaker and Jeannie, staggering down the steps with baskets full of food, and rugs, and nursemaids carrying the babies, and the little children all carefully clambering up into the beech wood, bringing their toys. Perhaps it would be so. But then she realised that Deaker would never do that. She would be too old, by the time Tilly herself was married. "I'm going to be a bride and a mother by proxy, I've decided. You'll have to do it all for me," she said.

"You can't say that. You can't imagine what you're missing." Ros was already in a position of being able to queen it over her friend, her engagement had already brought her a status above that of Tilly. And her marriage would remove her even more from her friend, who would herself have to marry if she were ever to reach that elevated rank. Besides, Tilly would be missing more than that, the love and honour of a devoted man. "Anyway, it's all nonsense. I'm sure you will find someone you love, very, very soon." Ros was now stripping the bark off another little twiglet which she had pulled from an adjacent branch. "But you might have to think of it seriously, I mean, seriously, Tilly. Perhaps tell your Pa that if he wants another clerk there are plenty of good men he could employ. After all, you can't go on clerking for ever, you've already learned enough to oversee a manager, if that becomes necessary."

"You mean, if Father died?"

"I don't know. I didn't want to say that. I mean, if anything happened, anything at all,"

"You see, you're doing it again, now. It's so false to talk about something happening. I'm sorry, Ros. What you mean, you should say, outright ...' if he died, or had an accident.'"

"I don't know that I do mean that. I mean anything, anything at all, and you had to take over. Don't be cross."

"I'm not cross, Ros. I just wish people would use the right word. It doesn't help to dress things up, or flannel over things. Anyway, something has happened, as a matter of fact. It's nothing bad, just that he's going away for a week to London, and he's left me to manage."

Ros stopped fiddling with the stick. "Good gracious. You mean all on your own? In charge of the factory."

"It won't be difficult, Mr. Robert Willoughby will be there. And nothing untoward is likely to happen. After all, the strike is over. They won't come out again. And we know what we're doing, orders and so on."

"Tilly!" Ros hugged her friend, then held her at arm's length. "You're so clever, I'm sure I couldn't manage a factory, not now, not ever. Will you wear a top hat, while he's away?"

Tilly pushed hard, and they both collapsed in a heap on the ground. "Race you down the slope." Down they went, through the new, tussocky grass, slipping and sliding to the bottom.

They stood, panting, surveying the stream, and the tiny, uncurling, leaf buds.

"Oh, it's so gorgeous, so, so beautiful. I could die, right now, and you could bury me here," Tilly gasped, "and you'd have to find a new bridesmaid."

"Don't do it, I forbid. There's no-one else."

"Hello? Hello?" It was Edna's voice. The girls ran to the stile. There she was, in the field, huddled up on the grass, nursing her leg. "Oh, oh." They could hear her groaning.

"Mama! Whatever's happened?" They both clambered over the stile, as quickly as possible, then took off towards Edna, who was lying on one side, her leg bent awkwardly beneath her.

By the time Tilly and Ros rushed up, Edna had pulled herself up, and was half sitting and nursing her left ankle. All the blood had drained from her face, and she felt dizzy.

"Lie still, don't move, Mama." Tilly felt perfectly cool. "I'll run for help."

"I'll go. You stay. Take my coat." Ros quickly slipped off her jacket, and they put it over Edna. "Shall I get your smelling salts?"

"Yes, yes. Get them," Edna moaned.

"They'll be in her reticule," Tilly said. "Ask Deaker. And tell George. She won't be able to get back up to the house." Ros set off at a run. "What happened?"

"I don't know. I was just walking along, and then my leg went from under me."

Tilly looked at the ankle. When she went to touch it, Edna flinched. "You can't walk back like this."

"No." A few tears were rolling down Edna's cheek. She smiled ruefully up at Tilly. "What a silly Mama you have."

"Nonsense. You're the best mama in the world. It's the hole where the water comes up when it's wet. You must always take care, just here. I thought you knew."

George's head suddenly appeared over the edge of the slope. He put down the rake. "Wait there a moment, Ma'am,.. Jim!" His voice carried across to the wood, and echoed back.

Shortly, the two men were coming down with a chair,

"Now then, Ma'am, if we'll get you set down. That's it, now then." The two men skilfully hoisted Edna up on the chair, then, with Jim on one side, and George on the other, each of them with one hand on the back of the chair, and the other underneath it, they bore her aloft. "Put your arms on our shoulders, Ma'am. That's it. You'll be safe with us." George spoke gently but firmly.

Edna did what she was told. The pain in her ankle was still intense, but she felt reassured and safe. Steadily, chair, bearers and Edna, with Tilly behind, processed up the steps.

Edna's fingertips just touched the rough cloth of the mens' jackets. Her head, slightly inclined away from Jim, was a little nearer to George's curly beard. She looked straight ahead of her, but from the corner of her eye, she could see Jim's eyelashes, his small moustache, and his forelock bouncing on his forehead as he climbed.

George began breathing heavily through his mouth as they reached the landing half-way up, where the steps changed direction.

"Just give me a whiff," George murmured to Jim, as they paused. Jim's breathing had not altered with the effort, but his nostrils were slightly flared. There was a smell of tobacco and sweat, which Edna did not find unpleasant. It was an adventure. Already, she was beginning to cope with the pain in her ankle. Her body went limp, and the men noticed the difference in the weight when they took up the chair again.

"Might as well take you right to the door, if that's your wishes, Ma'am" George blurted.

"Beg pardon, Ma'am." Jim said. "Was it them moles? I know they've got into the grass. That or a rabbit. You'll be all right now. Nearly there. "His voice was soothing.

"It's that hole, where the water gushes when there's a storm. It needs filling. It's been there for ages. It needs filling." Tilly commented.

As they passed the morning room window, Edna saw Deaker looking out, a horrified look on her face. But Edna managed a smile. At the French doors to the sitting room, the procession halted.

"This all right, Ma'am?"

Edna couldn't speak. As the chair was lowered, she found herself gazing at Jim's mouth. He had full, pink lips, showing beneath his moustache. For an immeasurably short moment, she felt the wish to put her mouth to his, to put her arms round him, and pull him towards her.

The chair came to rest on the grass, and George was helping her to stand up. Deaker had come to the glass doors and was opening them.

"Thank you both. Deaker and the girls will get me inside. Very good" Edna murmured, turning away.

Jim took off his cap, and brushed his hair back into place with his fingers, before putting it on again.

Deaker had come to the glass doors, and was opening them.

"Help me in, Deaker. That will be all, George."

It was Deaker who piloted her up the steps into her armchair.

The two men went off down the terrace. Jim began whistling.

"Cut that out," George said.

Inside the drawing room, Edna continued to look at the terrace, bathed in sunlight. Once more, the feelings she had just had, welled up in her. She tried to fill her mind with something else. The image of the man's mouth came back. Her breath became faster.

Deaker was speaking. "I brought your smelling salts. But maybe you'd be better with tea?"

"I would. I'll sit here for a while. Don't fuss." Edna said."

"I'll get you some water for that, and bathe it," Tilly said.

"Not at all. Deaker can do all that. In a moment. Go and enjoy yourselves. I don't want to spoil things for you."

"You wouldn't at all. I would like to help."

"And me. I mean, I too," Ros added.

"No. Just go off." Why did they have to go on so? "I'll just sit here quietly on my own."

"If you're quite sure," Tilly said. She wouldn't have minded at all helping her mother. But evidently she would rather have Deaker to minister to her. Well, so be it. She and Ros left the room, and Deaker hurried away to make the tea. Probably the Mistress had felt a little faint, that was why she'd fallen over. It did seem more and more likely that she was heading for the change..

That evening, in Tilly's room, both the girls were strangely excited. Ros was talking. "Your poor Mama." Ros said. "Fancy having to be carried about like that."

"Oh, you don't know her very well. She actually likes that sort of thing. Being made a fuss of."

"My Mama's quite the opposite. She won't ever be ill, nor let anyone else be ill."

"It's a bit different when you've got something broken. It's not exactly being ill, is it? But I suppose her ankle isn't actually broken."

"Anyway, I wasn't suggesting your Mama hasn't cause for wanting some extra attention.

"Anyway, you're right. She could have walked up the steps. After all, we were there."

"It was more fun being carried. Must admit that. Though if it had been me I would have insisted on two dusky warriors with turbans."

"And a palanquin?" They both laughed.

"Not much chance of that round here."

"Just old George, and Jim."

"And they're so sweaty."

"Ros, you shouldn't say that. That word. It's a good thing Deaker isn't here."

"Oh, Deaker. She still rules you all, like she did when you were a little girl. 'Now Miss Tilda you must always this,' and 'Now Miss Tilda, you mustn't do that.' I remember. Anyway when I'm married, I'll be able to tell you...everything. And I'll say 'sweaty', if I've a mind to."

"Will you?" Tilly paused. "Do you know already? About it, I mean."

"Mother says she's going to have a talk with me. She will. One day she'll come into my bedroom, and then I'll know it all. I'll tell you, of course I will."

"You're the first one of my friends to be married. Do you know that? You've got a big responsibility. I'm sure my Mama won't ever tell me anything. So I rely on you."“

Ros was sitting propped up on the pillows, smoothing her long blond hair down over her shoulders, first one side and then the other. "There isn't much to know anyway. I know how babies are born as it happens. Mother's had seven others besides me. I've told you about that."

"But still, that doesn't explain."

"I think I can guess. I just want to know if I'm right."

Tilly was hugging her knees under the soft feather eiderdown. "Aren't your frightened, Ros? Just a bit. I mean, suppose you don't like it, whatever it is. Then what will you do?"

"I shall like it. I'm sure I shall. Mother must like it, or she wouldn't, keep on having babies, would she?"

"I don't mean having babies. That's just part of it. I mean everything. Being under a man."

"Under a man? What do you mean, 'under a man,'?"

"You know exactly what I mean, under his orders."

"I thought you might mean 'underneath.'"

"Whatever gave you that idea? You do have some strange notions. I mean under his dominion."

“I don’t know it is such a strange idea. Because I think that’s what happens. The lady gets on her back, and then the gentleman gets on top of her, and that’s when IT happens.”

Tilly turned her head to look at Ros with round eyes. She began laughing. “You can’t be serious. Is that what you really think? I can’t believe it. That’s so funny.

“It may be funny, but I’m very nearly sure, that’s what happens. Anyway, you must have known, or you wouldn’t have said ‘underneath’ like that.”

“I did not say ‘underneath’. I said ‘under.’ Under his orders. That’s what I said.” Tilly pulled the covering right over her head.

“Underneath,” Ros gasped.

“Under,” Tilly screamed, her laughter stifled in the dark cavern of her bedding.

Next morning, Deaker, coming into the morning room, heard muffled explosions of laughter. The girls were swaying backwards and forwards, their heads together, tears rolling down their cheeks.

“Oh dear, oh dear, “Ros said, as they let go of each other.

“Oh Deaker, we had such a joke.” Tilly explained. “It was just something Rosalind said last night.”

“You said it,” Ros said, giggling again.,

“Well I never. Just like two schoolgirls. I never did. Come and have your breakfast. Really Miss Tilda, no-one would think you was being trusted by your Papa to look after the whole business while he’s away. And you, Miss Rosalind, soon to be married. Such goings on!”

“We’ll have some porridge.” Tilly was still gasping and panting and gripped the back of her chair, in a paroxysm of gasps.

“I won’t ask what you were laughing about.”

“No, Deaker, don’t. You wouldn’t understand anyway.” Ros let out another hysterical shriek. Tilly had to turn her back, to control herself.

“Get on with you.

“There’s no sense in you this morning.” Deaker swept out again. When she’d gone, Tilly and Ros fell in each other’s arms, tears running down.

It was cold again, back to winter. Gertie, whose table was next to the door, had her feet on a little box and wrapped in a small piece of blanket. Even so, when anyone went in and out to the workshop, she felt a draught catching her back and shoulder. She knew she’d feel it when she was in bed tonight. There was a good fire burning, that’s true, but she couldn’t catch the benefit from where she sat. It was thanks to Miss Manstone, anyway, the fire, since she’d insisted with her Dad that he provide a good supply of coal for the women’s decorating shop. She said it was no good if their hands trembled and spoilt the line. After all, it was fine ware wasted, if the painting was wrong. She did seem a good sort of lass, that Miss Tilda, even though she was one of the bosses. Perhaps her father would listen to her when he wouldn't listen to his own conscience. He was supposed to be religious, that one, he'd founded the new church in Epsilon It seemed he could put money into that, but as for making things better for the workers, they might as well sing for their supper. Gertie's thoughts turned back to Rob. In fact they didn't really turn, because they never left him, or they hadn't done recently. She'd felt something wasn't quite as usual. He'd been late coming to see her, sometimes, and he'd been downright bad-humoured when they'd been out together last Sunday. True, it hadn't been warm, and she'd shivered when they were under the railway bridge, up at Moor End. But it hadn't been like him to be cross.

"It'll be all right, when we're married, Rob," she'd said, with her arms round his neck. "I'll mek thee a good wife, I will, tha'll not find a better."

"Willt, Gert? Willt?" He'd kissed her, then pushed her away, it seemed. They'd stood like that for a few minutes, waiting for a rain squall to pass, and he hadn't said more, but they'd linked arms, and walked home, with hardly a word between them. Gertie had felt all hollow inside, as he turned at the end of the road, without looking back.

"Robert not coming in, lass?" Mother had said, but when she'd seen Gertie's face, she'd known better than to enquire any further.

The door of the workshop blew open. The wind was getting up, and evidently whoever went out last, had not closed it properly. Gertie disentangled herself from the blanket, and got up to close it. Looking down the steps to the yard she saw Miss Matilda, with her back to her, talking to Robert. The Manstone gig was turned round, near the gate. It must be time for the young lady to be off home. Miss Matilda gave Rob a piece of paper. He nodded and spoke a few words, the girl wrapped her long coat tightly round her, and got up into the gig behind George. As she left she raised her hand to Rob.

Gertie caught her breath. She had felt a slight pain in the chest. She must get inside.

"Wait." It was Robert shouting. As the gig rattled out of the yard gates, he sprang up the wooden staircase, to where Gertie was standing with one hand clasped round her throat, the other on the rail.

"What's up?" he said.

"It's cold, it's nothing."

"What's the matter, Gertie? You're always cold."

"It is cold. It is always."

"Take this." He unwound his scarf, and wrapped it round her.

"I cannot take that, it wasn't knit for me," But she didn't take it off.

"It's just borrow. That's all."

He took her hand. "I came to apologise - for last time. You must'na get me wrong. You're my lass. You know that." He drew her down the two steps towards him.

"I get tired of waiting, I do, and all. Why must we keep waiting?"

"Hush. We can't talk now. Anyway, we've been through all that." Robert's voice was low, and he kept looking over Gertie's head, towards the door of the decorating shop.

"I just want you by me, that's all. Mother's said we can have the front room." Gertie couldn't prevent her voice from trembling.

"We'll see, we'll see."

The door of the workshop opened, and Alice came out.

"Oh. Tis you, is it Mr. Willoughby. We cannot get on with that order, which is promised, if Gertie isn't here. She's holding us all up. We shall all have to work late." She went in, slamming the door.

Gertie looked dismal, frowning." She's worse than a man, she is. Why don't we have a man over us, like the other shops?"

"Take no notice. Listen. I've just heard from Miss Manstone. The Mistress wants me to go round once a week. Listen." He took the letter from his pocket, and unfolded it with care. *"Dear Mr. Willoughby,"* he read,

"As I stated before Christmas, I shall be pleased if you can accompany my violin playing, and some singing practice for Miss Manstone, at our mutual convenience. The fee will be one shilling per hour, with train fare.

Yours truly,

Edna Manstone."

He re-folded it carefully. "What do you think?"

"Is that what she said at her musical evening? Why didn't you tell me?"

"She didn't say anything then. She just asked me the price, but nothing was arranged. I didn't tell you, in case nothing came of it."

"I don't see how anything can come of it. She don't expect you to go all that way of an evening after work, do she?"

"No, of course not."

"Well then? What other time is there? Saturday you're practising with Dick and them others. And what other time have you got? I don't suppose she means Sunday, do she. They're strict Church folk."

"Well, she said, 'mutually convenient' so she'll have to fit in with me Church or no Church."

"You aren't going to give up Chapel, are you? For the sake of a few shillings from her."

"Don't worry, Gertie. She'll have to come to some accommodation with me, if she wants to be suited."

"What do you mean? Accommodation?"

"Give and take. Make some changes if she seriously wants it."

"I should say so. And what about me? What about us? If she's going to make accommodations, we'll have to give up our Sundays too. Is that what you're saying?"

A face appeared at the window.

"I'll have to go now, Gertie. Don't worry. Think how much I could earn, if I only did it for one year. Just think."

"A year!"

"Think how it would add up. It'd help get us settled. Towards getting married, I mean."

Gertie shook her head, and turned to go back up into the shop.

"We'll talk later. I'll come round," Robert said as he ran down the steps.

He was glad to get into the office. It hadn't been good with Gertie. Too bad she'd seen Miss Matilda give him the letter from Mrs. Manstone, otherwise he'd not have told her about the arrangement to go to Terrilea, until he'd actually started. He'd have made some excuse or other if he hadn't time to meet her so regularly. At any rate till he'd saved up a few shillings. Perhaps then he might be able to give her some money to buy something for her bottom drawer.

Even as he thought this, Rob caught himself out deciding that he wouldn't give Gertie anything towards the wedding purchases. In fact Rob dug deeper, in his mind, and came to flint. He wouldn't give her anything, because he knew, now, for certain, that he wouldn't be getting married to her. There was nothing more sure, than that he wouldn't wed Gertie. Sitting at his desk, in the little dark office, the thoughts came crowding in on him, like rats round bones. He was motionless, despondent. He should be cheerful, now he'd made up his mind, but he couldn't be. He couldn't move, to get on with his work. He just stared out of the window, not even aware of the sky and the clouds, and the steep roofs. His prevarication about the marriage, the reason for Gertie's tears, and his bad humour, the reality of his own feelings, the fact that he had to lie to the woman, his pity for her, his shame about the fact he wasn't recognised by his own father, all were all reasons gnawing at the back of his mind. He had felt like this before, but usually at night, never in the daylight, with the sky showing through the window, and a fire alight in the grate.

He put his arms on the desk, and leaned his head on them, with one hand across the back of his neck. After a moment he became aware that his jacket was becoming damp, with the moisture from his breath. He felt the wool fibres under his lips, he heard the faint murmur from the fire. He stirred, he was aware of himself, of his life. He heard Mr. Manstone clearing his throat next door.

"Come here, Willoughby."

When Rob entered, Enoch leaned back in his chair, and pushed against the desk, laying down his pen. "Sit down, sit down. We have to make arrangements for when I'm away."

"Away, sir?"

"It's time I took a trip down to London. I've made me mind up. I've various clients to see down there, and I'm going with Barker on the Committee of the Science Club. I'm a member now, you know. I was elected last month. Yes, I was elected. Well, I'm going down there, with our secretary, and we're to meet Sir James Leavy. He's giving the MacDermott lecture. I shall be introduced."

"You must be well pleased, sir."

"Oh yes. I am well pleased. The fact is, I shall be doing more of that kind of thing now, Willoughby. It won't be just going to meet Leavy. Mixing business with pleasure, it'll be, more travelling, that is. I may join a London club, as a country member of course. My scientific friends will stand up for me."

Enoch was looking into space, and Robert considered the import of what he was saying. He felt a gleam of optimism.

"It will mean more responsibility for you and Miss Manstone. I don't go lightly away from my work here, as you well know. But I feel now, you two can manage adequately. Of course I'll leave explicit instructions, as usual."

"Yes, sir, I'm sure of that. I shall endeavour to come up to your expectations."

"Of course you will. We've a job to do here, and the livelihoods of all rely on getting the orders, and then fulfilling them. The first part of that is my task, Willoughby. We have to put ourselves about. Competition from Germany, and the States. Pressure is mounting, and it's not getting easier. It's no good cutting corners, and getting soft. I don't want any of this here slacking off. Or we'll all suffer. Do you take my meaning?"

"You can rely on me, Mr. Manstone."

"I must do, or I wouldn't be leaving you here."

"May I ask when this will be, sir, this trip?"

"The end of the month. Just one thing. You're on trial now. In recognition of extra duties, I shall be raising your salary by £4 per month. And Miss Manstone has been here six months now. She'll be receiving a salary too, put her down for £10 per month."

"Yes, sir. Thank you Mr. Manstone."

Robert went out, closing the door softly behind him. He sat down at his desk and scribbled some figures on a piece of scrap paper. Then he walked over to the window. There was a small yard, then the roofs of several rows of terraced houses. After that was farm land, sloping up to wooded hills. Beyond the hill, some four miles away, was Epsilon, and just beyond, Terrilea. Robert, standing with his legs apart, and his hands clasped behind his back, realised that his earnings, by dint of his salary increase, and the contract for the accompaniment, had increased by nearly 15 per cent. He wasn't going to marry Gertie and saddle himself with wife and family. He could save, now, and get away from this place, away, beyond those grey streets, and wooded hills. He sat down to resume work. Not yet, but soon. But what of the working men he'd wished to help when he first had come here? What means could he find to break the power of the Masters?

12

Enoch completed the arrangements for leaving the management with Robert and Tilly.

Nothing was left to chance. He had been away before, of course, to see his agents in London, but this time it was to be for longer. And this time, Matilda was to be in charge, as Mr. Manstone's deputy, and Robert would have the title of Office Manager, who would outrank the Clay Manager, Mr. Gurdy, and the Decorating Manager, Joseph Moore.

It was Thursday, the busiest day of the week, and Enoch was to take the London train on the following Monday. Gurdy, and Moore, as well as all the various Little Masters and Misses, journey men in their trades, were in the office to collect their payments.

In the wages ledger, the names with their work and numbers, were listed according to their workshops. Alongside each name was the amount of money payable to that individual.

Gurdy and Moore had already inspected the ware to make sure that Mr. Manstone wasn't paying for anything that wasn't perfect.

"Mr. Gurdy, for Elijah How, Dennis Could, Albert Glass." As Robert called out the names, each man stepped forward and took their money. This would then be paid to the workers under them, who were employed by themselves, on a daily basis.

Tilly had already checked the figures for Rob and was now sitting at her desk in the inner office. She was studying the Pottery Gazette, comparing prices for two specific glazes.

"Miss Manstone, please." It was Robert's voice. He was holding out a brown envelope. "You are to have this. Mr. Manstone's orders."

She frowned slightly, and took the packet. Back at her desk, she opened it to find two sovereigns. She looked at them, turning them this way and that in her hand.

After a few moments Robert came in through the door. He'd finished paying out, and the outer office was empty. "Give you a surprise, did it? Didn't Mr. Manstone tell you?"

"Of course he did." Tilly was cross with herself for showing surprise, and annoyed that Robert had seen through her. Why hadn't father warned her? Was it just a present, as he was going away, or was it...like wages? He'd never said anything about giving her wages. And if she'd ever thought about it, she assumed that her status was more like that of an apprentice, and that she should really be paying him for all that she was learning. But then, she couldn't do that, as she didn't have any money. Mother paid for everything, even for little gifts she might want to buy. In any case, she made most of the presents which she gave away. Mother always said that it meant so much more, if it was one's own handiwork. Tilly couldn't imagine what she could do with all this money. Would she be expected to pay her mother something, or even her father? Would it all just disappear?

"I thought not," Robert said. "Any way, you're on the pay roll now." Of course Manstone wouldn't have said anything, crafty old devil. He'd been having the girl here all this time for nothing. Well, now she was getting paid, there'd be no more of this having time off.

Tilly wondered whether she'd now be working full days. If she was to learn everything there was to learn about the pottery business, she'd have to spend more time here. At the moment, she still felt she was between two worlds. She really did not understand the chemical processes involved. She knew what happened when glazes were fired, but not how. Would she ever be able to make decisions herself, about the business side of the trade? How could she ever be in charge, if she didn't grasp all the most basic principles of management and technique? Would her father ever teach her? He always seemed too busy even to speak to her, let alone educate her. She went back into the outer office. Robert was alone again, writing in one of the ledgers.

"Mr. Willoughby. Have you a moment?"

"What is it?" He wiped the pen and replaced it on the ledge.

"What is your opinion of my work now? I want you to be frank."

Robert frowned. "It's not for me to say. It's Mr. Manstone's place to say. It's obvious what he thinks. Since you asked me to be honest, I will be." He paused, "I think you have learned the business remarkably quickly. Obviously only experience of the industry will allow you to take real responsibility. I hardly feel I have that yet. But one thing, you have. You have a feeling for the work people. I would never have believed that could be possible. Perhaps it is because you are of the gentler sex." His voice became so low, the words were almost indistinct as he spoke the last words.

Tilly blushed.

"I do not wish to give you cause for embarrassment. But you asked me to speak out. I noticed your attitude, then at the fire....."

There was the sound of heavy footsteps. It was Mr. Manstone. "That Silas. He caught me down there, or I'd a been up 'ere to tell you about your wages, my lass, I did mean to talk to you, but it slipped my mind"

"Thank you, Papa. You know I've been working here for my education, and to help you," Tilly said, primly. She couldn't believe that such an important thing as two pounds a week on the wages bill could have slipped her father's mind. "Of course I'm grateful for it. But you mustn't think I expect it."

"I should think not. You're not trained yet, by a long way. But I think it's right for you. You've more responsibility now, with me going away."

"Yes, papa,"

"We'll go through the order book, and the ledger, at once, if you please."

"I have them here, sir," Robert interposed.

They proceeded to check out invoices for glazes and clays, as well as the orders from customers. This took them until one o'clock. Tilly was getting hungry, as it was past the time at which Tom usually collected her. At last Enoch closed the ledger.

"Put them back now. I canna see anything amiss there. I want them kept like that. Go for your snapping now."

Robert put the heavy books back.

Manstone's words annoyed him. When had he ever had reason to find fault about the way the ledgers were managed? He wished his words with Tilly had not been interrupted.

Enoch told Tilly to put on her hat and coat as he was taking her to lunch. They would go by tram to the Station Hotel.

"Papa, if I had known I wasn't going home for lunch, I'd have dressed accordingly." She had on her usual blue serge coat and skirt. "I could have worn my green dress."

"You'll do very well as you are." He took his own top hat off the hat-stand, and clumped down the stairs, Tilly behind him. Outside, it was warmer than she expected, and she felt too hot in her long jacket. Why hadn't Papa told her he wished her to stay the afternoon, and have lunch out? One never knew what to expect from Papa, it could be annoying.

As they came out of Manstone's tunnel into the lane, Tilly felt the sun on her face. Even here, in these smoky streets, the sun occasionally penetrated. She thought with longing of the fresh, heady air, in the woods at home.

"Did you tell Mama I wouldn't be home for luncheon?" she asked Enoch, slipping her arm through his.

"I telled Tom to bring the gig at three o'clock. I've no doubt your mother will have made the appropriate arrangements. It'll be the same now, every day."

Tilly did not respond. It seemed strange to her that her father couldn't tell Mama directly of his plan. She suddenly wondered if Mama even knew about her wage packet. She decided not to ask him if he'd told her.

The tram stop was at the end of the street and as they reached the corner they could see it swaying along the rails in the distance. Enoch stuck his umbrella out, advancing right onto the track to make sure it stopped.

Once aboard, the bell clanged, and off they went.

The Station Hotel was at the bottom of the hill, by the railway station. As they went into reception, the clerk recognised Enoch, and sent to inform the head waiter that Mr. Manstone was on his way through.

The restaurant was practically empty, its rows of tables, clad in heavy white damask, and festooned with glittering table ware, waiting like submissive virgins, to be ravished by the conquering heroes of the manufactures.

Tilly sat nervously on the edge of her chair, while waiter after waiter offered enticing food and drink. She didn't feel hungry. now, but in deference to father, she was eating her way through mulligatawny soup, poached turbot, compote of pheasant, lemon pudding, cheese profiteroles, and peaches. She sipped ginger beer, while her father drank two glasses of champagne.

"What was the matter with Silas, father?"

Enoch was munching, and didn't speak for a moment. "Oh, it's nowt. He's allus going on about that machine."

"The engine? The engine itself?"

"Of course I mean that. What other engine is there?"

"I thought perhaps you meant the pugmill."

"How could I mean that? That's nobbut five years old. I should hope that won't need replacing for another twenty year. Should see me out." He pushed his plate aside.

Tilly persevered. "If it's the engine itself, that could be serious, father."

"I know that, my girl. I'm not stupid, though your mother may think it."

Tilly held her tongue. Her father seemed to be ill-tempered, all of a sudden. Perhaps it was the trip to London, which was worrying him. "Of course she doesn't, father. She admires you. We both do. Where would we be without you?"

"Aye, you can say that, where would you be? Or any of those folk which are working at the Pot-bank," Enoch said. On the other hand, Tilly was learning the business fast, and she would soon be able to do the job, as far as a woman could. "Perhaps you should come with me to London, one of these trips. There's more to running the business, than just managing the factory." Sitting opposite to Tilly, her hair peeping out from under her hat, her cheeks flushed from the food, and her eyes bright, he realised that she was now a very attractive young woman. "You're not thinking of doing what your friend Rosalind is doing, are you? Getting yourself wed?"

Tilly blushed, "What on earth gave you that idea, father? I'm quite happy with what I've got. I'm glad you've seen fit to pay me. I didn't expect it, really, I didn't, but it means a lot to me, I won't let you down, I won't." She meant what she said, it came from her heart. But at the same time, she knew she was coming more and more under his power, this father of hers, with his strange autocratic ways, his unpredictable decisions about what should or should not be done, and when. She didn't ask why he hadn't told her or her mother about the lunch, or about the wages, or even about her working longer hours, from now on. No, it was up to her, now, to just go along with his wishes, whether or not, and smile about it. She was an employee, now, and as such, she was as much in his power as is a wife to her husband, as Ros would be to Cyril. "It's lovely fish," she said, delicately separating flesh from bones. "This is a treat."

"You could have a glass of wine, if you wish." Enoch saw the wine waiter approaching.

"No thank you Papa, just this ginger beer."

A few days later, after leaving Enoch at Epsilon station, Tom and Jimmy took Tilly in the carriage to the factory. Edna insisted on accompanying her as far as the factory gates, and she then went to lunch with Mrs. Dawkins. She said she would call for Tilly after lunch.

"I may not be ready by then, Mama. But please come if you don't mind waiting." Not pausing to wave her mother goodbye, she strode purposefully through the gates, down the tunnel past the lodge keeper, into the main yard. As soon as she had entered, the metal gates on the factory end of the tunnel were closed. She paused in the yard before going up to the office.

It was twenty to eight. The engine was throbbing, the chimneys smoking. Lads were running to and fro between the mould sheds and the kilns, there was a group of women sitting near the pile of withies, weaving baskets, ready for the finished ware, and labourers were shovelling clay and ground bones from two wagons near the stores by the slip house.

Although Tilly normally came to work at the same time as her father, she had followed meekly in his wake, oblivious of the impressions which she now had. Now, alone at last, the works seemed like a huge beast, sprawling in its den. People, like ants, were scurrying hither and thither over its limbs, unaware of its power and menace. Now she, and only she, was its master. She just had to say the word, and the creature would stir into fevered action, blowing hot savage breath, roaring up its throat, fiery flames coming from it like a three headed hydra. Another word from her, and it would lie down to sleep, quiet and dreamless.

Tilly didn't feel afraid, on the contrary, she felt excitement. Her blood was up. She was in charge, and she felt the strength coming to her, from what she governed.

"Good day, Silas" she said, putting her head round the door of the engine room.

The old man was standing at his work bench, filing at a piece of metal held in the vice. He was startled when she appeared, and stopped what he was doing, nervously wiping his hand on his leather apron.

"Everything running smoothly, no hitches?"

"Good morning Miss. Nothing unusual. See this." He held up a small strip of metal, which he was grinding at with a file. "Canna make the old lady run without this. We shall have to replace her. She's getting old. Master'll be losing money, if this go out again. She wasn't young when she come here. There's better ones now. There's only so much I can do."

Tilly was surprised at this long speech by Silas. She'd never had three words from him up to now, and here he was telling her all about the engine. Evidently he knew about Papa's absence, else she was sure he wouldn't have favoured her with this intimacy.

"Have you spoken to Mr. Manstone about this?'

"Have I?" He picked up the file again. "Excuse me, Miss, I've work to do." With no further words, he stepped away.

Tilly followed him into the middle of the engine shed, hoping that he would say something else. This was the heart of the monster, throbbing away endlessly. It was shiny green, with brass. Silas made sure it was well oiled and polished. It was his pride. Surely he couldn't be contemplating that father would replace it. It looked so beautiful, as good as new. She didn't know quite how old, but not very old, surely. This was another thing she didn't know anything about...engines. She had the impression that Silas cared for it in the same way that George cared for his horses. She felt humbled in the presence of this man and the machinery. What did she know about power, and energy? That was what dominated the world, the people who controlled the energy. Silas was the true master of Manstones, not her father, and certainly not herself. She suddenly realised that the engine was probably nearly as old as Silas himself. He had probably been hired as the engineer, when the engine first came. Perhaps if they needed a new engine, they'd need a new man. So then what would Silas do? People...that was another complicated area that she didn't know much about. The face of David Lockyard flashed into her mind, and she remembered that he had said he would be a student all his life. She would be, too, but she would like to start off by being a real student, with books and teachers.

Tilly saw that there was to be no more from the old man, and she went across the yard, up the stairs and into the office.

Robert rose from his stool as she came in.

"Good morning, Willoughby," she said.

Robert had never stood up when she had come in before, unlike all those other men whom she called gentlemen. He had always affected not to notice her comings and goings.

"The fire's been going an hour,' he said.

She wondered why he said this. The fire was always lit well before she came. Was he drawing attention to the fact that he'd noticed the time she arrived?

"Mr Manstone's gone, then?'

"Yes," she said, and went into the inner office, closing the door behind her. On her father's desk was the sales and purchase ledger, and the record of processed orders. Normally on a Monday, she would be writing out postcards to send to various firms in different parts of the country, apprising them of the date and time various travellers would be arriving to take orders. She had only met the salesmen on infrequent occasions. Most of her father's business was done by correspondence, and each salesman only appeared in the office when a new itinerary was being discussed. She remembered Mr. Goodrich vaguely as a thin young man, with a jolly manner. However, his life was familiar to her. She knew about the places which he visited, the shops and stores where he took orders, even the inns at which he stayed on his journeys. Through these letters, which flitted backwards and forwards across the country, she felt that Manstone's was the centre of a huge web, fanning out across the land. Recently her father had established a contact in the United States. She'd overheard him talking to Robert about the agent out there.

She opened the record of processed orders. She wanted to work out in what respect sales were improving, and where they had dropped off, during the last three years. She began by making a list of the various firms which had placed orders with Manstone's over the period. After a moment she went into the anteroom, carrying the huge ledger.

"Have we an analysis of these?' she asked.

"I think not. Mr. Manstone's never asked me to do that."

"Well, I'm sure it's essential. No doubt he has a good idea of which line is going up, and which down, and which firm is dropping out, and so on. But I don't know that, or why it's happening. I wish to have an overall picture. Then we may put things right.' She finished rather breathlessly.

Robert put his hand on his chin, pen poised.

"Has he asked you to do this?"

"Of course not. If he had, I'd have known it was already done. That's why I asked you." Robert Willoughby was exceedingly obtuse sometimes. Or was he just warning her off, because she was encroaching on his territory? "And what's all this about the engine, Silas was saying?'

"That! There's no call to take notice of that. That's not so old, that engine, that we need a new one. Old Silas would be out of a job, any road, if he got a new one, that didn't need mending. Any lad can cope with a new machine."

Tilly doubted that, but she ignored it. "If it's wasting time, it's wasting money, I should have thought.' she said, and swept back to her father's desk. It wasn't surprising Father trusted Willoughby so much. They were as like as two sparrows. She pulled a crisp piece of paper out of the pile, and continued with her analysis. This would be finished before Father returned, and she could surprise him with it. She'd also talk to Silas herself and perhaps learn more about the engine, maybe even read some of the machinery catalogues, which must still be about somewhere in the office. That way, she'd know better what Silas was talking about. She pulled the chair round to the end of the desk, so that a weak sunbeam was falling on her back, and settled down contentedly to the task she had set herself.

The morning passed quickly. By one o'clock Tilly was tired and hungry. She stood up, to look out of the window, and stretched. Everything was going well, so far. She would have a glass of lemonade, and the bap with cheese which Jeannie had put in a packet for her.

Just then, she saw the gate man come out of the tunnel into the yard, and with him was a tall man, with a smart velour hat, and umbrella. After a moment she recognised David Lockyard. The gate man was directing him towards the steps up to the office.

Tilly was rooted to the floor. He must be coming to see her father, and her father wasn't here. What should she do? She suddenly decided she would prefer better to meet him in the yard, rather than up here. She flung on her mantle and was half way down the wooden stairs before he reached them.

"Mr. Lockyard! What a surprise. I am afraid my father is away, on business. I expect it was he you came to see?"

"Miss Manstone. What a pleasure!"

"Did you have an appointment?"

"Not really. I have come on a little errand from Mr. Lugando. Concerning the church pews again, I'm afraid. We were in the area, and he hoped to have a word with him. It is of no account."

"I am so sorry you've come out of your way."

"Not at all. We are only two streets away. Mr. Lugando may have a commission concerning the site of the recent unfortunate fire."

"Really?"

"Naturally the owner is anxious to rebuild, and I think he wishes to have some advice from Signor."

"Is Mr. Lugando there now?" Tilly had been smitten by a great idea.

"Indeed. I am returning to him."

"Would you mind very much if I came? I would very much like to see what is happening. One of our maids, her mother lost her home in the fire. I should like to know what is being done for them."

"I would be very happy if you were to come with me, but I'm afraid there is not much to see."

Tilly raced upstairs to get her hat, and they set off together. The streets behind the factory were unpaved, and muddy, with puddles in the potholes.

"May I?" Mr. Lockyard said, offering his arm.

"Thank you." Tilly was grateful for his help over the rough ground.

A crowd of small children were splashing about in the mud, and Tilly realised that she would have some explaining to do about the hem of her skirt when she saw Deaker. Any worries on this score were forgotten when they arrived at the ruins of the burnt down streets. All the roofs had fallen in, and the insides of the houses were simply charred remnants of blackened timbers, and shattered slates. All the furniture was missing, either destroyed at the time, or rescued by the homeless owners.

"What is to be done, here? Do you know, Mr. Lugando?" Tilly asked when the greetings with the architect were over.

"It seems that the owner wishes to replace these old tenements with more modern and spacious houses. We have a good site here, as you can see, gracious lady." He pointed to the view, far away, of distant moors. "South facing, too, and well sheltered by those trees."

Indeed, if you looked for it, Tilly thought, you could see how beautiful the countryside must once have been. Wooded valleys, and rolling moorland must have been here, once, instead of these dismal terraces and streets. It was a shame to rebuild on it. But the people must be housed.

"So will the former inhabitants be able to come back?"

"Well, of course, we shall have to wait and see what the owner wishes, Madame."

Tilly had the impression that Lugando did not want to speak more about it. Perhaps she had already overstepped the mark.

"I must be going back, now. I know you have much to do, as I have. Thank you for your time."

"I will walk back with you?" David Lockyard glanced at Signor Lugando, who raised his eyebrow and nodded.

Tilly said nothing, as they went back to the factory. She was astonished that nothing had yet been done about rebuilding the houses. Why could not the roofs be mended, and work begun to reinstate the tenants. Surely it could be done? To her, it seemed as if the owner of the properties had already decided that he was going to rebuild, and not to rehouse. As they came towards Manstone's Tilly saw the gates of the factory being opened. The carriage, bearing her Mother was just turning in. She saw her mother's face and the astonishment when she recognised Tilly and her companion, arm in arm, coming along the road.

For some reason, Tilly realised, she did not wish to speak to her mother just now, especially if it meant justifying her action in leaving the factory for a few minutes, on the arm of David Lockyard.

The next day, Robert asked Miss Manstone to convey a letter to her mother.

"If it should be convenient, I could come tomorrow, to accompany your good-self and Miss Manstone, at half past six o'clock." He would do what he wished without further reference to Gertie.

Mrs. Manstone agreed, to the time suggested, and so the next evening Robert was striding along the lane from Epsilon station, a bag of music over his shoulder. He arrived at Terrilea just before time. Jeannie answered the door, and led him into the morning room. Edna had had candles lit on the piano. The music stand was up, and there were daffodils on the mantel piece. .

Robert stood by the window. He hadn't seen the woods and the stream before, as when he had been here last, the curtains had been drawn. Now, there was still faint light outside, and he could see the peaceful landscape, and the dark trees, climbing up the bank to the horizon. He began to feel apprehensive. What was he doing here? He was being paid to spend his time, part of his life, with these two spoiled creatures, who didn't even know what life was about. Why should he waste time with them? Why should he humble himself like this? His time was more precious than any money they could give him. By rights, he should be an honoured guest in their house, not a skivvy. For that is all he was, a skivvy, like the maids. Perhaps he should just walk out. Why were they keeping him waiting? It showed their attitude. He supposed they would just expect him to give them extra time at the end. Well, he wouldn't. He took his watch out of his waistcoat pocket, unclipped it from the button, and put it on the piano top, face up. It said six thirty-five. Five minutes gone already. They'd have to pay for that too. He wouldn't walk out. That might work against him with Mr. Manstone, but he'd make sure they knew who was calling the tunes.

Edna came in. "Mr. Willoughby, I'm so glad you've come, the maid has only just...apprised us."

"Good evening, Mrs. Manstone. I'm sure I don't know why. I've been here a good ten minutes."

"Oh dear me. We shall have to work all the harder." She went over to the window seat, where her violin was lying. "My daughter will be here directly." She took the violin out of the case, dusted it off, and then began to rub the bow strings with resin. She tightened them, put the violin to her chin, and played a scale.

Rob sat down and picked out an A on the piano keyboard. Edna tuned to it, then tightened the strings. She lowered her violin and stood in front of the music stand.

"I have 'The Minstrel Boy,' Mr. Willoughby, if you please."

Rob found the music, propped it up, and began to play. The song went well, with only one false start, and they both reached the end together.

"We'll try another." Edna's colour was rising. She was feeling elated. Her initial nervousness was beginning to evaporate.

They played four more songs.

"I think that was quite...commendable." Edna said at last. "Thank you. Do you think we might try something a little more taxing?" She opened the drawer of her music cabinet. "I've been practising this, and I managed to obtain the piano part." She showed Robert the music of the 'Dance of the Blessed Spirits.' "Shall you need to familiarise yourself with it?"

Robert's bad temper seemed to have dissolved, He took the music off her, and began to sight read. He was aware of Edna standing behind him, watching and playing, and he stumbled twice over the same few bars. He stopped for a few moments, shaking his hands, and then attacked the music again, with gusto. This time he got it right.

"Good, good, well done. Now we'll try it together."

Rob felt so inspired he began playing with vigour.

"You're swamping me. I think we'll have to recommence," Edna said.

"Oh, I apologise. I would not wish to swamp you."

"I expect it's you who are normally the soloist. Perhaps?"

"I always accompany, as I did at your concert." Rob said.

They started again, and this time Edna kept making mistakes. "Let's do that again. From the second rest. Where I come in."

They tried again, and again. Soon, they were playing well together.

At the end, Rob swivelled round on his stool. "I think we're improving, Mrs, Manstone."

"I'm improving. You're very good, anyway."

"Thank you," Rob murmured. "What shall it be now, some Mozart?"

"Yes. A good idea. 'Eine Kleine Nachtmusik'? Your part is on there." She came up to the piano, bow in one hand, violin in the other. As she lifted her arm to tap on the pile of music, Rob was aware of her scent, a faint smell of perspiration, mixed with lavender. Her breast was on a level with the piano top and pressing against it. Her cheeks were flushed, her lips slightly parted. He took the pile of music from under the tip of her bow, and leafed through it.

"Here it is," he said, looking straight into her eyes.

"Yes." Edna turned back to the violin stand, and Rob sat down on his stool. He could see her reflection in the polished wood of the piano lid. He watched her, arranging the violin under her chin, then holding her bow up ready to strike the strings. There was the curve of her breast again. Now he had the scent of her, more strongly. He began playing the familiar music without attending to it, almost automatically. Edna too, seemed to be under a spell. This must be a piece of music she had rehearsed and practised a hundred times, perhaps.

In fact it was Edna's show piece. Tonight she was playing it as if it was the only music in the world. The cadences swelled and trembled, and Rob answered them on the piano.

Tilly came softly through the door, but neither player made a sign of noticing her. The repetitions were played, then played again. Tilly made no movement, but listened, and watched. Her mother seemed like a stranger, so deeply involved was she in the music. Tilly hadn't often seen her like this, except perhaps, recently, when she'd watched her sketching by the stream. For a moment Tilly felt a pang of anxiety. Was her mother still her mother, was she still there? Her mother now appeared to be someone else, a stranger, foreign to her, with a life and feelings which she couldn't share. It was as if she had somehow withdrawn, into a world of her own. Tilly couldn't go there, she thought.

The music ended, and Tilly gave a little clap. "My goodness, Mama, that was wonderful."

Edna sighed and put down her bow. "Thanks to Mr. Willoughby here. He's to take the credit. Your turn, my dear. I mustn't take up all the hour. What time is it?"

It was already twenty past seven. "Quickly, my dear, or you won't have any time. My daughter is going to sing," Edna added, turning towards Rob.

Tilly dutifully put her music on the piano, and Rob began again, with "Drink to me only." But Tilly's heart wasn't in it. Somehow, she didn't want to compete with what she'd heard as she came into the room. After a short while, she began to cough. "Oh, dear. I think I'll have to stop. It's my throat. I think I'm a bit tired, Mama. It's been quite hard work at the office since Papa's been away".

“Of course, dear. I was forgetting. It’s the same for Mr. Willoughby too. I mustn’t be selfish.”

Robert was seated at the stool, waiting for a signal from Edna. She nodded, and he at once packed up the music, rose, and wound up the piano stool to its normal height.

“Next week, Mr. Willoughby?”

“Of course.”

As soon as the front door was closed, Rob broke into a run. How had they managed it? He had stayed beyond his time, in the end, in spite of his determination not to be late getting away. He heard the train whistle, and as he came to the station, it drew in. He flung himself on board, breathing fast. After a moment, he ceased watching the smoke billowing past the window, and the landscape, fading fast in the twilight. He was gazing, in his mind, at Edna, with the violin under her chin, and her round breast just touching the piano lid. The smell of her lavendery sweat was in his nostrils. He blew his nose, vigorously, forcing himself to think of something else. He would plan the programme for next time. He’d give them their money’s worth, he would.

13

Enoch sent a telegram that he would be back on Tuesday, not Saturday as originally envisaged. Edna had told the maids to leave some cold cuts for supper. She herself went to rest in after lunch. Tilly said she was going for a walk round the field.

Deaker decided to walk over to Edgethorne to see her sister. She hadn't seen Daisy for a month and was looking forward to her day off. Recently she had been feeling tired and anxious, she realised she was worrying about the Mistress. She'd been so different recently, probably it was just a phase, connected with her age. She must be going through the change, Deaker was certain. She'd been like it once before, soon after Tilly was born. She'd had a reason. It was hard on her, to be told she wasn't to have any more children. But she'd got over it after a few months. Deaker thought in some ways it was a good thing there hadn't been any more children, especially since Miss Edna was such a slip of a thing. She'd been happy enough with just the one, and that one had turned out well. She herself could take some credit for that, and for Miss Edna, too.

After a short while she turned into her sister's cottage gate, and an hour later, replete from a good tea of cold boiled bacon, pickles, bread and cakes, Deaker and Daisy were sitting convivially talking in the parlour, enjoying a glass of last year's plum wine. Deaker held it up to the light, appreciatively. "Aye. I feel better for that."

"I thought you didn't seem yourself, our Millie. You're not to worry about Miss Edna. I expect she's just missing the Master. She must be missing him, for sure. I'd miss my Tom, if he were called away, sudden. You don't think you will, but there, you do.'

"You don't know the half of it."

"What do you mean by that? Not what I think, surely."

"I'm not gossiping with you, sister. You know I don't hold with tittle-tattle. But I will say this"

"What's that?'

"Things is different for some people than they are with you and your Tom."

"Oh, I see, I see. Poor woman." Daisy stretched out to refill her sister's glass. "It's like that, is it? Poor woman."

"I don't know as you do see" There was silence. Outside, William was sitting on the step. Deaker could smell the smoke from his pipe. She suddenly felt she wanted to be up, and moving about. Her legs were coming on to ache. She even wished, for a moment, she hadn't come. In her little room at home, she felt comfortable, with all her things around her, her photos, her pressed flowers in frames on the walls, her rag rugs, the dressed dolls she had made for Miss Edna, and then reclaimed. There, everything felt right and solid, as if it would last for ever. But from here, things looked different. Now, Daisy, had forced her to become aware that things were changing. There was something in the air, something was happening at Terrilea. Edna seemed to be pre-occupied very often, and Enoch was distant, even absent. As for Tilly, she was changing too,. Growing up, probably.

Deaker felt she must recognise that times were changing. And where would she be, if things were to change?

"Shall we go out, sister, I fancy some fresh air. That is if William will take me back, later."

"Of course he'll see you home, my dear. We could just go a short way, down the path to Marlpark, as far as the Dissenters' chapel."

The two women put on their bonnets, and were soon engrossed in conversation about Daisy's offspring.

"I dare say our Agnes will be married soon, and probably young Jack. He's sweet on a girl from the pot-bank at Chalders. Nice little thing. What do you think of that?"

"They're a rough lot, some of they lasses."

"I do think I canna say much either way. 'Tis his choice, and 'e'll have to bring her to his ways. Besides, if your Miss Tilly can mix with them folks, I reckon he won't come to any harm."

"She don't exactly mix with them." Deaker snapped. Once again, the affairs of the Manstones seemed to be the target of criticism." She's managing well. Her father is right proud of her, I do know. That's why he's able to take off, just now, he trusts her all right. Like a son."

"I know as I wouldna do that, if I had a big factory to run. Still, I suppose that clerk of his, what's his name again?"

Robert Willoughby."

"I do hear he's a union man. Been seen at the meetings. Quite open he is about it."

"I suppose you got that from young Jack?"

"I don't know where I got it from. But it's true."

"He may have been to the meetings, but that was on the Master's business. I happen to know that. Any road, the Union's busted now. That strike didn't do them no good."

Deaker wondered to herself why she was protecting that Robert from gossip. After all, he was nothing to her. He must be all right, if the Master trusted him. "There's a lot of gossip about, and I don't hold with it," she continued to Daisy.

They had come to the end of the lane, where a five barred gate blocked the way.

A tiny chapel, newly built, stood in the corner of a small plot, enclosed by a make shift fence. A notice board proclaimed it to be 'The

Peculiar People's Chapel, founded by Miss Eldridge of Witherstone House.'

"Here it is." said Daisy. "It looks as if service is just over." As she spoke, the door of the chapel opened, and people began to emerge in ones and twos. After a few moments, a tall man, with an old fashioned full beard, and whiskers, came down the steps, and turned sideways, to shake hands with the people leaving. There seemed to be a large number of young men, and their lasses, as well as older men, and a few matrons. All of them were working folk, clean and tidy, but shabbily dressed, quite unlike the congregation of elegantly clad people who attended St. John's where Deaker had been to Matins that morning.

The two sisters began to walk back up the lane, and behind them, the chapel goers surged through the gate, overtook them, and jostled excitedly back up the track. The lads and girls had arms entwined, the older men were engrossed in intense conversation. There was an excited, festive air about this exodus.

Suddenly Deaker felt a hand on her arm. Turning, she saw a tall man alongside her, smiling down at her, hat in hand. For a moment she didn't recognise him. Then, she suddenly knew who it was. Speak of the devil.

"Mr. Willoughby," she gasped. "This is a surprise."

"It is, Mrs. Deaker. What brings you so far afield? Have you been to service?"

"I have not. I attend St. John's, of course. Mr. Manstone's church. I was just out walking with my sister, here, when the chapel came out."

"Oh, I beg your pardon, Missus," Robert said politely, raising his cap, again.

Whatever else could be said about him, Daisy decided, his manner could not be faulted. He was a well-set up man, too, didn't seem to be from these parts, judging from his voice. Quite refined, she thought. Happen he'd go a long way. All this passed through her mind in the second it took to nod and acknowledge his greeting.

A young woman was walking along by the side of Robert, but he did not introduce her to the two old women. For a few paces he kept abreast of Daisy and Deaker, then he pulled his watch out.'

"Excuse me for hurrying, the train goes at six o'clock."

"You best get along, then, Mr. Willoughby."

"Enjoy your walk," he said, raising his cap again. He hurried off up the lane, dodging through the throng. The young woman held her skirt up with one hand, and her bonnet with the other, and darted along after him.

Deaker put her hand on her sister's arm. "Let's bide a while, it do make me breathless, running. Let the young folks go, for goodness' sake." They stood back to the tall hedge while the crowd hurried past.

Soon there were only a few stragglers coming along and Rob's tall figure was lost in the bustling throng of youngsters, who were turning out of the track onto the lane which led to the station.

Gertie, who'd by now caught up with Rob, put her arm through his. "You could have waited. Did you want to get away from them? Slow down now."

They were crossing the railway by a road bridge, and far up the line, perhaps half a mile away, they could see a tiny puff of smoke.

Rob slackened his pace to walk round the bend from the bridge to the wooden platform near the rails. Gertie was panting. She leaned against a milk churn. Rob stood to face her, legs apart. "We're only just in time. That's why I was hurrying." He took her hand, the finger tips between his thumb and forefinger, and stroked them gently. "They're looking better, my wench, since you made more of washing the colours off. You're looking better yourself."

It was true. The blood was in her cheeks, from hurrying to the station, and her eyes were shining. She took her bonnet off, smoothing her hair with her free hand. "I thought maybe you were ashamed of me, Robert Willoughby. That was why you didn't tell my name to them two. Who were they?"

At that moment the train came in, letting off steam so loudly that conversation was impossible. Doors were opened, late comers were running into the station, doors were slammed, the guard blew his whistle, and signalled with his flag, and they were off.

"Who were they?" Gertie persisted, sitting close to him in the crowded carriage.

He felt her hips pressing close to him. Smoothing his moustache with his left hand, he could still discern the smell of her fingers on his. He remembered the last time he had sat in this train, when it had been the thought of Edna, the smell of her lingering scent, which had aroused him. Once again. It made no difference who or what had caused it. He was a man. He should have what he needed, he had to have it.

He spoke gruffly. His breath was coming fast.

"They ain't nobody. The old woman is Mrs Manstone's maid, and the younger one, she did say, that's her sister. I don't know why they were there. You tell me."

The more he thought about it, the more annoyed he became that he'd run into Deaker. He didn't want his private life to be the subject of speculation on the part of anyone connected with Manstone. He knew that Deaker would be wondering about Gertie. He realised suddenly that he had been ashamed of introducing her. How could he have done so? If he had said anything, he would have had to say who she was. He didn't want to say anything, he didn't want to make public his relationship with her. Secretly, there was an arrangement between them. Gertie, and her mother, saw him as the future husband, the future son-in-law. But no-one else knew, so he thought. His livelihood would be at stake if he made a public promise, and then dishonoured it. He closed his eyes, aware of all the people in the carriage, who seemed to be watching him.

"How did you know her, if she's the maid? Has she been to the Works?"

"No, of course not. Just drop the subject." He did not wish to bring up the subject of the musical accompaniment.

Gertie recognised a harsh tone in Rob's voice, something which she'd heard more of, recently. She took her hand from where it lay under his, and laid it on her own lap. She looked at the other passengers, wondering if they had heard Rob's words. Two other young men were happily entwined with their lasses. At the opposite end of the carriage, two old men were sitting dozing. Outside, a darkening embankment showed blurrily through the window. Everyone seemed totally pre-occupied with their own thoughts. She wondered if they were happy. The two couples looked happy. The girls had their eyes closed, their heads on the young men's shoulders, their lips slightly parted. The two old men, eyes shut, were snoring. Gertie had a hollow feeling in her chest. She wondered why Rob had suddenly become anxious and cross since he had met that woman. Besides, where had he met her before? She glanced at Rob, but now he too had his eyes closed. He seemed as remote from her as the other occupants were. She wondered whether she knew him, really knew him at all. Was he asleep, or what? He seemed withdrawn, unaware.

Robert was thinking that his idea of the accompaniment assignations was beginning to go wrong. He didn't want Gertie interfering. He wasn't her slave. Not yet, anyway. Not ever, if he could help it. He put his hand over hers again, and squeezed them. She was a good girl, he didn't want to be unkind to her. She relaxed against his shoulder.

"Thank you" said Tilly, as the fire boy heaved a large bucket of coal from the office door to the grate in Enoch's office. The day was cold and rainy. All signs of spring had gone, if they had ever arrived, in this little office, set as it was in the middle of the huge expanse of factory buildings, mighty chimneys, bottle ovens, rows of tiny terraced houses, and acres of wasteland covered with dumps of broken pottery, weeds and mud. Tilly had ordered the fire to be well made up, and extra buckets of coal to be taken round the various workrooms. If she was to be sitting all day long in this gloomy room, at least she wished to be comfortable. She also thought the workers would work better if they were warm. In fact, with all the doors and windows being open to allow rapid entry for the mould runners, and rapid exit for the clouds of mineral dust which the various trades used, the extra coal made no difference at all, except in the minds of the workers. Some people appreciated her concern, others, the majority, thought it was the act of a soft, sentimental woman

"That be all, Miss?" the lad asked.

"Yes, Daniel." Tilly now knew everyone by name, in the factory. She'd made it her business to call in at all the different shops, and speak to the journey men and women at least once a week. It was she who had, in the first place, persuaded the Master to allow more coal and light on the premises, for the same stoppage of wages as before. She thought, that to stop anything at all out of the wages to pay for light and heat, was an old-fashioned, and somewhat insupportable practice. Her father declined to change the system altogether, in deference to the opinion of the Masters at other pot banks. But he also valued his daughter's opinion of him, so he had become a little more generous, for the same payment. Tilly felt marginally more assertive and confident in her dealings with her father. She wanted to prove herself more and more valuable in running the factory. He was trying to expand the business, he'd told her as much, and so his trips away would become more frequent. His need for her would increase. That would give her the basis for her next request - the purchase of a new engine. It would be more reliable, more economical of fuel, and best of all, it would be less taxing on old Silas. He had a couple of youngsters working for him, that was true, but as long as he was in charge, he took full responsibility on himself. How long could he last?

Orders for dinner services seemed to have dropped off recently. After half-an-hour looking at the order book, Tilly decided that they gave no clue as to the reason why. "Make sure we bring the matter up when the salesman next comes, about the orders," she said to Willoughby.

Perhaps it would be a good idea to look at the orders given to the engraver, over the last few years. Were certain patterns going out of favour?

Tilly got up and stood by the fire for a few moments. There were two wooden armchairs beside it, and in between them, on a low table, was the pattern book. She began turning over the pages. There was no indication in the book how popular the pattern was, how many times in one year it was used. And what about new designs? As she turned over the pages, she was struck by the similarity of patterns. And how many potters, within a mile of Manstone's were turning out such ware?

She thought of Mr. Dreyd, the designer, upstairs in a small office. The room was always full of tobacco smoke, and seemed cluttered and untidy. She'd only been in a few times, as she felt uncomfortable. Mr. Dreyd smelled slightly, of what, she did not know. She had an idea it might be brandy. Perhaps he could do with an assistant, to inject some fresh air into the place. She suddenly realised that Dreyd did as little work as possible, just using and re-using the same old ideas that had been going the rounds for decades. Not creating, but copying. Perhaps this was why the sales of table ware were decreasing. She wondered if she should go and see him. How much could she do herself, how much should she leave to her father? Probably the best thing would be to concentrate on one thing, the purchase of a new engine. She realised that if she overstepped the mark with Enoch, she would get nowhere at all.

Tilly went back to her desk and began flipping through the machinery catalogue again. The names were so wonderful, what a sense of power they gave. They were beautiful too, beautiful in their strength. After a moment she decided to go down to the engine shop and see Silas. Which engine would he think was necessary? Was the engine they had too old for the job, or was it just not big enough, now?

She hesitated near Rob, whose head was bowed over the ledger.

"Mr. Willoughby. Do you know anything about the Noxious Substances Committee? I read something about it in the paper this week."

"I do. A little. There's some who wish the law to be changed as to what we burn in the chimneys. They're thinking a different kind of coal, maybe anthracite, might make the difference."

"That would be very expensive wouldn't it? I don't believe it's local."

"It isn't. It's from the South Wales coalfields. And it won't make more'n a ha'p'orth of difference, anyway."

"Are there many in favour of a change?"

"Not many. The masters wouldn't have it anyway."

"I wonder if they would have to change the engines, too, if they had different coal."

Robert didn't answer, so Tilly nodded, and went on down the wooden steps. Above the towering chimneys, blue sky could now be seen. The wind was blowing so hard that the smoke was streaming away from the yard, all across the serried roofs of houses around the pot-bank. The rain had stopped. Labourers were unloading clay from a cart, and pushing it through the locker shutters into the pugging shop. Young boys were darting across the yard from the mould shop to the drying room, with full moulds, and back with empty ones. Tilly was greeted with smiles as she made her way to the engine shop. She felt charged up with excitement by the preceding effort of battling with figures, orders, designs, and descriptions of machinery. She pushed open the engine shop door. It was warm in here, and smelled of grease. The piston of the engine, a great brass rod, was pushing in and out, in and out. She watched it, her heart was beating loudly.

Enoch went straight to his office from the train on his return from London. Everything was in good order, no disasters, orders were in hand, and there was the sense of well-ordered bustle. Monday absenteeism had dropped during the time Tilly had been at the Works. This was due partly to the fact that she had insisted that wages were made up in exact amounts to be paid to the master of each workshop in small denomination coinage. This obviated the necessity for the Little Masters to go to the bars of the public houses nearby to have large denomination notes changed for small ones and coinage. By this method alone, a simple change, the Friday night drinking spree had been curbed, and since the workers could now take their wages straight home, without a diversion to the ale house, the women's household allowances were less likely to be spent by their men folk, before they had even sight of them. Formerly, Friday night drinking had been repeated on Saturday, and the effects were still being felt on Monday, hence the absenteeism. It had taken Tilly's persuasiveness to make Enoch aware of the economic soundness of the arrangement. Less drunkenness meant better work, more consistent, steady work, within regular hours.

So it was no great surprise to Enoch to find his factory operating at full tilt, Monday though it was. Pleased with what he saw, he walked round all the workshops, still dressed in his London frock coat and best hat. In the engine shed he slapped Silas on the back.

"How many breakdowns this last week, Silas? How did ye manage without me to let off to?'

"Aye we managed not so bad. Your lass she's been in here. She'll have me learning her about the engine. She seems fair fascinated by it.'

"Miss Tilly? What does she want with that? Have you been telling her some tales, eh?'

"I have, Maister, and you may hear the same from her.'

"How many stoppages have you had? That was my enquiry.'

"We've had too many. I'm here altogether. And if I weren't your factory wouldna run. And that's the bottom of it."

"Well now! But you are here, my old friend. And she's good for a year or two?" Enoch turned to watch the engine for a few minutes. It seemed to be running smoothly and sweetly. What on earth had Tilly been up to? He'd have to say that her mother wouldn't want her in the engine shed. That was going too far.

He went out of the door, and up the stairs to the office

Robert, sitting at his desk, nodded as the Master came in.

"Morning, sir.'

"Good morning, Willoughby. Come into my office.' He passed into the inner office.

Tilly was at work.

"Father,' she said, jumping up. She stood before him at the desk.

"That's right," he said. "I'll look through the day book, Willoughby," he said as Robert came in. "And what have you been doing, Miss?"

"Was it a successful trip, Father?' Did you seen Mr. Duskins, and Mr. Goodrich? What orders are there? New ones, I mean?"

"Steady, steady now. I'll look through these figures. You can tell me how you've been occupied.'

Tilly went back to her work. She'd been making a fair copy of her analysis of the past three years trading. She wanted to bring up the question of the decoration designs, but first she wanted to show her father the facts. She felt excited and nervous. Her father was back rather earlier than she had expected. She had hoped she would be quite ready for him. Now he was actually sitting at his desk behind her, the idea of approaching him about the new engine seemed daunting, even impossible. After all, how could she possibly set herself up as knowledgeable enough to challenge him? She'd only Silas' word to go on. And if he hadn't managed to persuade her father, with all the knowledge he had at his fingertips, how could she hope to influence him?

"What's all this I hear about you being down in the engine shop? Am I to believe this?" Enoch's voice came booming over. Tilly still had her back to him, and he was gazing down at the day book in front of him.

She turned round. There was no chance of putting it off. She'd have to face him, now. "Yes. I have been down there. Nearly every day, Father. Silas has been teaching me about engines. I've been going through this." She rose and held out the catalogue to him.

Enoch did not look up. He was tracing a column of figures with his forefinger.

Tilly stood in silence, with her arm outstretched.

At last, he raised his eyes, but still did not take her offering.

"And why, pray, are you wasting my time with that, Miss. Your time is my time. I pay for it. And I expect you to do what I wish to be done.'

Tilly was silent for a moment. "I thought you wished me to learn all about the business, sir.'

"I do, I do." He slapped his hand hard on the table. "That doesn't mean I wish my daughter to go into every dirty and unsavoury place, with the workmen. You have no call to be down there. Your place is here. Here."

"I beg pardon, father. But to me, the engine is the heart of the factory." Tilly's heart was pounding. She was aware of a tremor in her voice. She took a deep breath. "Unless I understand about this, about engines, how can I be able to know about the factory itself. Besides, I like it."

"Oho. You like it. That makes it all right, do it? Tha' likes it, dost tha'? I never heard such talk. Do we do what we do because we like it? We do not. We do it because it is our duty. Our duty! And it is not part of our duty to hobnob with the workmen in the dirtiest trade of them all."

"Father, how can you say that of me! I was not doing what you describe. I've been learning about the engine, and who better to teach me than old Silas. If you are not pleased with what I do, please say so immediately." Tilly felt tears coming into her eyes, and began blinking furiously. "I do it for your sake, for the factory's sake. I must know all about everything, if I'm to serve you and the factory" She turned away slightly. "Shall I leave now?" She let the catalogue fall out of her hand onto the floor, then stooped immediately, and replaced it on her desk. As she turned away, she hastily wiped the incipient tears from her eyes. "If you are not pleased, or you don't trust me, will you kindly give me permission to leave?"

Enoch said in a low voice. "There's no call for that, lass. Tha'st done well enough. Calm yourself." He picked up the day book, and went into the outer office. "Have there been any stoppages, Willoughby?"

"Just the three, sir. One on Monday, then again two on Friday. Mr. Silas worked till ten on Friday to finish off."

"Thank you, Willoughby. That will do." Enoch went back into the inner office, and closed the door. Tilly was sitting at her desk again, apparently reading through the entries on the paper in front of her. "What else have you been doing, aside from moithering old Silas?" Enoch's voice was soft.

Tilly looked round. Then she rose and went over to him again.

"Preparing this. I thought it would be helpful to you." She began to explain why she had prepared the analysis, and how it would help Enoch to decide the cause of falling sales in table ware. He glanced at it, then put it down.

"I'll see to that tomorrow," he said. For the first time since his return, he had a good look at her, bending over him. Her cheeks were flushed, and there were tear stains on them. He was suddenly reminded of Edna, as she had been a few years ago, only a very few years. But this one had more spirit, she was more like him. Going into the engine shed! Learning about machinery! Well, a son couldn't be doing better. But Tilly wasn't a son, she was a girl, a chit of a girl. Somehow, the thought of her in those dirty surroundings, even dangerous..... it wouldn't do. He took up the papers she'd written. "You've done well enough with this." He walked towards the coat-rack. 'We shall have some luncheon now, and I'll put you on the early train back."

Tilly said nothing, but marched to the hat stand, and pushed her hat onto her head, stabbing into her thick hair with the hat pin. Her heart was pounding, not only because of her father's words, but also because she could not think of a reply which would show him how she felt. If he didn't want her to know all about the business, not just the artistic, decorative bits of it, but all of it, then she wasn't interested. He'd better get someone else.

Robert watched the Master and Tilly leaving. The shouting and the tumult had died down. That wench could get the better of the old man any time. It was strange that she could manage him so well, but the mother... she was different altogether. The woman seemed afraid of the Master. But then, she was a sensitive soul, she was fond of her music, that was certain. How the devil did a woman like that come to be in the possession of such man as Enoch? How did that fellow deserve such a prize? He hadn't deserved her. There was no such thing as just deserts. 'To the rich, shall it be given?' If people had their just deserts, he himself would be a wealthy landowner, with a large house, and servants.

Rob laughed. That would be a fine thing. If he had the money, he'd go in for politics. He'd not be a Whig or a Tory, he'd go in for the Socialists. He took a book and bun from his bag. Munching, he opened the book at the first page, smoothing down the page tenderly, and began to read.

There was a clatter of boots on the stairs. The door flung open, and a fat, elderly man came in, breathing heavily and apparently holding onto the door handle for support. His moustache and beard were stained with nicotine, and some long grey hairs protruded from beneath his cap.

"Dreyd!"

"Where's that wench? Is she here?"

"She is not. She's gone with her pa."

"Thank God for that. He's back then."

"Sit down." Robert removed a ledger from the chest, and pushed the old man down.

"I canna abide women like that. She's a know-it-all. Why cannot she stay with her sewing, at home?"

"Here, have a drink of this." Rob groped for a bottle in his bag, and handed it to Dreyd, who at once drank a long draught. Wiping the back of his hand across his lips, he then rubbed his beard and moustache, and brought a long clay pipe from the inside pocket of the smock overall he was wearing.

"You canna smoke here. Best tell me why you're here and then be off."

"Oh, I will then." Dreyd made to rise to his feet, then collapsed again, heavily. "She's been in and out, all the time. Looking at this, that and the other, and I can't bear it, I cannot. If the Master wants her in the office, so be it. But she's no right to keep onto me, in my work. What do she know about patterns and designs? It's a liberty, it is."

Robert said nothing, and Dreyd proceeded to finish up the bottle of beer. "Confound the whole tribe of them. What do you think of it all, young man? A scrap of a girl, in and out of everywhere. My place ain't my own anymore."

"I'll speak to Mr. Manstone, I will. But now he's back I doubt she'll be down there so much. Take no note, Dreyd, it's just like spring sun, here one day, and gone the next. Come Autumn time, she'll be gone altogether, mark my words." Robert was surprised at himself for using the metaphor. After all, Tilly wasn't like spring sunshine, she was more like a March wind, blowing everywhere, disturbing the dust.

"Well, she ain't sunshine to me. She's been asking me questions about these designs. I've been doing the job thirty years, ten years before Mr. Enoch took over, and I' ve always done right for them. I canna change now."

"There's no reason why you should. Your work's good and sound, and Mr. Manstone relies on you." Rob looked at the clock. Enoch and Tilly wouldn't be back for another hour, if they returned at all. He'd have to get rid of Dreyd if he was to have time to go over to make arrangements with Dick about tonight, as well as collect the stationery for Manstones.

The old man was still muttering under his breath. "Has she been down today?"

"Today, Friday, every day. She's up and down them stairs, borrowing pattern books, from the old days, or watching me at work."

Rob wondered how Tilly ever managed to catch Dreyd at work. Whenever he'd been over to the design office, the old man was either down the street at the engravers, or contentedly puffing away at his pipe, feet up on his table. But he still managed to churn out a succession of different patterns, how, Rob couldn't imagine. But that was the creative environment, for you, wasn't it? Relax and let the ideas pour in, and suddenly, there it all was, to the last loop and curlicue, on paper. Tilly's enthusiasm would pass, she'd disappear, and old Dreyd would no doubt carry on till he killed himself with drink and tobacco.

Rob stood up. "I've got to fetch some stationery. Will you walk down there with me?" He knew perfectly well what the answer would be.

"I will not. I've quite enough to do, up and down, up and down." Dreyd rose laboriously to his feet, and lumbered down the stairs, without another word.

Rob put on his bowler hat, locked the office door, and followed behind.

Outside the office it seemed warmer. On the way to the stationery shop, he went along the canal for a way. He had to cross it by a small hump backed bridge. He leaned his arms on the parapet. A long boat, filled with clay was coming towards him, pulled by a horse walking along the opposite tow path. The main part of the boat was filled with whitish earth, brought from Cornwall. The little cabin doors were painted brightly with floral designs and polished household items could be seen arranged on shelves in the tiny living quarters. A man was leading a muscular horse, with feathery legs, and a plaited mane, and a woman was sitting on the side of the boat, just outside the cabin. Further up, on the other side of the bridge, was the dock area, where several barges were tied up, to be unloaded. Probably some of the clay would be going up to Manstones.

Rob lifted his face to the sun. He felt a faint stir of excitement. It was as if he were a spider, sensing the presence of an insect in his web, by the slight vibrations. The whole universe seemed to be revolving round his little world, the throbbing world of the factory. People and materials were drawn from far and wide, and after that seemingly magical process in the kilns, wonderful objects would be produced, and sent back into the world. He himself was at the centre of all this. He felt very powerful. There was nothing he couldn't do. Anything he wanted, would happen. It was his life, his life, in his own hands. His decision it was, to come to Manstones, and it had been the right one. He'd left behind that solicitor's office, and all the sordid business of his parentage, and he'd made his destiny was his own. He didn't know what he would achieve, but achieve it, he would. He lingered a few more moments to watch a barge negotiating the lock just beyond the bridge. A full bosomed woman, about forty years old, with thick arms, got out onto the tow path, and was turning the handle to close the lock gates. The horse was standing patiently, and the bargee was steering. Skilfully, without a word passing between the couple, the barge rose in the water, until it was level with the surface beyond. Robert could watch this feat of engineering as often as he liked, but never got bored with it. He wondered if the barge people ever took passengers. For a moment, he thought he would like to slip away, far from this heap of coal waste and pot shards, and bones, and rats, and hunger, and disease. But as soon as he thought that, he realised that this was the place where he must and would find his fortune.

"Off to Ethburstone's then?" Enoch asked, as he and Tilly left the restaurant. He had his hand under her elbow. She was a smart young woman now in her well-fitting jacket, frilly white blouse with high collar, and small straw hat, decorated with feathers. He was proud to have her with him, and hoped he'd run into one of the pottery masters. He was so confident that none of them had a girl the equal of his daughter.

"I suppose you've been spending that money I gave you on hats and gloves, and such like", he remarked, tenderly.

"As a matter of fact, no, Papa. I have a scheme which I shall ask your advice about, if you like. And I forgot to mention, that Mr. Lockyard came to the office, while you were away. He had the drawings with him, amended. About the church benches."

"He didn't tell me he was coming. Did he leave them?"

"No. He says he'll bring them shortly. There was something he particularly wished to ask you. About them."

"Now then, what shall we buy for Mama? A little gift, as I've been away."

Tilly was amazed at her father' sudden concern. Also, it was obvious to Tilly that her father had forgotten already that she had mentioned a scheme of her own to him. Perhaps that was just as well. "Father, if you want to really please Mama, I have an idea what she would like very much."

"What is that?" "I think she would like a new box of oil paints, and the piano accompaniment for several pieces which I know she wants to practise."

"You mean play over with Willoughby?"

"Yes. They've been through all the old music now."

"Have they indeed? That's fast work - how many times has he been?"

"Only once Papa, but I think he's due again on Saturday. It would be nice to have the music by then, so she can practise a little."

"I can see there's been a deal happening since I was here." Enoch began to feel vaguely uneasy. In the few days of his absence things had not only gone quite as satisfactorily without him, but a few new shoots were appearing on that sturdy little tree of life, of which he thought of himself as the main stock. He looked at Tilly, puzzled, his sharp eyes piercing, under the heavy brows.

"We'll get her those oil paints." They set off, walking fast. "Now tell me your plans."

"You asked me whether I'd spent my money. I haven't done Father. In fact since my birthday last year."

Enoch stopped in his tracks, looking appreciatively at the girl. "That's good now. That's very well. And may I know what you wish to do with it? Perhaps I might contribute, if I think it's worth it."

"Oh, it will be worth it, Papa. I can assure you. But still, perhaps I should wait a little before telling you."

"You're a deep one. I'm beginning to think. Don't be so sure that I will help you."

Tilly turned away from him. She was breathing deeply, to control her annoyance. She would not reveal her plans until they were properly formulated.

Once the paints were purchased, they set off at a quick pace in the direction away from Manstones Ceramic.

"Aren't we returning, father?"

"Of course, I am. You're to go home. You'll just catch the three o'clock." Tell your Mama I'll be home before dinner. And give her this."

He gave her the parcel. The station wasn't far and having seen Tilly safely onto it, Enoch headed back to the works. He was humming a little melody. One he'd picked up at the music hall on Saturday. He was content with his action in getting the present. Edna would be fair pleased with that. By the time he got home, she'd be busy with her paints. She wouldn't care he'd delayed coming home, even though he'd been back at the works since this morning.

It was as Enoch supposed. Edna was delighted with the present, and overlooked Enoch's late return.

14

Enoch was wrong. For the next few days, Edna was absorbed, not in painting, but practising her violin. She was determined to have at least two of the short pieces by heart, before Willoughby came again.

By the time Robert turned up for the next session, Edna felt she had been quite successful.

"I have been getting one of these ready," she said, showing him the piano part. "We'll try this first."

Robert nodded, and tried out the accompaniment. It was time for Edna to show off. But as soon as Robert started playing, she began to lose concentration. What on earth was the matter with her? The simplest sequences seemed to be beyond her.

"Perhaps we should try one of the ones we did last week. Just to warm up?" Robert's voice was gentle. It was obvious the woman was flustered.

"Yes, of course." The new book was put aside, and she rummaged through the pile of music. There it was.

"Ye banks and braes..." Immediately the familiar notes sounded, Edna's poise was restored. The playing was fun, and she was going to enjoy herself.

"Very well," Robert commented. "Let the music speak to you, through you. You are a person who can." He smiled at her. When he did so, Edna felt revived.

"Yes, I hope so, indeed." She shook her head, as if she didn't really agree with him, but it was a nice compliment.

They played another folk song, then it was time to try the new music. This time, it went better. After the third attempt, Edna put her violin in the case and her bow on the table. She hadn't finished yet. She just needed to compose herself a little.

"Will you step out in the fresh air, Mr Willoughby. We're in need of refreshment."

He folded the music up, and followed her outside into the cool hall, then through the French doors onto the terrace. It was fine and sunny, a real spring day. There was no one about and the sun was brilliant after the dimness of the house. They both stood on the step, and Edna breathed in deeply.

"That was quite acceptable I thought, Mr Willoughby. What's your opinion?"

He turned his head. Why did these women want reassurance? Like mother, like daughter. In other ways they seemed unlike. This one had been a beauty, was still a beauty. No-one could call the other one a beauty, but she had an inner spirit which was lacking in her mother. But they both wanted something more from him, more than just plain truth. What could he say which would encourage and yet be truthful? The woman was hurrying too much, as if she were striving to complete the piece. Where she should linger, she scurried. What was the point of rushing? "You need to practise it. Know it so well, you won't worry about being right. Then linger, linger. Let the music speak. As I said."

Edna said nothing, but stepped down towards a small conifer on the edge of the terrace. There was a row of them, framing the wild trees on the other side of the valley. She'd longed for him to say some more.

"I do need practice," she said in a low voice. "It's so different when there's accompaniment."

Rob walked up and stood beside her, gazing across the valley to the wooded slope beyond. "I don't know what to say to you, you know what you have to do, to be a musician."

"I don't expect to be a musician. That's out beyond my reach. I play for myself."

"It makes no difference. I play for myself too, but mainly it's because of the music. I can't help it. I need it."

Edna smiled. "I know. Have you been playing long?"

"Not really. In my first position, where I was lodging there was a piano. I taught myself. About ten years ago, that is."

Edna studied his face, still in profile to her, as he looked out over the valley. For the first time, she noticed tiny lines round the corner of his eyes.

He turned towards her. "I never had lessons," he said.

In a flash, she pictured him as a small boy. She wished she'd had a little boy to embrace, to hold in her arms. She wondered how his mother had felt, when she first held the little boy on her lap. She visualised a woman, smiling down at her infant boy. She recognised the woman as herself. For a moment she felt an undeniable urge to touch this man, who was telling her what she should be doing. She put out her hand, and put her fingers on his sleeve. "You are a good musician. You didn't need lessons."

"Everyone needs lessons. About everything," he said.

"I know I do." Her voice was very soft. She turned away from him, towards the house. "Shall we go back?"

They came back into the shadow of the house, and then up the stone step into the hall. Only that morning she had put a large bowl of primroses on the table by the door. Their fragrance filled the hall. It was like the cool, faint scent of flowers in a church, in which there has been a recent wedding. "We'd better get on with practising, if that is what we have to do." She turned her head to smile as she went past the marble stairs.

Robert followed her. She needn't think because she had needed a rest, that he would make the hour longer. He was being paid for an hour and that was what she would have. Nevertheless, he realised, he would stay longer, if she asked him to. He recognised the contradiction in his thoughts, but he couldn't help it. Now, he did want to stay longer. He hoped she would ask him.

"Mama!" Tilly called. Her face appeared over the banister above. "Oh," she saw Robert. "I thought you'd finished. I won't interrupt you."

Edna turned back, put her foot on the bottom step and called. "We're waiting for you, my dear."

Immediately Tilly's head reappeared. "Mama, I asked to be excused today." Why hadn't Mama listened when she had especially reminded her mother that Ros was coming and on account of that she would have to miss her singing lesson? She was to be the Chief Maid of Honour at Ros' wedding and they were to look at some patterns together.

Edna turned back. She had forgotten about Ros' visit. She blushed with annoyance at herself and the fact that Willoughby had witnessed her discomfiture. But time was pressing. Already they were well into the second half of the lesson. She'd come to think of her arrangement with Robert as a lesson, with him as the master. In a strange way she was no longer in charge, he was. This was not due simply to the fact that he was the better musician. There was something else. He was decisive over what should be done and honest with her in his criticism of her technique and he didn't treat her in any way as his superior. She was a client of his, that was it, and he implied that he demanded respect, as any professional man would. And there was still something else about him she felt, as if, though his manner was cool, even remote, at times she caught a look in his face, of amusement, was it, or scorn. Behind that outwardly calm and courteous exterior, there was someone of whom, she had to admit to herself, she was a little afraid.

"Excuse me for not letting you know, Mr Willoughby, my daughter did tell me. She won't be able to come today. We could take on another piece."

"Certainly," he said, in his low voice. "If that is what you wish." The sun had gone round a little and was no longer shining through the big bay window in the morning room. It was dim and even gloomy, after the bright garden. Rob took the book of pieces and opened it out on the table, to get the best light. He turned it over, leaf by leaf, while Edna stood waiting. She picked up her violin and bow and played a scale, then another. She performed both meticulously.

Rob spoke, "We'll try this one." He put her part on the music stand, then his own on the piano. He set the metronome and counted three, then they were away. After a few bars, Edna lost her way. "Wait a moment," she said. He sat, with his hands poised over the keys. "Take your time. Try on your own first." She did the same few bars again, this time perfectly. "You see." Robert said. "You can do it. You just need to relax, and enjoy the music."

"I do, I do. I really enjoy it." Edna felt the perspiration under her arms and on her back. This dress was really too constricting. When on her own she always wore a loose robe for practising, but she obviously had to dress more formally when Willoughby was here. She was getting so hot, and her heart was pumping. She reflected that she would have been able to do the whole piece, perfectly on her own, in the privacy of her room, but with him, well, it was completely different. The bow felt sticky in her hands and it fluttered unevenly on the strings. She took a deep breath. She was nervous. She recognised it but she would not let him see it. She tried to concentrate on the music, gripped the bow harder, clamped down her chin on the violin and said, "Let's try again."

This time it all went better. She managed to get to the end of the piece, and they finished together. "Oh," she said, smoothing her hair with the back of the hand holding the bow.

"That was very good. Excellent," Robert said, swivelling the piano stool towards her.

"Thank you. I'll practise that one, for next time." She had been going to suggest they should do it again now. But she felt she should not detain him. She was afraid he might be angry if he was kept over the hour.

"I know you've a train to catch."

He got up from his seat, and she put down her instrument, going over to her handbag on the chair by the table. "Thank you again," she said, holding the money towards him.

He took the money. Their fingers lightly brushed.

"It is my pleasure, Mrs Manstone," he said, stressing the last word. "You are progressing." He put the coins into his waistcoat pocket

"Will next Saturday be convenient, Mr Willoughby? Perhaps afterwards you might like to take tea with myself and my daughter and Mr Manstone of course?" Edna found herself issuing this invitation without having realised that that was what she was going to do. Immediately, she regretted it. She hadn't consulted with Enoch. He would undoubtedly criticise her, categorising Willoughby unsuitable as a guest a mere clerk. But that was ridiculous. Tilly worked with him every day at the office. And Enoch himself had humble origins, as he could not help displaying. She wished however that Robert would decline the offer of tea.

"I shall be honoured to come," he said.

Edna's heart raced. It was too late now to revoke the invitation. "That's decided. And I'll practise very hard, to make it worth your while."

Again, he smiled. "Good bye, till Saturday, Mrs Manstone."

"Good bye, Mr Willoughby."

He was gone, and Edna wiped her violin and bow, replacing them in the case. She did up the fastenings, closed up the music, and then sat on the piano stool. Her fingers rested lightly on the keys. This was where Robert's fingers had been, running up and down, gently stroking and pressing, evoking chords, trills, and cadences. Music. Robert. Robert. She murmured the name to herself. It was an aristocratic name, deep, austere, strong. She suddenly felt that her blood seemed to be draining towards her fingertips. They were leading a life of their own. She kept them still, feeling the pulse in them. Her breathing quickened, her lips were moist and then there was a warm feeling in her belly, creeping upwards and outwards. She recognised it, putting her hands to her cheeks. She caught sight of herself reflected in the shiny wood of the piano. She pressed her cheeks, and peered into the polished surface. She thought, "I am still beautiful. He thinks so. I am sure he does."

She was planning next Saturday. She heard the door open, and caught a whiff of cigar tobacco. She realised it was Enoch.

"There you are. I take it Willoughby's gone?"

"Yes, Enoch." She turned towards him, putting her hands on her lap. "The hour was up".

"And how are you progressing? Do you find it helpful?"

"Yes." Edna rose, smoothing her skirt.

Enoch noticed her bright eyes. She still had a trim waist. In fact, he recognised with a pang, she had the look of a girl about her sometimes. This was one of those occasions. "I can see the music does you good. You look bonny."

Edna's colour rose again. "It's wonderful. Thank you for paying for it. Your clerk is a good musician."

"Do you think he is wasted on clerking?"

"No, of course not, Enoch. To be Chief Clerk in Manstones is a job any man would be proud of. Especially a man of his background."

"His background?" What did Edna know of Willoughby's background? Did she mean, 'his breeding'? Did she know anything about that? "I don't know owt about his background, except he was recommended to me by Elijah Winterbotham. It seems he was working in a law firm in Chester. That's all I know of him. But in the two years he's been with us, he's been a steady man. I don't know owt about his breeding either."

Edna was silent for a moment. "Will you be here on Saturday afternoon next week, Enoch?"

"I don't know if I will. I might just take a ride out, if Matilda wishes to come, or you yourself. You haven't been out riding for a while."

Edna said nothing. She could say nothing. She knew she wouldn't go riding. That was nonsense. She hadn't been riding for years. Enoch knew she wouldn't go riding. There was silence.

"Why do you ask?" he continued.

"It's not important," she said. No doubt he would have forgotten this conversation by the time next Saturday came. He'd be off in the field, or in his study. Willoughby's coming would be of no consequence to him, and if it were to come to his notice that Willoughby stayed for tea, she would face that issue if it arose. Perhaps Enoch wouldn't object anyway. There was no reason why he should object. He seemed to like and respect his clerk. He hadn't mentioned anything about his breeding when she had talked about his background. In the event, probably Robert wouldn't come. That was the way things were. Whenever one worried about future events, or looked forward to them, they did not transpire.

"I'll ring for some tea."

She got up from the piano stool, pulled the bell rope by the fireplace. Jeannie came in. Enoch noticed her red cheeks. No doubt she'd been curled up with the cat somewhere. Edna ordered, then Enoch said,

"None for me. I'll be in my study. Get the fire lit, and bring me some whisky." Jeannie bobbed and went out. Why had he said that about the fire? It was Mavis' job to do that, and it should have been done long ago. Back in the scullery the new maid was washing saucepans. "Master wants the study fire lit." Jeannie shouted. "You'd best get about it. Else he'll be in a temper, and you'll be losing your fine new job. And hurry up, before he gets in there."

Mavis turned, without a word, dried her hands on her apron, went to fill the wood basket with sticks and logs. Jeannie went into the kitchen, and squatted for a moment, by the range, to warm her hands.

Enoch retired to his study. Although the sun was shining outside, in here it was cold and damp. He stood by his desk, sorting out various papers appertaining to the household. The price of everything seemed to be rising....coal, candles, feed for the horses, everything. The books kept by Edna all told the same tale. And at the same time, profits from his factory were dropping. He'd read the correspondence from the new representative at his sales office in New York, and it was obvious that the fellow wasn't doing so well as had been envisaged. Was it the chap's fault, or was trade just as bad there as here?

The door opened, and in came the new maid, balancing a wicker basket of sticks on her head, and with newspaper, rolled up, under her arm.

She said nothing, but dumping the loads, immediately returned to the door.

"What's your name?" barked Enoch.

The girl jumped, like a shot rabbit. "Beg pardon, sir, I didn't see you, sir. Mavis."

"Hasn't no-one told you to knock before you come in?"

"Yes sir."

"Well do it then. We're gentry here. We likes our privacy."

"Yes sir."

"You're the new girl, I take it."

"Yes sir."

"Well, Mavis, the new girl from the fire, mark my words."

"Yes sir."

Enoch became aware of a strange smell. Was it the girl? He looked at her, standing with her hands behind her back. She appeared to him to be very young, much younger than Jeannie. She was also paler and slighter. Could she really be menstruating? "I have work to do. Hurry up with your task. I require whisky and soda now."Why could not Deaker ensure that the girls were clean? It was disgraceful. "Send the housekeeper with it. I wish to speak to her."

By the time Robert's train pulled away from Epsilon Station the clouds were coming in, but over the west there was still a patch of blue sky. He gazed out of the dirty carriage window, at the cows peacefully chewing the cud or grazing, and sheep further away on the undulating hills, sprinkled about like carelessly scattered mushrooms. Soon, however, there appeared ramshackle huts and patches of worn out grassland, covered with docks and thistles, makeshift sheds, tumble-down barns, and rough cinder tracks connecting one dwelling with another. Then the houses grew more numerous and soon were laid out in straight, tight rows, striping across the contours like bars; the dirt tracks became cobbled roads, larger and longer buildings appeared, factories, pot banks, with bottle shaped kilns, till the whole landscape was nothing but a conglomeration of red brick buildings with slated roofs, grey and sooty, stretching in all directions as far as the dark moors in the distance.

Robert's spirits sank. Here he was back again, this was where he had his whole being,... here, in this wretched festering pustule on the face of the earth. Why was he here? He hugged his crossed legs, bending forward over with both knees. It was as if he was sick to the stomach. But there was nothing really the matter with him, he knew. It was just getting back to it all, after that brief gap out in the country. Why was he here? Why was it that he had to spend his few precious days on earth, in this place, of all places? Yet he'd come here of his own will, hadn't he? He could have been happily returning to a little cottage in Cheshire, working as a Solicitor's Clerk, in a much more salubrious place than this. Probably he'd been a fool to feel his pride needed him to make his own way in life, not owing anything to that mysterious patron of his, a man whom he'd never seen, who would not see him, who yet felt it his duty to help him along life's way. Well, he wasn't beholden to anyone, least of all to someone who wouldn't recognise him face to face.

The train drew into the station. Robert took up his parcel of music, put his hat on after a glance in the little mirror above the compartment seat, let down the window by its leather strap, reached out for the handle and was opening the door, jumping out, before the carriages jolted to a halt.

As Rob hurried along the platform, the engine let out a blast of steam, doors slammed, the guard's whistle blew. A group of girls met some passengers and they all started shouting and laughing. A news vendor was crying out the late sports edition. Rob felt more cheerful. He knew why he liked this town. It was the hustle and bustle, the people, that was why he had come and why he stayed.

He gave his ticket to the collector at the barrier, walked along up the familiar street to the canal bridge at the end. He'd promised Gertie he would meet her there, but he hadn't said he'd be coming from the direction of the station. She'd be expecting him to come from his lodging, further up the hill.

For a moment Rob considered whether he would make a detour so that he would appear to be coming from home. He didn't want Gertie to ask awkward questions about where he had been. He wasn't sure why he did not want to reveal all his comings and goings to the girl, but the fact was, he didn't.

He felt a hand on his arm. "Robert. You're early. Why have you come this way?" It was Gertie.

"Why have you come this way, come to that?"

"I heard from Maisie, she saw you going into station yard this morning, dressed for out. So I knew as you'd gone to Epsilon, though you dinna tell me."

Robert stopped and turned towards Gertie, as she breathlessly explained all this. She was really very pretty today, her cheeks flushed from hurrying, she was panting hard. "Rest yourself, my wench. It don't do to get like you do. I'm here now, and there's nowt you need to worry about. Come here." He pulled her towards him and kissed her full on the mouth. "There now. That'll stop your carry on."

Gertie jerked away, holding her hat on with her free hand. "Mind, what you're about Mr Robert Willoughby. You forgot you was to take me with you next time you went piano-ing at the big house. I wouldna be in the way. I could ha' gone and spoken to that old woman, Deaker, the maid if that what she is."

Rob turned round, keeping her by the arm. "Come on now. I didna say I'd tek ye this time. I said, sometime or other. Well, today wasn't right."

"Oh, that's it. Is it?" She stopped. "Are ye ashamed of me in front of your friends? I don't see why. Miss Tilly and the Master, they both know as we're to be wed. They wouldn't mind if I came along and waited for you."

"All right, all right." Robert was walking faster and faster. "I will do, Gertie. Don't mither me. I will do it. Now tell me, how is your Ma? Is she better today?"

"She is a little better. But, I'm worried about her, Rob. She's been coughing again. It don't seem to leave her."

"We'll go straight to the pharmacy this minute and we'll tek it back straight away. And I'll buy you some oranges. We'll have them for our tea, some for her too. She'll like that my wench."

"You think of her more than of me, Robert."

"I only think of her because she's your Ma. You know that."

"I wish you were there to tek care of us all the time."

Rob was looking to Gertie with only part of his mind. He registered what she was saying, enough to know that it was the same as what she always said. He gripped her arm more tightly. "We'll go for the medicine when we get home. Before the rain comes, let's catch the tram for Elbow Ridge. I've got a spare shilling."

"Could we?"

"That's why I do it these lessons and such like.... to spend a bit on you."

"That's not true, Robert. You do it because you've a mind to." Gertie knew Robert was set on improving himself, it had nothing to do with her, she was convinced. Quite the opposite, why should a man like him with his brains, bother with her?

Rob ignored her remark. "Be smart now, and we'll get the half past five tram. It's due now. Run." He propelled her forward and they started to run.. It was only a few hundred yards, but they kept up the pace. When they came to the stop they were breathless.

Gertie leaned her whole weight against Rob. "Oh, you'll do for me, you will," she said. "I told Ma you might come back for tea."

"That won't matter at all," he said. "You didna say 'would'".

"How can I ever, I never know with thee!"

The tram drew up clanking and they climbed on board, Robert helping Gertie on first. "Best keep close to me, I'll keep thee warm." They held hands and she leaned her head on his shoulder.

Soon they were leaving the streets. The tram terminal was at the end of a leafy road. Twigs from the branches were almost at arm's length.

"Do you remember when we came up here the first time, Robert Willoughby?"

"I can't forget that, can I?"

"That was the second time we met."

"Aye." And nothing had changed, Robert thought. That would be the next thing she'd say. When she did say it, he added nothing, except "Aye," again.

The tram stopped and they clattered down the stairs.

"Thank you Sir, Miss," the conductor said. "Last tram returns 6.30 sharp."

"Right ho." Robert got off the platform, Gertie stepped down, taking his hand. "We'll go up the path, Gert."

He had hold of her arm and they set off purposefully down a track between high hedges. The sun was still warm, and in the shelter of the hawthorn bushes, the air was heavy. The nettles were beginning to grow, and the brambles were coming into leaf. Robert held Gertie closer and closer to him. They were walking in harmony, he could feel her from her waist down through his hip to his thigh. They came to a field gate. He stopped. "Woulds't like a rest?" he halted by the gate and leaned his back against it. "There, shall I lift thee up?"

"I'll stand here," she murmured. Her face was against his chest. He opened his jacket and she leaned her cheek on the soft wool cloth of his waistcoat. He stroked her cheek then laid his hat on the grass. She remained standing. Her heart was beating, and she watched him as he bent over with his hat. When he turned back she turned her face towards his. He took the pin out of her hat, and carefully laid it on top of his own. He took her face in his hands, and kissed her, very gently on the mouth. Her lips were soft and succulent. Her body was warm and yielding. Her arms came round him, pulling him closer to her. The world was closing in, concentrated in this moment. The presence of the gate against her back was forgotten. All she was aware of was his body, his strong, firm legs pressing against her through her thin dress.

After what seemed a long time, with his mouth against her, Gertie drew her face back. "I love you, my Rob," she lifted her face again, clinging to him.

"Come and sit down in the field for a while. We'll have a rest before the walk." With his free left hand, he pressed in the spring latch on the gate. He pushed against the heavy bars, but they were stuck in the long grass. He guided her through, his hand still around her waist. "Sit on this." He took his jacket off and put it on the ground.

"It'll get wet, this grass is damp." She remonstrated.

"It'll dry." He sat on the coat, patting the place beside him, and pulling her down. They sat together on the coat, arms round each other. With his right hand, Robert felt her breasts, first one then the other. He began gently stroking them, with a circular motion, in turn.

Gertie let her head fall onto his shoulder. It seemed as if she could feel the earth turning. She was magnetically drawn to it, deep onto the revolving sphere. They were rushing through the universe, she, Robert, and the rotating sphere. The feeling in her breasts was seeping downwards and along, into all the secret places of her body like the salt sea tide rushing into hidden crevices and fissures in a rocky pool. Down, down, she was sinking. "That's nice," she murmured. She moaned. "That's lovely....oh, oh."

"Do you like it?" He stopped and lay backwards on the grass, pulling her onto him, so she lay with her head on his chest.

She said nothing. A few moments went by.

"We shouldn't be doing this," she said as she drew breath.

"I can kiss you, can't I?"

"That with your hand." She lifted his hand away. "It makes me feel funny."

As she rolled over, she saw his face blank, his eyes shut. "That's right, that's what it supposed to do."

Gertie sighed. She let her body relax against his. She undid his waistcoat, and put her head to his chest, on top of his shirt. Under her cheek, the heart was beating fast and loud

Rob lay quietly, for a moment, then his hand came up to her thigh, pulling at her skirt. The cloth was rucked up round her waist. He could feel the skin of her belly. It was so soft and smooth, smooth and silky. His hand moved downwards.

"Don't" she cried out, jerking away and gripping his wrist. She wriggled herself onto her side, away from him. He was on his face, now, his forehead on his arm. She knelt beside him. He seemed to be suffering. She put her cheek to his, but he did not respond. At last he rolled onto his back.

"You did for me then," he murmured.

Gertie frowned. Was he cross? Her heart was still racing."We shouldna have come. It was just a walk." she whispered.

"Just a walk, just a walk. Dinna you know what a man is?" Ferociously he brushed and rubbed at his trousers. "We'll be off."

Oh, must we? It's so nice here, with you. "She turned towards him again, pulling at him.

"Don't." He shrugged her off. "First you want me, then you don't. Dost know what that does to me. Dost?"

"I do love you Rob, I do. But you must bide your time."

"Oh yes. You know what love is, I suppose. Like all silly wenches. "

"How can you say that? How many have you known? It's true love, I want, not just some silly fancy in the wood. You know that." She sat up, decisively.

"I wish we hadn't come." Rob had rolled away from her, fanning his face and rubbing his hair. "These midges are biting me."

"Go away, go on with you," she said flicking at his face with her fingers.

He grasped hold of her hand. "Leave me be. You won't do owt like that."

Gertie felt a sudden loss of breath, as if someone had hit her in the chest. "I'm only trying to help."

"Well, you're not. I'm not a baby. I don't know why we came."

Gertie jumped to her feet. "You do. You wanted to come. I said as we should've gone home for our tea. And what about the oranges?"

"Go home for our tea! That's all your world, isn't it?" Rob had his knees hunched up to his nose. "Don't you ever think there's something else besides 'home' and 'tea'? I brought you here to see how...."

"To see what? What?"

"Oh, never mind. You wouldn't understand."

"So I'm not clever enough for you then, Robert Willoughby. Well, tek me home then, and we'll not see each other no more." She had her back to him, and then turned sideways to squeeze through the gate.

"There. We'll go home if you've a mind. But there's a long walk for the tram.

"We can walk, can't we? It's nobbut two or three miles. If we ain't going to the Ridge we might as well."

"All right." He handed her her straw hat, and jammed on his bowler. "Be sharp, and we still might catch your Ma's tea."

"She won't be giving you tea, not ever again." Gertie bolted off, running, her hat ribbons flying behind her. She was struggling to contain her sobs, but every now and then one escaped from her. "Oh. Oh."

Robert marched along at his own pace behind her. She couldn't get away from him, however hard she tried. Walking fast, his long stride would be a match for her breathless attempt at running. His hands were clasped behind his back and he began whistling. He now felt completely in control.

After a hundred yards, Gertie had tired. As he came up to her, she said "You've done me a mischief, I've got a right bad pain in my side."

"Not half the mischief I might have done you, my wench." He was smiling, Gertie's show of temper had banished his ill humour, and he wanted her all the more. He caught hold of her and brought her hand up against him. "You're a silly little missy, what are you?

"Let me be, Robert Willoughby. You don't love me."

He kissed her eyes, each in turn, then wiped her wet cheeks with his fingertips. "Th'art a silly wench. It's just because I love thee, I want thee, in a way you'll never know. Never. That's why I was so cross. It was wrong of me, Gertie, but I canna help it. I want thee so much." He pulled her close, pressing her to him, his hand on her waist. "But I canna have thee. Whenever I want thee, I canna have thee."

They clung together.

Gertie whispered. "I didna say tha couldn't have me. I dinna say it, Robert."

"Tha didst not. But I know it. Tha must be wed first. Or if not, we must be if we mek a babby."

"Well, we will be wed. Then we'll mek a babby. We will, Rob, we will."

"I know, I know." He kissed her again. But he knew then they wouldn't be wed. He couldn't tell her they'd never be wed. How could they, how could he every support a wife in one of those tiny cottages, with squealing babies everywhere and old Ma to be taken care of? He couldn't do it, he couldn't. But he couldn't tell her either or take advantage of her trust either. Now was the time, now, to tell her honestly and make an end of it. But he couldn't do it. He couldn't. "We'll work it out, somehow, my wench. We will. Now dry your eyes. What will folk think else?" He put his thumb to her eyes, carefully closing the lids, and wiping away the remnants of tears. Then they were kissing again. This was as good as he would get, he said to himself. Why wasn't he satisfied with it? Of course, he wasn't. He was a man, and he wanted her, entirely. Yet, he himself wouldn't give up any of his own freedom, his life, his destiny. "Let's go on," he said, taking her arm. "We don't want Ma to think there's owt amiss."

15

The music lesson, for so Edna now considered it, came and went on the following Saturday. Edna concentrated from the beginning, and the music went better. She would make it sing through her, and, as she had been practising hard, some of the pieces did indeed, seem to have a life of their own. Enoch had announced his intention of going riding that afternoon, Tilly had gone with him, and Edna was expecting her to be back in time to do some singing. However, she did not appear, and so, when Robert and she came out of morning room following the lesson, Edna had to make excuses again.

"I expect you think my daughter has given up, Mr Willoughby."

"Perhaps as a young girl she needs some relaxation.

"Perhaps," Edna was surprised that Willoughby described Tilly as a young girl. It made him seem so much older, more her own age. She wondered how old he was. Perhaps he was older than she had first thought. "I expect they'll join us later, after the ride. My husband enjoys the exercise after a day in the office."

In the drawing room, a small table had been laid with a cloth, plates, knives and cake forks. Edna pulled the bell. "Do you ride Mr Willoughby? Please sit down." She motioned to a chair without waiting for an answer, and she continued. "The weather has changed. I don't suppose they will be long."

A splatter of raindrops whipped against the French windows. Clouds had blown up from the west during the night, and now it seemed that the fine spell was over.

"I used to go on horseback when I was a boy."

Edna noticed how he described himself. He talked as if it was so long since he was a boy. She wondered whether, she felt the same, that it was so long since she was a girl?

"Used you to live in the country, Mr Willoughby?"

"I did." He took the tea cup she proffered. "I was brought up in a village. We had need of horses. Since I've been living here, I've got used to the trams and trains."

"I expect you miss the country, being raised as you were."

"No." He stirred his tea. "I haven't missed it. If I did I shouldn't stay in the city."

"Tell me what you like about city life."

"It's the place for a man like me. There's plenty to interest me."

"Do you mean, your music?"

"That. And there are other things going on. Lecturers and the like, Evening Institute."

"Are you a member?"

"Not regular. My schooling was enough for me. But there are visiting speakers I go to."

"Are you a church goer, Mr Willoughby?"

"Chapel. But I'm not a man who is prejudiced. Besides there's the singing. A man doesn't always have to worship one way alone. It's my belief...," he trailed off.

"What is your belief?"

"I think where people are together, in the name of good, that's the best."

"In the name of good? What is that?"

"Responsibility to each other. That's my religion, Mrs Manstone."

A bell jangled. A moment later Jeannie announced Mr. Lockyard.

"Show him in, of course." This was indeed fortuitous. Robert's presence in the drawing room would not seem so strange to Enoch, if there was another young man here with him.

"How very nice, Mr. Lockyard. I was afraid you had forgotten all about us." Edna was so pleased at this turn of event. "I am sure you remember Mr. Willoughby, whose group performed for us so beautifully at my musical event."

"Very glad to meet you again." The two men shook hands and sat down. "I must not prevail upon your time, Mrs. Manstone." Lockyard continued. I have been meaning to bring a book over which might interest Miss Manstone. She showed an interest in the works of Mr. Ruskin."

"Indeed. A book! Well, of course. My daughter will be back presently. She and her father are out riding. Will you have a cup of tea?

The next moment Enoch entered the drawing room. He was in his stockinged feet, and was wearing his riding clothes except for the coat. "Oh, there you are!" He saluted his wife with his riding crop. "And Willoughby. And you sir. I am sure we've met. Are you partaking? Mrs Manstone didn't say we had guests or I would have made sure to be on time." Enoch felt completely confused by Willoughby's presence, and now, by the fact he couldn't put a name to this stranger.

"Mr. Lockyard. He was at our soiree. With Mr. Lugando, the architect."

"I'll tek these wet things off and I'll tell Matilda," he hurried out of the room. He'd had a shock to see the clerk sitting in the drawing room, sipping tea with Edna. He'd felt at a disadvantage in his soaked clothing, while Willoughby was sitting there so neat and composed, taking tea from his own porcelain service. Not to mention the other fellow, sitting there as brash as brass. Architect! Why was he always turning up when least expected? He'd wanted to see Lugando, not his assistant. He stamped upstairs. His leather boots had leaked a little and now his feet made wet imprints on the stone steps. As he passed

Tilly's door he knocked on it with the flat of his hand. "Be sharp. Your Mama has guests. The tea's poured."

The front door bell jangled, and the sound could be heard all over the house.

"More visitors," Enoch muttered, as he went into his dressing room. He wouldn't have time for his usual bath. He'd just change and go down immediately. He had determined to try and please Edna with punctuality.

As he came out of his door, he was aware of someone in the passage. Turning, he saw that Mavis had come out of the servant's door into the master bedroom. When she saw him, she shrank into the shadow, away from the dim light still coming through the belvedere.

"Come here. I know you're there. No need to be afraid of me."

"Yes sir." The girl came out.

"Now, then. Come here and stand in front of me."

Mavis did what she was told.

Enoch looked down at her, then raised his nose in the air, sniffing. "Aye. That's better. Did Deaker tell you?"

"What sir?" Mavis whispered.

"About keeping yourself clean. You're in a gentleman's house now. Wash yourself. Wherever necessary. Otherwise you won't be here much longer."

"Please sir, I do my best."

"I'm sure you do."

"Will that be all, sir?"

"Come here." Enoch put out his hand towards her head.

Mavis flinched.

"I'm not going to hurt you." He touched her cap, to straighten it. "No that's not right. You'd better do it yourself." He removed it. "That's better." Now, he could see that she was pretty. Pale, and thin, but those eyes. And nice little paps when she lifted her arms up. "Go and tidy yourself. And bring me my whisky when the tea party is over."

"Please sir, it's Jeannie's job. That is. Deaker says."

"No matter. Do as I say."

In the drawing room Edna was only half listening to the conversation between the two young men. Robert's seemed to be bored. His face was set and distant as if he had withdrawn into his shell. She wanted to turn the conversation away from him. She was aware that he was being regarded as some kind of curiosity.

Enoch came in, and immediately Lockyard rose. "I fear I must be leaving you, Mrs. Manstone. I have prevailed on your hospitality too long already." He held out a small parcel. "May I ask you to to give this to Miss. Manstone?"

"Do wait, just another moment, I am sure she will be in directly."

"So gracious of you to suggest it, but I must indeed go. Thank you so much."

Edna held out her hand. "Do please call again. We should be delighted."

Just as Jeannie was showing Mr. Lockyard out, Tilly was coming down the stairs. "Mr. Lockyard!" she cried out.

He turned immediately. "I thought I had missed you. I gave Mrs. Manstone a book for you. It is by the lady who copies the works of John Ruskin. Octavia Hill. But she isn't just a copyist, even an artist. She is well known for her work to do with the housing of the poor of London. Forgive me, I am sure you know all this. If you remember our conversation at your lovely soiree."

Jeannie stood awkwardly with Lockyard's hat.

"Really? Of course I do. How kind of you. No. I haven't heard of her. But of course, I have heard of John Ruskin. Please come back in, and tell me the rest. Have you had some tea? "

But David Lockyard stretched out his hand for the hat. "Thank you for asking me. But I have to be home before the light fails. It will take me an hour."

He bowed to her, and went through the door. Propped against the pillars of the porch, was a bicycle.

"I'll read it, and return it to you, at the church?"

"Very good. Don't be in a hurry. Goodbye."

Skilfully, he heaved himself onto the high saddle, and was away, without a wobble. Tilly and Jeannie watched him down the drive.

"Well, Jeannie, what do you think of that?"

"I don't know, Miss." Jeannie couldn't remember ever seeing such a handsome young man, come calling on a bicycle. She couldn't wait to pass on the news to Deaker.

Tilly realised why Lockyard was behaving like Cinderella. Of course, to cycle would be dangerous, in the dark.

In the drawing room, her father was talking to Robert.

"My chapel is in Epsilon, Raven Lane, sir."

Edna recognised it as a Dissenters chapel, but said nothing. She had no wish to embarrass Robert, although judging by his cool smile, nothing would seem to discomfort him.

The conversation dragged on, all about Whit picnics for the children.

"We don't have a sponsor. We just have a walk at Whitsun - there's no picnic," Robert Willoughby was saying.

Tilly tried to show interest. "That's a shame. Why don't we find sponsors for them, father? It's a shame for the children not to have a picnic. Mama, let's do something for them." Tilly passed her cup for more tea. "It can't be that expensive Papa, what would it cost to hire a brake? Mr Willoughby - you'd know." Tilly had a vision of little children crammed on benches on a wagon, being taken to a wooded glade, being fed with lemonade and buns, then frolicking in the fields.

Enoch began reminiscing about Sunday school picnics he'd been to as a child. At that time his family had been chapel goers. He now seemed to be in a jovial humour. He hadn't been put about to see Mr Willoughby taking tea, after all. Tilly knew her mother had been worried about Papa's reaction. On the contrary, he was more relaxed than usual. And Mama too was smiling and happy, Tilly noticed. Her thoughts returned to the idea of a picnic. Why shouldn't they use one of the works' drays? Cleared out from clay and bone it could accommodate at least a dozen children. And why not have a picnic for the children connected with Manstones? Why should everything be done under the auspices of church or chapel? "Do any of the pot-banks arrange picnics, father?"

"Yes, sir. It would." Robert sipped his second cup of tea. "An expensive one."

"That's right young man," Mr Martin said.

The conversation turned to ways they could organise a picnic.

Robert put his cup on the occasional table. "Will you excuse me?"

After brief goodbyes he left. He was glad to get out of the stuffy atmosphere and walked hurriedly through the rain.

Tilly dashed up the stairs. Now, she could enjoy opening the parcel. Inside, was a small book entitled. "Our Common Land" by Octavia Hill.

Immersed in this, Tilly spent several hours on her own, for the next two days. Her horizons, formerly bounded by the factory, her home, and the various good works which Mother and the other ladies would initiate and then organise, had suddenly widened.

16

A few days later, Edna was to have a fitting for the dress she was to wear at Ros' wedding. Spanglow, taking the last pin out of her mouth to make a final adjustment to the hem of the sweeping train, said, "Miss Matilda's is coming along nicely Ma'am. But I'm having a bit o' trouble with they sleeves. If so happen she could come in, I could settle it, you see. Now then." She held a long mirror up so that Edna could see her back by the reflection in the cheval looking glass.

Edna twisted this way and that. The dress made the most of her slim waist and shapely bust. "Yes. That's very nice, Miss Spanglow."

"It's a real pleasure to see the clothes I make setting you off so well, Ma'am. I'm sure Mr Manstone will be pleased with that, won't he now. Yes to be sure." She began unpinning the dress at the back and undid the bustle tied round Edna's waist.

"I'll try and arrange for my daughter to come in."

"That will be very convenient, Mrs Manstone. I'm right busy, but I like to oblige my customers you see. It's a matter of juggling things about a little." She put the dress back on the tailor's dummy, and helped Edna back into her own dress. "Now then," she said, handing her customer's hat to her.

"Good day, Mrs Spanglow. I may be returning after luncheon." Edna swept out.

Tom was waiting with the trap outside. She smiled graciously to him as she climbed in. She held her head high, as the trap bounced over the cobbles. She'd surprise Enoch and Tilly. She hadn't mentioned her visit to the dressmaker. Already she felt warm and excited, as if she was indeed wearing the beautiful new dress.

Within a few minutes the pony was clattering through the tunnel, past the lodge and into the yard of the Pot Bank. Silas was standing in the doorway of the engine shop, as George brought the pony to a halt.

The old engineer touched his forehead to Mrs Manstone. "Good day, Missus. Out for a drive? It's the weather."

"Good morning, Mr Silas." Edna greeted him warmly. George helped her down from the trap, and she went up the wooden stairs to the office. She opened the door. Robert was sitting at his desk, copying letters into the copybook.

"Mrs Manstone!" he said, rising. "If you want the Master, he's out, and so is Miss Tilly. They're visiting the engraver. Then for lunch. That's how it is, Mrs."

"Oh." Edna felt totally deflated, as if all the energy had suddenly poured out of her. "Oh dear, a wasted journey." She turned to go.

Robert pulled his stool out from its position by the desk. "If you'll wait a while, Ma'am. He'll be back soon. That is, if you're not in a hurry."

She looked around the neat little office. "Well, well. Perhaps I should. It's Miss Tilly I really came to see. I'll wait in Mr Manstone's office. Don't disturb yourself."

"Very well, Ma'am." He opened the door for her, and she went over to the desk. "If there's anything you require, I'll be at your service, Mrs Manstone. As always." He closed the door gently, and went back to his stool.

Edna stood by Tilly's desk, at the window. It seemed cosy and comfortable in here. There were letters written in Tilly's hand lying in a tidy row, and beside them Tilly's inkwell, and pen. Pattern books were lying open on one end of the table and there was a row of issues of the Potters Gazette, propped up by bookends. Enoch's desk was empty except for a wooden tray containing some opened letters, a blotter, pencil and pen.

Edna wondered whether to sit on his chair, which was of well-worn brown leather, or on Tilly's stool which had the advantage of being near the window. She turned one of the pattern books towards her and began turning the pages, one by one. The patterns were pretty, but all very similar. After studying a few of them Edna closed the book. She was beginning to feel hungry. She looked at her watch. It was a quarter to one. Was Robert going out for his lunch, or would he have it here? Probably Enoch would not allow him to leave the works in his absence. She began to calculate how long Enoch and Tilly might be gone. At least two hours, probably. It was fanciful to suppose they would be back before three o'clock. She sighed. It was unlikely that she would be able to fulfil her promise to the dressmaker to take Tilly there this afternoon.

There was complete silence from next door. Edna wondered whether Robert had gone out. She sat without moving, holding her breath, to see if she could hear his pen scratching. There was nothing, no sound at all, of breathing, of paper turning, nothing. She imagined him sitting there, his pen poised, held between his long fingers, motionless. She wondered if he was listening for her. Perhaps he knew she was listening for him. She stood up, and went over to the bookshelf, picking a Potters Gazette, at random. She walked to Enoch's desk, and slapped the magazine on the table. It was really too bad to be trapped like this, waiting for her husband. Why hadn't he hadn't told her he wouldn't be at the works at lunch time. Surely she had mentioned she was going to town. He might have guessed she might call in. And Tilly was as bad. But then she never did call in, or only seldom. Tilly and Enoch seemed like conspirators sometimes, their world was secret to them alone, and she was an outsider.

Well, she was an outsider. As she looked through the Gazette she realised here was a whole language she didn't understand. From the inner office she couldn't see into the yard, as the only window faced onto the lane behind the factory. But she was aware of everyone working round about her. But who they were, and what they were doing, she couldn't conceive.

There was a slight cough. Mr Willoughby had his head round the door. She hadn't heard him open it.

"As Mr Manstone isn't here, is there anything you wished for? I could send out for it."

"Yes, please. I would like some tea."

Robert didn't answer, just retreated, closing the door gently. He hadn't expected her to ask for tea. The women in the pot bank brought a drink with them, lemonade or ginger beer, home-made. The men brought beer or bought it in jugs from the alehouse. She'd have to have ginger beer. He went down to the Lodge Office. "Slip out for me for two bottles of ginger beer, Barlow," he said to the clerk.

"Yes, Mr Willoughby." Why couldn't Robert go for himself?

"Mrs Manstone is in the office, and I canna leave her. She's thirsty."

"Oh, is that it? Well, I'd best be quick, eh." He grinned at Robert, taking the proffered threepenny bit. Rob stood in the gloomy lodge, idly flipping through the day book which recorded details of traffic in and out through the tunnel. Today, there had been a cart load of withies for making the baskets which contained the finished ware. Also a load of straw had come in for packing, and a tray of finished ware had gone out, to be transferred to a canal long boat for the journey through the Midlands to the South of England.

He wandered up the tunnel to the yard. Outside the basket weaving shop a man and two boys were busy with baskets for the next delivery.

"All reet, Mr Willoughby?" the old man asked.

"Aye. For the present, any road." Rob said. He watched them for a moment. He knew it was hard on the fingers, but in this sporadic sunshine, at this time of year, it seemed a pleasant enough task. He thought about his own job, which confined him to the gloomy office, and he pictured Edna, up there. She was waiting for him, he supposed. Well he couldn't be quicker than quick.

"Here you are." Barlow, breathless, had come up behind with two stone ware ginger beer bottles.

Rob took them, with a nod, and went off up the wooden steps. "All reet for some of us," he winked at the old fellow. "Ain't it?"

In the office, Edna was waiting by the window. When she heard Rob's foot on the stairs, she resolutely kept her back to the door. There was a knock. "Enter," she called, faintly.

"Here you are. That was the best I could do. We don't make tea here, and it would take too long to go up to Kardomah. I hope that will suit."

Edna turned round. She didn't know what to say. She hadn't really wanted a drink at all. She'd only asked him to go in the first place, because in a strange way, she wanted him away from her. But now, he was back, so quickly, and she would have to make a show, at least, of drinking.

"Excuse me," he said, softly. He went out of the door again, and was back in a moment, with a glass and a white napkin. "Mr Manstone does have a drink with his luncheon, sometimes. But it's not ginger beer." Rob smiled. "Here, I'll pour you some." He carefully tilted the glass and poured in the golden, fizzy liquid. "Was he expecting you?" he asked as he passed over the drink.

"No. That is to say...."

"I thought not. Or he'd have been here." He paused, in the doorway.

Edna smiled. "Won't you have some, Mr. Willoughby.....I suppose you like something stronger?."

Rob said nothing, but looked her full in the eyes. "You supposed wrong. I'm not a drinking man. Life's too short for that."

Edna felt herself reddening under his gaze. At this distance she could feel the heat coming from him. She lowered her head holding the glass with both hands, in front of her. Her mouth was slightly open and her breathing quickened. She felt her hand shaking.

"You're very beautiful." Rob said, taking a step forward. He took the glass from her hand and put it in the table saying, "You don't like that, best get rid of it."

Edna had not moved, her hand was still outstretched, as if the glass were still there.

Robert took her fingertips. "I beg your pardon, I should have brought tea. Nor should I have said that. Did it offend you?"

She hung her head. Every thought went from her, except for the sensation of his cool fingers, holding hers. She should move, but she could not. It was as if the hand didn't belong to her, as if she could see what was happening, and couldn't alter it, as in a dream.

"I'm sorry. Please excuse me. There." He let go, and she curled her fingers inwards, and held them to her mouth.

"You mustn't," she managed to get the words out, but she still could not move away.

Every bit of her flesh was sensitised. She was sinking deep into darkness, and there was a roaring sound. It was so sudden, so intense, she had no notion of what was happening, she could not resist it.

Robert's watched her. Her eyes were closed, the eyelids fluttering.

"Mrs. Manstone! Are you unwell?" He was on one knee beside her.

She stared at him, unable to focus. She put her hand to her forehead.

"Oh. you're there....!" She sighed. "It's nothing. Just a little faint."

"Please do not be distressed. Compose yourself. They are returning."

There was the noise of footsteps on the stairs. Robert stood up, and when Enoch and Tilly entered, he was waiting at the entrance.

"Mrs. Manstone is here sir, she's been here a while. I sent out for some ginger ale, but it didn't agree with her. Best see to her, Miss."

Tilly rushed into the inner office to see what was the matter. Edna was standing by the window.

"Mr. Willoughby said you weren't well, Mama."

..... Edna turned round. "I am perfectly all right. I just don't fancy that drink. That is all."

She did look pale, Tilly thought. "If you're sure."

"I'm all right." Edna heard herself saying. "I've been waiting to take you to Miss Spanglow for the fitting."

"You must go, of course. I'll return on the train," Enoch said.

The two ladies went downstairs, and soon the gig was clattering back through the tunnel, on the way to Madame Spanglow. The road took them past the site of the fire. Seeing the ruins of blackened houses, she touched her mother's arm.

"It seems so long ago. Do you remember? Do you wish to see for yourself, Mama?"

Tom halted the pony. Both the ladies gazed out. Little had changed since Tilly's visit here with David Lockyard. However, a few weeds were now poking their way up through broken posts, slates and red clay.

"It's all disgusting. Why had it not been cleared up?" Edna said.

"And what has become of the people who lived here?" Tilly felt suddenly ashamed that she had done no more to help out. She'd had all those ideas of doing something, but in the end, she'd done nothing. Those decisions that she had made, after her words with Papa, had been forgotten. She had not even acted on her resolution to go out on her own, sometimes, anywhere, except for her occasional ride out on Silver. And her mother had done more for the dispossessed people, than she had, by employing the new maid. At least one person had been resettled.

"Are you satisfied? Mrs. Spanglow is waiting."

The visit to Spanglows was not a success. Tilly seemed preoccupied, and uninterested in the dress.

"Anyone would think you are not looking forward to your part as a bridesmaid. The chief bridesmaid." Edna commented on the way home.

Tilly looked at her, but said nothing. How could she say that she hated the idea of Ros getting married, especially to Cyril? She had told Ros always to be open and truthful, and not to fake feelings. But here she was, doing it herself. She wasn't looking forward to the wedding at all, and as for the dress, it wasn't to her taste. She liked herself best in darker colours, without all those frills and bows. But she wasn't going to argue about it. She had more important things on her mind. She would reserve her strength for those.

Robert, busy that afternoon over the books, or responding to Mr. Enoch's demands, was living his real life at a deeper level. The fleeting satisfaction he'd ever had at Gertie's hands, was totally insignificant in the light of what had just happened. Edna's reaction to his taking her hand had been a revelation. Now, he knew what he could do with her. He could possess her. Soon, he was sure, she would be all his. He'd always thought she was a beauty, but a cold one. He'd thought she was frigid. How wrong could he be? Now, he knew, he could conjure the passion in her. She'd revealed herself to him, in those few minutes, and she'd never be able to go back. It was up to him, now. She would not refuse him or put him off, and through her, he would get everything he needed.

It was Sunday afternoon. Nothing was moving at Terrilea, except for the water in the fountain. It faltered, picked up again, shot up three feet, then dribbled to a stop.

"What the devil?" Enoch grunted, something had awakened him. He shifted in the basket chair, rearranged the cushion under his head, and determinedly closed his eyes again. But it was no good, the dream had gone. He tried to catch its tattered remnants, something about being asleep in bed, someone coming to his side, he'd been trying to say something but his eyelids and mouth had been glued together. He couldn't speak.

Now he was fully awake, his eyes wide open. Shimmers of blue showed through the branches of the Himalayan cedar tree. He stirred in his chair restlessly. When he was not asleep he didn't like lying about. Normally, on a weekend, he'd be walking round the garden or estate. On a Sunday in between services, he might sit for a while, but usually inside, in his study. All this, the fountain, the terrace, the ornamental gardens, he'd done all this for his family, and yet he, he felt almost as if he were an intruder. When Edna and Matilda were out here together, sipping lemonade or tea, they'd always be welcoming, sure enough, when he joined them. But they would change the conversation, and then one or other of them would rise, smile, then leave..... Women's talk! Well, he could do without that.

Enoch smiled to himself, smoothing his waistcoat and patting his stomach. That girl he'd chosen in that house in London. She'd seemed to appreciate him. She'd wanted to be close; almost too much, the way she'd wound herself round him, from the very first minute. Those Cockneys were different, that was it. He'd liked it anyway. No wonder she'd fancied him. He'd a good mind to make a regular thing of it with that lass. No need for her to be in a place like that. Maybe he could set her up somewhere. Well, that'd have to be looked into, it might be too expensive.

But the way things had been going with Mrs. recently, well something had to be done. He'd fix up with Dennis Goodrich soon for another visit to the Capital.

The fountain gurgled, and with a sudden splash, out came the water again. Enoch watched the drops shining in the sunshine. It was really very pretty. He didn't know anyone else who'd got a fountain like this.

"Papa." There was a light touch on his head and he turned his head upward. Tilly was standing behind him, a book in her hand.

"Are you coming to keep your father company for a while?" he asked. Bless her, he thought she'd have seen enough of him for a while without seeking his company out on a Sunday afternoon. "What's that you've got there?"

"It's about the living conditions of poor people. In London. The author, or should I say authoress, is Octavia Hill. She's spent her life working to improve their housing."

"Sounds dry stuff to me. I thought you ladies liked novels and the like. Besides, that's not something as should concern you. Your work is helping to provide work for them. That's what matters. As long as they've a job, they'll do well enough."

"I know you're right father." Tilly bent down to trickle her fingers in the pool. "These lilies are very fine this year."

"Aye. I fancy George did what I suggested. Re-potted them in cow dung. They liked that."

"Exactly. You gave them better conditions and they've rewarded you by growing better. That's just what I mean."

"What are you trying to say? Speak up. I don't hold with this sermonising. Say what you mean, not with silly stories."

"You're right, father. I try to do that. But it's difficult, sometimes."

"Not with your old father? Come out with it, young lady. What have you in mind?"

"It's this, sir. I've heard that it's Mr. Dudley Shepperton who owns those houses that were burned down."

"Who telled you that?"

"It's common knowledge, father."

"Who was it? I wager it was that young Locksmith."

"Mr. Lockyard, sir. No it wasn't. You know that the new maid, Mavis, came from those houses. It's a distant cousin of Deaker, who lost her house there. That's how I know who is the landlord."

"So that's how we come to have a new maid, all of a sudden."

Tilly was silent for a few moments, watching the fountain, listening to its splashing. The shade from the cedar tree was spreading nearer. Soon the spring afternoon would be over. She could not let this opportunity go. She thought of the tiny dirty houses she had seen, the smoky, dark back yards, the rubbish strewn open land. It was hardly credible that all that existed so near to where she was now sitting. The lives of those people who lived there were so different from her own, yet it was by their labour that she and her family could live like this. She abruptly rose from her chair, and went to the edge of the bank to look out over the stream and the valley beyond. A kestrel was soaring towards the wood. Having hunted all day, it was soon going home to roost.

"Getting a new maid, giving one person a better life, is not enough. We must be involved in improving their conditions generally. We owe them something, Papa. It is up to us to take the lead in this. I am asking you to let me help them."

Enoch stared at her, shaking his head. "I cannot make you out. Where do you get all these ideas from, my wench?"

"You are my father. You are a man of imagination, and purpose. You have seen the way to running a prosperous business. The scheme I have in mind will make you rich in another way." She knelt down beside his chair. "I want you to lend me a little money, Father. Just enough to buy a street of houses."

"A street of houses! You don't know what you're saying."

"They can be bought cheap, at the auctions. People like Dudley Shepperton, they can't be profiting much, with the low rents they charge. They sell them, when they can."

"Now, you are talking sense. He don't make much at all."

"That's why he'll probably build something else, much better, which the people can't afford the rents for. Then they won't be homeless for just a few months. It'll be for ever, father."

"And what would you do? How could you manage if you had the ownership of these old properties? The people in them, they won't be any different, from what Dudley has got. And they're all the same. They'll ruin them, even if they had new ones."

"I want you to read this book, Papa. You'll see how it can be done. Miss Hill has made a great success of it, in London. All sorts of well-known people have asked her to manage their houses, and she's been able to improve the conditions and the people too, even. They get educated, and then they can set up their own businesses, and...." Tilly ceased in mid-flow. "What are you looking at, father?"

Enoch smiled. His irritation at Tilly's words had suddenly evaporated. She was looking so bonny, standing there, with her eyes shining, and her colour rising.

"You're becoming quite the orator." Enoch stretched his legs out and lay back in his chair again. "You should have been a boy, my wench, you know that."

"Father!" Tilly stood up abruptly. "How can you? I'm me. I want to be me. You shouldn't say that."

"Ee, lass, don't take on so." The girl had flared up, he liked to see that, but it wasn't right to answer him like that. "Mind how you speak to your father." He liked the girl to have some spirit, but to contradict her father, well that wouldn't do.

But Tilly would not stop. Her colour had come up and she stood over him. "It's God's choice what I am. I'm a woman. That doesn't mean to say I can only get married and be servant to a man."

"Tch, tch. Let's not bring in 'the Almighty'. It's this world we're talking about, and women's place in it."

"Oh, Father. Really." She wouldn't listen to this homily. "I didn't mean to be rude. I beg your pardon."

"Well, I give it. But mind your tongue. This is just what your Mama said would happen."

"What?" Tilly flared up again.

"You'd get wrong ideas."

Tilly looked down at her father, who now had his eyes shut again. His straw hat was pushed back and his face was pink, with a damp glow of perspiration on his forehead. She gazed at him for a moment holding the book tight in her fingers. He didn't know what he was talking about. He just wasn't conscious of what was going on in the world. He had no idea how the rest of the world was living. This was his world, just this, this house, its artefacts, and and the factory, where all he cared about was how much tableware was fired and sold every week. He had no conception of her mother's life or of hers, what went on in the minds of the people he thought he knew best. For a moment she hated him. She felt like kicking him hard in the shins.

"Will you excuse me Papa? I promised to wake Mama when it was time for tea."

Enoch was evidently still awake. "I'm coming. We'll see if there's a piece of cake."

Tilly did not hold out her hand to him, and he extricated himself from the garden chair as best he could.

"There now," he said, tweaking at the knees of his trousers.

Tilly picked the book up off the grass. It was no use asking him again if he would read it. Would he ever take her plans and ideas seriously? Still, she knew she must try and persevere with him, by whatever means.

Insides, the cool hall, they could make out the faint sound of Edna, practising her scales. “Mama’s doing very well with her lessons, isn’t she Papa? Have you heard her recently?”

“I didn’t know it was lessons - I thought it was called accompaniment,” Enoch paused. “Any road, she is getting better. I can listen to her now, I can.” Tilly said nothing. “Why dinna you keep on with the lessons, if you must call them that. Your voice is worth ten of anyone else round here.”

Tilly shook her head. Obviously, he was trying to be nice to her now. “You’re prejudiced Papa. I have only a moderate singing voice. In any case, I haven’t any interest really. It was only for Mama I did it. But she doesn’t mind anyway.”

Enoch was looking at himself in the hall mirror, smoothing his hair where it had been squashed down under his garden hat. “I dare say you would like to be married, like your mother says. Tell me the truth now.” He turned to face her, where she was sitting, unlacing her outdoor shoes.

“The truth, father.” She pulled off one shoe. “Well, now.” She looked across at him. “I don’t know. That’s the truth. Of course I would. I suppose, one day.”

“But there’s other things in life, that’s what you’re thinking?”

Tilly frowned. “You know what I want to do.”

“I know what you think you want to do.”

Edna came out of the morning room. “Where have you two been?”

“Just talking, Mama, in the garden.”

17

"Only a week now," Tilly said to Ros. They were walking arm in arm down the out-lanes to Epsilon. "And you'll be a blushing bride." She felt sad. It was only Midsummer, but she felt there was something in the air, as if the warm weather was nearly over, and would not return, this year.

"Don't be like that," Ros said. "You know you're being silly. It's not going to be like that at all. You'll be able to come and see me, heaps, if you want."

"Of course, I shall want to. But it won't be the same. He'll be between us. And you'll be too busy. Babies. And the house. Menus - Dinner parties. The Church. Everything." The words left Tilly's lips like plum stones, spat onto the rim of the plate.

"I won't have you talking like that. It's not true." Ros squeezed her friend's arm. "I've told you before."

"I'm a realist, Ros. Whatever else, I know about things."

"Well, I don't envy you then. I don't know about things, but I do believe."

"Yes, I know. You're a dear. It's people like you who make the world go round. You know.... keep on turning. If everyone was like me, we'd all give up before we began. It would all look so impossible."

"I don't know why you're speaking like this."

They had come to a little stream and where the water was shallow they were able to cross on a row of stones. They loosened arms and tip toed across, quickly, Tilly following. In the middle she stopped, looking at the glinting pebbles. Ros, from the bank, watched her friend. Was she really unhappy? Why was she speaking like this? A thought dawned on her. Was Tilly jealous? She spoke more softly. "It's all right, darling. You'll find the right man soon."

Tilly, still standing on the stepping stone, looked at her and shook her head. "Really, Ros. After all I've said. I can't believe it." She continued to gaze at the glimmering water running clear between them.

"Come on, do. We'll be late. It opened at two o'clock." They were on their way to St Donat's fête. Tilly joined her friend and they continued on their way.

They were entering an area of newly built houses, identical terraces of small red brick dwellings. "It's all changing. Have you noticed? These houses are different," Tilly said.

"They're bigger now, and they each have a little front garden."

"Oh, that's better, much better. But other things aren't changing so much. Have you ever looked inside any of the houses in town?"

"No. I haven't. Have you?"

"Of course. I often see through the window when I come home from the Works.. There are some streets we have to go through."

"I don't know why Tom takes you that way."

"I asked him to. It's quicker, and I want to know how the people we employ live. It's not fair, Ros. It just isn't. To see how they live. Some of them have had to sell everything to get enough money to eat. Can you believe? And all of them work, even the children, who should be going to school. Even some of our own workers, they get their own children to come into work, rather than send them to school. I know it's against the law. It's not fair.""

"What is? What is fair, when all is said and done? Nothing is. It wasn't meant to be."

"Some people don't think that. What about the Americans for instance?"

"America! They have got some strange ideas. That's for sure."

"Well, I believe they're right. All men are born equal. And I believe more than that."

"It took them long enough to free their slaves. They didn't think they were equal."

"What do you think our workers are? I sometimes think they're no better off than slaves, if you must know. They don't have any choice how they live their lives."

"Watch out!" Ros put her hand out to guide her friend onto the side of the lane. A large dray was coming behind them, pulled by four horses. It was laden high with bricks. The driver saluted the two young ladies with his whip. The horses were struggling with the load up the slight incline. When it had gone past the girls stopped for a moment looking out over the village spreading in all directions below them. The spires of the two churches, one old, one new, stood up tall amongst the crowded streets.

"You're becoming quite grand here, Til. Soon you won't lack for anything. Churches, town hall, station," Ros went on. "You'll have it all. It's I who'll be envying you.

"It's me who should be envious, Ros. You've got everything, but the best thing is you're happy with what you've got."

"You have got everything."

"Do you think so? The trouble is with me, I see underneath. To you, maybe, and most people, you think this place is bustling, busy, prosperous. So it may be, in some ways. But underneath it all, there's meanness, squalor. There's no freedom here, unless you've got money. And you can't compare conditions here, to Saghead, and other big cities. How can folks be free when they're breathing smoky air? Do you know, when the kiln is first lit, the smoke comes out dark black, and huge pieces of soot in it, the size of saucers. It blows right down over the lanes by the Works, and I've seen the women rush out and take in all the washing. Deaker says even my clothes need washing every day. Can you imagine what it must be like to live there all the time?"

"I suppose the smoke goes up higher, when the fire's drawing properly."

"Of course, like it does in any grate. But even if there's no smoke, they've got no space, even to sit in the sunshine. I went with Mother to the photographer's yesterday. She was asking about us all having our photograph taken. Papa wants it and the man there, he takes other photos, not just portraits. I was looking at some of them. It made me think, really think. You can't believe how those people live, it's really, really horrid. They're human beings like us. But they get these terrible diseases, and it's all from how they live, bad air, and bad water. It's all been in the papers. You must have seen it. I've been reading about the efforts in London that are being made, to give people open spaces to take the fresh air."

Ros said nothing. Sometimes Tilly did go on so. They were getting late, she was sure. Her mind was on other things. "I expect you're right darling Tilly. You really understand all about it. I just stick to what I know myself."

"That's just it. I need to find out more. I really do want to know about it."

There was silence and the two girls marched on. "Do you think it's strange? That I want more knowledge?"

"I don't know. You usually seems to do what you want. But this - well. Anyway, how would you go about it? I don't know how you could do it."

"Maybe I could get more education, go to University." There, she had said it. Now it was out. What had just been first a vague notion somewhere in the back of her mind, deep in her being, now it was in words, it was real. She had a goal in her life. But as soon as she had said it, she doubted if that really was what she wanted. What about the plan about the housing project she had brought up with Papa? What did she want?

"Oxford! How could you? It's only for men."

"Oxford, isn't the only place. What about London University? They take women. It's been open to women for ever such ages."

"I've never heard of anyone going there."

Tilly said nothing. She sometimes wondered how Ros could be so totally incapable of stepping outside her own little world. She herself couldn't name any famous people who had been to London University, but she knew there were women who had been, who were there at the present.

Ros went on. "You'll have to find out all about it. Get all the information Tilly, then ask your father."

Tilly said nothing. Father was considering other things. How could she now say that, she was having different ideas? "I'll race you across the common, Ros," she shouted, picking up her skirt and darting off down the path. In the distance two young children were playing with a hoop, bowling it along with a stick, but long before the girls reached them they were quite out of breath. They walked sedately down the main street.

"He won't be able to come Friday. Willoughby sends his apologies." It was Tuesday. Edna was accompanying Enoch into Saghead, to collect some music. Enoch glanced at his wife as he spoke. She was sitting next to him, but gazing out of the opposite window of the carriage, with her head turned away. He could see the line of her chin, and her neck, but not her expression.

After a moment, she asked, in a low voice." Did he give a reason?"

"Just hoped it wouldn't inconvenience you too much."

"And next week?"

"Well, I expect he'll let us know. If he doesn't want to come, no doubt there's others."

Edna did not reply, but continued to stare out of the window. The carriage was now passing towards the stretch of the road she loved the best. There was a precipice of rock on one side, and on the other a brook running through a grove of trees. Edna had her gloved hands folded on her lap, but the carriage now rushed around the first of a series of bends and she quickly grabbed the strap by the door to retain her balance. Enoch slid against her as the carriage rocked. "Oh." Edna gasped.

"Take care, Tom," he shouted. Tom called out to the horses and reined in.

"How many times have I told him," Enoch said. "Are you all right, my dear?"

"Quite all right," Edna managed to say, in spite of the feelings boiling inside here. Why had Rob cancelled the lesson? It was unbelievable after what had happened in the office only four days ago. Since then she had thought of nothing else but of their next meeting. She had accompanied Enoch this morning so that she could go to the music shop in Firth Street to collect some pieces, which Robert had recommended. Now, what was the point? If he didn't come, she might never pick up her violin again. She would not. She hung on to the strap grimly. Somehow she would have Robert back at Terrilea again. He could not treat her like this. She wouldn't have it. What was he thinking of, suddenly to cancel his appointment?

Tom, cracking his whip, encouraged the horses to pick up speed again, and the road home was straight and broad.

"I'll come in with you to the office before I go on to Ethburstone's for the music. I need to know what is the matter." She said to Enoch.

"That won't be necessary. I should think you needn't trouble yourself. Whatever the man's reason is it can be said to me?"

"Of course, you're right. Say nothing more about it," Edna murmured. She suddenly realised she didn't wish to demean herself by appearing at the office. Perhaps he was ill. "Is his work all right?" she asked.

"Eh. Well he's a good man. I do say. I don't think it's anything to do with his health."

There was silence again. Edna thought of the long day, yawning ahead and the visit to the music shop, a call on Aunt Vera, and then back home to an empty house. Tilly was away staying with Ros, for a few days, before the wedding.

Edna felt herself blaming her whole predicament on Ros, and the wedding. As Saturday this week was booked up with the Manstone family going to Rosalind's wedding and reception, she had asked Rob to come on Friday evening instead. He had promised to come, but in the event he had shied off. Surely, surely, that must be the true and only reason why he was not coming. She gave a deep sigh.

Enoch looked at her enquiringly, but now, she was leaning back against the leather seat with her eyes closed. Her face was blank, yet, in some way, it struck him that she was sad. Her hands were folded, on her lap. He gazed at them, wondering whether to pick one up. But he wouldn't. There was nothing he could do about his wife's moods. They were getting worse - what was the matter? Perhaps it was that time in life. He stared out of the carriage window.

Here, new streets of terrace houses were being built, some on sites formerly occupied by shanty dwellings. The City was steadily engulfing the low hillsides around. Only one hilly ridge remained between Epsilon and the suburbs.

A few minutes later the carriage rolled in through Manstone's gates down the tunnel and into the yard. Enoch got out. "Good bye my dear," he muttered to Edna and hurried up the steps to the office.

"On to Ethburstone's, Madam?" Tom asked and she nodded. As the carriage wheeled through the tunnel she turned her head to glance towards the office window. There was no sign of anyone. The glass was dark and blank. But the feelings she had had when she had come here before came back to her in a rush. She put her hand to her forehead, bending over and hiding her eyes.

"What is it about him?" A strange conviction gripped her. It was love, she felt. Love. She turned the word over in her mind. It was like a crystal ball, glinting. It was a magnet, drawing out her feelings. She recognised it, but at first she could not name it. "It must be that. It is, it is, it must be." She whispered the word. "Love." How else could she have degraded herself like that, in the office? She'd been living with that moment every minute of the day and night since. When she'd knelt to say her prayers, she'd asked forgiveness, for what she knew must be a sin. Her feelings must be obvious to him. To feel like that about a man who was not her husband! Yet she didn't feel it was a sin. She didn't feel she needed forgiveness. Why should her religion say that such a thing was wicked? It seemed to her that through Robert's brief touch, she had become herself. She was snatching something from life, for herself, alone. Not because anyone else expected her to do it, or to enjoy it. Yes, she was in love. Not with a clerk, but a man, a real man, who could make her into a real woman. The question she had been asking for the last two days was answered. The deep ache she had when she glimpsed that empty office window, now engulfed her. She wrapped her arms round herself trying to stop herself shivering. Why, why was Rob not coming on Friday?

At Ethburstone's Edna climbed slowly down from the carriage as Tom put down the step for her. Inside the shop it was warmer, but gloomy.

"Good day, Mrs Manstone. Always such a pleasure." The portly little shopkeeper came hurriedly from behind the counter to bow and bring up a stool."

"I came to collect the music pieces ordered by Mr. Willoughby. Thank you." Edna smiled wanly.

"Not such a nice day, Madam. I dare say you're cold." The little man was opening and shutting drawers behind the counter. "Oh, beg pardon ma'am. They've already been collected. The gentleman himself came in. Just. Not a half-hour ago."

Edna took a few moments to take in what was being said. Evidently that was where Rob was when she had called at the office. He must have been here, while she was there. She had only just missed him. Speechless, she gazed at Mr. Ethburstone. So! She'd missed Robert by seconds. Fate was dealing her a cruel blow. How had she deserved to be so unhappy? Was it punishment already for the feelings she had experienced when Robert had held her hand? Tears began to squeeze through her eyelids. She turned quickly to the door. "Thank you, goodbye," she managed to mutter, as she went towards the carriage. What had she done to merit this horrible deadening pain, right in her midriff?

When she arrived back at Terrilea, the faintness she had felt in the music shop had not left her, and she went straight to bed.

Later that afternoon, Mavis was in the scullery, scrubbing. She had a large bar of yellow soap in her left hand and the bristle brush in the other, applying them alternately to the snowy wooden ridges of the draining board. There came a shout from the courtyard.

"Miss, Miss."

It was a messenger boy, with a parcel for Mrs. Manstone

"Well I never," said Deaker, sending the boy off with two apples and a penny. "I'll mek the tray now. Jeannie, you get on with that ironing. Make the fire up and put the irons to heat. Happen I'll give you a hand later if Missus hasn't anything for me to do. Go on now."

Mavis went on scrubbing. Her legs were aching, and it was hours before bed-time. She thought about her mother and her brothers. She had not seen them for a month. It was all her mother could do, to persuade her to come back to Terrilea, after that visit. But she had to, after all.

A few minutes later Deaker was on her way up the back staircase towards Edna's bedroom. She had the small tray balanced on her right hand and in her left hand she held the parcel in the hem of her skirt.

"Come in." Edna's voice was loud and clear, and when Deaker came she saw her mistress was sitting on the armchair by the bay, wrapped in her dressing gown."

"Now then, don't you be getting cold. You might have stayed in bed till I came with your tea."

"It's all right, I'm better now. I must get dressed. I've plenty to see to, till we go to the wedding on Saturday."

. "There's a parcel for you. Will you have it now?"

"A parcel? Edna looked round to the bed. Sure enough, the brown paper packet was there. "Bring it here, please."

Deaker handed over the packet, which Edna looked at for a minute.

"Oh, of course," she said after a minute. "I think I will get back in bed for a while." She took a cup of tea and put it on the bedside table. She laid the parcel beside. "That will be all, Deaker. I will have another rest."

Deaker went to the door. "Now ring for me if there's anything at all - otherwise I'll wake you at six.

"Yes," Edna said. She climbed back into bed, and heard the door close. Then she sat up again, leaning on one elbow, and gazed at the parcel. She listened for Deaker's footsteps going down the corridor. There was silence, except for the sound of her own heart beating. The packet was from Robert. She had to put off the moment of opening it. Somehow, this seemed to be a moment in her life which she had to live fully, now, and it would last forever. There would be a message, there must be, something about how Robert felt about her, about his plans, about wanting to see her again. She stretched out under the sheets, feeling for the cool corners of the bed with her toes. She folded her arms round, clinging to herself. "Robert, Robert," she kept saying. "Robert, Robert." She reached for the parcel, and put against her breast, under the covers. The string felt scratchy and the sealed knots bore into her flesh. She pressed them against her. Then she took the parcel out of the bed, read the inscription again, then she was kissing it, feeling the smooth paper on her lips.

At last she could wait no longer, she flung herself out of the bed and frantically dragged open the drawers of her dressing table. She snatched a tiny pair of embroidery scissors and began furiously hacking at the tough string. But the scissors were too frail and blunt and she began biting at the string with her teeth. At last it parted and she could tear away the paper

Inside were the music books. She'd known all along that's what was inside. She dropped them, one by one, on the floor. There was no letter. How could there be no letter? It wasn't possible. Where was the letter?

She stood in the middle of the carpet shivering, then sank on her knees, with her head on the floor. "Please God, make there be a letter. Please God, please." She swore that if there was a letter, if by some miracle, a letter appeared, she would burn it at once. "I won't keep it. I won't even read it. Just let there be a letter." She took up the first book again, 'First Sea Songs,' and held it by the spine, shaking it, like a terrier shaking a rat. She waved it around, and leafed through it. There was nothing. She took the next book, 'In the Drawing Room' and did the same. She shook and shook it. Nothing. There was only one more book. Her heart sank. She prayed again. There must be a letter this time. As she picked it up, suddenly she saw his writing. It was a letter but not a loose one. It was written on the flyleaf. It looked like a few lines of a poem. "Oh, God, Oh God." She moaned, tears pouring down her face. Why had he sent a poem, why not a real letter, from him to her, a letter which would tell her why he wasn't coming on Friday and why he had taken the books from Ethburstone's and now, had had them delivered?

Why had he gone to all that trouble?

Suddenly she realised that he had taken all that trouble because he did want to send a message. Perhaps the poem was the message.

She read through the few lines of poetry on the flyleaf.

Take,
This slave of music, for the sake
Of him, who is the slave of thee;
And teach it all the harmony

In which thou canst, and only thou,
Make the delighted spirit glow.

She read through the lines again. "Him who is the slave of thee." She got back into bed again, with the book pressed against her cheek. She recognised the lines of verse, of course. It was from a poem by Shelley. How strange, that Robert had found this to say to her. It was beautiful, beautiful. But somehow, she wished it hadn't been poetry, she wished, she had written just an ordinary note. And not in the book. She fell back onto the bed, her head buried in the pillow. "Him who is slave of thee..... him who is slave of thee," she kept repeating the line to herself. If only, if only, he had sent a letter. She grabbed the book again. There it was, his handwriting, strong, definite. She kissed the page. It must be love, it must.

It was half-past seven before the Manstones returned home after Ros' Wedding reception.

"I shall go straight to my room, Enoch," Edna said.

"Will you excuse me too, father? I wish to change." In fact, Tilly couldn't wait to step out of her bridesmaid dress which was becoming uncomfortable.

"I'll ring for Jeannie to help you, "Edna said. "Then she may come to me."

"Mama, I heard you telling Deaker that she could go to her sister, and that Jeannie should have the afternoon off. You thought we would not be home till nine o'clock."

"Did I indeed?" Edna passed her hand over her forehead. "Why was she becoming so forgetful. "I did. Then we'll have to help each other. Come up with me." After all the excitement, she had a headache. She hadn't slept well either, and all through the wedding ceremony, and the reception, she'd had the strange feeling that she wasn't really there, she was watching it all, like a bird, perhaps a canary. There it was, all going on, but it was meaningless. She had been dreading it, especially all the remarks which she knew would be directed to her, about the bride's appearance, and how it would soon be Tilly's turn. Now, she'd found that none of that was of the least importance. She was totally concerned with matters of her own, her own marriage, and her feelings towards Robert.

"Good night, Papa." Tilly knew that she could not face talking to her Papa, alone, in the condition he was in. As usual, after drinking champagne, he was irritable, and then, somnolent. Well, he would have to cope on his own. Sometimes, when she would have liked to talk to him, he hadn't been there. Now, the position was reversed.

Both ladies glided up the staircase.

"I suppose I must manage as best I can, then," Enoch grumbled. With none of the servants about, whom could he send for his whisky, and fresh logs?

He went into his study. There was no fire lit and it seemed cold and uncomfortable. He sat down in his usual armchair, took up the morning's paper, and almost immediately, he was asleep.

Half an hour later, there came a knock on the door. Enoch woke with a start.

"Who is it? Come in."

In came Mavis, with the log basket.

"Beg pardon, sir. I was told by Mrs. Deaker to make sure your fire was lit."

"Fire? Lit?" Enoch struggled to recognise the small figure in black who was standing by his chair. "What are you doing here?"

Mavis was silent, and transferred the log basket from her head, to the floor.

"Come to see me, have you?" He stretched out his leg, to bar her way to the fireplace.

She went round the back of the chair. As she came beside him, he reached out his hand and grabbed her arm. "Since you've come, you're welcome."

"Oh, sir!" Mavis tried to pull away. Before she had time to struggle, he half rose, put his other arm round her waist, and fell back into the chair, with her on top of him.

"Ride a cock horse, would you? That's it, that's it."

Enoch's knee began vigorously pumping up and down.

"Oh sir, leave me be, please sir...." The girl tried to squirm away. As she wriggled, Enoch grasped her more tightly.

"Now, then," he breathed hoarsely into her ear. "Don't be taking on so, that won't do, that'll make me want you even more, hold still, you!"

"Please sir, please, let me be." She could smell his breath, hot and fumy, and felt his beard against her neck. His arms were round her shoulders, his two thighs holding her leg fast. She felt a wet warmth spreading under her skirt. She put her hands against his shoulders, and pushed.

..... The more she pushed, the tighter Enoch held her. He had her skirt up, over their heads. Thus, he could not see her naked bottom, but he grabbed it, pulling it towards him, struggling at the same time, with his trousers. "I'll have thee, I'll fucking have thee, I will do," he gasped. In a moment, with a terrific exertion by himself, he had her on the floor. He forced her legs apart.

Mavis' eyes were tightly shut. Of course, she knew what was happening, what had happened, although, for her, it was the first time.

She gave one scream, then it was over. It had all been so sudden, and unexpected. Her tears were flowing, but her pain was not too great. She had struggled away, at last, as Enoch relaxed and was huddled on the floor. Quietly, she sobbed. She gazed at him. He was breathing heavily, with his eyes closed. She clutched at her knees. She had stopped shaking, except for the occasional shudder, and her tears were drying. She knew she would be able to bear it, she would not die.

Enoch turned on his back. A huge wave of relief came over him. That would do. And he would make it worthwhile for the child. A moment of remorse came. She was only a child. Had he hurt her? He stretched out his hand to touch her back.

"Art thou reet?"

Mavis shrank away from him.

"Dunna be a baby. Tha knowest it's for the best. I sall look after thee now." He sat up, and took her face in his hand. "Tha'rt a pretty wench, if thou hadst new clothes, tha would be. Wouldst like a new dress?"

Mavis had her eyes covered, and the tears were coming again.. He began stroking her hair. "I'll see thee all reet now. Dinna you fret, tha sall be all reet. Thou sall not be lonely no more."

Gradually her tears stopped again. She stayed perfectly still, a few inches away from him, on the carpet. She hardly breathed, she felt anything might set him off again.

At last Enoch said, "Get the fire lit, else we'll both starve of cold."

Slowly, she bent forward, so her knees were under her, and and knelt by the grate. She fumbled with paper and sticks, long deep shivers occasionally affecting her. When the fire had taken, she stood up, reaching for the log basket.

"Go and get my whisky now. Didna' Deaker tell thee that? Where are they, any road?"

She could not answer, the words would not come.

"Wait." Enoch was fumbling in his watch pocket. Out of it he produced a half crown. "Put that in your money box, and you shall have another to add to it, if you hold your tongue, and be a good girl."

With her head turned away, she took the coin from him, and slipped out of the door. In the hall, it was cool. She leaned against the back of the door, drawing deep breaths. She looked up to the belvedere, far above. The bedroom doors opened off the landing, up there. Had anyone heard anything? She began to cry again. Why wasn't her mother here, or her brothers? No-one had heard anything. She was all alone, no-one cared about what had happened to her. They didn't know it, and they wouldn't believe her. If Jeannie had been here, it wouldn't have happened. Jeannie wouldn't have let the man do that to her. Now, if she told her, Jeannie would just say it was her own fault, letting him taking advantage. But what could she have done. Jeannie was so big, and strong, she would have known just what to do. She would have turned on him, with her nails.

From this thought, Mavis received some strength. Sometime, that man would have his punishment. Somebody would serve him what he deserved. Like a shadow, creeping along the wall, she went upstairs, to the bedroom she shared with Jeannie. For a moment, she looked out of the window. She had to get away, before anyone should come back, before he came searching for her. She went to the door and listened. Everything was quiet. She must hurry. From under the bed, she dragged her carpet bag, and bundled in her few things. She took a drink from the jug on the washstand, and, wetting a rag, she rubbed her face. She scrubbed her fingers, with their bitten nails, and dirty from the coal. The rest of the water, she put into the bowl, and squatted over it, to wash. How could she ever feel clean again? With the half-crown clutched in her pocket, she ran out into the yard.

Behind her, the moon was rising, and, under the trees along the driveway, it was already dusk. An owl was hooting. Mavis wrapped her shawl more tightly round her. As she hastened along, each step seemed to jolt more tears out of her. It wasn't until she was on the train, going to Saghead, that she managed to calm down. Mother would know what to do, she would help her. If only she had never left home. How she had missed them. At least now, she would be with them again. She pressed her face against the glass, looking out for the first sight of bottle kilns.

18

The day after Ros' wedding, it seemed as if summer was over. By the Monday the bad weather had really arrived. A strong wind was lashing scuds of rain across the window panes in the office. Tilly couldn't settle to her work, and kept looking out through the streaming glass, picturing what was happening at Ros' home. The workmen would be taking down the marquee if it hadn't already blown away. The servants would be busy packing up the extra china and cutlery. No doubt all the children would be back at their lessons, all their wedding finery safely stored away, next to be worn, possibly, at winter parties. And what about Ros? She was due to have taken the boat to Ostend today, then on to Brussels and Germany for the marriage journey. Surely, the boat would not be sailing in this weather. She'd be spending an extra day in the little hotel, with her new husband. Tilly nibbled the top of her pen trying to concentrate her mind on her work.

Enoch was sitting at his desk, going through some letters.

"I'll be away next week, for three days. You and Willoughby will be in charge, like before," he announced.

"Will you be going to London again, father?"

"Yes, I wish to see someone about our operation in New York"

Tilly's heart sank. How could her father take any interest in her own hopes and plans if his mind was continually occupied with the business in faraway places? She went on with her work of totalling cash entries for the last month. Her mind turned again to Ros in Dover. She thought about the hotel, the maids serving tea in bed. Would Ros be embarrassed the first time a strange servant saw her in bed, a married woman with a husband? She couldn't imagine how that would feel. But no doubt there was some kind of magic which changed you, when you got married, so you wouldn't be shy. Or perhaps you just lay down in the bed, and covered your head with the sheet and pretended not to be there. Ros certainly wouldn't do that. She'd sit up in bed and show off her frilly nightie. Nothing would make her shy, she'd be too proud and happy in her new situation. It wasn't fair. Without a husband, Tilly would probably never ever go on the channel ferry. Why, she'd never visited anywhere further afield than Chester! Oh, the excitement Ros was having! Tilly looked gloomily out of the window.

"Father?"

"What is it?"

"Could I….."

"Could you what?"

"Would you..... would you take me on one of your business trips? I could help you such a lot. And I'd learn from it too. About the business, I mean."

"Go to London! And who'd manage here while I'm away. I need you here my girl. You know that."

"You could trust Robert Willoughby, Sir."

"Oh. I know that. But there's such a thing as trusting someone too much, you know. He's got the know-how, he has. But you, well you're family, that's right, isn't it?"

Tilly didn't reply. She was too disappointed to speak. She had had plans to write to Octavia Hill, and ask for an interview. She bent again to her work. Enoch looked across at her. "Happen you're a bit put out, are you, Miss?"

"No. Well, yes I am, a little. But I want to do what's best for you and the business too. I need to learn about the outside world too."

"Tell you what. Next time I go, I'll make arrangements for you too."

Tilly looked up, her eyes shining. "And mother too? Could we stay?

"Well, I don't know. It'd have to be a posher place than my usual. You wouldn't be wanting to live near Kings Cross Station. Happen we'd have to go Bloomsbury way."

Tilly jumped up and put her arms round her father's neck. "That would be marvellous, Papa. If we were in Bloomsbury we'd be near University College. I've always wanted to look at that.

"University College! Well, I don't know."

"And the British Museum. That's near there too, father. We could see the Roman remains and the Greek frieze from Athens. Oh. I'd love that father. So would Mama."

Enoch smiled. "Where've you been finding out all this? From your magazines I'll be bound."

It was true. Tilly had been reading the "Family Leisure Hours" since she was a young girl, and most of her knowledge was gleaned from the stories and articles in it.

Enoch went on, "So if business still goes on as it is, and everything all right here, maybe I will take your mother for a spell down to London. Do you think she'd like that?" His tone was dubious, slightly wistful.

"Of course she would, father. She'd love it."

"I dunna think she's herself at the moment, my wench. What dost think?" He felt he could hardly voice his concern but the words had to be spoken.

"You mean, because she has headaches sometimes?"

"That and other things besides. Do you think she's not well?"

“I think she’s very well, father, but life isn’t the same now. She hasn’t so much to do. Perhaps, she’s a little bored. She would like to have something to plan for, like Ros’ mother did. With all the excitement, you know.”

“Well, happen you’ll give her cause?” Enoch laughed.

“Not for a very long time father.” Tilly sat down again at her desk. This wasn’t the time to approach him again, about the housing plan. She knew he’d be disappointed, even angry, if she knew now, without doubt, that she didn’t want to spend her life running Manstones, even as a very junior partner. She disagreed with so many things, yet she couldn’t see how they could be changed. There might be ways of changing, if she understood more. Knowledge was the key to it. Without knowledge she just felt like a stick being hurled along on the flood tide of a torrent, powerless to choose her own direction. Of course, she had gathered some information from Mr. Lockyard, at her brief meetings with him. One day, they would meet again. Ros hadn’t been any help in making her define her plans. Ros wouldn’t see why Tilly should choose anything else than marriage for her future.

“I’m off now to see about those engravings,” Enoch said, rising from his desk. “I won’t be too long. Then we may go home together.

“Yes, father.” Tilly continued casting up the figures, able to concentrate at last. Outside, the rain was ceasing. The sky was clearing. If she had looked she would have seen a break in the clouds. But her head was bent over the ledger and her lips moved as she mouthed the numbers “One and sixpence, two and ten, five shillings, seven and three, ten shillings nine plus seventeen and two pence, carry a pound.”

Tilly felt stiff, after crouching for so long, at her desk. She glanced at the clock. It was more than half-an-hour since Enoch had gone out. If he didn’t return soon, they would be too late for the next train. She yawned and stretched and went to the window. There was the usual bustle going on in the yard. The glost kiln was being stacked, and men were hurrying hither and thither with tall columns of baskets on their heads, containing biscuit ware which was to be fired. The complicated task of actually filling the kiln was just out of Tilly’s field of vision. She decided to go and have a look, nearer to the centre of action. Just as she arrived at the foot of the wooden steps, a sharp squall blew her skirts in all directions. She took shelter in the doorway into the fettling shop, standing with her back to the women workers within. As she stood there, she heard one of them say

“Here ‘e comes now, Jan, don’t forget what we said. It do get ‘im put about.” There was a piercing squawk of laughter, and Tilly turned to see what was happening.

At that moment, a lad of about nineteen was coming through the doorway at the end of the shop. Balanced on his head was a long board, resting on a rolled-up sock. On the board itself was a row of pots, being brought in for the fettlers to see to. As the lad came through the doorway, he skilfully turned his head, then manoeuvred the whole load through the gap, without hesitating. By this time, his hands were occupied above his head, managing the board, to put it down near the table where the women were sitting, in a long row. As Tilly was admiring this complicated piece of adroitness, the woman opposite to the youth suddenly reached forward, and seized his trousers. In a moment, she had undone the front flies, and put her hands, copiously smeared with clay, inside. Then she was rubbing her fingers, and working them as if she was kneading bread. The boy shouted, nearly dropped the board, and backed away. The women all yelled with laughter, and Tilly caught a glimpse, for less than a second, of what the young man considered to be his prize possession, and what seemed to her to be curious kind of animal, with a long pink nose, and ginger fur, crouching between his legs.

At once, Tilly backed out of the fettlers shop.

"Tha shall have to have a proper wash for once," one of the women was shrieking.

"Go and clean thee in the yard, and tell the Maister what tha'rt doing with all that clay. Good clay that was, now it's all wasted."

The women went on jeering and shouting. Tilly hurried back up the stairs. The rain storm was coming in fiercely, but there was no chance of lingering.. As Tilly rushed back up the stairs, she got thoroughly wet. She could not look at Robert as she fled back into the safety of the inner office.

By the time she recovered her composure, Tilly had decided that she would not tell anyone what had happened. She felt sorry for the young man, those women seemed cruel to her. But she also felt sorry for them too, if their lives were so bleak that they could only think of horrid tricks to play, to make their lives more cheerful. But what was uppermost in her mind, was the vision of that strange growth, on the man's body. Were all men like that? Once again, she was aware that she didn't know anything at all, about the real world. How would she ever get this knowledge? And would she like it, when she got it?

A few days later, Enoch saw the salesman, Goodrich, in the office. He arranged to go down to London the following week.

"Same as last time, Mr Manstone?" Goodrich asked him.

"If your good wife can arrange it."

"And the other?"

Enoch took his watch out of his waistcoat pocket. "Of course," he said. It was ten to five. He'd better not stop late this evening. He had to get home early and see Edna. He'd have to put in an appearance and get it over with, sooner or later. She'd have to know about him going to London again.

"Yes, indeed. Now good bye."

"I'll meet the 10.30, as before, Sir."

"Very good." Enoch stood up as the salesman left and reached down his hat and coat.

"I'm going now, Willoughby," he said. "Mind you go through those bills of lading, I'm still not happy about that invoice from Curruthers."

Robert was sitting at his desk as usual, in the outer office. "I'll be here till locking-up, Mr Manstone."

"Good lad." Enoch hesitated by the outer door. "Missus say anymore to you about arrangements for the violin practice? It'd be a pity to give it up, now she's just started. Best come as usual this week unless she has other arrangements.

"I will do that, Sir, I just assumed she'd want to continue."

"Well, of course last week was different with all the shenanigans. Back to normal now."

"Yes, Sir." Rob opened the door, for his master and shut it gently behind him. He went into the inner office, threw all the rest of the coal on the fire and stood there rubbing his hands together. The fresh coals on top of the embers began to hiss and gave off a yellowish sulphury smoke. Robert began to cough a little, and sank down on his haunches seizing the poker to beat the coals into a better shape. The smoke lessened.

Silly old man, Enoch Marstone. Pathetic really. What was he trying to do? Was he so sure of his wife he could just throw her together with a young man and not be worried of the consequences? What in heaven's name did he think would happen? After all Edna wasn't old herself. By no means. 35 years old at the most, he reckoned. And he was 29. She was still a fine woman, and young looking for her age. Happen because she'd only ever had the one child. Perhaps Enoch thought she was past all that. But she wasn't, was she? No. She was a fine woman, indeed. Maybe Enoch didn't think of him as a man, certainly not as a rival. Why, he was only a clerk.

Probably to Enoch, Rob just appeared as a member of some other species.

Rubbing his hands and sitting on his haunches, Rob began to feel excited. The ensuing conflict with Enoch had had that effect. If he could get Gertie in here now with him, what a time they would have. But she was the same as all women, she'd cling to him and say she loved him, but what did she want really? A meal ticket, someone to look after her and the old lady. She'd never consent to anything but marriage, he couldn't get beyond that. Why hadn't he broken with her, ages ago? Well, he would, that was definite. Rob stood up. His mind was made up. There would be no more shilly-shallying. He'd go for the mistress, dear Missus Edna, for all he was worth. She could be roused, that one, it was obvious after what had happened between them. He'd get something out of it, that was for sure. She was a fine woman, and he'd have her.

He decided not to waste the fire, he'd bring his work into the inner office and use Enoch's desk. As he was rubbing his feet, he heard the clatter of feet outside on the steps, the outer door opened and the next moment, in came Enoch.

"There you are Rob. Forgot my parcel," Enoch said, panting heavily. "Shall miss the train now." He grabbed a small brown paper packet which was on the desk. "What a fire you've got there. Did you go and use all the coal up?" he shouted, turning to rush back through the door. Robert had no time to say anything as his master blundered back out of the office.

Stupid old fool, he thought. Worrying about a few coals. When he should have been keeping an eye on his wife. He gazed out of the window in the outer office. There was Enoch, rushing across the yard, with the little parcel in his hand. No doubt that was some little gift for Edna. A piece of seconds, most likely to put on her mantelpiece. But she wouldn't be worrying about ornaments and such like things. She'd be too busy with higher things, he'd see to that. He'd waken her up, he would, to what really mattered.

When Robert next came, Edna was cutting roses, from the bushes near the window. She saw him enter the room, and put his books down on the piano lid. Jeannie had opened the door for him, and as she left, she smiled and bobbed. Robert smiled back and nodded. Edna felt a wave of stony displeasure, to see this exchange. She resolutely snipped a few more buds, before turning to go into the house. She met Jeannie as she came to give her word that Robert was there.

"I know Mr. Willoughby is here. I saw you show him in."

Jeannie sensed a reprimand in her voice. "Yes, ma'am. I were just coming to get you."

Edna swept into the morning room.

"That'll be all. Put these in water." She put the thorny bundle into Jeannie's hands, removed her own gloves and held out her hand to Robert.

"Mr. Willoughby," she said. "What have you got for me today?"

He took her hand, and bowed slightly. "Good morning, Ma'am."

Jeannie, negotiating with the flowers, gloves, and Edna's scarf, retreated through the door. As soon as her footsteps had died away, Robert came up close.

"May I?" Without waiting for an answer, he took her hand again, and kissed it, first on the fingertips, then, up her hand to her wrist. "There." He smiled." When I saw you come in with those roses, I thought you were more lovely than ever."

Edna's head was bowed. "Thank you for the books. I went to collect them. But you'd already been there." The anguish of her disappointment that day, came back to her.

"Did you not read the poem?"

"I did."

"Well, what did I say? Don't you believe it?"

Edna turned away. "I don't know. I don't know what to think. It's so sudden. Besides...."

"Besides?"

"I wish you'd written a letter."

"What's better than Shelley? Aren't you satisfied?"

"Yes, yes. Of course."

Very softly, Robert said, "I can show you how I feel. Let me." He came closer, and took her waist with both hands. She was so little, and he, so tall. She stood there, head averted. He put his hand on her cheek, It was soft, very soft. He let his hand rest there. Her body was rigid, she was hardly breathing. He closed his palm over her lips. Gently he turned her face towards him. "There, there," he murmured. As if it was being pulled by an invisible wire, her own hand came up, to touch his fingers. She settled herself against him, her thigh against his.

So, they stood together, for a moment.

Robert moved his hands to her shoulders. He could feel her bones beneath the silk. He put his mouth down, to her neck, the little hollow, which was just available, above her collar. His tongue came out, into the dip. "There, there"

The feeling was beginning, rising from the base of her spine

"Do you want me to make you happy, happier than you have ever been? I can do it for you." Robert's voice was coming to her, from a long way off.

"Can you? Can you?" she murmured.

"I can." His grip on her shoulders tightened, he could feel the plumpness of her upper arms, then her elbows, and her lower arms. Suddenly, he let go and turned away.

"Yes. I will."

"Trust me. He's going away again." Robert repeated.

"Going away again! He's told me nothing."

"Well, he's told me. He was arranging with Mr Goodrich. It'll be next week."

"I can't believe it." Edna felt a pang, was it anxiety or anticipation? "Are you sure?"

"Certain. I'll get a message to you." He moved his music off the piano, and opened the lid. "Now," he said. "We shall have some music. I shall play for you. Do nothing. Just stand there, where I can see you."

Slowly, she moved towards the piano, to stand in its curve. "Here?"

He gazed at her. "Yes." He began to play.

Edna was content to stand, where he told her.

After a while, Robert asked, "Where's that old woman, this afternoon? And the other, the maid?"

"They're about. Somewhere. Deaker won't be going far if she knows you're here."

"I'll be bound she won't. She looks after you well, doesn't she? She's more like your auntie than your maid."

"I suppose she is. She brought me up you see, and Matilda." Edna had hesitated before mentioning her daughter's name. She didn't want to do that.

"Where is she? The young one?"

"Oh she's upstairs."

"Cannot you send them out somewhere? Next week. That way, we won't need to worry."

"I'll try. It's very difficult."

"You're the Mistress, aren't you? Just do it. Do it."

"I'll try. I will." Edna's legs felt weak

"Next week. He'll be going next week. That's the time."

"All right. I will do it." There was silence. Edna suddenly felt a burden. How could she manage all this? Her life seemed so complicated. But she would do it, she must. She couldn't imagine going back to the old state of affairs. She was troubled for only a moment. God would help her find a way. Then she gasped, and her heart raced. Of course, she could not ask God. Already she'd desisted from prayers. How could she kneel and ask for strength? She didn't want the kind of strength which God would send. She wanted her own strength, coming from herself, to be herself. She could not pray. For the first time in her life, she could not pray. She stood looking out of the window. There were birds flying round the tree tops over in the wood. They were rooks, looking for a roost for the night. They soared and banked, hardly moving their wings. They had the freedom of the air. She would be as free as them, following her nature. "I will do it," she said, turning towards Rob.

"Would you like to play a little?"

"I must."

Edna took her violin from the case, tightened the bowstring and went to stand by the piano.

She had not played two lines, when Tilly came. “Oh,” she said and stopped. There was something about the sight of her mother that made her feel she was intruding.

“Come in, Matilda, you can join me. I’m sure Mr Willoughby won’t mind if we recommence.”

“A pleasure,” Robert said.

They played two songs, and Tilly sang. Then Robert looked at his watch.

“Is it time to go?” Tilly asked.

“It’s nearly four o’clock, Miss.”

“I shan’t be requiring you next week, Mr Willoughby,” Edna said in a low voice. “Saturday is inconvenient, I’ll let you know.”

Robert bowed and went out.

“Why did you say that Mama?” Tilly asked, as soon as the door shut. “That’s the second time. He’ll think you’re not to continue.”

“I don’t know that I can. I haven’t decided yet,” Edna said. “I shall see. She put the violin back in the case, gently dusting off the resin, with a flick of her duster. “Now then, shall we walk up and see the new calves?”

They put on their outdoor boots and walked up the gravel path which went round the orchard. It had been raked that morning by Tom, but even so, the first few leaves falling had made it look untidy.

Tilly dragged her feet enjoying the rustle. Soon would be the season of bonfires. How she savoured the smell of wood smoke, curling up through the damp air. Why had mother cancelled her appointment with Willoughby and why had she sounded so cross? Tilly glanced at Edna’s face and was surprised to see her lips were slightly parted. She was almost smiling. “I should think Mr Willoughby will wonder what to expect next, Mama,” Tilly suddenly blurted out. “It isn’t as if there’s anything special on next week.”

“Oh, isn’t there? Edna said. Then pressed her lips.

“Well is there?”

“Apparently your father is going away again. He hasn’t told me in so many words.”

Tilly was silenced. How had Mama found that out? Evidently Papa must have told her before he even mentioned it to Willoughby. He certainly hadn’t mentioned it in the office. Well, she didn’t care. She’d enjoyed it the last time she’d been left in charge. But then she remembered something else, her plans for the autumn. Tilly had a vague sense that she was already entered on a path onto which there were no turnings. And she must hurry along it, if she were to initiate change, this year. Her father had promised to take her, some time, to London and also she must talk to him again about her idea of managing some houses for him. She was sure she could do that. It would be her own, her very own project. But it must all be sooner, rather than later.

They'd reached the kissing gate into the field. Tilly held the gate open while her mother squeezed through, first one way, then the other. In the field the turf was damp, and here and there little white blobs were sprinkled about.

"Puff balls," Tilly said.

"I'm surprised Tom hasn't been up here."

"Shall we get them, Mama?"

"What in, we've no trug?

"I could use my scarf." Tilly had a silk scarf round her neck. Without waiting for instructions. She had it off, knotted the corners to make a bag, and proceeded to pick the fungi into it

"What will Deaker say when she sees that. I don't know. You're just a child still in some ways." Edna looked on. She couldn't help but be pleased as she watched Tilly stooping and bending, darting from one clump of fungi to the next and filling the make-shift bag.

"Anyway, I'll brush the earth off. She won't know. I think we worry too much about what she thinks."

Tilly was right, Edna decided. Deaker could reprimand as much as she liked about mushrooms and scarves. She had no idea at all about what was happening. And whatever Deaker was to say, there was nothing to be done about it. Edna was aching, aching everywhere, in every bit of her body. And what could she do? Nothing. Nor would she. She had to see this through. She felt as if she was living at second hand. Again, it was as if she was looking on, at what she was doing. Talking, walking up the path with Tilly, squeezing through the gate, all that was being done by someone else. The real person, the real being inside her, knew only one reality and that was a desire for Robert.

They came to the barn-yard and went through the gate, across the brick paving to one of the low stone byres where a cow was standing nosing through a hay manger. In the corner, on a large pile of fresh straw, was a small calf, its brown eyes alert at the sound and smell of strangers. The cow gave a gentle low and turned to nuzzle the calf, whose ears twitched.

Tilly put her hand over the half door. "Come on then, girlie, come on," she whispered clucking softly with her tongue. Together the two women gazed at the baby animal. "He is lovely, isn't he, Mama? He's beautiful."

"Yes." Edna said. Her anxiety was suddenly forgotten, in contemplating the animals. And yet, no sooner had the pain of separation from Robert, and dread for the future evaporated, like dew in the sunshine, than it returned, more forcefully than ever. What was she doing, what had she done, what would happen next? She'd actually welcomed the news that Enoch was to be away next week. It would give her a chance to be with Robert. She was already laying plans, that was why she had cancelled his lesson, in the knowledge that Tilly had taken note that the lesson was cancelled. But of course she would see him, oh yes, and she'd make sure no one else was about. It would all be so easy. As she stood in the old barn, her mind was working, working. At the end of the row of byres, entered by a separate door, was the hay store. Once the cattle had been fed, no one would go there.

The calf had struggled to its legs to suckle and the cow stood patiently enough. Animals, thought Tilly, they just lived naturally. There was no pretence, no covering up, no hiding. Why couldn't humans be more like that?

"Mama, did you ever wish to do something quite different, which no-one expects you to do." Tilly said. She hadn't known she was going to say this. She'd just said it. She rested her chin on her arm as she leaned against the high gate. There was a warm, sweet smell coming up from the animals. A bird was singing loudly in the hawthorn tree which shaded the big stone trough in the corner of the yard. She turned her head to see what bird it was and, as if showing off, it flew out of the foliage and perched on the half door of the next door byre. It was a robin, its breast swelling as it began to sing again.

Both women stood stock still, watching the bird. It cocked its head, eyeing them boldly.

Edna put her hand on Tilly's arm which she held for a while, gazing at her daughter. At last, she smiled. "You must do what you wish, I would not stop you. I didn't wish you to go into the business but you would do so. Do you now wish to leave it? I do not know what your father will say, but no doubt you've already consulted him?"

"I don't exactly know what I wish to do. But, yes. It may be that I shall wish to leave the business. I find him so busy, I can hardly speak to him." Tilly was amazed that her mother had guessed her thoughts.

"You are a grown woman now, but not of age of course. Whatever you do, you will have to get your father's consent."

"Yes. I will need his support too. Will you speak to him, Mama?"

"How much does he know? Have you already asked him?"
She gripped her daughter's wrist, then turned the hand over. "Your father's hands," she continued. "I do not think you have much of me in you."

"Oh, Mama. I do. I hope I do." Tilly turned her head, smiling, up to Edna. "It's just something I really want. I don't want to leave you, I don't, but there are things I need to do."

"Do you mean to have a training? Will you be a teacher?"

"Perhaps, Mama. But I want to learn, first. Not for what I will be, it's because of what I am. I want to learn, and to help. Why the world is what is it, what it should be even."

"What do you mean, what it should be?"

"Since I've been working, I've seen things, Mama, which you wouldn't believe. About the people who work at the business. They're so poor, some of them, and they work so hard, and the children too, and yet they are so poor. You know, really, really poor and unhealthy too. They haven't much to be happy about, or laugh about."

There was silence. The robin had fluttered off. The cow was standing motionless with her head lowered over the calf.

Edna shivered and turned to go. "You must do as you will. But first you must decide what you really truly want. I'm not sure that you know yet, what that is." Do people ever know, she wondered.

"But will you speak to Papa for me, please." As she said this Tilly thought that she would have a better chance of getting her way with Enoch, than would Edna. She suddenly saw her parents' relationship as a hollow, brittle thing, which might shatter with too much talking. "Will you, Mama?"

"I'll see. When you tell me exactly what it is. But I'm not sure it will make much difference what I say." Edna's voice was low, almost as if she didn't want what she said to be heard. She knew she would have no success with Enoch. If he didn't want something to happen, it wouldn't happen, however much she tried. And by the same token, what he did want, would happen, in spite of her. She didn't want to think about Tilly and her little plans and schemes. Her own path was set. That was all that now mattered.

They walked back along the gravel path over the young trees in the orchard the sun was now setting, sending red streaks over long, thin clouds.

In the yard, George was standing just inside the door of the wood store. He had the wooden saw bench in the threshold and was cutting up logs, which lay in a pile, waiting to be split. .

"Evening, Ma'am, evening Miss." He stopped sawing for a moment to touch his cap. For an old man he was very muscular and fit.

"It's very fine, but autumn will soon be here," Edna said. "We'll soon be needing those." She smiled and went on.

Tilly stayed for a few minutes in the drawing room. The gas lights over the fireplace had been lit, and the fire was burning. She warmed her fingers by the blaze. Why had her mother seemed so abstracted? She didn't seem to be bothered, one way or the other. But one thing was certain. Something would have to happen quickly. Autumn was nearly upon them. There must be some decision made soon, surely, about what was to happen about the site of the fire. She felt as if the vultures were gathering, to pick her hopes and plans to pieces.

Tilly yawned and became aware of an unpleasant sensation in her stomach. How could she organise her life, and set off on her quest? Who would give her some advice, sensible advice?

Enoch left as planned, for his trip to London, and on the second day of his absence, Edna was in the garden. She held a deep red petal to her nose.

This rose had a particular scent which, she realised with a pang, would remind her, all her life, of this moment. There were several, hanging down within the trellis arbour, at the end of the rose garden. In the last eight years, these bushes had matured, and new varieties had been added. Enoch had had the garden laid down for her on the occasion of her twenty eighth birthday, two months before Tilly was ten years old - Edna standing there, sniffing the bloom above her, was aware of what the garden meant. How pleased she had been when Enoch had first shown it to her! He'd had hurdles put all round it, while the gardeners had been busy laying out the beds and planting up. On her birthday, all the hurdles had been removed, and she was led in, to this very arbour, to this very seat, to admire and savour the delicious scent. She had often come in here over the years, during hot days in the summer, to be out of the sun. She would read here, or paint the flowers. It was her favourite place.

Today, she would meet Robert here. It was fitting she had come out here stealthily, although she knew no one was about. She sat down, facing up the path to the little cupid on a plinth, near the house. She had a tartan rug under her arm, and she put it carefully on the stone seat.

It was quiet, apart from the hum of a bee, which was doggedly buzzing from rose to rose, sipping, sipping the nectar. Then came the sound of a cock crowing. His arrogant voice blared out from the chicken run, beyond the walled garden. Otherwise, nothing. It seemed as if she was the only person alive in the whole world. How alive she felt. The warm sensation in her belly was spreading again, gently pervading all her limbs. She recognised it. The blood was beginning to pound in her ears.

"Where are you, where are you?" She whispered to herself, gripping the edge of the marble seat, so her knuckles showed white. Wasn't he coming? Didn't he have her message? She gazed over to the left, then the right. There was no sign of anyone. Even the birds seemed to be hiding. She closed her eyes, and took a deep breath, then another. She began to count. She would wait until she had counted up to a hundred before she would look again. Suddenly she smelt something.

She opened her eyes immediately. There he was, coming across the grass towards her. She had known he was there.

She remained completely motionless on the seat. He was standing in front of her, and took both her hands. "There you are." He pulled her up. His cool cheek, and the soft hairs of his moustache were against her skin. They were kissing. He had her mouth in his, she was completely enfolded by him, his arms round her, his head bearing hers downwards.

"That's it, that's it now." He was gripping her shoulders.

"I knew you were there; it was as if.............the air became more solid. I'd have known it was you if I was blind." The warmth of his body burned hers. She was tingling all over. "I had my eyes shut, but with my inner eye, I knew you were there."

"I can play your fiddle now, can't I?" He stroked her cheeks and hair and ran his fingers over her mouth. Her lips opened, "Yes, that's right." He kissed her again. Now they were in the arbour. He had her on his knees. His hand was on her left breast. She pressed towards him so that both her breasts should feel his hand. "Are we all right? Did you do what I asked?"

"I did. They've gone down to Epsilon. Tilly and Deaker. Only Jeannie is here this afternoon. George and Tom are gone to the horse fair."

"And have they left you all alone here. All alone?" he murmured the words in her ear. "And the master, well, we know where he is."

"Yes," she did not want to speak of Enoch. She would put him out of her mind. At this moment he didn't exist for her. She was leaning against Rob, her head against his neck. "If you like, we could go somewhere, quite private."

Robert sat up and drew away from her a little. "Now then, do you know what you mean?"

"I do. Robert, I do. I've thought about nothing else. Please. You cannot disappoint me."

"I won't. You'll have all you want from me." He was stroking her forearm. "You are the most beautiful woman in the whole world. That's right, you are."

"I love you," she breathed. "Oh, I love you." She leaned against his cheek again. He held her tightly, making no further movement. He felt her shuddering and the beat of her heart.

"Where is it, this private place?"

"I found it a few days ago." Edna had a momentary picture of herself and Tilly leaning on the gate. "It's up by the byres." Edna knew that after today, after this afternoon, what would happen in the next hour, nothing would ever be the same again. There would be no going back. Tilly and Deaker were down at the village and they would be quite unaware of what had happened. Already, it seemed, she'd made the choice. But she'd had to make the choice. It became her to make it, by making it she became herself.

She felt her cheek damp on Robert's collar. For a moment she rested, unmoving. The world had stopped at this moment. Then she sat up, slipped off his knee, took her bag off the bench, found her handkerchief, dabbed her eyes and nose. Standing apart from him with her head bowed, she said, "Take the gravel path up by the garden to the field to the cow byre. It's the door to the right. There'll be no one there till evening." She turned away and walked up the path towards the cupid.

Robert stood in the deep shadow at the back of the arbour. When Edna had disappeared round the side of the house he took a cigarette out of his pocket, lit it and sat down on the seat to smoke. The sulphurous smell from the match and the scent of tobacco now mingled with the perfume of the roses. When he'd finished the cigarette, he stubbed it out on his shoe heel, slipped out of the back of the arbour, down the steep steps towards the bottom meadow, and then by a circuitous route towards the cow byre.

Inside the dark, warm shed, it seemed that there were no humans in the world. From here, where Edna stood, it was so still, as if all the creatures were hiding, waiting, to see what the humans would do. Edna had left the half door slightly ajar, and mild light dissipated itself on the golden hay, and trickled through the dust mites floating where she had trodden. She stood still, her mind blank, her mouth dry. She was poised, between one world and the other. She could fly back, or stay, do nothing, just accept what would happen. She was breathing quickly, all her senses fully engaged, with the scents of the hay and the animals, the comfortable sound of the cow and her calf next door, moving in the straw, and the pale rays of sun from the door. Her back was to the door, so she did not hear Robert coming. By the time she was aware of the half door being pushed open behind her, his arm was round her waist, and it was too late.

She let her body relax onto his. He put his hands over her two breasts, holding them, each a round fruit, which he was feeling for ripeness, pressing it with his fingertips, holding each up, as if he were afraid they would fall to earth before he could taste them. She was ready for him. He turned her round. Her lips were moist, her skin delicately flushed.

Rob stroked her cheek, with the back of his hand. "You're so lovely," he said. "So lovely." He took her face between his hands, drawing his fingers up towards her hairline. "You deserve everything. I will give you everything. I will give you love, in a way you've never had it before. Let me see you, like he sees you..." He began pulling out the hair pins. First one lock of hair came down, then another, till there were bundles of it, round her shoulders.

She hung her head, and shook it, then looked at him, through the hair.

Rob laughed. "That's right. " He began to undo the buttons which ran all the way down her bodice. "One, two, three," he was saying. As he went downwards, she began at the bottom, going upwards. Underneath was her undergarment. This too, had buttons. She smiled. Together, they worked away at it.

At last, there she was. Now, he could feel the skin. He bent his head, and kissed the nipples, one by one. Oh, he must hurry, with all this undressing. Otherwise it would be too late.

She raised her hand, and put it over her eyes, but next minute her eyes wide open, she was kissing the top of his head. His dark hair smelled so sweet, she plunged her mouth into it.

"Come on, my beauty," he said. He put his arm under her bottom. There she was, her dress trailing on the floor, her breasts bare, her arms round his neck. She managed to sink her face into his shoulder, before he had placed her, carefully, on the hay. "Wait," he said. As she lay, on her side, her head on her arm, he took off his jacket, then his other clothes, till all he had on was his shirt. She gazed at his white, tall body, and saw, for the first time in her life, a penis erect. She closed her eyes immediately. Enoch had never shown her this. Even when she had lain with him, before Tilly was borne, it was all under cover of the dark, no candles, no lamp. He had fumbled with her, in the warm, moist den made by the bedclothes, and she had never held, or beheld, his member. She peeped through her fingers, at Robert. There he was, and there it was again, oh, and how she loved it, she wanted it. She half sat up, holding her arms towards him.

"Let me see you," he was kneeling beside her. She went to feel his arm through the linen, then she felt his thighs. They were hard, and slightly furry. He had his hands on her ankles. He had one in his left hand, and with the other hand, he was smoothing his way, up the calf, up the thigh. All the time he was speaking softly, "Come on, now, there now, you're so lovely, now then." The words ran together, like music, like a stream, as he was kissing her, all the way up her leg. Next he was astride her, and he had her long skirt right up round her waist "There you are now...let me see you." He arranged her dress, so it came up behind her head, making a pillow. "Yes, a rose."

She closed her eyes again. He would come into her, now. She knew it. She wanted it. "Come," she said. "Come."

He entered her, and he was right. Edna experienced the most exquisite pleasure she had ever felt. The thread of her life seemed to snap, and shiver into thousands of tiny golden shards. In a moment, then another, and another, these fiery messengers delivered to her, the intimations of eternity. She called out, "Oh, God, oh God." At the same time, she heard Robert's voice too, and she knew that this must be the hour of her life, which she would look back on as the very meaning of her existence. Whatever happened, she would have this.

Next door, the cow had stopped her munching, the calf was looking with large eyes at his mother. Edna and Robert lay unstirring on the hay. Gradually, she became aware of his legs on her, his weight. He rolled away, and lay with one arm across her belly. She touched the little hairs with her fingertips. She smoothed them, up, up towards the elbow. She gazed at his hand, then picked it up, and put it to her cheek, this hand, which she had watched so often, caressing the keyboard.

He opened his eyes. "Well?"

"I love you," she said. She could hardly breathe. Already, she was thinking of the next time, and all the hours before he would come back to her. He turned towards her, taking her face in his hands. He kissed her gently on the lips. She was limp, a cat, lying on a sunny window sill.

He spoke slowly, savouring every word, his voice deep and melodious. "Do you know that poem, written by Christopher Marlowe? It was written for you. 'Thou art more lovely than the evening air, clad in the beauty of a thousand stars.'"

"I love you so much." She was amazed.

"It was about Helen of Troy. The most beautiful line in English poetry."

"Oh," she sighed, as she lay in his arms again. "You know so much. Poetry, everything. "

"Now I know you, I feel as if I do know ....everything. You are my book. I shall read you, through and through, and learn you, line by line."

She kissed him passionately. "Will you see me again?"

"Of course."

It was time to go. He pulled her skirt down, and helped her up. She watched him dressing, his white limbs disappearing in black serge. She longed to enclose him again. Silently, they stole out of the shed, the sun as bright to them, as it would be to night animals, disturbed in their burrow. Back in the hay, there was no sign of their passion left, but a deep hollow, and the dust mites floating in a sunbeam.

19

In Epsilon, Deaker had a few errands, and Tilly had come for some fresh air, and to buy some ribbon for her hat. Mother had told them not to hurry back. They had to pass by the little park which had just been laid down, near to the station. There were flower beds, a bowling green, and two grass tennis courts, on which two ladies and two gentlemen were playing tennis.

"Well, I do believe it's Nancy Westerham, and her brother, and....and...." Tilly cried. She saw that the other man there was David Lockyard, and another girl she did not recognise. She looked quickly at Deaker, but it was obvious that she had not recognised Lockyard. Tilly cried. "It's ages since I saw them. "I'll wait here, till they finish, Deaker, and we'll walk home together."

"All right then, Miss Tilly. Promise you won't stir from here."

"Deaker. I am not a child now. I suppose I can be trusted."

"Of course, Miss. I'm just thinking what Miss Edna would say, if she knew I was leaving you all alone here."

"I spend every morning in the factory on my own, except for Willoughby, and she doesn't quibble at that, when my father is away."

"I don't know as it is the same. it's more like your own home there, I suppose."

"Oh go on with you, Deaker. I might be living on my own very soon now, if I get the chance. You know I've told you about that."

"God forbid, I don't hold with it, all this....modern way of going on."

"Just be a good thing, and go, will you. Look, I'll speak to them. They'll make sure I'm quite safe. Hello, Nancy!" she shouted.

Nancy turned to shout back, and missed her return. David was serving. "Hello...Oh it's Matilda" Nancy shouted. "How are you? Wait there, when this game's over, you must join us." All the others raised their rackets to her, and the game went on.

Tilly settled herself down on a seat.

Thump, thump, thump, thump. The ball went flying back and forth. They seemed very good. Tilly wondered how difficult it was. Suddenly she felt a pang of envy. How was it that Nancy and her brother knew David Lockyard and were having such a good time? She never seemed to do these things herself. Love all, fifteen love, thirty love, thirty fifteen. They were calling to each other across the net. What did it mean? What were they doing? It was all very mysterious. And who was the other girl? Tilly felt strangely put out. Why wasn't she ever invited to make up a party like this? Because she was working, she decided, ruefully.

The match was soon over. Everyone came over to speak to Tilly. Nancy introduced her cousin Edith, and then the girls went to fetch their things, in the pavilion.

"Did you come on your bicycle, Mr. Lockyard," Tilly asked.

"I did. I use it as much as I can. What do you think? Do you want to try? I'll help you."

"Oh, thank you. That's very kind of you, I don't think I could." Tilly realised that her dress would get caught up in the big wheel, even if she could get on board. Everything was against her; this was just one more area of life, that she, being a woman, couldn't explore. "I'll have to wait, till they invent something a little more convenient."

"That won't be long, I am sure. This is the greatest achievement in transportation, since the first railway engine, and it's bound to revolutionise our lives. No more feeding horses, or having to control the wily things, just two metal wheels, which don't even need water, and everyone can go anywhere."

"How fast can you go?" Westerham asked.

"I came all the way down here, from the site, in about an hour. That's twelve miles at least."

"As fast as a horse! Still, I would prefer my horse."

"Yes. Of course. But still, they're a responsibility, and very expensive. Not something most people can afford."

"Well, they won't out do the horse, ever."

"You'll see. Within ten years, this will have ousted the horse, for working people."

"Not so, they don't have horses anyway. Maybe they'll have ousted Shank's pony."

Tilly was tongue tied. What could she contribute to the conversation? She thought of her own life, flowing down a rigid course, unable to deviate, or meander along unexplored routes. Besides, she recognised that the two young men actually wanted to argue. Just for the sake of it.

David Lockyard turned to her. "Have you had time to read Octavia Hill's book?"

Tilly was mortified. "Of course. It was so interesting. I have really wanted to see you about it."

"How?"

"I've been concerned, all summer, about the people who lost their houses in the fire, that night of the Ball. Do you know yet for certain, what is happening there?"

"I believe that there will be some development. More houses. I'm not sure yet, who is putting up the money. I don't think our firm is concerned. Mr. Lugando is not interested in that kind of commission. Workmens' houses, that is not his province. Now had there been a new church there, that might have been different."

"Oh. Of course."

"You sound disappointed."

"I am." Tilly smiled at him. "But in a way I'm not." She hesitated. "I was hoping that my father might be involved. I want him to....."

There came a shout from the girls.

"Ginger beer," Westerham said. "Come and join us." He walked off.

"Do you think your father might be interested?"

"Perhaps. If he did he could institute the kind of ideas that are outlined in the Octavia Hill book. You know, a kind of estate which the people who live there can manage, or at least co-operate in managing."

"Interesting, but it wouldn't bring much profit to your father."

"Maybe not, in money terms. But in terms of having happy and industrious workers, it would. And he would be fulfilling his duty."

"Quite so." Lockyard thought Tilly sounded rather prim. "Have you spoken to him? Perhaps he has plans."

"Perhaps he needs persuading to have plans. He never looks beyond the factory."

"I see. Well, I'm sure, you are the best person to talk to him about it."

"He won't even read the book. I thought you wouldn't mind if he did so, before I returned it."

"Not at all. It is a great pleasure to me that you have found it inspiring. You must keep reading, as much as you can. And talking to people. You will soon find what you need to do. "

Tilly sighed. "I am determined to improve my education. I have spoken about it to my family, but so far, nothing has transpired."

Lockyard looked at her intently. "It is difficult for older people, parents especially, to understand what it is that young people need, - need in order to survive. I had a problem. My father wanted me to join the army. He didn't think I would be able to make a good living out of architecture."

"How did you persuade him in the end?"

"I didn't. But I managed to find a sponsor, another relation who is prepared to invest his hopes, and some finance, I have to admit, in me. He will be repaid."

"I don't know of anyone like that. Really, unless my Father agrees, I don't know what I can do."

"It is more difficult for ladies. But in London, now, there are many women who are supporting themselves, as I told you, and they study part-time. Just like working men do. There is education for all who wish to profit by it, men and women. You will see women working in the civil service. Others are teachers, and there are also women who work on the Settlements. You might consider one of those options."

"Do you mean the Christian missions, in the slums? Teaching and medical care?"

"Precisely. I know some myself. They are very clever and dedicated people. They are doing very good work. Fulfilling too. You would enjoy their company, Miss Manstone."

"Please call me Matilda. Tilly"

"Thank you." Lockyard smiled and bowed slightly. "My name is David."

Tilly smiled. "David and Goliath. You seem to have met the powers that be, and bent them to your will. Like your father."

"Well, hardly." He laughed. "He soon capitulated, when he knew I was financially secure."

Tilly sighed. "You've given me something to think about."

By the time Deaker came back she was surprised to see Tilly animatedly talking in the middle of the tennis group. She sat down on the bench to wait, her basket on her lap. It was good to see the dear thing enjoying herself. Life had been dull for her, all the attention had been elsewhere, on Rosalind, or on the Works. She must feel she needed more company. Once again, Deaker thought of how life would have been different, if Tilly had not been an only child.

Nancy and the others waved goodbye, and went down the path with their racquets and balls. David Lockyard turned to Tilly. "I shall be leaving very soon, as the job is finished. I am not waiting for the official opening of the church, as Mr. Lugando wants me to start some work back in London. May I write to you? I may be able to give you some information about some highly respectable ladies, who have already found work and accommodation in the big city. I also know of a College, which can help people to matriculate, with a view to going to University. Maybe that would be of interest."

"Certainly. Of course. I do so want to do something, to help change things. Children here...." she hesitated. "Even though they're supposed to go to school, they don't. Most of them work to help their families, and many, many of them don't even have shoes. It can't be right. But I mustn't bore you. Oh, and I must return the book. How shall I do that?"

"Of course. I shall send you my address, and you may send it, if you wish. But I am sure we shall meet again and you can give it to me then." Lockyard's eyes were shining as he looked into hers. "And you don't bore me at all. I have the same thoughts. I'm particularly interested in the question of housing for the poor. Some people in London, philanthropists, have ideas about clearing the slums. For that is what they are, just slums, some of the old courts still exist from the last century, and before. We must talk again. I could introduce you to some of my friends." He held out his hand. "Good bye, and may I say, Au revoir?"

"Au revoir."

David mounted his bicycle and was away.

"Well, Miss Tilly. I never did. That was nice, wasn't it?"

Tilly took the basket, grasped her by the arm, and marched her away. "Oh, Deaker, that was fun." She felt that at last, something was happening. "Let's go."

Soon, they were out of the town, going down the hill towards the bridge.

The canal stretched away beyond them for a hundred yards in one direction. In the other direction a bank of weeping willows hung over the tow path, and a sinuous curve prevented them seeing any distance. They settled on the parapet facing the long open view, with their backs to the dark willows.

"I may want to go to London, Deaker.To get my education."

"Good gracious me, Miss Tilly. So that's what that was all about. Well you've quite taken my breath away." Deaker had started and flinched, and her head shook as if she had received a smart slap.

"Yes, that's what I may want. It depends on my father, of course. I may stay, and help him with a new project. It all depends. Now you know, what do you think?"

"What can I think? It's not what I expected, no. I thought you'd got your mind set on something very different, I did. And so did your Papa."

"You mean, take over the business? Or marry a pottery master?"

"Perhaps. I thought you really like working there, you never said nothing about this, did you? No, you haven't, not at all."

"Well, I do like working, but I want to do something for myself."

"But you're a lady, Miss."

"I'm a woman. Even more, I'm a person. And I want to do what I think is right for a human person. I'm not just a lady. Can't anyone understand that?"

There was silence. Tilly slipped off the low brick wall.

"Do you wish to go on, Miss Tilly?"

"I'm just going up there for a few blackberries." She went up the slope a little way to some brambles growing in the hedge. Deaker watched her reaching for the fruit and then eating them, a mouthful at a time. "I'll bring some for you. Don't come up. Just wait there."

She went on picking and stretching. Then she suddenly froze and was gazing at something, out of view to the old woman, evidently near the canal in the other direction.

Taking care not to rick her neck, Deaker turned her whole body round to see what the girl was looking at. A man was standing on the path looking at them both. He was stock still, with his hands in his pocket.

It was Robert Willoughby.

At the same time as Deaker saw him, all three of them moved. Tilly moved her arm, Robert came forward and Deaker heaved herself up.

"Oh, Mr Willoughby."

"Good gracious what a surprise" Deaker said.

"Good day, Miss Manstone," Robert nodded at Deaker. "I see you're after blackberries. Nice for a pie those. Shall I get those up there?" He went towards the brambles, reaching up beyond Tilly.

"There's no need." She turned away. "We only wanted to taste them."

"Nice day for a walk," he said. He fumbled in his pocket, bringing out a piece of folded newspaper. He made this into a cone and began picking into it. "They're good and fat with all this rain."

Both women stood watching him. Deaker felt rooted to the ground.

"Here you are, Deaker, these are for you," Tilly said. She gave Deaker the few berries she still had in the palm of her hand. They had made a little purple stain. "Good day to you, Mr Willoughby." She turned and went off up the lane, towards home.

Robert didn't pause in his picking. "Good day, Miss Manstone. Take these back for Jeannie, if you like."

Deaker hesitated. Robert turned to her. "I canna walk with them. There'll be sufficient for a pie." He handed her the newspaper cone.

"Enjoy your walk, Mr Willoughby," she said and walked off after Tilly. "That was strange, meeting him, Miss Tilly, wasn't it?" She muttered breathlessly. "He's come far afield." Then she remembered seeing him down at the chapel, that day. "Still, he do come this way sometimes."

Tilly said nothing, and was walking quickly away, and Deaker had a struggle to keep up. Suddenly an idea occurred to her. Was it because of Willoughby, Miss Tilly suddenly wanted to leave the office? There was something about that man Deaker couldn't quite place. No one knew anything about him, but there were rumours about his birth. He was a stranger here. He seemed polite and helpful, and he was good looking too, neatly dressed and all. But still, there was something .

"If you went to college, Miss Tilly, is there anything special you'd study? I thought it was more for people who could read Latin and that. Is it open for ladies? I've never heard that."

"Of course it is, and it isn't all about Latin nowadays. It hasn't been for years." Tilly walked a little faster. She wished she hadn't brought up the subject, now, and something else had started niggling in her mind. Why was Robert here? Hadn't Mama cancelled the accompaniment today?

"I suppose it's very expensive. That's why it's mostly the noble who go there. Is that right, Miss Tilly?"

"That is so," Tilly sighed. "Why did you bring those Deaker? I can't think they'll be very nice, out of that newspaper."

"That's right, Miss." Deaker emptied the blackberries out into the hedge and screwed up the newspaper into a ball. "I only did it because I thought I'd hurt his feelings, else."

About ten minutes later, they reached home.

Deaker had a key for the back door and she let her young mistress in.

Jeannie was sitting in the big chair in the kitchen which she had pulled up by the range. The cat was on her lap, both of them were dozing. As Tilly and Deaker came through from the scullery she jerked awake and pushed the cat off her knee.

"Come on now my girl. We are cold after that walk and Miss Matilda here needs her tea. So does Missus I'll be bound. Has she rung?"

"I haven't heard anything. It's only half past four.

Tilly went out into the long back hall. It was cool and dim here and she shivered. As she went past the row of bells hung up high near the ceiling, one of them suddenly jangled, making her jump. She looked up. It was the drawing room bell. Mother must be ringing for tea. She skated and slipped along the highly polished Minton tiles. The bell could still be heard jangling, even after she had closed the double baize doors behind her. As she reached the stone floors of the part of the house leading to the drawing room, she couldn't slide any more but jumped from rug to Persian rug, like a shipwrecked sailor, making for shore across the rocks.

Mother was in her usual armchair beside the log fire, which had evidently only just been lit. She smiled at Tilly. "Come and warm yourself," she said. "It's cold out."

"It isn't really. In fact it's a nice day."

Tilly settled herself on a cushion in front of the fire, at her mother's feet. "Did you have a nice afternoon? What did you do? Did you practise?"

"Oh, a little, just a little."

"By the way, you'll never guess who we saw. On our way back. It was Robert Willoughby. He was walking along the canal."

Edna's hand became still on the top of Tilly's head. After a moment she continued stroking. Tilly went on speaking. "I couldn't believe it was him, at first. What was he doing hereabouts?"

"I've no doubt he has good reason. I can't account for it. But then I don't know what Mr Willoughby should or shouldn't be doing." Edna's voice was loud and firm. To Tilly her mother sounded rather annoyed.

At that moment the drawing door opened and Deaker and Jeannie entered with the tea trays.

"Deaker thought it was strange too, about Mr Willoughby." Tilly went on. "At first we supposed he'd been here, but of course that couldn't be the case."

"Really Tilly, I know nothing about his arrangements. Now let us drop the subject." Edna began pouring out.

"I might ask Father myself." Tilly continued. "I think he should know if his Chief Clerk is all over the place."

"You're to do no such thing. I'm sure your father knows everything he needs to know about Willoughby and business. It won't do at all to interfere." Edna put her cup and saucer on the table.

Tilly was silent and stirred her tea. "Well, I do think it was strange, and so did Deaker. He gave us some blackberries. But I didn't fancy them, out of newspaper that had been in his pocket. Besides they're hardly ripe. We threw them away." She began poking the fire again.

"Please stop doing that, Matilda. The fire is burning well.

Tilly put down the poker on the hearth. She spread another scone with jam and munched in silence.

Edna was resting back in her chair, her face in shadow. Tilly looked down at her stockinged feet. Why did so many of her conversations with Mama end like a sailing boat that goes aground in shallow water, the sail flapping?

"Where are your shoes?" Edna asked at last.

"I took them off, they were so muddy."

"Well go at once and put on your slippers. You will catch your death like that."

"Very well, Mama." Thankfully Tilly rose and made for the door. Her mother's eyes were shut now and the rosy flush which had been on her cheeks when Tilly entered, had completely disappeared. There seemed to be an impenetrable barrier round her, once again.

On the train, Rob just had time to have his tea with Mrs Jakes before his meeting with Frank Borthing. Then he was having a practice with the others in the singing group. Mrs Jakes set down a large plate of stew and boiled potatoes in front of him.

"Get that inside you. You need to put on some weight, you got to build up for the winter now."

"That's very good, Missus," he said, sticking his napkin into his shirt collar.

Mrs Jakes sat down by the fire, which she'd lit earlier. She took out her crochet work.

"Days drawing in now, we'll be seeing some frost soon."

Rob said nothing. He knew Mrs Jakes' remarks were a preliminary to some long diatribe, probably about some political issues. He didn't want to get involved in that. He had to hurry to be ready for Borthing.

"Not doing so good, our boys. It's my belief they shouldn't be fighting out there. Use the natives, is my belief."

"They do, Mrs Jakes." Rob wished he'd said nothing.

"I knew that they do, don't forget my Sam was in the army. He did tell me. All the ordinary soldiers are natives in those parts. but he did tell me the sergeants and such, they're all our men. And they're the ones who're in the most danger. They've got to lead the others, they're in the front."

"That's so, Missus. That's how it should be. It's up to the Officers and the N.C.O's to lead the way."

"Well, it's my belief, the natives should fight for themselves. It's their border, their frontier, when all's said and done. What did they do before we was in there to protect them, I'd like to know. Of course, it don't mean much to you, now do it. You're too young to remember the mutiny, weren't you? That was a shame, a real shame. We should have left them to their own devices."

A knock came at the front door.

"Happen that's your friend, Mr Robert." The old woman stood up, smoothed down her skirt.

There appeared a short, square young man, with blond hair, moustache and cap in his hand.

"Evening, Mrs Jakes. There you are, Robert,"

"Fine evening."

"I were just saying, if this fine weather keep up, we're in for early frosts. I was just saying that to Mr Willoughby."

"You were," Rob pushed his plate aside and rose to go.

"Eh, you'll wait for your tea, will you not, young sirs. The kettle's just boiled. Now then." She hastened into the scullery and they could hear the clink of cups on saucers.

"Come on Frank. We haven't got time for this," Rob stood up and made towards the coat stand.

Mrs. Jakes returned with the tea things. "We was just talking about the war, Mr Borthing. I was saying it's a shame they don't use the natives to fight their own battles, wasn't I Mr Robert?"

"Yes. You were," Rob said shortly. He couldn't imagine how he had managed to let Mrs Jakes get away with this misconception for so long.

Borthing contented himself with placatory remarks, and compliments about the home-made biscuits. At last the pot was emptied and only two biscuits remained.

"I expect you're in a hurry now. You must go if you have a mind to," the old lady said, as she realised that without her contribution the conversation was withering on the bud.

With alacrity Robert got up and in a moment they were both outside, Borthing following his friend.

"She's a daft old brush," Robert remarked, cramming his hat on his head.

Borthing was struggling to keep up, his long coat flapping about him. Yes, it was colder, there might well be a frost.

"You're in luck to have such a woman. Happen she's sweet on you."

"Why cannot women leave you alone? They always on about something. Her and the Afghan war. What is to her, or us? This is what matters." He pointed at the wasteland they were now crossing. It was barren, ringed by shacks, and smoking chimneys. The whole ground underfoot was a mass of broken pottery shards, and mounds of dirt and waste. It was a general dumping ground from the surrounding pot-banks. A rat ran across the path which wound along between the filthy hummocks. "This is what we need to worry about. With the present state of trade the masters will never clean up their own backyards. They won't spare the money to do it and the Council canna do it on the rates paid. This is what's wrong, not border quarrels in India and who fights for whom. Can't anyone see that?"

"It's not going to matter much what the old woman say. It's the young ones that need to see what's the matter."

"The young ones are just the same. How many years have we been struggling in the Union to get something moving, to get people to sign up. If the trade stays craft, it's in the hands of the journeymen. We won't have better condition till we've adopted modern methods of production. To be honest, I feel I've had enough sometimes."

They'd crossed the canal by this time and were walking up the hill towards the Union Chambers in Tolley Street. The door stood open, and the light fell out onto the pavement. From within came the sound of an accordion.

"Maybe young Buckley's inside," Borthing said. "He telled me he'd find us here, if we were going to meet."

Borthing disappeared inside but Robert turned away. He suddenly felt a deep pervasive gloom filling him up. Here was he in the middle of this huge city, at the heart of it. All around there were lights, there were people, crowds of people. Lamps would soon be lit in parlours, pianos would be played, songs be sung. Yet he could not bestir himself. He thought of the meeting with Edna that day. Her soft compliance, her kisses, had astounded him. He'd promised her a new life. What had he meant by that? He'd aroused her, enjoyed her. She had been ravished with him, and by him. She'd been overwhelmed by him. Yet he couldn't be content. He wasn't ashamed of himself. No. Not at all. He wasn't amazed either. It had been so easy, so easy to move her, possess her. Yet what did it all mean, how could it change things? His own situation couldn't change because he had stolen the master's rights, usurped his position. He would still be poor Robert Willoughby, a nondescript clerk, whose struggles to better the lot of the pottery workers were quite unrewarded. How could possessing the Master's wife, make any difference really, to the state of things? Where was he going, what was he doing with his life? And now, he would have to lie low for a while, at least until Matilda left home, if ever she did.

Buckley and Borthing came out together. "It's been postponed while Wednesday."

"Postponed again! When are they going to grow up? How'll they ever take any real action, if they cannot even decide on a meeting time? "

"Afraid of the women, that's what it is."

"Aye." Robert grunted. If they didn't know how to handle the women, to get what they wanted, they must be poor things, by any standards. "See you then." He turned off down the street.

20

Edna was snipping roses off the bush at the end of the terrace. Fallen petals lay on the grass like drops of blood. The remaining blooms had a weather beaten look, like frowsty matrons after the ball is over. Really, it would be impossible to find enough to fill the rose bowl which all summer had stood on the hall table, providing a pool of scented warmth, to radiate up the stairs right along the top corridor. She laid her secateurs along the stems in her basket and went over to the edge of the terrace. There was a cool damp spreading up from the stream. Soon, it would be time to go in and change for dinner. She thought of the fire lit upstairs and her dress laid out for her ready. She shivered and hugged her arms tight to her breasts.

Yesterday, it was only yesterday, she had been with Robert. Since then, it had been as if one whole life had passed away, a life of someone she did not know, her life as the true wife to Enoch Manstone, Mrs Manstone. Now, she was not his wife any more. She knew this with the innermost knowledge of her being. Everything she had been, up until yesterday, she did not recognise any more as being a part of her true, real self. That self was now growing, growing, and the old self lay behind her, like a blown rose on the grass. The petals would scatter in the breeze, the scent would vanish and her new self would ride, rough shod, over it, and that was how it should be.

She had talked with her daughter, she had smiled, given instructions and walked about, and it had all been as if she was doing things in a mirror. Her other self was watching what was happening. In spite of herself it was indeed still happening. She could not help catching sight of it, but only as a dancer might see herself, reflected in a ballroom looking glass. She would see a smiling, gracious woman, but she would not recognise that person as herself. And soon she would be out of the ballroom, and there would be no reflections to catch sight of, just herself. Edna was moving towards a new reality. She saw everything around her, the lawns, the flowerbeds, the world, the rooms filled with polished furniture, paintings and porcelain, the stables, the horses, the servants, yes, even Tilly, all was receding from her. As she moved away she was pulled by that gravitational pull that couldn't be gainsaid; the pull exerted by her love. She had to be with Robert, she had to be, and he could not be here, so she would have to go to him. She would tell him next time he came. He could not refuse her.

"Miss Edna, I've brought your cloak. Best put it on." It was Deaker hurrying across the grass. "These dews don't do you no good, wouldn't do to catch cold, now would it?" The old woman dexterously slid the cloak around her mistress' shoulders.

Edna shook herself, apparently shivering. "I'm coming in," she turned. "The roses are over, you'd better ask George for some dahlias to go with them." She gave Deaker the basket.

"Your fire's lit."

"I'm coming," Edna repeated, nodding vigorously. "I want to see the moon come up. It was early last night, but I missed it." When the moon was over the beech trees, huge and low, Edna would watch it climb, till it became smaller, shrinking from the size of a giant orange to that of a penny piece, as it rose in the sky.

"Well, I don't know," Deaker hesitated. "I'm not catching my death here. Miss Tilly was looking for you." She added, faintly spitting out the words. Missus was still so strange and moody. When would it end?

"There it is, Deaker. Look. Stay and watch."

"Oh, well," Deaker had turned to go, but was held back by the tone of Edna's voice. In a gap between the huge beech trees, at the edge of the wood, the massive golden ball was gently hoisting itself above the skyline. Brilliantly shining, it was so bright that it seemed to be ablaze with liquid light, which spilled out bathing the branches, and flooding the evening atmosphere.

"Isn't it beautiful," Edna whispered. "Have you ever seen anything so wonderful?"

Together, the two women watched. There was complete silence over the whole valley, as if all the animals and birds were mesmerised by the sight, and had lost their tongues with wonder. Slowly, slowly, the ball moved upwards, floating towards the top of the trees; Edna could hardly breathe. As they watched, the moon cleared the treetops and, apparently lifted by the warm scented air, appeared to sail diagonally towards the darkening sky. As it went higher, it diminished in size and turned silver.

"It's going, it's going," Edna said softly.

"It makes you wonder, doesn't it? Deaker spoke at last.

Together, they went indoors.

A week later, Ros came over to Terrilea for the day. She'd grown plumper since her marriage, giving rise to speculation. Tilly and she had come out to the stables after tea, and now her friend had gone to the kitchen to beg for carrots for the horses. It was the first time the two young women had met since Ros had returned from her wedding journey. They'd had a little time to talk when Ros had arrived, but the conversation had been strained. It was as Tilly had expected, nothing would ever be the same again between them, at any rate, not until she herself was married.

"Here you are, Miss." It was Jeannie who'd come back with the carrots, which she now held out for Ros.

"Thank you, Jeannie. Where is Miss Tilly?"

"She'll be out again in a moment, Miss, Ma'am, I mean." Jeannie blushed. "She's gone to fetch her shawl, and one for you. Mrs. Deaker did say as it was getting cold now."

"Well, I don't find it so, but still." Ros took a carrot, stuck it out over the half door for Dimple to nibble. Her yellow teeth snatched it out of her grasp, and it fell on the floor. "Serves you right, Dimple, for being so greedy," Ros said. "Here you are, here's another." She proffered another. Jeannie stood patiently with the basket. "If you drop that, it shall be your last," Ros said. "Serve her right won't it, Jeannie?"

"That it will Miss, Ma'am, I mean. I beg your pardon. I ain't got used to it yet."

"I know, Jeannie. It is difficult, isn't it?" Ros laughed but inside she felt slightly annoyed. She felt everyone should be aware of her new status, surely it must shine out of her for all to see. "Please try to remember."

"Yes, ma'am," Jeannie whispered, holding the basket a little higher, to be nearer to Ros' hand. It was a good thing Miss Tilly wasn't like this Mrs. Arbuthnot, or whatever she was now called. She couldn't imagine Miss Tilly being a cross-patch like that. What was in a name anyway? Deaker often called the Mistress Miss Edna, instead of Mrs. Manstone, and she never got told off. Had she been getting it wrong ever since she was Miss Edna's nurse? Times must be changing if people thought so much of themselves. Who were they anyway? Common folk like all the others, at root. In fact the Mistress had come from a landed family, come to that, and she had less airs and graces than this young upstart, whose father, so they said, had started up as a printer's clerk.

"Will that be all, Miss?" she asked, "Ma'am....Oh I am so sorry, Ma'am. There I go again." Jeannie blushed with anger. She was so annoyed she'd put herself into a position that Ros could tell her off again.

"You may go," Ros said. "Good bye, Dimple" she murmured, stroking the horse's muzzle. "You are the loveliest girl, aren't you? But you mustn't be greedy, no, no, no." She turned away, her back leaning against the half-door. Wherever was Tilly? She was indeed beginning to feel chilly and bored. Soon, the carriage would be here, her carriage to take here back in time to change for dinner, and resume her place as mistress of her new home. She'd come this afternoon to talk to Tilly and tell her all about her wedding journey. She'd brought her sketchbook with her to show all the places they'd been to, on the South Coast. But Tilly hadn't really been interested. She'd only been interested when she'd been talking about London. Ros and Cyril had stayed at a fine hotel in Kensington and they'd visited the new museums. It was very grand and quite the thing to do and Cyril wanted it, but frankly, Ros had been bored by all the display cases full of stones and stuffed animals. She'd rather have spent the whole time in the shops but she'd had to fit in with Cyril's wishes, of course. And, of course, Tilly would have found those museums entertaining.

"I shall go to them all - I'll spend my life here, when I go to London, you'll see," she'd said.

"Well, of course you will, if you go. Have you asked your Papa yet? What does he say?"

Tilly hadn't replied, but she'd just smiled.

Where on earth was Tilly? No sense in waiting here any longer. Ros decided she might as well go back to the house. Just as she reached the gate dividing the big yard from the little one, she saw her friend, standing on the top of the steps, looking out towards the woods on the far side of the stream. She was standing quite still, with the two shawls, over her arm, watching something intently.

Earlier that afternoon, Edna hadn't been aware of the front doorbell ringing or of Tilly going down to meet her friend at Deaker's summons. So she had had no reason for not going to her assignation with Robert. It was a whole week since their last meeting in the stable. As far as she knew, Tilly was in the library, reading, or upstairs in her room. If anyone had noticed her going down the steps towards the stream, they would have assumed she was going for a little walk.

Now, an hour later, she was standing further up the valley, where the brook went through a limestone gorge. She had her back to Rob and he was squatting on his haunches, checking her over for marks on her coat. He gently smoothed the soft serge, slipping his hand softly up and down, from her waist, over her buttocks to the hem, then again all round. She stood meekly, while he did this and turned when he told her to. At last he straightened up, brushed the fur collar of her coat, then took her cheeks with his hands and kissed her on the lips. "You are so beautiful. I keep telling you. But it's true."

"Oh, Rob," she said flinging her arms round him, pulling him so tightly she could feel the buttons of his coat pressing through to her skin. "I hate it when you have to go away. I feel dead, dead inside. It's terrible. I can't think of anything else, but when we'll be together again." Her face was against his. She could feel the silky hair of his moustache with her cheek. She kept nuzzling against him, to feel the hairs again. Already she was dwelling on what was happening between them. She could picture their hollow in the hay. The mice would be able to come out of their little nests, now there were no humans about. She wasn't afraid of mice when Robert was there. Surely there must be mice in the hay, but she never gave them a thought. But they must have been witnesses to their love. Perhaps they cowered in their holes waiting for peace and quiet to resume. She smiled.

"If mice could talk, or cows, our secret would be out, Rob."

"They'd never tell on us, my girl. They wouldn't dare. You're the Mistress, aren't you? They'd keep their counsel."

"Yes, I am. I'm your Mistress too, Robert, aren't I?"

"Of course, Madame." He went over to the brook and bending down, splashed his face with water from his cupped hands. Then he shook his head like a dog. "We'd best be going, before there are questions asked. You go on first, that's best."

Edna clung to him. "Don't go yet. No one will wonder where I am. In any case, I go for walks in the afternoon, even when you're not here. It's all right. Hold me close again."

Robert shook his head, then took her in his arms. "We must be careful. It's best if we don't meet always meet here. I've been thinking."

"What?"

"It's this. Maybe we should go somewhere else for once." He was thinking of the woodland walk he'd been on with Gertrude. Things would be easier with this one, she'd do anything for him, this one would. Not like that stiff little wench with all her promises. "We could go into the country on the tram."

"Oh, I don't know. It would be difficult to get to Heathersham. I couldn't take the carriage."

"You could make out as you were going to that friend of yours."

"I don't know. I don't know. Why cannot we just meet here as usual?"

"That's when it becomes dangerous, when you keep doing the same thing - stands to reason. That's how robbers get what they want, they watch people to see what they always do - then they've got them. Perhaps someone's watching you."

"Oh, Robert. Don't say that. Who?"

"I don't know. That maid of yours - the old one. She's all about, that one is. Then there's your young lady, Miss Tilly. She's bright. You wouldn't want her to know, would you?"

"Oh, Robert. How dreadful." Edna, for a fleeting moment, realised the enormity of what she was doing. Supposing, supposing, Tilly was ever to know. She shrank into herself, but as suddenly she recovered. What if Tilly did find out? She'd realise her mother was doing no wrong, or if she was, she'd forgive her. But perhaps Rob was right. They should be more discreet. But for how long? What would be the eventual outcome? Surely it would be better if they did disclose to the world the relationship between them. It was beautiful, and it was true, why hide it? "I'll think about what you say. I'll send a letter to your lodging. It won't be long before you get it." She gave him one last fluttering kiss and went off down the path towards the meadow. As soon as she came out from beneath the trees, she looked up towards the terrace. There were two figures standing there. One of them waved but the other turned away and hurried back towards the house.

Edna couldn't move. Who was it over there? Had she been seen? Her whole being froze, a sharp pain went through her head. Suddenly she had remembered that Rosalind was due to come that afternoon. She stood motionless, staring fixedly at the two figures. One of them was already nearly out of sight, and the other was definitely Rosalind. Why had Tilly not waved? Perhaps she hadn't seen her. Or perhaps she had, and was hurrying away before facing her. After a long pause, Edna gathered her skirt up, and turned back along the path where she had left Robert. She could not see him. He must have begun the long climb back. She began to tremble. There was the old log where she had been so many times before. She sat down, holding her head in her hands. Suddenly she smelled tobacco smoke. It was Robert. He was there.

"What is the matter?" he asked softly, emerging from the shadows.

"I think someone saw us." Edna could hardly speak.

"Never." Robert gathered her into his arms. "Don't worry. It isn't true, it's impossible. No-one saw us. "

"I saw them. Two of them." Edna clung to him.

"No-one saw us. Perhaps they saw you. Not us. That is all. They saw you. You were out walking." He kissed her eyelids. "Now then. Trust me."

"Yes, Robert, yes." Robert's arms held her fast, and kept her warm. She stopped shivering. She was safe. No-one had seen them together, and she had just been out walking, as usual. God was good to her, he had given her a few more minutes with Robert. Thus they stayed, while the last rays of the sun went down behind the hill.

On the terrace, Ros set off after her friend. "Why are you hurrying away? It is your mother. Didn't you see her?" Ros panted.

Tilly marched on, her face set.

"Didn't you see her? It was her, of course. Why didn't you wait?"

"I'm cold. I've got to go and get my jacket," Tilly darted away and Ros was left behind.

She turned round to wait for Mrs Manstone, but there was now no one there. Dismayed, she went after Tilly, but slowly. As she came into the hall, she was met by Deaker.

"There you are Ma'am. Your tea's just ready. Miss Tilly's gone upstairs for she's cold. I don't know," Deaker sounded severe.

"I'll come in. Miss Tilly won't be long." Ros went into the long drawing room and sat down by the fire. It was such a beautiful room this one. She would give anything for her and Cyril to have a room like this one. Their house was nice enough, but there was nothing like this. So elegant and peaceful. The late sun shone through onto the gilt sconces over the fireplace and picked out the soft lines of the Persian rugs. There were bowls of roses, which perfumed the air. It was all so orderly and peaceful, the still heart of the house. To achieve this room needed the work of all the people at Manstones but with all the servants here and the meticulous supervision of the owner of the house; the room was still hardly used. It seemed to be waiting for something to happen, for people to come, to enjoy and admire it, briefly, and then to go away to the real, interesting business of their lives. Tilly was one of those, Ros reflected. She never sat in here, except when there was company. Mostly, she took herself off to her own room, to read or write, otherwise she'd be outside in the fresh air, walking or sometimes riding, when she wasn't at Manstones, that is. Ros realised that she and her friend were growing apart. Tilly seemed more and more distant from her and it wasn't just her own marriage which had caused this. Tilly herself was different. Where was she? She was being so long coming down.

Ros had a sudden presentiment that something was the matter. Perhaps her friend was unwell. She looked at the clock on the mantelpiece. It was ten to five. She got up and walked to the French windows. There was no sign of anyone on the terrace. Where had Mrs Manstone got to? She had been coming out of the woods when they had seen her, or rather she had seen her. Ros still wasn't convinced that Tilly had seen her. Surely it would not have taken her all this time to climb the steps back to the house.

The tea, in a teapot with a padded linen cover, was fast getting cold. There were only two cups. That must signify that Deaker hadn't expected her Mistress to be there for tea, only Tilly and Ros.

Ros suddenly decided to wait no longer. She would have to be leaving soon, she'd said she would be home by half past five and she didn't wish to keep Cyril waiting. He expected her and she would be there. She rose and pulled the bell by the fireplace. Within a moment, Jeannie appeared.

"I'm going up to Miss Tilly's room," she said. "This tea has gone cold, you may as well take the tray. Miss Tilly can ask for fresh if she wishes. I shall not have any."

To Jeannie, the new Mrs Cyril seemed stern and cool. Why should it make such a difference to these ladies when they got themselves wed, she wondered?

"All airs and graces," she said to herself as she expertly manoeuvred the heavy tray out of the door. "Airs and graces," she grumbled to Deaker back in the kitchen.

Upstairs, Ros knocked tentatively on her friend's bedroom door. There was no answer, so she knocked more loudly.

"It's me. May I come in? Please."

"Come in." Tilly's voice was barely audible. Ros poked her head round the door and tiptoed in. She didn't see Tilly at first, but then spotted a lump on the bed, a bump covered by the eiderdown. "Tilly, is that you?" she went up to the bed and gingerly reached back the covers to reveal a head. Tilly's face was buried in the pillow and her feet, with the boots still on, emerged at the other end, hanging down to the floor. "Why whatever is it?" Ros took her by the shoulders, and put her face close up to Tilly's. "What is it? Tell me."

"It's nothing. I've just got a stomach ache."

"Oh, dearest. No. How awful. Why didn't you say anything? When did it come on, shall I call Deaker?"

"No, don't," Tilly said vehemently into her pillow. "I'll be all right, in a minute. It's getting better all the time."

"Very well. You just rest here." Ros began rearranging the cover. "Your boots. Shall I take your boots off?"

"No. No. I'm getting up in a minute."

"Will you, really?"

"Yes," Tilly mumbled.

Ros stood staring at her for a moment, then looked at the small gilt clock on the mantelpiece. She really couldn't stay much longer. She'd have to go, or she'd be late. But she didn't like to go without even a goodbye. She walked to the window. The sun was now setting and the clouds near the horizon were turning pink. "It's going to be a lovely evening, Tilly." Somehow she didn't believe that what was wrong was a mere stomach ache. Tilly never got aches and pains, as far as she knew. Why now, all of a sudden? "Oh. There's your mother coming along the terrace, now. She's finished her walk. Shall I go and tell her you're ill?"

Tilly suddenly sat up. Her eyes were wild. "Don't tell her anything. I'm all right. I don't want you speaking to her. I'll tell her myself." She strode over to the dressing table and let her bun down and began brushing vigorously. The hair fell down over her face and Ros couldn't see her properly.

"Well, Tilly. I won't tell her. You've no need to shout at me. I only thought it might be for the best. She should know, if you're ill."

"I'm not ill. I'm not ill. It's nothing."

"Well. I don't know, really Tilly. I think I'd best be going. I'll see you again when you've fully recovered." It was too bad of Tilly to behave like this. She had never seen her in such a state before. She turned round to make for the door.

Tilly flung down the brush and caught her by the shoulders.
"I'm sorry. I'm so sorry Ros. You're my best friend, I didn't mean to be rude."

Ros turned again and saw Tilly's eyes swimming with tears. Then she realised these were not fresh tears. Her face was all steamed and puffy. Now she could see it properly it was obvious from Tilly's face that she'd been crying for several minutes.

"There, there," she said pulling her friend towards her, patting her back and smoothing her hair. "What is it? What is it? Tell me, please." She led her back to the dressing table stool, and sat Tilly down. Then she knelt down beside her, putting her arms round her waist. "What is it? Can I do anything?"

Tilly said nothing, her eyes were open and blank and tears just kept rolling down her cheeks.

"Did your Papa say you couldn't go to London? Is that it? Why didn't you tell me before?"

Tilly was gulping, she just kept flicking the constant tears off her cheeks.

"It's nothing," she whispered at last.

Ros continued to hold her close. The minutes ticked by. From the hall came the chime of the grandfather clock. "That's the quarter," Ros said gently, "I've got to go. I shall have to. Otherwise Cyril will make a fuss."

"Yes, go, go," Tilly went over to the washstand, dipped her face flannel into the cold water jug and began dabbing at her cheeks.

"Shall I come and see you again soon, when you're feeling better?" Ros asked.

"Come again?" Tilly looked puzzled. "Yes, if you wish. Oh, I don't know." She had folded the flannel to make a pad for her eyes. "Goodbye, Ros." She squeezed her friend's arm, then climbed back on the bed, lying flat on her back, the wet cloth over her eyes.

"That's right, dear. Have a rest." Ros began tiptoeing towards the door. She was just about to open it when Tilly removed the pad, opened her eyes and fixing her with a stern gaze, said, "If you see Mama will you please tell her I'm having a rest and will not require any dinner, I do not wish to be disturbed."

"Not even your Mama, or Deaker?"

"No one," Tilly said in a resolute voice, sinking back on the pillow.

Ros went out, closing the door gently behind her.

In the kitchen, Deaker woke up with a start. Her mouth had fallen open and her modest snores had reached a crescendo and it was the last, overblown snore, which had been enough to jolt her awake.

"Oh dear, dear," she murmured wiping her mouth on the corner of her apron. "This won't do." She glanced at the clock. "Good gracious!" She suddenly wondered if it had been the bell which had wakened her.

Looking out of the passage door at the row of bells on the ceiling of the corridor, she saw that one was, indeed, still vibrating. But it was not the drawing room bell. It was the front door. Jeannie came running down the back stairs.

"That'll be Miss Ros' carriage, Mrs, I should say." She hurried through the baize swing doors.

Deaker came back into the kitchen. The fire needed making up and she stooped to put on more coals, holding the small of her back. It was strange that Miss Edna hadn't rung for tea yet. It was nearly half past five, where was she? She went to the windows to pull the curtains. The house seemed unusually quiet. Somehow, she could tell when no one was about. Then she heard footsteps.

"That'll be the Missus," she said. The clatter of steel tipped heels were going fainter as the wearer of boots walked away along the tiled floor in the domed central hallway. She must have come from her walk. She ought to take off her boots. Jeannie took an hour polishing that floor this morning. Besides it wasn't safe with those boots on, she'd skid and fall, then there'd be a howdedo.

It was already dusk in the yard, which was hidden from the light of sunset by tall trees on the bank and the bulk of the house itself. A cock with glossy blue black tail feathers was stretching his wings out, first the left then the right. His wives had all gone in to roost. He was evidently making sure all had gone in, before he followed them into the hen house. Suddenly he stretched his neck out and gave an aggressive squawk. He turned round and addressed himself for battle, chest feathers upstanding, head down and wings raised.

Deaker peered round, cramming her neck to see what had frightened the rooster. Out of the shadows at the end of the yard, there coalesced the figure of a man. The old woman frowned. It couldn't be Tom, or George, they would have approached the bird, calling him by name, or kicking out if he came to peck at them. Deaker could now see the man more clearly, but he was just standing without moving. Who was it? It must be an intruder. Her breath was coming short and fast, as she tried to decide what to do. Where was everyone? Suddenly she remembered that Jeannie was at that moment opening the door to Ros' coachman. Perhaps this person, whoever it was, was something connected with her, a groom or footman, who'd been talking to George and Tom. That must be it.

She went to the back door, flung it open and shouted. "Mrs. is going now. You'd better hurry up if you're to ride back with the carriage."

There was no response, as she watched the shadowy figure moved out of sight. But Deaker had had a chance for a better glance at the man.

Jeannie came back into the kitchen.

"Has she gone?" Deaker asked, the words catching in her throat.

"She has, Mrs Deaker. And they took no tea. I come back in here with the tea tray untouched, but I didn't wake you being as you was resting."

"No tea? Didn't Miss Tilly neither?"

"No, she didn't. She's in her bedroom and Miss Ros, Mrs Arbuthnot, I should say, went up there with her some time, they were talking but Miss Tilly did not come down with her."

"Well, well." Deaker took a last look out of the window, then drew the curtains vigorously so the curtain rings rattled.

"Did anyone else come for Mrs Arbuthnot? Has she a footman?"

"Just the groom and her coachman. He's a nice man."

"That's as may be." Deaker settled down again in her armchair by the fire. "Make the fire, my girl, and then we'll be having our tea. They won't be wanting nothing now till dinner, unless Master does come today."

"Aye, that'll be it. Happen he'll be home soon."

Deaker wished the Master would be home soon. He was still in London. She wanted him back here, now. This was where his duty lay, this was his home and he should be with his wife and daughter. She felt uncomfortable about the shadowy figure in the yard. Who was it? Suddenly she felt a tingly sensation, goose pimples came out on her arms. She suddenly knew who it was, who'd been lurking there. It was Robert Willoughby, Mr Manstone's clerk. Impossible. There was no lesson today. Why was he there? And why hadn't he come over when she'd called?

"Where's Madam?" she asked Jeannie. "Didn't she want no tea, Jeannie?"

"She never rung the bell. I fancy she's only just come in, any road. I heard her door go."

Deaker continued to gaze into the fire, where the coals which had just been added, were sending out bright new tongues of flame."

Jeannie, up first next morning, was on her knees on the upstairs landing, wiping dust off the banister rails. She'd already swept and laid all the grates and lit fires in the morning room and kitchen. It was hard work, now Mavis had gone. There had never been talk of replacing her, but for the few weeks she had been here, it had been wonderful. Now, she was back to being scullery maid and housemaid. And parlour maid, too, for that matter. It was too bad. Why had the girl gone off, sudden, like that? Deaker had been to see her ma, but she'd had no joy out of that. Just said the girl was needed at home. A likely story.

The water was on, heating up for the morning ablutions. Deaker was in the kitchen, preparing porridge for breakfast. It was half past six. In another hour the household would be awake. Jeannie noticed a light shining under Miss Tilly's room. She frowned. Sunday, it was unusual for the young lady to be up early of a Sabbath. She dipped her cleaning cloth into the sudsy water, wrung it out, then meticulously wiped round the rails again. There was no noise coming from the bedroom. She wondered if she should go in and light the fire. If Miss Tilly was out of bed already it would be cold up there. Happen she was up early to go somewhere for the day, but no one had mentioned it. Jeannie crept up to the door, put her ear to it and listened. From within came the sound of gentle snoring, which as she stood there, suddenly ceased.

Tilly had wakened for a long moment. She had lain there, struggling to orient her mind. She'd only been asleep for a few hours and now she felt as if she was floundering through a sea of mud which threatened to engulf her. Her soul felt heavy, nearly drowning. Suddenly she remembered what had kept her awake so late, what had sent her mind into corridor of nightmares. It was her suspicion, even realisation, that her mother was no longer her mother, a loved, real, generous, beautiful person, but a stranger, someone who had secretly met, in her husband's own house, a man who was under contract to her husband, as she was, and who, like herself, was betraying him. She was certain that the two people whom she had seen in the wood were her mother, and Robert Willoughby. They had been together, and she knew that it wasn't the first time. When she had seen Willoughby by the canal a few days before, he must have been involved in some assignation with her mother then. Tilly had turned these thoughts round and round in her mind, all night long. But she was sure that she knew the truth. This woman was no longer her mother, but a treasonable despicable wretch. The iniquity of it, the dire wickedness. Tilly lay there, nauseous, she couldn't bring herself to put her thoughts into words, these dreadful thoughts which were like indigestible toadstools in her stomach, making her retch, and gasp. She moaned a little...struggling if only she could get rid of this awful sick feeling. Her limbs fell paralysed. She moaned again.

The lamp was still burning, as she'd left it when she'd gone to sleep, vainly hoping leaving it alight would dispel the shadows. Now its feeble glimmer was fading as the dawn rose.

There was a tentative tap on the door. Tilly pulled the cover over her head, she had a moment's horror that it might be her mother. "Go away," she muttered, but softly and without conviction. If only it would go away, all go away, if only she could wake up, properly, and it would all be a dream.

The knock came again. "It's me, Miss Tilly. Jeannie. Can I get your tea for you, Miss, and light the fire, being as you're not so well?"

Jeannie had remembered Tilly hadn't been down for dinner the previous night.

Tilly took her handkerchief from under her pillow. It was still damp, but she wiped her nose with it, again, pushed the hairs out of her eyes and with her lids closed tight, said, "Come in..."

Jeannie entered. "I don't wish to disturb you, Miss," she whispered. She tiptoed to the fire and threw a few sticks from the basket onto the embers. In a moment the flames were leaping up. "There now, that's better. Shall I let some light in Miss Tilly? I'll send for Deaker if you like?" She drew the curtains and then made up the fire with small logs and some coal. "That's coming on, nice now, Miss. Shall I be telling Deaker for some tea, Miss?"

For answer Tilly put her arm out of bed and grasped the young girl's hand. "You're a good girl, Jeannie," she said. Tears were at the corners of her eyes.

"Oh Miss," Jeannie sank down by the bed. "You're not well. What is it? Should I let your Mama know?"

"No. No. I'm all right. Go on now and get me some tea." Tilly squeezed Jeannie's hand and gulped, then turned on her other side. "Bring me some water and ask Tom to get Silver ready, I'll take her out. Tom will come too. Tell him I'll have a ride in fifteen minutes. I'll have breakfast later and let Deaker know." As she heard Jeannie going down the stairs, she dragged herself out of bed, slowly and ponderously, like an old woman.

By the time Edna came down for breakfast at nine o'clock Tilly had still not returned from her early morning ride. She was alone with her thoughts but she was not lonely. Her night had been as wakeful as Tilly's, but in her case, she'd been fully conscious, retracing the events of the last few weeks and dwelling on her dream for the future. Her mind kept going round and round, her thoughts always reverting to the same theme, Robert, and their future. She'd tried to relax herself, stretching her feet to the bottom of the bed, then turning again and again, trying to recollect, through her finger tips, the satin warmth of his skin, the tickly softness of the hair at the nape of his neck.

She wanted him again, already. When she'd at last drifted into sleep, she'd had that dream again, of floating, with her tiptoes just above the floor. She was in an enormous room, and every so often, she swooped up to the ceiling. It had seemed so easy, and she'd looked down on everyone below her, why couldn't they do it too? Now, she stretched out her arms. If only he was here, with her, in this comfy warm bed. She wanted them to be together, but not secretly. She could see the light through the curtains, and she remembered it was Sunday. She would have to be going to church. How could she avoid that? She felt she couldn't possibly go through with that, an extra burden of deceit. She would have to tell a lie, and say she had a headache.

In fact Edna did not know when Robert would come, possibly it would be days before she would see him again. He was right to have concerns about their meeting here. Even if no-one had seen them together yesterday, it must only be a matter of time. What was she to do? She would have to put on a false face, and wait patiently. So she had to accept the fact she was in a world of toast and boiled eggs, not of roses, waterfalls and fountains. It would change though, she must be patient.

The clock struck nine o'clock; then, like the figure on a mediaeval clock, which appears on the hour, the morning room door opened, and in came Tilly in her riding-habit, her cheeks flushed from the ride and her hair squashed down where her hat had kept it flat.

"Good morning, Mother," she said, throwing her gloves and riding whip on a spare chair.

"Tilly, my darling," Edna said smiling and turning her face upwards for a kiss but Tilly sat down, without greeting her. She arranged her habit carefully and drew her chair up to the table.

"I'll ring for some fresh tea," Edna continued, as if she had not noticed her daughter's action.

"No, thank you," Tilly said. She folded her hands in front of her and stared at her mother.

"Tilly what is it? Have you had a fright?" Edna asked holding her napkin in front of her mouth. "What is it?"

Tilly just stared at her. Unblinkingly she knew the moment had come. It could be a moment of courage or of cowardice. It could change the future of everyone she knew, forever. She must pull out the serpent's sting, even if it killed her. Now. Now. "Mother, I know..."

Edna half rose. Her lips parted. "What do you know?" She gazed at her daughter and caught the stare in her eyes. She pushed her chair back abruptly and went over to the fireplace, her back turned towards Tilly. "You don't know anything."

"I do. I know it all. Don't tell me what I do or don't know," Tilly sat bolt upright but with her head bent, looking at the table. "I do know. I've been thinking all night, I've hardly slept." She glanced round at her mother.

Edna's face was flushed, her eyes sparkling. "I've done nothing wrong. There's nothing I'm ashamed of. Tell me what I've done wrong."

"I can't. I cannot bring myself to that. Please do not make me do that. Please." As Tilly spoke the last word, she brought her two hands up to cover her face.

"My darling child." In two strides Edna was over to her, clasping her round the shoulders, with her cheek against the girl's fingers. "Please don't."

For answer, Tilly's shoulders heaved as she struggled for breath which came and went in great sobs. "How could you do it?" She managed to ask, through clenched teeth. "Of course it's wrong. You know it is. How can you say that? Don't touch me." She shook Edna's hands away. "He's just a common clerk, and he works for Papa. It's all too unbelievable. How could you, how could you? Such a man."

Edna was standing quietly. "You don't know what you are talking about. He has more about him than your father ever had. He's kind and gentle and a gentleman, I know he is. More of a gentleman than..."

"What are you saying? Is what he is doing gentlemanly?"

"You don't know anything about what he's doing," Edna's voice was raised.

Suddenly the door opened and Deaker appeared, with a tray. She stopped at the sight of the two women, facing each other's, eyes blazing. Tilly immediately rose and went towards the window and Edna sat down again at her place.

"Excuse me, Ma'am. I thought as how Miss Tilly would like some fresh tea." She put the teapot on the table and removed the old one.

"Thank you," Edna said.

"Will there be anything else?"

"I think not."

There was silence as Deaker collected up some soiled plates and cups. She went out again with the tray.

Tilly turned back from the window. "You must promise not to see him again." There was a pause. Edna's face was impassive. "I saw you, I saw you both together. Yesterday."

Edna turned her eyes on her. "You don't know what you are talking about," she said again.

"If you don't promise me, I shall inform Papa. For his sake, and yours and mine, if it comes to that," Tilly announced this, pausing between every few words. "I mean it mother. It has to be so."

Edna said nothing and Tilly came back to the table, placing her hands on the edge and leaning forward. She looked into her mother's eyes. "I mean it."

A low moan came from Edna's mouth. She put her napkin to her mouth, then rose, thrust it down and went towards the fire.

There was a silence then, in a low voice, Tilly said, "Well." She left the room.

Somehow, Edna felt very calm. Now it had come to this, she was cool. Silly girl. So, she would tell Enoch then. Just as well. She sat down in the armchair by the fire. The clock was ticking gently on the mantelpiece. Edna remained quiet for a moment, she felt empty inside. She couldn't lie to herself. Now, the truth was out, and it had to be recognised. What she couldn't grasp was that the person, who every day for eighteen years had taken her breakfast in this room, sat in this armchair, listened to the clock on the mantelpiece, had been herself, the very same person who now sat here. She knew she, Edna, had been a child before she'd fallen in love with Robert, a child, anxious to please, demure, quiet. Now she was an adult at last. She'd made a decision and she would stand by it. She sat there thinking for a long time, every now and then her mind coming back to look at objects in the room, the candlesticks on the mantelpiece, the sampler, framed and hung on the wall opposite, the mahogany occasional table, the Persian rug. She knew the provenance of all these things. The past, through them, called to her. At the same time she was comparing herself to Tilly. Tilly had decided what she wanted to do and had done it. She'd worked in the office with her father and now she wished to leave and go to College. No doubt she would achieve that too. For a tiny moment, Edna felt a pang. Would what she was doing interfere with what Tilly wanted? She did not wish this to happen. Her decision should be for herself alone. She dismissed, as soon as it occurred, the realisation that no decision can impinge on only one life. She stood up and looked at herself in the mirror above the mantelpiece. She smoothed the skin under her eyes, and pushed her hair back where it had escaped from behind her ears. She turned her head sideways to catch a glimpse of her profile. She ran the back of her fingers upwards from her chin over her cheeks. She looked into the reflection of her eyes. Deep in the pupils she could see her face. She felt she was seeing herself for the first time. Yes, she was young, beautiful and strong. She must see Robert.

Edna pulled the bell and could hear it jangling in the corridor. She waited. No one came. She pulled the bell again, and again she waited. This time she heard running feet. Jeannie came breathlessly to the door.

"Excuse me Ma'am. I was upstairs. Mrs Deaker isn't well Ma'am. She's fainted, I think."

"Fainted. Whatever next?" Edna stood bewildered for a moment. "Where is she?"

"She's in the kitchen, Ma'am."

Edna hurried out into the passage and along the corridor to the kitchen. The old lady was slumped in the wooden armchair. Her face was grey and her eyes closed.

"I've been upstairs Ma'am and I come in to wash my hands, Ma'am, before answering the bell and there she was."

Edna was bent down over Deaker, listening to her breathing. She could scarcely hear it, but it was there. She took her limp hand.

"Wake up, Deaker, wake up. It's me. It's me, come on now, wake up."

There was no response. "Get a damp cloth Jeannie, and then get my smelling salts, from the cabinet by my bed." Edna felt completely cool. She could face anything, manage anything.

Yes, Ma'am," Jeannie rushed out of the door.

"And ask Miss Tilly to come at once. We'll have to send for Doctor Makepiece, if she's no better."

As the door banged behind Jeannie, Deaker stirred. Her eyelids fluttered, they opened wide. "Where am I? What happened?" she said.

"You're with me, dear," Edna said, stroking the old woman's hand. "Don't worry, don't worry. You're all right."

Deaker shifted in her seat, pulling herself into a more upright position.

"Oh, I am sorry, Miss Edna. I don't feel too well."

"I know, I know. You'll need to rest for a while. I'll tell Jeannie to see you into bed."

The next minute Jeannie and Tilly came into the kitchen. Tilly stood back as Jeannie handed the sal volatile to her mother. "There you are now, sniff this."

The effect was immediate. Slight colour returned to Deaker's withered cheeks and she managed a warm smile.

"There now, I'm all right."

"Nonsense," Tilly's voice came. "She must rest."

"Of course you must," Edna said. "Jeannie will take you up and you must stay in bed all day. I won't hear of anything else. Matilda, you go with them."

The two young women got hold of Deaker and supported her across the room into the corridor, while Edna held the door open.

"You rest there. I shall go myself to Doctor Makepiece to put you up something."

Tilly looked over her shoulders at her mother, but did not smile.

"I'll take the trap," Edna said. She went out into the yard to find Tom.

"Sit with her, Jeannie," Tilly said, when they had managed to get Deaker upstairs. She went down to the empty kitchen and put the kettle on the range. The hob was hardly warm and she realised she would have to make the fire up. Why had she not sent Jeannie to these mundane tasks, while she herself tended Deaker? Somehow, she found herself unable to cope with the old woman's illness. She'd rather occupy herself with doing something active. She filled the hod with coal and rattled it onto the smouldering fire. Almost at once the lumps started smoking, then caught light.

Tilly settled herself in Deaker's chair waiting for the kettle to boil.

It took Tom nearly an hour to take Edna to the Doctor's, near Westham Park.

"Here you are Ma'am. Shall I pass the message, or will you get down?"

"Of course, I'll see him myself." Why on earth should she have come, if she had not planned to see the doctor? She climbed out of the trap and rang the front door bell. The maid answered.

"Doctor Makepiece?"

"Beg pardon, Ma'am. He's away out on a call. Will you wait?"

Edna was paralysed. Suddenly she saw the solution. She turned to Tom

"Wait here for the doctor. I have some errands to make. "

"Yes, Ma'am," Tom raised his whip in salutation and Edna turned out of the gate, to go down the hill. Her heart was thumping. She knew fairly well where Robert lived. She had to take the chance that he would be at home. She had to see him.

There was no one about in the main road in which Makepiece lived. Large houses in their own gardens were sheltered from the street by sturdy plane trees. The slope went down steeply towards the valley where the river and the canal both flowed. Edna crossed one bridge, then another. Children were playing on the tow path. They were occupied with their games and did not notice her. Along the canal bank several men were casting their lines. They were gazing steadfastly at the water and once again, Edna passed unnoticed. The road began to climb and smaller roads lined with terraces of houses gave off at each side. Edna remembered Rob's address. She'd had a discussion about the naming of streets when Enoch, as a Parish Councillor, had been asked to suggest names for the new terraces of houses being built at Epsilon. She had thought he might use the names of battles, and he had then said.

"My clerk lives in Crimea Road. I don't know, as we want another so near."

But Edna didn't know the number. However she pressed on, somehow she was sure she would find him and she would not have to ask. She walked on quickly, her veil pulled down over her bonnet. The street was quiet. Her breath was coming quickly, as she hurried along. For a moment, she wished she hadn't come on this mission. But she dismissed the thought. She needed to see Robert and tell him what had happened with Tilly. She was scanning the curtained windows as she went, trying to discover some clues as to Robert's whereabouts. She felt he must be here, he could not be out. Surely he would sense her presence, and come out to her. He must do so, he must.

The road flattened out. She had nearly come to the junction with another street running across. She wondered whether to cross over and look at the houses on the other side, or to continue over the next road. But perhaps this was the end of Crimea Road. She hesitated. There came the notes of a piano. Softly but surely, the music tinkled out from the very window outside which Edna was standing. A rush of tenderness came over her, she leaned forward, almost fainting, her breath coming short. It was Robert, she knew it. It was his way of playing. She was certain it was him. She felt again a surge of warmth. He was here. In a moment he would be with her. She braced herself with her fingertips on the low brick wall round the tiny front garden. Should she open the gate and walk down the path?

She stared at the lace curtains. The playing went on, it was a piece she knew. She was gathered in by the melody and floated on it, like a petal of cherry blossom on a stream.

The music stopped with a crashing chord, dissonant, extreme.

The next moment the door opened. It was Robert, fierce eyed. "What are you doing?" he asked hoarsely. "Come in!"

She immediately pulled up the latch of the gate and in a moment he had grasped her arm, pulling her inside.

"Why are you here?"

"I found you," she said, drawing his face down towards her. He kissed her, hard, on the mouth, then their bodies relaxed against each other. Edna smelled the tobacco on his clothes. She suddenly thought of his smell being on her, when she went home. But it wouldn't matter. Concealment was over. She leaned her cheek against his shoulder.

"Matilda knows."

His body grew tense. He pushed her away, holding her at arm's length.

"She must have seen us, both, together... Yesterday."

"Come in here." He opened the door into the front room. It was small and dark. The piano was against the wall near the window. The dim daylight was trapped into insignificance by the heavy net curtains and the pot plant on a stand in the bay.

"I heard you playing. That's how I knew which house. Don't you feel surprised I found you? I knew I would."

"I am. Very surprised."

"I liked what you were playing. I wish I could bring my violin here. Couldn't I visit?"

Robert shook his head in disbelief. What nonsense was this? He indicated a chair for the woman. Edna sat down her hands clenched on her lap, her head bowed.

"What does the lass know?"

"Oh. Everything I suppose. She's very angry. I had to see you. She says, she'll tell Enoch if I don't promise not to see you. Can you believe it?" She smiled ruefully.

He stretched out his hand to her cheek. "What are you going to do?"

"What can I do? I don't think I can manage without you? It doesn't matter about them. They're both strong enough people. But I'm not, Robert. I'm not." For the first time, there was a catch in her voice. "You tell me what I can do." She grasped his wrist, turned the palm of his hand towards her and held it to her mouth. It was warm; she could feel her breath moist against it. She bent her body against his, half falling from the chair. "Oh," she moaned. "Oh." The tears were coming.

"Now, now," he said, his arms round her. "Now, now. We'll see. We'll see. It will be all right. It will."

Her sobs contained, her body was shaking at long intervals. "I don't know what to do. Deaker's ill. That's how I managed to come. I came for the doctor, but he wasn't there. George is waiting for him. I haven't long. Deaker's bound to think it strange if I don't go home with Doctor Makepiece, if he goes." She now felt more muddled than before.

"Come on," Robert held her more tightly. "Deaker will be all right. If she's ill, she won't notice. What happened?"

"She just fainted. It's probably nothing. But she hasn't been looking well for some time. She's quite old, you know." Edna blew her nose. "I must be going."

"I'll come with you."

"No...no. I had to tell you. But there's nothing you can do now. I have an idea about what to do. If Matilda goes to College, that's what she wants to do, I am sure we can manage. We must, we must, Robert. She won't tell Enoch, I'm sure."

"Don't think about it anymore now. Be very cool. Say nothing. No-one can prove anything. No-one will accuse you. You must trust me. Just trust me." He pulled her to him again. "I can't have you unhappy like this."

Edna's face was ravaged with tears. She smiled briefly, then turned her head, holding her hands over her face.

"You must be brave and go home now. See to Deaker. Act normally with Matilda. I shall arrange everything, you shall see. Wait here." He went out of the room, and Edna sank down on the stool with her back to the piano. She looked round the little room, with its dark wallpaper and fringed curtains. Out of all these things, only one of them had a soul, everything else was dead and muddy like jetsam on the tide line. Only the piano had an inner life and that piano, she knew, was Robert's. If only she could be standing here with her violin, while he played. If only she and he were married, even a little house like this would be paradise. But she'd make it light and airy with flowers, and rich colours, it would glow and radiate, and come alive. Perhaps she could do it. Perhaps it would happen. Then she would look back on this morning like a bad dream, or another life, a memory of another person.

Robert came back carrying a small tray with a glass of lemonade; also, on a dish was a folded napkin. "I damped a serviette for you," he said. "You must wipe your face."

Obediently she unfolded the cloth and dabbed her face with it. She surveyed her reflection in the shining wood of the upright piano. Yes, that was better. She took two sips of the lemonade. Already she was distancing herself from the room, from Robert, from her dreams. She put on her hat again, adjusted the veil.

"I'll be in touch," he said squeezing her fingertips, as she went in to the hall door. He signalled to her to wait for a moment, as he opened the front door. He glanced up and down the street. There was no one in sight. He beckoned her forward and she went down the path and through the gate without a glance.

At the bottom of the road she passed an elderly woman, hurrying the other way. It was Mrs Jakes, Robert's landlady.

There wasn't a sound as Mrs Jakes turned her key, and walked softly over the threshold. Robert had been tinkling on the piano when she went out. Now the silence in the house was thick and cloying. A slight smell wafted along the tiled corridor from the kitchen. The stew which she had put on for the Sunday meal before going out, was now emitting an enticing aroma. Where was the lad? She'd had thought he'd still be practising. That was what he did on a Sunday, prior to going out, dressed up, probably to see that young woman he'd been walking out, or, maybe, to sing with those friends of his. She stood ruminating for a moment. There was something strange, not quite ordinary. She sniffed. That was it. As well as the scent of best end of neck onions, and carrots, there was a slight fragrance. It was lavender, lavender water. A woman's perfume.

Without bothering to knock, after all, it was her own dining room, she turned the door knob and went into the room. Rob was seated on the music stool, with his back to the piano; his feet flat on the floor and his hands on his knees. He met her gaze without smiling, then, nodded slowly.

"Well, Mr Willoughby. I never thought you were in here. I guessed you'd have been upstairs in your room by now, getting ready to go out."

There was a pause. Robert still gazed at her. "Dinner won't be long. If you want any, that is." A slight note of sarcasm had crept into her voice and she came into the room, panting slightly and sat down heavily on one of the upright chairs by the table.

"That hill I wish someone would iron it out. They can do that for railways. It's killing me that is."

"You should wait for the tram, Mrs Jakes."

"That's all right for some. Now then, Mr Willoughby, we can't keep chatting here all day." She rose, leaning on her stick. "Has there been a visitor? I didn't expect no one."

For a moment a sign of alarm passed across Rob's face. "Yes, as a matter of fact. My cousin called by. My uncle's been taken very ill. I have to go to Cheshire tonight."

"Your cousin?"

"My cousin Ruth. She'd come on the train. But she didn't stop. She had to go straight back. I'm to follow later."

"Oh there. Well, I am so sorry. No doubt it's very serious, if she was to come all the way out here."

"No doubt. No doubt." Rob rose and straightened the music stool, putting down the lid of the piano. "She had to inform another relative at once, as well. But then she'll be returning."

Mrs Jakes suddenly remembered the veiled lady she'd passed as she came up the street.

"Well, I believe I may have seen her at the crossing. I am truly sorry."

Rob felt relief he hadn't lied about the visitor. He'd guessed the old woman must have noticed Edna. His fabrication had proved to be the right thing to do.

He rose. "I won't be requiring dinner, Mrs Jakes." He had to act quickly if what Edna had told him was true. The best method of defence was to attack. He'd learned that from his days playing chess with one of the other clerks at the Solicitors' office where he'd had his first job. Attack, attack, when or where it was least expected.

They both went into the hall. The savoury stew would have been tempting enough in other circumstances. Now, Rob noticed, it merely made him slightly queasy. "I'll be home very late, that is, if I can get away at all," he said.

"God be with you. I'll pray for the old man. What is his name, Mr Willoughby?"

"Robert," Robert said. "Same as mine. Robert Willoughby." No point in wasting the old girl's prayers; he laughed to himself, as he slammed shut the front door

Outside, it was cold. He turned up his coat collar. He'd gone out without his muffler though his cap was in his pocket. He put it on. He hurried down the hill and within a few moments he was in the street where Gertie lived. Shivering, he knocked at the front door.

"What is it? Good gracious. I didn't think you were coming till later." The door opened straight into the living room, where the fire was lit.

"Oh, Gert. Let me in - there's a good girl."

"Come on then! You're all of a shiver, what's up with you?" She led him through. "Sit down now and I'll get you a mug of tea." Robert stood back to the fire as she went into the kitchen. "What is the matter? I know there's something."

"Nowt to worry about. I just heard from Master he's got a special job for me. He can't trust no one else."

"Special job?" She came back into the doorway. "I don't know what you mean. It's Sunday.. He can't want you today, surely."

"It's nowt to do with the factory. Well, it is and it isn't."

"You're always artful, Robert Willoughby. That's you. I don't feel you're ever clear with me. Do you know or not what it is he wants?" She went back to the singing kettle, mashed the tea, refilled the kettle from the pump by the stone ware sink and replaced it on the hob.

Robert stood and watched her, as she wiped her hands on her apron, then, on second thoughts, untied the bow at her waist, removed and folded it to hang on the line over the range. She came and stood in front of him, the teapot in one hand and the cups in the other. He barred her way. She put her head on one side, raising her eyebrows and pursing her lips."Let me by, if tha want th' tea."

He moved aside, clasping his hands behind his back. "I cannot say more for I don't know any more. Mr Manstone sent a message to me to say he had to see me urgently. I don't know what about."

"Well, did he send a telegram?"

"A note, with the lad."

Gertie gasped. "Are you going then?"

"I have to, haven't I?"

"Why can't he wait till the office, he'll see you then?" She said, and poured the tea out.

Rob took his cup and began, still standing to drink. All of a sudden, he felt parched. Now, he realised he was hungry too. How foolish he now felt, at having missed his dinner, for an attack of nerves. What should he have to fear, even if Tilda did have some idea of what had happened between himself and her mother? What had happened anyway? Precious little and nowt anyone could prove. There was no chance at all, she could have seen anything. It was all surmises.

"Woulds't like a pie?" he asked Gertie. "I could get a pie and a cake for us, if tha will."

"Where from, this day? I've had my dinner. Haven't you?"

"No. Mrs Jakes wasna well. So I said I'd eat out."

"I've had a good meal, thank you Robert. And I wouldn't have a pie anyway. It seems to me...Have you forgot tha was coming over this afternoon for tea? Ma's got something special, but I shanna tell thee what."

"Tisn't my wish to have to go to see Manstone, I keep telling you. I won't be here later. That's why I came, to tell thee."

Robert turned to go. As usual, Gertie was beginning to irritate him. She'd always go on and on, nagging about this and that. He couldn't imagine why he'd come round to see her. It hadn't been to tell her of the true nature of the message from Manstone's household. God forbid. Somehow or other his first thoughts had been to fly to Gertie, when he realised what a scrape he appeared to be in. But now, he felt she was just another part of the whole problem. He'd made up the whole story about the message from Manstone. He couldn't abide having to see her tonight, and eat the old woman's tea. .

"Good bye Gertie," he said, putting his cap on again. He did not make to kiss her, he just strode away on up the hill, towards the centre of the town.

Gertie closed the door and locked it. She poured herself another cup of tea, then gazed into the cup. Tears began to ooze out from the corners of her eyes. Her lips were trembling. She put her head on the table, her shoulders began shaking as she drew choking, sobbing breaths. Robert had gone off in a bad temper, he'd lost patience with her. How often had that happened? It was always happening. But she loved him so much. It was because she loved him she'd been angry with him when he said he'd be at Manstone's instead of coming for tea. It was always Manstone this and Manstone that. It was his whole life, and there was no place for her.

She knew, she knew for sure, he was drawing away from her. Why didn't he just go and leave her for good, if she wasn't good enough for him? He must know more than he would tell her. Why didn't he trust her? If he loved her as she loved him, he'd tell her everything of his plans. He didn't even want to talk of what their plans would be when they'd get married, where they'd live and whether Ma could live with them. There was no possibility that she'd ever go and leave her mother. Robert knew that, and Gertie thought he'd accepted it. But he never made plans about their future, whereas she thought about it all the time. It was what she dreamed endlessly, when she was painting hour after hour in the decorating shop.

There came a knocking from the floor above. It was Ma, ready for her drink. She'd been poorly all morning and kept to her bed. Gertie filled a stoneware hot water bottle, which stood on the windowsill, and took it upstairs. "Here you are now, Ma. Here's a nice fresh hot bottle for you," she said, turning the covers back from her mother's feet.

The old woman smiled weakly and her eyes fluttered open briefly. Gertie sat on the bed, and chafed the cold feet and then put them gently on the bottle. "That's not too hot."

"That's lovely my girl. That's a kind wench."

Gertie supported her and pumped up the pillow in the other hand.

"Robert won't be here for tea."

"Robert's a happy man to have thee promised to him. You're a good girl. I don't know why he's waiting. Happen it's for me to go. It mustn't do for you two to find me in the way."

"I don't, Ma. Of course not. I'm not leaving you. That's all I know. Now rest a while," she said after a moment. "Put your cup here when you've finished cans't?" She cleared a little space on the bedside table.

Shutting the door gently, she clambered back down the narrow stairs again. There was still enough tea in the pot for her to have a second cup. She sighed, poured it out, and sat back in her chair, with her eyes closed. The tears were beginning to ooze, and she wiped at them fiercely, with the back of her hand.

21

Dr.Makepiece went to Terrilea on his own, when Tom said he had to wait for the Mistress to return from her errands. Jeannie told Tilly that the Mistress wasn't back yet, but the Doctor had arrived. Tilly was stunned. Mother was returning later, and Tom was waiting for her? It must be that she'd gone to see Robert. Tilly raced up to her mother's boudoir.

"It's impossible. She wouldn't have done that," she breathed, leaning against the door jamb. She had a vision of the lovers in the wood, that foul man's arm round Mother's waist, her face turned up towards him. She clenched her fists and beat on the door.

"Why aren't you there? I've got to talk to you." There was no answer and she opened the door. The room was empty. Tilly pushed through the room, to the bedroom door. She flung herself on the bed, weeping, clasping the pillow to her and moaning.

Where was everybody? She was deserted. Why was not father here? He would know what to do. She sat and bit her lip, clenching her fingers against her forehead, and now she was holding her head in her hands, gripping it tightly, snuffling, and tasting the salt tears on her lips. "Oh, come back, come back," she kept repeating. "It's not too late. We love you, we love you."

Suddenly she heard a man speaking outside in the corridor, and for a moment she thought it was her father. The voice came nearer, now she could make out the words.

"I'll leave a note for your Mistress and you're to make sure, Jeannie, Mrs Deaker doesn't get up today. You'll have to do her work for her."

"Oh, I will, I will Sir," Jeannie replied. She already did, any road. "I'll look after her. I do. I always do."

"I'm sure you do your duty and will be rewarded when your time comes. Now then, I'll go into the library and write the note."
The footsteps went past the door.

Tilly sat down at her mother's dressing table and looked at herself in the triple mirror. Her hair was dishevelled and her eyes swollen. She took her mother's brush, undid her bun and ran the bristles through her long hair. That was better. She brushed and brushed, tossing her hair along her shoulders, as she did so.

Well, she could manage, and she would manage. They could all manage, that was certain. She took the lavender spray and applied some to her forehead, and behind her ears. The cloud of perfume made her sneeze. There, she felt better. Her hair was tied back on top of her head. She stood up, brushed her skirt down and left the room. She felt hollow inside but at the same time, resolute and calm. She knew now she could cope and she knew what she was going to do.

In the hall Doctor was just leaving.

"Ah, Miss Matilda," he said, raising his top hat, "your old servant is quite comfortable now, thanks be. I think she should have a few days complete rest. Would you kindly pass on the news to Mrs. Manstone? I understand from Jeannie here she had a sudden errand in town which prevented her returning with me. Nothing else serious, I hope?"

"Not at all," Tilly said in a firm voice.

The doctor had no sooner left, than the front door bell tinkled again. It was the telegraph boy delivering a telegram. Tilly, who was just on her way back upstairs was summoned back by Jeannie. "He wants to know if there's a reply, Miss," she said, in a hushed voice. Everything seemed to be happening today, just when Mrs. Deaker was ill and father was away. Tilly tore open the little yellow envelope which was addressed to Mrs Manstone.

"Returning tonight, arriving at 10.40. Tom to meet train. Enoch."

"No reply, thank you," she said to the lad. "Wait a moment. Jeannie fetch my bag. On my bedside table."

Jeannie hurried off, her cap bobbing and the boy stood with his legs apart and his hands behind his back. He'd never been out to this house before, and he tried to steal a glance into the hall. There was a deep red rug on the floor, bowls of flowers, and a smell of wax polish. How these people lived! Jeannie came back with the purse, and Tilly gave him a threepenny bit.

"Thank you, Ma'am. Very much obliged." He touched his cap and went off. She was a nice woman and pretty too. Well, she could afford to be generous. What did she have to worry about?

Tilly watched him go. It was a tidy way for him to have walked, and a cold afternoon.

"When George comes in, he'll have to go out again tonight. Mr Marstone is to be picked up from the station at 10:40."

Jeannie went off. Tilly went into the dining room, where the fire had been lit, but the table was not laid. With Deaker being ill, everything was upside down. She wondered whether to recall Jeannie and tell her to lay the table and make some sandwiches. But she sat there without stirring. She didn't feel hungry. Why should she take it on herself to keep the routine running? If Mama needed food, she'd surely arrange for something to be done. An awful dread came over Tilly. If she ever did come back? But she was so sure Mama would come back. She must do so. In an hour or two, she would glide into the room, in her old accustomed way. Then everything would return to normal. By tomorrow it would all be as usual. The events of the last twenty-four hours would be as if they'd never happened. She knew, if

Mama were to come through the door now, they would cling together and she'd feel her mother's soft cheek against her own. Surely, she would be home in a moment, presumably with George, when he'd returned Doctor Makepiece to his house. Tilly had to decide what she was to say to her. Should she ask her outright whether she'd been to see Robert? And what if she got the reply she dreaded the most? Would she have the resolution to tell her father of the situation? Perhaps it was not too late to save the day. If, somehow, she could be with her mother, as she had been, they would never let anything come between them, ever again. If only it could be so.

Tilly realised that if her mother did come back now, it would mean she certainly hadn't been to see Robert, and the river of her own life would also to flow back into its usual course. She herself would never be able to pursue her ambition of pursuing her studies, and, perhaps, having a career of her own. She might have to give it all up. In the crisis of the last few hours, she'd seen her mother as a separate person, someone who had a life in her own right, not as someone in the family. And if Tilly wanted Edna to revert to being a true wife and mother, she too would have to resume her own role as dutiful daughter. If she were needed here, in the family, then she would have to stay. She knew with clarity that she couldn't snatch her own liberty, and expect her mother to continue shackled to an existence she hated. It must be that Mother hated it. Otherwise why should she have been captivated by that man? After all, he wasn't much. Yet Mama had found in him something which was missing in her life. How empty must her life be, to find solace in such a person! How unhappy she must have been to find happiness in that quarter!

Tilly gazed round the room. She saw it all as she'd never seen it before. The black clock, the carved marble flowers over the fireplace, the brass fire irons, the heavy-fringed drapes. All of them seemed as weighty and stuffy as sodden clothes encumbering a drowning swimmer. Most of the things in the room had been here as long as Tilly could remember. How many of them, she wondered, had actually been chosen by her mother?

Very many of them, now she came to think of it, had been bought by her father before he even married Edna. Did she really like them, or did she just accept them, as she had appeared to accept all the routines and structures of her life - the twice weekly visit to Church, the annual bazaar and fêtes, the tea and dinner parties with neighbours?

All the time Tilly was gazing into the fire. She let her head fall against the back of the chair. She must have slept, and was wakened by the noise of wheels on the gravel outside. She sat bolt upright in her chair, her heart beating, hardly able to breathe. She heard the front door open, footsteps in the hall. She sat still, waiting. Now, the door must open. Her mother would come to her. She heard Edna's voice in the hall. Then Jeannie's. Then there was nothing. Silence. After a few more minutes, Tilly opened the heavy door, and peered out into the hall. It was empty. There was a faint scent of lavender. Obviously Edna had just passed through; she hadn't heard her, but it was apparent she had gone straight up to her room.

Tilly stood by the stairs, her heart racing. Hadn't her mother even thought about the dinner? It was unbelievable. She would not go and find her. She would not. If Mama did not want to see her, so be it.

The hall clock was striking midnight as Tom finally delivered Enoch to his front door.

"Come at ten tomorrow," he ordered. The train had been late and then Dimple had cast a shoe, making a swift pace back from town impossible. The house was in darkness, save for a lamp burning in the porch. The wind was up and Enoch gave a glance upwards to the tall chimneys and central lantern. The builders had assured him they'd always be a match for any gales, but sometimes he wished he'd opted for a less pretentious, simpler roof to this, the mansion of his dreams.

"Night Tom. Get Dimple seen to in the morning."

"Of course, Sir." Tom raised his whip to tap his hat. What on earth was the Master on about? As if he didn't know his business by the horses. He led the limping animal back into the courtyard.

Enoch let himself in, no point in disturbing the maids, but no sooner was he in the hallway than a white clad figure materialised near the grandfather clock. It was Jeannie, without cap and apron but with a shawl round her, carrying a candle.

"Oh, Sir, I'm glad you're back safe. We was expecting you half an hour ago. Is anything wrong?"

"Nothing at all. Go on back to bed, I can manage myself."

"Mistress, no, I mean Miss Tilly telled me to leave you sandwiches. It is in the dining room, Sir."

"Very good." Why was the girl hovering? "What is it? Be off to bed. I'll not be wanting anything more."

"Yes, Sir," she curtsied. "It's just that we're all upset Sir, Mrs Deaker is ill, Sir. She had a funny turn. And I've had to manage, while the Mistress went for the doctor and Miss Tilly...," her voice trailed off.

Enoch frowned ...what was she saying? Deaker so ill that Edna had to go for the doctor herself? "Well, well. I'm sure the doctor has made certain everything's all right. Doctor Makepiece?"

Jeannie nodded.

"Ah, a good man. If she can't rally with him, then there's not much we can do. Now then, I'm sure I'll find out about it all in the morning."

“Yes, Sir,” she bobbed and let herself out. Enoch helped himself to the cold cuts, then took his tranche of bread and meat, and his wine, and went to the fire, warming his back. He grunted and cleared his throat, then quaffed his wine quickly.

He did not mind the fact that no one was up to receive him with a host of silly questions. How could he explain that he'd come home early without admitting that it was not business, which would have kept him over the weekend, in any case? When he'd seen his companion on Friday night she'd been so sweet and appealing he'd offered to take her to the Gardens on Saturday afternoon. In the morning he'd gone with Goodrich to the Chelsea Potteries, a busman's holiday if ever there was one. Then the girl had turned up for the lunch rendezvous, promptly enough, young and sweet in her huge flowery hat and bustle. They'd walked round the gardens for an hour and he'd bought her sherbet and put his arm round her waist. But when he'd suggested returning to her place, she'd stipulated a visit to a hotel, the Carlton, if you please. Suddenly he'd seen the light. It was quite unnecessary to incur such expense. A late dinner, yes - he'd go to that expense, but not a night in a hotel. She had a room in Islington, he'd been there of course, why should he not return there again? No, she would not. It had to be the Carlton, she'd set her heart on it.

“Be off with you, Miss,” he'd said. “I ain't made of money. You might as well know it. Where I come from, the lasses know when they're well off.”

He'd left her standing by the fountain, where the late sun had made rainbows through the water. After a meal in Holborn he'd had to hurry to get the last train back. He was annoyed about the girl, but he was tired anyway. These things happened. There would be another one where that came from.

Now he was home, and no one was up to welcome him. He thought of the wench who'd let him in. She was a fetching young thing. Without her cap and apron she seemed younger and vulnerable. He began to feel aroused. But he wasn't taking no more risks, in that quarter, after what had happened the last time, with that other one, the one who'd taken off, back to her Ma. He'd got away with that, all right, but this one, she was more about, she was, she'd get her money's worth.

He turned out one oil lamp, and took the other to see his way up the marble stairs. Out here, the chill of the evening penetrated, and it was even colder on the top landing where feeble moonlight shining through the belvedere made his lamp unnecessary. He opened the door of his dressing room.

The fire was lit and it was warmer here. The bed was turned down and the handle of the warming pan projected out over the foot.

Enoch divested himself of his collar, then sat on the bed to remove his boots. In stockinged feet he moved softly to the inner door connecting the dressing room with his wife's bedroom. He pushed it gently. It creaked, as usual.

Standing in the doorway he could make out the figure lying on the big bed.

The moon shone on Edna's face. She was awake and her eyes were open. She was gazing up at the ceiling and didn't turn to see him. He stood there, hardly daring to breathe. Then he felt a cough rising. He had to clear his throat. He swallowed hard, trying to quell the need to cough. It was of no use. Suddenly the cough came, Edna turned her head on the pillow and saw him.

"I'm back," Enoch said, padding across the floor.

"Yes," she said. Her left arm was lying on top of the covers. He went across the thick carpet and stood over her.

"What's all this to do?"

"I couldn't help it," Edna said, burying her face in the pillow. Enoch sat down on the bed.

"Now then. Don't take on." He gently stroked her face and then put her arm under the eiderdown. "She's an old woman now. Happen she'll get better and happen she won't."

There was no sign from Edna. Her eyes were closed and she was pressing her head hard down into the pillow. Suddenly, she turned on her back, and stroked Enoch's hand.

"Don't. Don't say anything," she gasped.

Enoch sat still for a moment. Then he got to his feet. "She'll be better in the morning. And if she isn't, well, there it is. Tha' hast still got me. Think on it. We're married and I love thee, ma wench. Whatever else tha thinkest."

"I know, you do, Enoch, I know. But you don't know who I am. You don't know it, and you never have," Edna sat up in bed. "You don't know who I am, and you never will."

Enoch stared at her. What was this? He coughed. "Well, it's time we did understand each other. If that's the trouble. As for me, I've always been a good husband. I've given thee everything tha would have. And I need summat in return, I do. A bargain is a bargain. I tell thee what, ma wench, I've a mind to claim what's owed me," Enoch was breathing heavily and his voice shook. Edna's behaviour about Deaker's illness was totally unacceptable. What about him and his wishes? Why should he have to pay some whore, or a sprog of a servant, for what was his due, his rightful due, from his wife, his lawful wife? Always now, when he turned to her, she was hiding behind some excuse or other now it was anxiety over the old servant. Well, he'd give her something to worry about. He took off his jacket and waistcoat, and then undid the belt on his trousers

"What are you doing?" Edna asked.

"I'm coming into my bed. If you don't mind."

Edna gazed at him, standing there in the moonlight. He removed his trousers, walked to the press and hung them up. His long shirt tail still covered most of his body, but Edna's eyes involuntarily gazed at his white thighs and legs, which protruded below them.

"Now then, Missus," he said, as he climbed into the big bed.

Edna lay down at full length and he turned towards her, feeling her body through her nightdress. She didn't resist him. What was the point?

"This will be the last time," she said to herself. "Tomorrow, I'll tell him."

Tomorrow, she'd hear from Robert what best to do. He'd come for her, and her life would begin. All these thoughts going round in her mind, made her almost oblivious of Enoch, who was enjoying what was so warm and sweet, and welcoming, in spite of herself.

Deaker had heard Enoch come in. In fact she'd heard Jeannie tiptoeing past her door, going down the wooden stairs, then coming up again, a few minutes later. She hadn't wanted the girl to come in and see her, because she didn't want her to know that she wasn't asleep. She realised she wouldn't sleep at all that night. When she'd come out of her faint a few hours previously, for that was all it was, she insisted to herself, she'd had to face the fact of what had made her faint. It was the realisation that Edna, poor misled woman, had formed some kind of liaison with Mr Manstone's clerk, Robert. It was obvious now, wasn't it? Violin lessons! She wished she'd personally taken that violin and taken it up.......up Mow Cop. She'd been there on an outing as a young girl and there was a cliff there. She could have got it there somehow, and she'd have thrown it over the edge. That would have put a stop to all that nonsense. Or the well. Down the well. She sighed, a deep, deep sigh, from her heart, she thought. Now it was as if she was watching herself in bed and judging how successfully this woman was managing this crisis. She saw herself sighing. She turned over and sighed again, this time it was more like a groan. She listened to the groan. Didn't she really feel the crisis? How could she be so objective about it all? She was watching herself in the crisis. Suddenly she had a moment of realisation, which hit her and made her gasp. She was actually enjoying what was happening. Suddenly she had become important again. The years were stripped away from her, she was in the centre of things, as she had been when Tilly was little and before that, when Edna was herself a child. That's what they were again, both children. It was up to her to save the situation, to restore order, to bring back the tranquillity of the household, where everything moved as it should and everyone performed as was expected. She, Deaker, would see that it was all put to rights, that everything was for the best, in the end.

She sat up in bed, took the ribbon off the end of her long grey plait of hair, ran her fingers through it, and re-plaited it, winding it then into a bun. She swung her legs out of bed, took a hairpin off her little table, and secured the braid. Then she wrapped a long shawl round her shoulders, put on her boots and opened the door. Soundlessly she went down into the kitchen, listening at every step in the stairs, to hear any unusual noise.

Everything was quiet. A faint glow still came from the embers in the grate. As Deaker came to sit down in her chair, the cat stirred from his cushion by the fire, stretched and then jumped onto her lap. "Come on, pussy," Deaker said putting her face down to him and stroking him. "We shall manage, shanna we? Missus'll do what her Deaker says, shan't she? She's nobbut a silly young lass. I don't know how she's come to do what she has, if she has done it, if, I say." Tears were trickling from the tip of her nose, onto the cat's fur. He shook his head impatiently, his ears flapping. She smoothed the top of his crown, with her fingers and wiped her nose on the back of her hand. "There now, we mustn't cry, must we? Deaker will sort it out, won't she puss. Deaker allus does." She went on stroking the cat, which began to purr loudly. "Yes, of course, she will. But oh, pussy….." She began to sob more loudly - her breath coming in deep gasps, her body shaking - how could the child do this to her old nurse? She should've known better. "She could have told me what was the matter. Does she think I wouldna have helped her? It's the secret way she's done it. I would have helped her through this. Oh, it was my fault, my fault, poor pet. She should never have wed below her like this. It was rash and foolish. I knew it at the time. All these years, I knew it pussy, I did, I did. But it seemed all right." The cat was on its hind legs and was kneading her shoulder with his front paws. "Tha had best go, my darlin', th'art too heavy for me." She put him gently on the floor. "I'll get thee some milk."

She went to the larder, where some milk left over from tea time stood in a little jug, on the slate shelf. She removed the beaded cover off the jug and poured a little into the cat's dish. He began to lap immediately, scattering little drops about him as he drank. "That's a good cat," Deaker said. Her tears had stopped and she sat upright in her chair, listening to the night noises, an owl hooting, the clock ticking and a sporadic murmur from the cooling embers. After what seemed to her ages, sleep came.

22

The clear moon of the previous night had spelled fine weather for the next morning. Tom had the trap under the carriage porch for half-past te. Enoch had told him he would be at the office late and would go by the trap.

"Morning, sir," Tom said as Enoch and Tilly came out of the front door. Tilly's spirits rose a little as they jogged along the road to town. She had hardly slept and the thought of Robert appalled her. But when she'd heard that father would be late going to work and was going by the trap, she suddenly knew what she had to do. She would have her father alone with her, but without making a great show of it. The horse was spanking along at a good pace and in a few minutes they were at the outskirts of the town.

"We could go and look at the new memorial to Sir John Brandon, father, if you haven't seen it," Tilly suggested. "We've just time."

Directed by Enoch, Tom took the trap round to the rear of St John's Church yard, where there was a kissing gate. A new bench now stood just inside the church wall, beside a recently planted young lime tree.

Enoch and Tilly climbed out, while Dimple was allowed to munch the long grass at the side of the lane. They went through the gate and Enoch read out the inscription on the seat back.

"In respectful memory of Sir John Brandon, generous benefactor of this Parish. In the service of the Lord, and his fellow citizens, Sir John's shining example is one, which we who knew him would do well to emulate." Enoch read out. "Aye. Very nice. Very nice." He sat down and Tilly sat down with him.

"I'm sure he hasn't done more than you, Papa."

"But I'm not dead yet, am I? We shall see, shanna we?" He put his gloved hand over hers. "Or thou shalt, any road. It's not for me to say."

"Father. You lead a good life. You know that. Everyone recognises it," Tilly paused. Now was the time. "I wish to know whether you have thought about my idea about the investment of money in properties in Saghead. Whether you have made a decision."

"Oh." There was silence.

Tilly wondered if he had heard what she had said. Then he continued in a low voice.

"Aye. Tis strange you should have brought that up just now." He took her arm. "I met Mr. Shepperton on the train. Going to London. And we were talking about just that. It seems he has plans for it. He's going to rebuild."

"Oh, Father. Is it too late?"

"He has some very good plans, so it happens."

"What do you propose? Won't he sell the site to you.....Father?"

"I dinna say that. I didn't ask him. He's so full of what is to be done with it. He's raising money for the project"

"So it's to become just another terrace of houses? With higher rents? Just what I expected. What will the people do who were living there?"

"What are they doing now? They've managed I suppose."

"You suppose! So you don't know. Doesn't it mean a thing to you, some of them are your own workers? You have a duty to them, to see they're all right."

"Oh, and they have a duty to me, too, don't they? What about when they come out on strike and jeopardise the whole industry? Who let them come back to work again, without any penalties, without hiring new workers to take their place? Who was that then?"

"They're poor and ignorant. What else could they do? They need education and better conditions, and you are the one to give those to them. Why don't you buy the land, and we'll build model houses, and help them to manage the estate themselves? That's the way forwards, Papa. That way, you'll be remembered far more than Sir John Brandon, and not with just a silly stone, but in the hearts and minds. Don't you trust me?"

"Who tells you he'd change his mind. Why should he?"

"Have your promised to help him, already?"

Enoch was silent.

"You have, you have. You must have. You've seen another opportunity to make money, and that's all you're concerned about. Not me, and my wishes, or the good of your own workers."

"Hold hard, young Miss. I've a right to spend my money where I think will be best. And tha shouldst not talk to tha father like that. Be silent"

"I asked you for that loan, that now you're giving to that man.....that landlord, Shepperton. What right has he to be heard, before me? I could have made money for you, and done right by those people as well. You didn't trust me."

"Tha'rt only a lass, still."

"I'm not so much of a lass that I haven't been helping you this six month or more, and you've said yourself I've done well. Just because I'm family, you feel you can ignore me, just like you do my mother."

"Dinna talk to me of thy mother."

"You neglect her, you go to London, when you should be at home, you don't know what's been happening....."

"What has been happening, I know Deaker is ill...."

"She's worried.....and I'm worried too...." Tilly could not get the words out, her throat was constricted, and without warning, the tears began to flow.

"Come now, my lass....dinna be like that," Enoch drew himself up. "I shall ignore this conversation. Here, make yourself look respectable. We should not have come up here. I want to get down to the Works and we're late already."

"I'm not coming with you. You can't make me. I'm never going back there. You've just shown me what you think of me and my ideas. So be it. I shall take up my studies again, and somehow, I'll get educated. I know where I can stay, and work, and you can't prevent me."

The solitary bidding bell above the church now began to clang. There must be a funeral here today. A carriage drove up, and sombre figures climbed out. "You've said enough. There are folk coming now. We must be going." Enoch began walking down a side path, to avoid the mourners.

"I'll not be returning to the office as long as Robert Willoughby is there. You must choose." She rose to her feet and strode past him, not looking back.

"So that's it then!" Enoch muttered. "You'll not say more?"

"Do not ask me, father."

"Then I'll be thinking the worst of the man. But he's a good clerk, at least."

"Do not ask me, father. You cannot know what I feel."

"Feelings, feelings!" Why was it only women had feelings? There they were, all coming up from the gate, with their long veils down to hide their faces. They made such a fuss of feelings, grief, love, loneliness. He'd felt all those things, but life went on just the same, he hadn't the time or energy, or indeed, inclination, to indulge them. Nevertheless, he felt disinclined now, to go straight to the factory. Tilly's tirade had hurt him.

"I'll be taking you home. It's late now. We'll talk again." It was pointless to go onto Manstones now. He would go there after lunch.

Nothing was said in the trap on the way home. Enoch sat upright, his hands clasped on his stick. Tilly had her head back, to feel the breeze snatching at her small hat. She was gripping the rail of the trap. Inside her, right in her midriff, she felt there was a small lump she couldn't swallow. It was heavy, hard, and disagreeable. It would be so easy to give in to her father, and beg his pardon. Well, she wouldn't do that. Somehow, she would do what she wanted, and make her own way. She would do it. She would not be beholden to either of them. Her parents! Her own parents! They were both revealed to her, as totally separate, selfish, individuals. They would both have their own way. Well, so be it. She would have her own way. Suddenly everything seemed better. Whatever happened, a decision had been made. Somehow or other she would leave home. And nothing on earth would move her to return to the factory while Robert Willoughby was there.

The door was opened by Jeannie. She curtsied, took the wraps and said, "If you please Sir, Mrs Deaker would like a few minutes, Sir, if you could find it convenient."

"Oh, she's better, is she? Well of course, if it's something Mrs Manstone cannot deal with. Send word to come down to the study, Jeannie. And bring me a whisky and soda."

Jeannie bobbed and went off. Enoch turned to Tilly. Looking at her feet, he said, "We'll see, we'll see. I shall have to look into things."

"Yes, Father. But I wish to add that whatever happens between you and your clerk, I am not able to come to the factory later today, or tomorrow. In fact, ever again. I am sorry to let you down." She turned and went up the marble stairs.

"Well, well," Enoch muttered. He went into the study and sat down heavily in his leather chair. The arms were worn where he'd sat all the years, but it was still as comfortable as ever. He stretched his legs out, put his head back and closed his eyes. For a moment he craved for sleep, but he mustn't let himself drift off. Deaker would be here and Jeannie with his whisky. What was it all about, everything suddenly seemed upside down? He opened his eyes suddenly. Was there some connection with his visits to London? Had something occurred at the business, which Tilly didn't approve of? What about that incident with the maid? Had someone found out? He couldn't believe anyone would take that seriously. Perhaps young Rob had been involved in something and she had found out? If so, why shouldn't she tell him? Perhaps she'd found some anomaly in the books? Or maybe he'd taken up with all this union business. Even changed sides? That wouldn't explain her reluctance to go back to the office. Surely there couldn't be anything worse than that? Enoch's heart started beating, at the thought which had occurred to him. Had Robert been annoying her, in some personal way? The thought was too awful to put into words. The thought of his clerk and his daughter, his clerk insulting his daughter. No. It couldn't be. Enoch rose abruptly to his feet. Where was that girl with his drink? There came a knock.

"Come in," he shouted, "come in," more calmly.

Deaker appeared in her best dress, with lace apron and frilly cap. She came in, put the silver salver with whisky bottle, glass, and soda water on the desk, then stood silently in front of him, hands folded in front of her. "If you please, Sir."

"Yes, yes. Get on Deaker. I thought you were ill. Speak up, if you've something to say. Pour me out a tot." She gave him the glass and he sat down behind his desk. "Well?"

"Mr Manstone, Sir," Deaker began. Her voice was calm, her fingers clasped together. "I have been a faithful servant of yourself and the Mistress, for many years, a lifetime. I've always tried to do my best, Sir, without giving offence. Now then....," she paused, looking up at him. "Oh, Sir," she muttered. Her voice broke.

"Come, come, Deaker. What is it? No cause for alarm, surely."

Deaker shook her head, and pressed her mouth with her fist. "I don't know as I can go on, Sir." She put out her hand to steady herself on the table. Enoch half rose from his chair.

"You'd best sit down. I didn't expect you to bring me the whisky, being as you've been poorly. Don't excite yerself now."

"No, no, Sir. I'll be all right." She cleared her throat and a kind of grunt came from her. "It's this, Sir, I dunna think you had best be going off on your business, Sir, not so frequent, Sir. It's not my wish, nor my place, sir, to give advice Sir, but when I see things going awry, Sir, well, it's my Christian duty to speak up."

"Awry? What can you mean by that, woman? I think I know what my business is and where I'd best be."

"You dunna know, Sir. You dunna know. You'd best be here. This is your place, Sir. We cannot be doing without you."

"Really, Deaker. I do not know what I'm hearing. Am I to understand right, you're telling me how to run my own business?"

Deaker stood firm. "It's this, Sir. It is your business what goes on, here, as well as in the factory. You know that, Sir. I shouldna have to tell you."

"You should not. Indeed you should not. I think I know what I have to do."

"I've known the Mistress since she was a tiny girl, Mr Manstone. I've brought her up like a mother would, and since then I've tended her, tried to soften all the blows which Providence has sent her - it isn't right Sir, to leave her like you do."

"That's enough Deaker," Manstone rose. "I understand your concern. But you've been ill and see thing in a sorry light."

"Sir, I could tell you...."

"I do not wish to hear any more. It seems to me you need a rest. Isn't your sister still alive, you do well to pay her a visit, and get over all this? Get well, and when you are, you can come back. I'll tell the Mistress you'll be away for a few days. She and Tilly will have to manage with Jeannie till you return." Enoch suddenly saw the excuse he needed to give in to Tilly's wish to absent herself from the office. She could take Deaker's place for a while, and they'd all see how much she would like that. "Now, it's all decided. Be off with you to your sister's this afternoon and when you return it will all look better."

Deaker stood irresolutely, twisting her hands together. It was no use. She could say no more. It had taken all her resolution to get this far. "Very well, Sir." She bobbed and went out holding her hand in front of her mouth.

Enoch went to the window and took a drink from the glass which he had not yet touched. Something had indeed upset Deaker. Perhaps it was to do with Tilly, wishing to leave home. Deaker would certainly have found out about that. Probably she thought that if he was more at home, in Saghead or Epsilon, he could prevent the girl concocting these strange schemes. Well, well, the poor old thing had certainly tried her best. But it wouldn't do. He wasn't going to give up his trips to London. They would all get used to the idea, no doubt.

He'd better tell Edna of his decision to give Deaker a short break. He went back to the fireplace and tugged the bell pull.

Jeannie appeared at the door. "Tell Tom to get the trap out, to take Deaker. She's going to her sister's. After luncheon, I shall go to the pot bank."

When she'd gone he poured out another finger of whisky and drank it down quickly. He must go upstairs and tell Edna what he had done.

Edna turned over in bed, stretched, then folded her body up again, so that her knees nearly touched her chin. She had slept late, after staying awake long after Enoch had achieved release. She'd lain there stiff and dumb until, as dawn came up, he'd got up and gone into his dressing room. Then she'd immediately gone to sleep.

Now, refreshed, nothing seemed the same. He hadn't asked her why she'd allowed him to make love to her. After all the years of abstinence, suddenly she had allowed him. Why? Why? She had her answer ready. She would say that she was past childbearing age. She would explain to him, now, as soon as possible. Of course, she wasn't yet sure, if it was true. Deaker had hinted to her what might be happening. But if Enoch were to be happy with her, then....she would risk anything for Robert's child. Her body trembled suddenly with the thought of it. If only, if only. She would let them both make love to her. Even if she were to bear Enoch's child, she would risk that too. Whose ever child she bore, if it did come to that, she would go with him. It seemed so obvious. She knew now, that was what she wanted, another child. Had she always wanted that? She had, she knew she had. She wanted a son. Why shouldn't she have one? A little boy, just like his father, Robert.

Edna turned over. The clock said half past ten, it was long past the time Enoch usually went to the office. No one had wakened her. Why had Tilly not been near her? She had been so cruel, but then, she had been so unhappy. After all these years, she obviously did not understand her mother at all. She was a child, how could she understand? She had her life in front of her, a marvellous life it would be. Lucky girl, with the world as it was, there was nothing which Tilly could not have. She could be wise and clear in her choices, as she, Edna, had never been. Well, it was too late to see them off to work now. The day was established, the future was established. She knew she would say nothing to Enoch, nor would she say anything to Robert. Each would have their place, she would be satisfied, and be a wife, as well as a lover. She went to the dressing table, and sat on the stool. She brushed her long fine hair and it flew in clouds, away from the brush, like an incandescent halo. Her eyes were bright, deep blue and she studied them with rapture. She turned to see first one profile, then the other. She flipped her breasts, with one hand then the other. She stroked her cheeks and smoothed her neck.

She went over to the window. Outside, the grass was steaming. The wind had brought a slight shower, very early. Now the rain drops were evaporating under a brilliant sunshiny sky. She pulled up the heavy sash and breathed in the heady air. It was cold as she leaned out, but she stayed a few moments.

Down in the garden a blackbird was singing. A beautiful song, she wished she could play like that. She hurried over to her desk and wrote down the notes. She would try to find that melody on her violin. Robert could play chords to go with it. She hugged herself, "Robert, Robert." He could do anything.

She would have some breakfast. She pulled the bell and Jeannie came. "I would like some tea and toast. Up here. And bring the hot water."

"Yes, Ma'am."

"And is Deaker better? I'll be along to see her soon."

"Yes, Ma'am. She is very much better. Shall I send her up?"

"Not at all. She is to stay where she is until Doctor says otherwise."

"Yes, Ma'am."

After Edna had finished her breakfast and dressed, there came a knock on the door. "Come in." Edna gasped. It was Enoch. "Do you mean to stay at home today? You surprise me."

"Yes. It seems to me that there are things we need to sort out."

"I have rung for some tea. Will you join me?"

"Very well." He sat down on the armchair by the window and gazed outside. Edna's presence had excited him. He felt the first stirring of desire begin. She had been different, last night. But this other matter, with Tilly, he felt an irritation welling up, smothering his energy, like glutinous porridge. "Are you sure you're quite well?" A hint of sarcasm touched his voice.

"Quite well, indeed." She turned towards him, her eyes shining. Was this the moment? "I have something to tell you."

Enoch continued to survey the scene outside. There was level sunshine falling across the terrace, and in the distance the copper beeches were turning green and the green beeches were turning russet. Twenty years old now, they were fine strong young trees.

"I know what it is. Tilly has already spoken to me."

"Tilly!"

"I knew already. I've known for a long time. It wasn't likely that she'd want to stay in the office as an underling. I supposed it's for that she wants me to sack Robert."

"Oh." The word came as a long sigh from Edna.

"But I cannot just do that. He is a good worker. I have no complaint with him. He justifies his salary."

"You must do what you think right."

"She's got this notion of education. One time, the governesses were enough. And now this? Where does it come from? London, indeed."

Enoch thought better of mentioning anything about the scheme concerning house building and management. Edna said nothing. .

"She wants to leave the office?" she asked slowly.

"On account of Robert Willoughby. She won't work there no more."

"Robert," Edna whispered. She caught Enoch's eye. "The clerk."

"Of course. I shall have to see what's the matter. It won't do for her to go and live in London. Nor just to stay here, not working, idle. I won't have that neither. I will not."

A knock came at the door. Jeannie appeared with the tea."Oh, Sir. Shall I bring another cup?"

"Yes. Is Miss Matilda about? Ask her to come in."

The maid went to obey Enoch's orders.

"You're very quiet. Is there nowt to say?"

The moment hung in the air, like a bubble. How could she seriously imagine Enoch ever sharing her with his clerk? Impossible. She couldn't lead a double life. That left only one solution. She would have to tell him about Robert.

Edna knew she could grasp the bubble and it would break and the whole world would dissolve away, this world, as she knew it now. She could tell Enoch the truth. Or she could blow the bubble away and it would vanish, and Enoch would accept something else as the truth, that Tilly had taken some childish dislike of her father's clerk and that was all there was to it. It hung there, it hung there. The clock did not tick, the leaves on the trees did not tremble, Edna's heart did not beat.

Then came a tap on the door. "If you please, sir, Miss Matilda's gone out for a walk. And I brought the tea." She put the tray on the table, with two pots and two cups and toast for the Mistress.

"Very good. That will be all." Enoch dismissed her and Edna poured out.

"That reminds me. I told Deaker to have some time off. Tom is to take her to her sister's."

"Really, Enoch. You should have warned me."

"I thought I'd save you the trouble. I'll give Matilda a few days off to help out. Then she'll get over her fit, like as not."

Edna said nothing but drank her tea in silence.

After a few moments, Enoch put his cup aside and wiped his mouth with his handkerchief. "Now. I've got things to do. Excuse me my dear. Perhaps we shall see you at dinner time? For lunch, I shall just have a few sandwiches in my study to save Jeannie trouble then I'm going to the office. I brought Matilda back when she told me. But I must go, of course.". He rose and nodded at her.

Edna said nothing. The moment was past.

By the time Enoch was sitting in his study with his luncheon collation, Deaker had already been deposited at Daisy's place by Tom. She and her sister were sitting by the fire in the kitchen and Daisy was pouring out tea.

"I must have known you were coming. I did make a nice sponge yesterday and there's plenty left. It's as if I knew. I'm like that. I sense it, well, you're like that too, sister."

"I keep on telling myself I should have known." Deaker kept wiping tears from the corners of her eyes. "I should have. Since she was a tiny child. I knew when owt was wrong. She'd hide herself in her room and not play outside. Whereas, normal, she'd love to go out for her walk. She's been acting so strange, up and down, up and down. Then when Miss Tilly went off to her Papa's office,that did it. I know she wept many a tear. I felt for her, I did, I felt for her."

Daisy couldn't understand exactly what was the matter. All this fuss. Something to do with the Mistress.

The tears began to come thick and fast and Deaker felt it all welling up inside her. "Oh dear, oh dear," she moaned. Her arms were crossed over her bowed head and hot drops running under her fingers.

Daisy leaned over, to put her hand on Deaker's knee. She patted it and patted it. "Now then, now then. Dunna take on. 'Taint worth it. She's a grown woman now, she should be able to take care of herself. It ain't your place. Drink up this tea," she said, pushing the cup under her sister's nose. "It's Mr Manstone's place to worry. If you ask me he shouldna have gone off and left her, these business trips. What did folks do before there was trains, I don't know. When I was a girl that never happened. No. The men stayed at home where their place was."

There was no reply from Deaker who stared at the fire disconsolately, Daisy went on. "Tis strange, I do think. He's only just started doing it. Makes you wonder."

Deaker looked up. "What does it make you wonder?"

"What else we may find out about the Manstone family?

Deaker put down her cup with a clatter.

"I've heard other things about Mr. Enoch Manstone," Daisy went on.

Deaker's eyes widened. "Hold your tongue. I won't hear no gossip, not about him. He's a good man at heart, look at that church they got builded. A lot of his money."

"Well....." Daisy decided to let the matter drop. Nevertheless, there was talk about Enoch Manstone. But this wasn't the time to worry her sister with it.

Deaker stood up. "I'll trouble you for a dab of hot water. I'll have a wash. Mebbe I'll feel better." Her face was drawn and dirty, but now the old familiar glint appeared in her eyes.

"You're not going out?"

"I am. I'll meet the devil and turn him back."

"What are you talking about? Sit down this minute. You're going nowhere."

But Deaker had already refilled the kettle and put it on the hob. The coals were sizzling on its wet bottom. "There's a certain person who I have business with. And I'm going to find her."

"Leave it be, sister. You're not fit to go out again. And you're the one who's going on about gadding."

"Do not put me off. It's the Lord's business I'm doing. Do you mind when we ran into that clerk of Mr Manstone that Sunday. He was with a woman, wasn't he?"

"Gertrude Lambert."

"That's her. I'd forgot the name."

"I knew her as a young lass. She and Nancy Lambert were in service at Fergus Hall, as girls. It's Nancy's daughter. By all accounts, she's a good girl, looking after her mother. I ain't seen Nancy for many years. I never did know her proper."

"You've done me a service, sister. I'll be on my way."

An hour later Deaker was standing outside Nancy Lambert's home. Daisy had reminded her where it was, and there had been a convenient train.

Gertie herself came to the door. "Yes?"

With a shock Deaker realised that it was Monday. The girl should have been at work. "Good afternoon, Gertie. I will come in. In case you don't know who I am, I'm the housekeeper at Terrilea, known to your mother, many years ago."

"Of course. Come in." What else could Gertrude say? They went into the small dark front room and Gertrude hastily pumped up the cushions on the only easy chair.

In front of the window was a small table, flanked by two chairs. "I'll sit here, it's my back. I find it hard to get up these hills now. But I wish to see your mother.""

"My mother is ill, Mrs. Deaker, and should not be troubled. She's upstairs in her bed now."

"I am sorry to hear that. But you can hear what I have to say, as well as tell it to your mother. It's about you I've come. Sit down there, if you please."

Gertie did what she was told, and looked at the old woman, briefly, then out of the window. "How can I help you, Missus?" she said in a quiet voice. The street was quiet, no children playing, no carts passing, no clogs clacking of passers-by. Here, as in Epsilon and at Manstones, everything seemed stilled, and different. It was not a time for change and decisions, going forward, going back. Yet here, today, on this September Monday something had to happen.

At last, the silence was broken. "You've got to get a grip of that man of yours. I'm not a one for beating about the bush. So I'm telling you straight."

"What do you mean?"

"I've heard you're to marry your Mr Willoughby. Well, he's a good match. And he's got a good job. But it's best he was wed at once, Gertrude Lambert. It's not right to keep man like him too long on a piece of string. He needs to be settled down, now, with a good woman. So you'd best put it to him. It's Mr Manstone himself who's intimated that to me. He's a great pillar of the church, is our Master, and he sees a good man and wants him settled down, once and for all."

Gertie's heart was thumping. What had brought about this situation? Could it really be the case that Mr Manstone had made this decision about his clerk and had enlisted the help of his housekeeper?

"I don't really understand you, Mrs Deaker. My engagement with Mr Willoughby is long standing. But 'tis up to Providence when we are to be married. I have my duty to my mother. Monday is a day when I can have time, often enough."

"With due respect to your mother, Gertrude. It's your life and the life of that young man. You must do what is right and proper."

"I don't feel it right for you to come here talking to me like this," Gertrude managed to say in a stifled voice.

"I would see your mother. She would tell you your duty. But she's not fit enough to have do all that. I'm taking her place."

"It's Mr Willoughby you should be talking to," Gertie's anger was dissolving into tears. Why should this old woman be bullying her like this?

"I intend to see him. Yes, I will. If you'll please give me his address. Otherwise I'll catch him after business."

"I cannot do that."

Deaker rose. "In that case I'll not stop. But you're to know that Miss Matilda will be leaving her work at the office." She paused watching Gertie's face change. "Yes. She won't be going no more. She has told the Master, to my certain knowledge."

It was if Deaker had slammed a large heavy book shut, right under Gertie's nose, the Bible probably. "You mean....?"

"I'm saying no more. Will you give me that address? If you cannot get your man to do his duty, I shall ask him the reason Miss Tilda is leaving. Do you think he might know?"

"I don't know. I don't know," Gertie looked at the old woman, then looked quickly away again. "I'll ask him myself the reason. I am sure it is not what you think. It could not be," she added, softly.

"I certainly hope not. For your sake. And your good mother up there."

Deaker went out of the street door and Gertie watched her out of the window. Then she pulled the curtains. It was still early and broad daylight outside, but she suddenly wished to hide the view of the long narrow steep street. She knew that the pall of mist which shrouded the town every evening at this time of the year, would soon be rolling up and stifling the inhabitants who were outside, a yellow, sulphurous, choking miasma from which even the thickest curtains only partially protected the ground floor of the little house.

There came a knock on the floor above. Her mother was awake and requiring tea. Gertie sat at the table for a moment contemplating her hands, spreading the fingers and turning them this way and that. Would Rob ever fulfil his promise to her? Or would she be here, nursing her mother, on her own, forever. Surely, if they were married, Rob's pay would support them both. What was Rob waiting for? Suddenly, the truth, unbidden, erupted in her mind. Rob didn't love her. That was why he didn't name the day. He couldn't, that was it. She put her head on the table, unable to draw breath. It was as if she had suffered a huge blow in the stomach, her lungs wouldn't work. All his kisses hadn't meant love, and now Deaker had come with her insinuations that it was because of Rob's behaviour Matilda was to leave the office.

At last, she sat up. There were more knocks coming from the floor above.

"I'm coming. I'll make thee thy tea."

She went into the kitchen, put fresh coals on, then filled the oil lamp, which stood on the mantelpiece, lit it and set it on the table. She wouldn't go and ask Robert any questions. That would have to wait until tomorrow. But even then, she knew she wouldn't ask him. She knew the answer she would get.

23

Enoch had arrived at the Pot Bank about the same time that Deaker had been launching her harangue at Gertie. It was already three o'clock and the gas lamps were lit.

"Good day, Sir," Robert said. Before he had time to ask him about his trip, Enoch signalled him into the inner office.

"I imagine that everything is as it should be," Enoch said, settling heavily at his desk.

"Of course, but we've missed you, sir."

"I may as well come straight to the point. You've done well here, I can't deny. Credit is where credit is due. But I am going to have to let you go. "

"Let me go, sir! What is your meaning please?"

Enoch laughed. "Don't look like that, lad. It'll be in your favour. I've decided a good many things these last days, and one is that I need to expand the business, long past our shores. You know what I mean. Them as don't expand lose what they've already go. That's how it is in life. You'll learn that."

Rob stood perfectly still. He would wait and hear the old man out.

"For that reason, I've decided to invest some more in our overseas operation. It ain't good enough, what we're doing now. In the States. I've been looking at the figures. That is, myself and my daughter, and we're dropping behind, in some areas. We need a good man in charge. And I'm thinking about you. It'll mean a rise in salary, but you'll be leaving all this behind. Will you do it? Go there as my representative? It's a big responsibility. But then, you're a man to take chances, I believe."

Rob was silent for a moment. "I'll have to think for a while, sir. I've responsibilities here. I'd have to think about it."

"Hurry up then, you won't be asked again. And by the way, there'll be one short in the office for a week or so. I'm having my daughter take a few days off. But if you accept, I anticipate it will be sooner, rather than later, that you'll be off. I'm not a man to dilly dally."

So that was it, Rob thought. Enoch believed that there was something between him and the girl, Matilda. That icicle, that piece of lemon. Hardly. His heart began beating when he thought of what he had got, and that was Manstone's too. He could hardly repress a smile.

Enoch stared at Rob. The young man had his back to the fire, and his face was in shadow. It was difficult to see his eyes. "Do you understand what I'm saying?

"Perfectly sir, I understand you've a mind to send me to America. Is that correct?"

“Yes, perfectly correct.” But there was something in Robert’s tone. A slight insolence? Suddenly Enoch felt weary. Whether he had done the right thing or not, it was done now. He had raised the mirage of America, and if the young man was getting uppity, well, he could deal with that. He liked a man with spirit, anyhow. It was a pity that Matilda had taken against the young man. “Let me know, tomorrow, latest.”

Back at Terrilea, Jeannie was in the kitchen, sitting on a stool. She wished it could all be back as it was this time yesterday. What was the matter? Missus had kept to her room all day, and Miss had been in and out of the house, coming and going for walks and suchlike, unable to settle. No-one had been in the drawing room or morning room, those fires had been lit for nothing. Really, it was more than a body could stand. If things weren’t back into a proper routine by morning, then she, for one, wouldn’t stand it no more.

The cat was asleep on the armchair, oblivious of Jeannie, or of anything else going on in the huge house. “Get off, you lazy good for nothing,” Jeannie cried, tipping the chair up. The cat began sliding down on the floor, and desperately hung by his claws to the knitted blanket as it inexorably descended. “You horrible creature. How can you be like that, when your Mistress is so poorly, even dying? I don’t know what.” The cat tumbled onto the floor, clasping the blanket. “Oh, go on with you, go and catch them mice.” She seized it, and pushed it out of doors.

Outside, it was now quite dark, and there was a slight drizzle beginning. Jeannie turned with a sigh into the kitchen, and walked to the larder door. Mrs. Pedley had given her instructions about dinner but she wasn’t going to bother with all that. They were just going to have cold cuts. “Oh, Mrs. D. why ain’t you here now?” What was the matter with everyone? It was if there was a death in the house. “You’ll give them what for, won’t you Mrs. D, when you see how they’ve treated me.” She opened the steel mesh safe in which the meat was kept, and took out a large ham, which had already had a few slices carved off it. It looked delicious, pink, with a fine coating of breadcrumbs. She took it to the table and cut off a large slice which she ate in her fingers.

That was better. It wasn’t all bad, having the old woman away. At least, now she could help herself when she was hungry.

By the time Jeannie had worked single handed to lay the table for dinner, make up the fire, and serve the meal, it was late, and she was tired.

Edna had put on a soft grey wool dress and braided a ribbon into her bun, Tilly had on her plaid skirt, and green silk blouse, and Enoch was in his best Sunday jacket. It seemed that the whole family was making an occasion of it. Just before the gong was rung, they were all in the drawing room.

Without looking at her daughter, Edna asked "Did you enjoy your walk to the mill? Wasn't it rather cold?"

"Not at all, Mama."

Jeannie came in. "Dinner's ready, Ma'am."

Mrs. Manstone led the way. In the dining room, the soup was already in the tureen. "Very good, Jeannie." She lifted the lid and sniffed. "You've done well."

Jeannie scurried out to make ready the tray for the ham and baked potatoes.

"I suppose Mrs. Pedley left instructions."

"Perhaps." Tilly said. "Jeannie and Mrs. Pedley won't be able to manage, if Deaker doesn't come back."

"What do you mean? If?"

"She's very, very ill, Mama." They'd both been hiding from the facts. "You'll have to make some new arrangements. You can't expect Jeannie to do all Deaker's work. Deaker must be sixty-five, sixty-seven."

Edna, who had been feeling a little better, now put down her spoon. She still had the strange feeling, that she wasn't really here. All that was happening, in the household and in this room, seemed to be something quite outside herself, and had nothing to do with her. All she could think of was her situation with Robert. She had thought all day that she might have frightened him away, by blurting out her fears that their secret had been discovered. All day, she'd been waiting in her bedroom for some sign from him. How it would come, she didn't know. And now, here, they were talking about housekeeping. Tomorrow, perhaps sooner, she would be away from it all. How could she think about such things as housekeeping, when there was a flood gathering in the valley above, and the dam was about to burst? She was convinced that her life was soon to change for ever, for better or worse, and all this would be blown away, like last year's flowers. "I suppose she is very old now. I don't think I know her birthday."

"Not know it?" Tilly spoke with scorn. Then she realised that she herself had never troubled to find out, or even marked the occasion. Yet Deaker was a real person, as real as any of the factory workers, whom she often felt so sorry for, as real as herself or anyone in her family. Why had she never bothered with her, except to rely on her loyalty and service? Now, she was gone, and they would never be able to show what they felt about her.

Jeannie came in with the ham, and Enoch began to carve.

"I think I will only have a little, dear." Edna said.

He carved off a tiny sliver, and Jeannie then handed the potatoes. Edna took a half.

"Just a small one, father." Tilly took a portion of vegetables. It looked a minuscule helping on the big white china plate with the gold rim. "It looks nice, but I'm not hungry," she said when she saw the look of disappointment in Jeannie's eyes.

Enoch piled his plate high with ham. "It seems as if I'll have to make up for you two, or we might as well not have sat down to table," he growled. "Get me a bottle....." he was just about to ask Jeannie to go down into the cellar. "No, I'll get it myself. You won't know your way about."

Jeannie stood in the shadow, near the door. The Mistress and Tilly waited in silence for Enoch to return. Suddenly there was the sound of a dog barking far away down the other end of the house.

Edna stiffened. Who could it be? Perhaps it was the message she was waiting for.

Tilly sat back in her chair, fiddling with her fork.

"Go and see if anyone is there," Edna managed to say.

Jeannie's footsteps could be heard clattering back across the stone flagged floor. Then came the sound of the baize doors swinging open, and Enoch's heavy tread. He went over to the sideboard, and wrenched out the cork from the dusty bottle. He filled three glasses, and brought them over, one by one.

"Now, I don't want any excuses. You're both to drink that up. Doctor's orders. I won't have all this carry-on. It's not as if either of you is ill. But you're acting so. Now, drink up, and then we'll all have a good dinner. He raised his glass, tasted the wine, then quaffed half the glass in one go. Having done this, he wiped his lips on the starched napkin he had stuffed into his collar, and began to take forkfuls of meat. "Eh, that's better. I were ready for this. Nowt so much to eat today, with what's been going on."

For a moment Tilly thought she would just rise and go away. Once again she had the sensation she could not swallow. But after a moment, she raised her glass, and sipped. Edna did the same. In a strange way, Enoch's words were having a comforting effect. He seemed so oblivious of the turmoil which was inside both of them, that, somehow, it seemed less important. In a few moments they were beginning to pick at the food. The dread of the moment, of seeing each other for the first time, with the new perception of each other, was beginning to evaporate. They were beginning to assimilate it into their understanding of their own private worlds, of their comprehension of the others, and of themselves.

Jeannie reappeared. "There was no-one there, Ma'am," she said.

Edna glared at her. How could she be telling the truth? She was absolutely sure that someone was there, perhaps a telegraph boy with a message, from Robert. Or even, Robert himself. But the dog's barks had ceased. No-one was there.

With the dessert, the little family seemed almost restored to its accustomed existence. The foundations had shaken for a few terrible moments, the tremors had been felt. But now, the earth was still. Perhaps they could begin to sink new ones.

After that the meal proceeded normally. Tilly watched her father attacking the food with his usual determination, and was amazed he could carry on his life as if nothing had happened. But had anything happened? Apart from her mother's pallor, there seemed nothing, now to give any indication of a substance to Tilly's suspicions. She wanted to believe there was nothing to them, and she buried them.

It was Enoch himself who brought everything to the surface again, like a dog digging bones out of a flower bed. They were all comfortably ensconced by the fireplace, after dinner, with the tea poured out.

"I'd best tell you my decision now. I'm changing things at the business. My clerk, that's Willoughby. I'm sending him to America. He'll be there a while. It's where we have to expand now that the German market is going down. And you, Matilda, will be doing his work."

Edna brought her cup down, spilling a little into the saucer, as she banged it down.

No-one spoke.

"Is that all you have to say? It'll be best for the business. The other firms are engaging staff over there. We'll be left behind, else."

There was no reaction to Enoch's words.

"What's to do? Is there owt you have to say?"

"If that's your decision, Enoch, we cannot question it." Edna knew that this was what she was waiting for. Robert would never accept Enoch's plan to go to America. Somehow, this would give him the chance he needed to prove that he loved her, and would be everything for her. He would have to declare, and that would be the way forward, away from the tangle of deceit which enmeshed them. She suddenly felt light-hearted. It was all becoming real again. She met Enoch's eyes and did not look away. She smiled. She could afford to be generous. Not much more of her life would be wasted on pretence.

Tilly stood up. "What you do with Robert Willoughby is no concern of mine, either, Father. You must do what you think is right for the business. But do not rely on me being your clerk. As you know, I intend to go to London, to pursue my education. I have told you that already."

"Oh, indeed! And how do you intend to go ahead with this plan?""

"I spoke about it, this morning." She should have said what she had to say, about her mother and Robert, then. Evidently her father still did not understand the true situation. Now, the longer she left it, the more it would seem, when he did find out, that she had been conniving with her mother. She would need time, now, to consider her own position in all this. If he trusted Willoughby enough to send him to America, then he must have thought that she was just making up a silly excuse for leaving the office. With Robert gone, her father would naturally think the situation was solved. Obviously, he had indeed solved the situation about himself and Edna. Ironically, it seemed he had sorted out the problem, without actually knowing what the problem was. But the problem of what Tilly wanted to do with her own life, the problem of seeing that his own daughter had some rights, had not appeared real to him. He thought her idea of going to London was just some girlish fantasy. "I cannot speak about it now, Papa," she said, her voice low, but steady.

"What shall I do, if Matilda is to return to the office at once? With Deaker ill...." Edna spoke. She found herself back into the morass of the present. What was she to do? She knew, beyond doubt, that Robert would not accept the idea of going to America. But how could he help her, now? If he refused to do what Enoch ordered, he might be dismissed. They would have to leave together. Once more, she realised, that she could not possibly continue in the deception of Enoch. But how would they live? Her dream of a little house, and a piano....where was it now? She had to see him, to be sure. How could she get to him? For the first time, she realised how much she was missing her old nurse. But at the same time, she knew she could never take the old woman into her confidence. She knew what her reaction would be, and that she couldn't face up to her. Perhaps Deaker knew the truth already. Edna felt cold, and shivered. She had cut herself off, for ever, from one of the dearest people in her life. They might never be on the same terms again. "I think I may be getting ill, myself, whatever you think, Enoch. I shall go to my room." But she did not move. She sat looking at the fire.

Tilly went to her father and put her hand on his arm. Suddenly, she felt sad for him. He seemed like a child, things were happening all round him, and he was making decisions, but he didn't have the knowledge to see if they were the right ones. Perhaps we are all like that, all the time, she thought. "When is Willoughby going?"

"I don't know exactly. As soon as he's made a definite decision."

So, Robert wasn't committed yet, Edna realised. Of course not, he would never agree to that. She knew he wouldn't. He could not. They must talk, then they could decide what to do, together.

"When did you tell him your decision?" Edna asked softly.

"Today."

"And if he won't agree to go?" Tilly asked.

"He'll have to do what I bid, or I'll have him out, any road."

So, Edna was right. She knew Enoch, and she knew that he would insist on Robert doing what he was told, or face the sack.

Enoch smiled up at his daughter. She'd soon come round to his decision about having her back in the office. He'd make it worth her while. Perhaps she could attend one of those new business schools. That would be better than any University. Whoever heard of such nonsense! He looked at his wife, sitting gazing at the fire. She was still a beautiful woman. Would she allow him into her bed again tonight? She'd been gentle and welcoming last night, in a way he hadn't experienced since the baby had been born. Why hadn't Edna stopped him? Wasn't she worried any more about what the doctor had said all those years ago? Women were a queer breed. You never could make them out. He now, suddenly, felt strongly attracted to her. He wondered whether it was because he'd been with that woman in London. He knew now the worth of his precious wife, in contrast to the other female. Greedy and grasping, that's all she'd been. Which of them had changed, out of himself and Edna? He was aware of something which had come into their lives, but he didn't know what, and he wasn't even sure whether he had just imagined it.

"Would you fancy a trip abroad? When Willoughby is well settled in, it might be necessary to go and see what he's doing. I anticipate he'll bring in plenty of trade. I shall want to know what he is about."

"Abroad? America?" What was he thinking about? Edna felt as if he was laying a trap for her, as if he had guessed her innermost thoughts. "Of course not. I wouldn't." She hesitated. Perhaps her decisiveness would seem suspect in some way. Whatever she was to say, now, about anything, she was sure she was giving away her thoughts. She even tried not to think about Robert, when she was with Enoch, in case he could read her mind. "I couldn't abide the sea voyage, I know that."

"It don't take long these days, and it's safe too. I fancy it's time we had a trip somewhere. It's going down to London that's made me think. We're all stuck fast here. The world's marching on without us."

Edna was amazed to hear Enoch talking like this to her, so frankly about his feelings. Too late, too late, she thought. "I wouldn't want to go anywhere. You go, if you want to." It was true, she wouldn't want to go anywhere with him.

The next morning, at about eleven o'clock, the door bell sounded. Edna was sitting at the window. At the sound she started up from her chair, her heart had begun to beat violently. Jeannie came in with a telegram, addressed to Miss Manstone.

"Take it up to Miss Matilda, Jeannie." Jeannie was just leaving the room, when Tilly entered. "This is for you Miss."

"COMING TO PAY RESPECTS MONDAY MORNING STOP WILL YOU COME RIDING STOP HAVE GOT A HORSE STOP BICYCLE OUT OF COMMISSION STOP LOCKYARD STOP

"Oh, Mama. Mr. Lockyard will be coming in a moment. He wishes to go riding with me." She rushed to the door. "May I go?"

"I don't know whether your father would approve."

"Father isn't here. I am asking you."

"Well, then....."

"Please do not make difficulties."

"I can't," Edna murmured.

Tilly rushed to the door. "Please tell Tom to have Silver saddled.

When David rode up the drive, half an hour later, Tilly was waiting for him, in her riding habit, and Jim had Silver ready in the courtyard.

Soon, they were hacking their way along the lane.

"Have you anywhere special you want to go?"

"Yes. I have. It may seem a strange request. I wish to go to Saghead, there is someone I wish to visit."

"Certainly. I shall be happy to accompany you."

"I know a pleasant route, I used to go that way sometimes with my father."

It was a fine morning. The first frost of the autumn was fast thawing out in bright sunshine. As they trotted along, hedgerow birds fluttered away and there was the song of blackbirds and robins.

David turned out to be a good rider, and kept his horse trotting briskly beside Silver. The first part of the ride took them near to the bone-mill, which Tilly had last seen with her father. She remembered it all, as if it was part of another life, or as if she was then another person. Now, she wondered when she would next go riding with him again. She felt she had crossed some kind of bridge in her life, and her father was back on the other side.

"Did you ever have the impression that there are some days in one's life, which seem to have a magic of their own, as if a spell was being forged, which would affect you all your life," Tilly asked

"I think I know what you mean, though I wouldn't have put it so well. There aren't many, but there are some."

Tilly said nothing, but trotted ahead. At the brow of the hill she reined in her horse, and David halted beside her. They could see down over the whole city. Bottle kilns were lit everywhere, and the smoke, in the still air, was going straight up. Over all the hills, the terraces of red-brick houses crawled in rows. Tilly quite liked the pattern they made, rather like the brown furrows of a ploughed field.

“It seems strange to think all those houses are full of people, and all the streets full of horses and carts, and trams. What do they all do, and what is it all about?”

“It’s about surviving. Working and living, and dying.”

“In the catechism it says that we are alive to honour and obey God, and live happily ever afterwards with him in Heaven. Do you believe that?”

“I couldn’t really say what I believe. It’s easier to say what I don’t believe.”

“Well, do you believe that?”

“It depends what you mean by “God. If you mean beauty and truth, and sincerity, yes, I do think that. We must aim for it. I don’t know if it will mean we can live for ever. I’m not sure about that. In fact, I could almost say I don’t believe that. But that doesn’t mean we don’t have to try. Just for its own sake, not for what it will bring as a reward.”

Tilly didn’t reply, just kicked her heel into Silver’s flank, and off they went again.

“What is the matter with your bicycle?”

“Nothing really. It just needed a rest. Or rather I did. Besides, I know you like riding. You wouldn’t have enjoyed it much if you had to worry about me, coming along on a bicycle. Also, we couldn’t have come on these paths. “

Soon, they were down in the lanes of the city itself. It was easier riding here, as the road surfaces were better, and there was little danger to the horses from the few carts and donkeys which were about.

“I want to visit the site of the fire, David, and see what is being done about it.”

“That will be interesting.” He was conscious of feeling rather saddle sore, they had been riding for about an hour.

They passed the end of the turning to Manstones, and Tilly was surprised at the sudden pain she had, when thinking of her father sitting at his desk, and all the hustle and bustle of the normal working day at the factory. Would it be better if she were just to turn round now, and go and tell her father she had changed her mind? Should she try to ignore what had happened in the last few days, and go back to normal? She couldn’t do that. She had at least to find out what she had come to find out.

They came to the blackened buildings, and the rubbish at the scene of the fire. Most of the timber had now gone, and there were the dead remnants of weeds which had grown up on the waste land. At the far end of the open ground a small boy was playing with a collie dog, throwing sticks for it, and trying to make it return to him. Waving her crop at him, Tilly shouted. “Come here.”

He came up slowly, rubbing his hands on the seat of his trousers. The dog followed him, and began to bark.

"I wish to know where Mrs. Turner lives. She used to live in one of these houses. Can you tell me where she is, now?"

"Yes. Ma'am. Mrs. Turner is staying with my auntie, it's just along of there. Number ten."

"Thank you. Now do you wish to earn a sixpence? I want you to help this gentleman by holding this horse for me, while he waits. I have to go and visit for a moment?"

"Please, yes, Ma'am. I can hold horses, I done that before, my uncle he's got a cart. I help him sometimes."

"That's a good boy. Take hold of her head now." Tilly slipped out of the saddle, and went over to David. "I shan't be long. The purpose of my visit was to see the woman, if she is at home. I will not be long." Without delay, she hurried along the waste ground in the direction of the next street.

"Can't you take the horse? I mean...."

But Tilly had already gone. She must obviously have her own reasons for not wishing to take the horse, David supposed, and turned his attention to the large patch of waste land, which, as he now knew, was to become the site of a brand new estate of better class houses. He could imagine they might make quite desirable residences here, well up on the hill. Quite suitable for the lower middle class type of person, who were becoming more and more numerous in the Potteries.

The door of number ten was open, and as Tilly approached it, a woman came out, carrying a small child. Tilly hesitated a moment. Would she have the courage to address her, a perfect stranger?

"Mrs. Turner."

"Well. If it is." The woman frowned.

"I wonder if I might have a few words with you."

"I suppose so." She turned towards the room onto which the door opened. "Mavis, come here, tek the child." Then she came out again, closing the door behind her.

Standing on the low doorstep, trying to control her voice, which sounded unlike her own, Tilly said "I don't wish to waste your time, I'll come straight to the point. It's about Mavis, I've come. And yourself. Your daughter was working at my father's house, as we wanted to give her employment after the fire. Then she left without notice. I never knew why. Our housekeeper is ill now, and we need help at the house again. I wonder if there was any particular reason she left, and if we could perhaps persuade her to come back to us, for a time, to help you in the circumstances of the fire, and so on....." Tilly's voice trailed off. The woman's face had gone red, and she was clenching her fist. Now she brought one up to Tilly's nose.

"Get out of my sight," she screamed, "if you're Miss Manstone. And don't you never come here again. There was a reason why my girl come back, firstly she was not treated right, she had to work all hours, and then, and then.....she come home...." The woman's face was red, and she was forcing herself up close to Tilly.

Tilly backed away. "Please, please, I did not wish to upset you, if there is anything to be done, we can sort it out. I just wish to be of assistance."

"That's it, that's it, it's you and your sort, with your assistance, which makes fools of us all. Leave us be, and especially our girls. Now go away, and dinna you ask me no more questions."

"What do you mean by that, 'our girls'? What do you mean?"

"You know what I mean. They rich men, they think they can do anything, anything they please, but they cannot do it to such as my Mavis. Do not think that. They cannot. That's why she left, now you know."

She pushed opened the door behind her, then slammed it shut.

Tilly gazed at it for a moment, unbelieving. What had she heard? It was past comprehension. A face appeared at the window. It was that of a small boy, he flattened his face against the glass, his lips making a grimace on the window pane. Then a girl looked out. It was Mavis. As she recognised Tilly, a look of horror and disdain came into her eyes. She didn't have to say anything, Tilly could feel her hatred. She pulled the boy aside. Tilly stared at her, unable to move. The curtain was pulled, and she remained, transfixed. At last she moved away. Weaving her way, in tottering steps, she managed to get to the end of the road. There in the distance, she could see David, the little boy and the two horses. Somehow, she had to reach them. If she could only reach them, she thought, she would survive. She only had to live through the next few minutes, and she would be better.

The sun had disappeared. A cold breeze had sprung up and was blowing across the shards and debris on the building site. Smoke from the nearby bottle kilns of Manstones was billowing ever lower, bringing the usual flakes of soot. How could she get as far as the horses? With a supreme effort, clasping her cloak close to her, Tilly fixed her eyes on Silver, and plunged through the weeds and dirt to get to her.

A moment later, she had taken out a sixpence from her pocket, and was giving it to the boy. "Hold her head," she said, and hoisted herself into the saddle.

"You weren't long," David said. "Did you manage to do your business successfully?"

"Oh. No." She could say no more, it was as much as she could do to turn Silver's head, and set off at a trot. She had to leave this loathsome place as quickly as possible. How could that woman have been so rude and horrible? She had only been trying to be kind. But what lay behind her words, that was what did not bear thinking about. She must not think about it. She fastened her eyes on the gap between Silver's ears.

David had wheeled his horse round and soon caught her up. "Not a wasted journey, I hope."

"No. No. Not wasted." Tilly was taking deep breaths, and urging Silver on, kicking her in the flank and touching her neck with the crop. Soon she was at a fast trot, and then, where there was a grassy verge, the mare broke into a canter. Silver's warmth and strength were comforting Tilly. But she knew the worst was yet to come. She had to confront her father. She did not wish to know the truth, but she had to have it.

David was a good rider, and could easily keep up. When Tilly pulled up to a walk, he did so too. "I wished to speak to you, today, that is why it is so provident that we could go on this ride. I have been finding out all about the possibilities for further education for women, in London, in case you still mean to take up that option. Several colleges exist to prepare ladies for Matriculation to the university. No doubt you can enquire into the details of this for yourself if you so wish." All this talking was making David pant, as he bounced up and down in the saddle, alongside Tilly. He groped in his pocket, and produced a piece of paper. "I don't want to waste your time now, but it's all in here. I wrote it down, in case I didn't see you. I would have left it with Mrs. Manstone."

"Oh, thank you. Please give it to me when we return."

"It's been a pleasure. There are also details of various boarding house establishments, highly respectable, where unmarried ladies may stay, if they wish to pursue their studies. Or even if they wish to take up some paid employment."

Tilly was hardly listening to David. All she wanted to do, was to ride hard, and try to put what had just happened out of her mind.

"That is really kind of you, David. I shall think about it properly later. Now, I wish to take you somewhere, you probably have never been before. We could have a proper gallop, if your horse is not too tired. It's on the way home."

He raised his whip to her, and in a few moments, they had turned off the lane, along a track which ended in a field gate. On the other side of it, was an expanse of open ground, with scattered gorse bushes, and clumps of dead bracken. A straight ride had been cut through, which led, in a slow gradient, to the steeper slopes of the rocky ridge beyond.

As soon as they were the other side of the gate, Tilly was off. Silver obviously knew where they were, and she lost no time in making the most of it. Neck and neck, the two horses raced along the turf, Tilly and David encouraging them with yells and shouts.

Too soon, it was over. Pulling the animals up, they let them blow for a while. Tilly stroked and patted Silver's neck.

David, alongside on his horse, sat back in the saddle, gently rubbing the bristles of the cropped mane. Then he leaned across to stroke Silver too. "She's a lovely girl, isn't she, your Silver. Not so beautiful as her mistress, but nearly." He caught hold of Tilly's gloved fingers. He felt the warmth of them, and brought them to his lips. "Excuse me," he said.

"Oh." Tilly was aware of a kind of shock running through her body, right from the fingers he had just caught, to her toes. She gazed at David, aware that she was blushing. She looked away, gathered up the reins, flicking them on Silver's neck. "Walk on."

No more was said, until they were on the drive to Terrilea.

"Please forgive me, if I took a liberty. It was just.....I have been meaning to say something to you for weeks now."

"It's all right. Don't say any more. You will be going soon."

"That is what I wanted to talk about. I really wish to see you again."

"You mean, in London? "

"Yes. If you come. You must come. There is so much about you... you must develop it. Please do come. For your education, or work. I would help you to make friends. Really, I wouldn't pester you. I would never impose myself. That wasn't like me, what I did just now. I wouldn't take any liberties."

"Please don't worry about it, David. I didn't mind at all.""

They halted. "Thank you. I will be your good friend." He raised his hat. "I must be going now. It's later than I thought. Thank you for the ride, too. We must do it again. In London perhaps. May I write?"

Tilly found herself smiling. David rode off. Jimmy came to collect Silver, and Tilly retired to her room. Without changing, she sat by her window, and read the paper which David had given her. Skipping the preliminaries, she read:-

"In the event of your father not agreeing to this, there is another option. When you are of age, there might be an opening in another field. Several Missions have been opened in East London, mostly sponsored by reputable educational bodies, such as the Cheltenham Ladies College. These bodies require people, such as yourself, who feel inspired to help those less fortunate than themselves, to act as workers in these Mission Settlements, providing basic education and medical attention, for the poorest of the poor. Some training is provided, for such workers, gratis, by these bodies. I doubt if the remuneration is very much but it might provide an opportunity for you

to advance your ultimate aims. I know one such person, who has dedicated herself to this work, and I could put you in touch with her, if you so wish.

It was such a pleasure making your acquaintance, when I lived near Saghead. Would that I had known you for longer! I hope that you do not find me presumptuous in passing on all this information. I feel very strongly that I would like to be of some service to a person with such interesting and unusual ideas. Please don't hesitate to let me know if there is anything else you wish to know. Perhaps one day, I shall have the great pleasure of meeting you again, - not necessarily with the bicycle!

Your sincere friend and servant,
David Lockyard."

24

When Enoch arrived at the pot-bank, that morning, Robert was working at his desk.

"Good morning, Mr. Manstone."

"Come in to my office."

Robert followed him and stood by while Enoch took off his hat, and coat. For a moment, Enoch had the notion that none of what had transpired in the last few months, had actually happened. It was as if Tilly had never been employed at the Works, and had not taken against Robert, as if he himself had never gone down to London, and seen the wench down there, and taken the idea of opening up a branch office in New York; as if too, he had not had the new found feeling for Edna. He caught himself wishing that it was so, that he could put the clock back, a whole year. But of course, he couldn't.

"Well, have you thought?"

"Yes sir."

"And what is it?"

"I'll do what you want, Mr. Manstone. I'll go to America. But it'll mean a big wrench for me. As I said, I'm due to be married. I shall have to provide for my intended, and for her mother who's sickly. Then also, I shall need proper provision for when I first arrive. I need to make a good start there, to reflect on yourself, sir. So I shall need £200 in cash, sir, before I go. And there's another thing. I've worked hard for you, to sort out the troubles the men are having. As I've mentioned to you many times before. They have complaints, quite valid ones, in my opinion. I've had all my work cut out, to keep your business going, through my contacts with the Union, I've always sorted things out as best I can. Now I think the best thing you can do, and you'll do it if you trust me well enough to send me off on your affairs, is to raise the men's wages, so they get back the Lord Hatherton's Penny. Which you can well afford to, as can all the Masters. In fact many of the Masters have already done that, as you must know."

Enoch had stood silent all this time. He had never heard such a diatribe, as this, he'd never even heard the man put so many words together. "You obviously don't understand me, Willoughby. I made you a good offer. I could have just dismissed you on the spot."

"Why don't you then? Why do you hesitate? You must have heard bad reports of me, to suddenly say that, when, just now, you were asking me to go to America on your behalf. What is it then? Out with it!"

"I have my reasons. I don't need to say them to you."

"I have a right to know, if it affects me. I've always been a good worker for you, Mr. Manstone. If you don't think so, tell me why."

Enoch stood rigid. "I wish you to go to America."

"I do not wish to go. But I will do it, for the sake of the workers here, to better our trade which they rely on, and because I can do a good job for you, and that is what I look to do, a good job, right. But I must have what I asked for. "

"Is there any reason, to your knowledge, why Miss Manstone will not work here anymore?"

"Miss Manstone! None. None at all. You dishonour me, saying that. I might as well ask you about your doings in London. I don't question you about any rumours I may have heard about goings on in London. I wouldn't demean myself by believing such things."

"What have you heard?"

"I've heard tales, but I don't believe them. Of course not. You're my employer. I respect you."

"Tales?"

"Of course, every man in a superior position to workers, or servants, you must have servants, young, ignorant people..." Robert paused here, and stared at Enoch.... "Some of them, they will misinterpret...people will try to find fault.....you know what I mean. People are like that...I don't believe them."

Enoch sat down heavily at his desk. He sat with his chin cupped in his hand, the fingers over his mouth. "It seems to me we have no cause for argument. "

Robert went over to the window. "You've a fine business here, Mr. Manstone. And a beautiful house and family. I respect you for it. You've prospered, with my help, and that of all your workers. Now, I want to be like you. I could do it, and take your business and reputation higher and wider. Give me the chance, and I'll see you right. I will, I promise."

Enoch was silent. This was blackmail. Would anyone believe him, if the truth about that maid got out? He'd never heard no more on that score. But then there was the London visits. If Robert was to talk, even if they didn't believe him, mud would stick. He couldn't afford to take chances. He'd have to get him away, far away. "We're both men of the world. I can see that. You may do well for me. But let me make this clear. If you don't do well, you'll not come back here, you won't be employed again. If I send you off, with this package, I'll expect results. Oh yes. You won't get a second chance. There'll be no more payments of two hundred pounds. Just your salary, don't think otherwise. And I promise you won't get another job, in this country or wherever, if you don't make a go of this. I'll see to that."

Robert stood over him at the desk. "You won't regret sending me to New York. I respect you, Mr. Manstone. I won't hear bad words about you. I shall go to do your business, and I'll do it for the welfare of those people who work here, as well as anything else."

By lunch time all the details had been worked out. Robert was to go to London for a week, stay with Mr. Goodrich, who would help him get kitted out, and arrange a passage on the SS Batavia, which sailed every month, on a Tuesday. By leaving straight away, he would catch the next sailing, and would be in New York by the third week in October. Enoch would arrange the finances, with the Manhattan Chase Bank. Enoch also agreed to reinstate the Hatherton Penny.

Robert was on air. He walked the streets after work, unseeing and uncaring. Nothing could go wrong. What had looked like being a disaster had turned into a success beyond his wildest dreams. His conversation with Manstone had worked a treat. He hadn't had to own up to anything. He'd just hinted at some gossip, which was going round. He didn't know the truth about the gossip, he didn't want to know. If there had been reason for criminal proceedings, he knew Enoch would never be prosecuted, a man in his position, and it would only be the girl's word against his. What chance there, of a conviction? Besides, it would do no-one any good, in the long run, to persecute and ruin the man. So many people were dependent on him. And Enoch's family would be ruined along with Enoch, if it came to that. Besides Enoch hadn't accused him outright, of any dealings with Edna. Robert couldn't really understand what had happened. Enoch seemed to know, but at the same time, he didn't seem to know. The only fact he'd gleaned was that Miss Matilda had told her father she wouldn't come to the office anymore. Anyway, it had all turned out in his favour. He'd asked for a return ticket, too, saying that he would be returning in the spring, as he had promised to Gertie that he would come back and be married to her then. Whether he would or not was another matter. He'd try out the salesman job for a few months, and if he didn't like it, he would change to something else. The sky was the limit, once he was in New York.

"I'm going South, on Mr. Manstone's business, for a few days. I'll pay you now for this week. If it's to be longer, I'll send you word."

Robert was back in his lodgings to pack. He was catching the first train to Euston the following day.

"London, is it?"

"Oh, yes. London." He wasn't going to let Mrs. Jakes know about his final destination.

The old woman didn't press him. She knew that he was as pleased as a partridge. No doubt he would divulge more in his own good time.

"There's your shirts, Mr. Willoughby. I washed them this morning, of course, but they ain't dry yet for ironing."

"I'll collect them when I return." Of course, he wouldn't be returning. But he couldn't tell her that, or it would be all over the Potteries. He'd have to go and tell Gertie, before she heard from someone else. He'd have to go and see Frank as well. As he walked up the hill, he realised that this would be the last time he and his friends would meet. But there was no going back now. It wasn't easy, but he knew what he was doing. There would be other fellows he could sing with. More than likely those Americans would have glee clubs, and such like things.

The city suddenly seemed to be shrinking, like a party balloon, a few days after the party. He came to the corner, where he could see the steps and railings of the Institute at the end of the road. There was a light burning on the ground floor. That would be the lads.

"I shan't be singing tonight," he said, standing in the doorway. It would have been a good night. They were gathered round the piano, going through some music.

"Rob, you're early, ain't you? We did hear as there'd been some trouble at Manstone's and you'd been sorting it out. We didn't expect you tonight."

"Well, I'm here. But I'm not staying. There's no trouble, but fact is, I've to go to London, for them, for a few days, and I've to do some business, first."

"Business! That what you call it?"

Robert ignored this remark. "Shall us have a glass? I'll treat you. Just the one, mind."

"My word, things have changed."

"Well, can't pass an opportunity like that." They hurried to put on their coats and caps, and made off down to the Duck and Doublet.

"This is a bit sudden, ain't it, Mr. Robert Willoughby. What is it you do right, we dunna know of? Is it something you do with those brown eyes, I ask myself?"

Robert had the glass to his lips when Blundell spoke, and he disdained to answer. He merely glared over the rim. When he'd finished drinking, he wiped his mouth with the sleeve of his coat, and raised his eyebrows. Then he smiled.

The young man took this as a signal to go on. They were into the chase now.

"And which one is it? Does the lady's name begin with a G, by any chance?"

"You're in for some lip if you go off to London."

"Ain't you trying to rise in the world? We're not getting a bit above our station, are we?"

Robert was too happy to be angry. Soon, he'd be away from these clods for ever. Let them have their bit of fun. He wasn't going to be drawn.

"I'll be back in a few days, and I'll tell you what London's like."

"Oh. Ladida."

"I might even go to a concert, while I'm down there, if I can stretch to it."

....."Lucky beggar!" There was genuine envy in Blundell's voice. By whatever means, it seemed that Robert Willoughby was on the way up, and good luck to him. He began singing, and the other two joined in. "For he's a jolly good fellow."

They sensed that times would never be the same again. Rob was leaving their patch, they knew it, and he knew it.

"I'll tell you one thing. Old Manstone's made me a promise. He's going to restore the Hatherton Penny. He told me today. Himself. You're not to mention it till I give word. But there it is."

"Robert, you don't say!

"Will all the Masters do it now?" Everyone was talking at once.

Robert shrugged, and turned to go. That would keep them quiet for a while, and if Manstone went back on his word, then they'd tell everyone.

He left them. He had no regrets. It had always been a struggle for him to keep the group going. In some ways they had always seemed irresponsible and unmotivated.

On the way back he ran into Frank, coming out of the pie shop.

"All right?" Frank said, his face in the newspaper.

"Canna stop, Frank. I've a train to catch."

"Going Epsilon?"

"London. Tomorrow." Epsilon indeed! It was certainly time he was off, if the rumours were getting round.

"Will you be back?" Going to London meant a one way trip.

"Need you ask? Would I leave you all? Give over."

"Ta, ra, then." Frank raised his free hand.

Rob felt a sudden pang. When would he see Frank again? He'd not been of much use in the Union negotiations, but he was a good fellow, just the same. He'd like to have told Frank what he was about, but it was impossible, without stirring things. He realised, after he'd left the shop, that he hadn't eaten yet. With all that had been going on at the Works today, and the visit to the Bank and all, with Mr. Manstone, he hadn't eaten all day, and he was starving. No doubt, when he got as far as Gertie's, she'd invite him for tea, though, being Monday, she wouldn't be expecting him. But he couldn't accept a meal. That would be too much, in view of what he had to tell her. He went back a few paces, and ordered himself a pie.

Slowly walking down towards the canal, he began to realise, fully, for the first time, what he was doing.

It was a damp evening, the mist making the cobbles slippery. The flares from the gas lamps hardly showed him his footing. When he got to the waste land, which separated the streets round Gertie's house from the centre of the town, there were no lights at all, and, sliding about on the muddy path, he wished he'd taken the long route round, by road. He hadn't come by this path for ages, and obviously he'd have done better to avoid this rat infested, litter strewn, no-man's land. But of course there wouldn't be a next time. He wouldn't be here at Christmas, nor in the spring, when all this rubbish of broken pots would be covered with yellow and red flowers, and tall grass, sorrel, and elder bushes, with their pungent creamy blossom. He wouldn't be walking down the canal tow path again, where it ran along through the meadows.

He stood in the dark, with the sounds of the town coming to him from all sides, the clatter of trams, the pounding of a pot bank engine, which was working late, dogs barking and the shouts of some lads playing in a nearby street. How often, he thought, would all this come back to him? There was nothing for him here. He wanted to be off, and he'd best get on with it. No turning back, no regrets. He strode over the tussocky ground, towards Gertie's house.

Suddenly he was aware of someone in front of him, on the shadowy path. She was standing out, so he could not get by.

"Robert Willoughby! So you've come." She wasn't about to let him get past him. She had her stick out, and now, panting and wheezing, she pushed her face towards his. It was the old woman, Deaker.

"I been waiting for you, this past three hours, and yesterday. I knew as you'd be by, I knowed it."

"Compose yourself, Ma'am. It doesn't do to upset yourself. Now, just tell me what I can do for you?

"You don't need to put on those airs and graces," she continued, hardly able to get the words out, for shortness of breath. "Be off with you, Robert Willoughby, and don't be seen in these parts again, if you've any decent feelings for those who've helped you along the way."

Robert was completely stunned by this tirade. How had the woman managed to be here, at this time?

"I went to see your young lady, last evening, Lord help her. You get married to her, now, you promised, no more taking any liberties with those above you." She raised her stick.

"Now then, Missus, calm yourself. You'll be doing yourself a mischief."

"I know very well what I'm saying, but you're not getting me to breathe a word. No, I know my place and no-one shall get my secret from me," she screamed. "Get gone out of my sight.. I waited here all these hours, to tell you what I think, now get on with you, and do your duty, and leave honest folks be."

"I'll be saying good-bye to you, Mrs. Deaker. I've never done you any ill, and I don't wish to be your enemy. You'd do best to keep your nose out of my affairs. Good night. "

Deaker pushed in front of him, barring the way with her stick. "You shan't pass till you've made me a promise. Don't you come near to Mrs. Manstone, or her young one, again. Do you hear?" She had her face pressed up to him, her eyes flashing. She was screaming as loud as she could, yet the words were hardly coming out.

Robert put his hand on the stick, and pushed it to one side. "Excuse me".

Deaker lashed out, aiming for his head, but he was too quick for her, and once more, he grabbed at the stick. Her breath was coming hard, as she grunted and gasped, trying to wrench the stick back. He let go suddenly, and she staggered back. "Be off with you then. I'll have the Master after you. He'll see you get what you deserve. Evil blackguard, you are, evil, evil, you're the Devil's work. You should let honest people alone. "

But Robert had turned away, and was soon out of sight. In a moment, she stopped shouting. She leaned both hands on the stick, her respiration degenerating to wheezes and gasps. "Oh, Miss Edna," she muttered. "Devil damn him Damn him." Then began a piercing and awful pain, between her shoulder blades. It crept upwards, to her neck, then outwards, to both sides. Her head began to swim, and she bent double, her hands clutched to her chest. The pain grew and grew, it seemed to be pressing into her ribs, shouldering away every bit of breath in her body. It was a foul monster, breathing fire into her, then gnawing, gnawing, gorging itself on her life. The groans she gave out were not coming from her, but from the horrible thing devouring her. The dim light was waning, she could no longer see the path, nor the glow of the gas lamps in the streets below. "Robert Willoughby," she whispered. But he had quite disappeared. Gradually, she doubled up. Desperately, she tried to save herself, reaching out with her stick. But there was no purchase on the slippery path. She fell over, into the mud and slime. Her hands were clawing at the muddy cobbles. Then her face came down, she sensed the wet on her cheek. There was hardly a sigh. She lay still.

As Robert strode on, he glanced about to see if anyone had heard the argument with the old woman. There was no-one to be seen, and he was alone. His heart was beating loudly, and he had to control his breathing. Had Deaker been to see Gertie? It seemed obvious that she had. He'd been on his way to tell the girl of his departure to go to America. But now....He had half a mind not to go to Gertie's after all. What good would it do? But somehow, he had to go. And what of the old woman? He was amazed at the strength of her anger. What did she know? What would she tell Manstone? Surely he would cancel his offer if he found out the real facts. He peered back to see if Deaker was still there. Perhaps he should try to talk to her, reasonably. But there was now no sign of her. Anyway, she'd be unlikely to see Manstone before tomorrow. And once she'd found out about the America plan, she wouldn't pursue the matter, anyway. She'd want to keep quiet about it, to avoid scandal.

"There you are," Robert said, when the street door was opened by Gertie. She'd been suffering all day, on account of him. Now, she'd have the truth.

"Let me in a moment." He could smell her fresh sweat.

"I were just sitting down." She led him into the front room. There was no fire.

Robert immediately sensed that Gertie had had some fresh news. Otherwise, they'd be in the kitchen. "Why weren't you at Manstone's today? There was plenty on."

"I know that, all right."

"What does that mean?"

"It means I don't know as I trust you no more, Robert Willoughby."

"Who's been talking? You been listening to gossip."

"That's as may be."

"You tell me what's to do, before you say that sort of thing." Robert could feel the sweat breaking out in the small of his back. But what did it matter what Gertie thought, now? He was going to tell her he was off, anyway. He had a mind to get straight out of the door. But he held back, it wouldn't do to leave the town till this was cleared up. Why should he care? He didn't know.

"The person who told me isn't a liar. It's to do with that Miss Manstone. You've been after her haven't you?" Gertie had difficulty getting the words out.

"Miss Manstone! That wench! Gertie, is that what you think?" There was such warmth and relief in Robert's voice, that Gertie took it for sincerity. "Who told you that? It's a lie, a complete lie."

Gertie said nothing, just looked at him. "It was someone who must know something."

"Whoever it was has a vivid imagination." Robert remembered the words which Deaker had shouted at him." It was that old maid, weren't it? Any road, I didn't come here to have words with you. It's to tell you what Manstone said. If you want to hear it, we'll go in the kitchen, in the warm. I'm starving cold."

Silently, Gertie preceded him into the other room, where the fire was still alight in the range. He sat down and she stood on the other side, leaning on the mantel piece. Rob held his arms out. "Come on then, come on. Sit down here, with me."

Gertie hesitated still. "Is it all lies, then?"

"Come here."

She went over, and he put his arms round her waist. "I love you, my lass. I wouldn't take up with anyone else. And as for that female who told you all that, she must have lost her marbles. See?" He stroked her cheek, and smoothed her hair. "You're a lovely girl, you are. You know I love you." He buried his head in her warm body, she put her arms round his shoulders, and her face came down onto the back of his neck. He was so beautiful. His black hairs curled on his nape, she kissed them.

One of his hands was feeling down her thigh, and then to the hem of her skirt. "Let me in, wench. You'll like it."

For answer, Gertie pressed him closer. It was not too late to draw back. But it was. In herself, Gertie knew that now, now was the time. "We'll be married won't we, Rob. Say so, again."

"We are married. You know. Marriages are made in heaven." he pulled his hand back, and began stroking her breast, under the tight cloth of her bodice. "Will you be mine, now and for ever?"

"You were right. It was that old servant of theirs. She told me you had to leave town. is it true?"

"Yes. I am going. Tomorrow. But it's not what you think. "

Gertie immediately stiffened, and pulled away. "Going away? Then we shan't be married? Where to?"

"Don't be like that, Gertie. It's for the best. Manstone has asked me to be his representative in New York. New York, can you believe it? It's the best thing that could happen for us. I'll be able to send you money home, and you can save up, and look after your mother properly, and when I return, we'll be wed. If I have to go back, then we'll go together, when I've saved up a bit. You'd like that, you would." He took her hand and turned it over. "We'll have a better life. No more time in the pottery, painting cream jugs. Just looking after your man, and the babbies."

Gertie went over to the sink, and stood for a while, supporting herself with her hands on it, while she gazed out at the darkening yard. After a while, she turned to look at him. He was bending over the fire, poking at the embers, to coax them to flare up, his face lit up with the soft glow.

She went up to him, took him round the shoulders and put her cheek next to his. If he was going away, she had to have him, now. She had to. She would let him do what he wanted. That way, she would bind him to her.

"We shall be married, Robert, we must be."

"We shall be, we shall. I promise." He put his palms against her cheeks. "I promise, see. I do. There."

"Will you swear it?" Gertie suddenly realised what she should do.

"I will. We can be married, now."

She held his wrists, pulling her head back "How."

"Don't you know? I shall show you." He peered round the dim room. There, on the table was what he was looking for. Arranged on the lace cloth was the family bible, and a candlestick. He picked up the candle, and poked it into the fire. It flared up and he put it back in the candlestick. "Come here," he said, and took her by the hand to stand near the bible. "We'll both swear. To be man and wife. That's all you do in church. We don't need a minister for that. We can marry ourselves."

"Now, do you mean? Now? I'm not ready."

"You'll never be readier. You're beautiful, and I love you," he murmured again.

Gertie's head was lowered but when he said this she lifted her face. She smiled. Robert put his arms round her again. "Wait," she whispered, and picked up the candlestick, sheltering the flame with her hand. She lifted the latch on the door at the bottom of the staircase and listened. Just audible was the gentle, regular sound Mother made, when she was deeply asleep. Gertie turned her head, and took the candle, to find her way up the dark stairs. Robert was left in the dim room, lit only by the fire glow. Hardly daring to breathe, Gertie crept into to her own bedroom. Under the window was a large oak box. She opened the heavy lid, and out floated the scent of camphor. All her most precious possessions were in this box. She lifted them out, one by one. Here was one of her father's clay pipes, here her own rag doll, and the slate she had been given as a tiny child when she went to school for a while. There were her hair ribbons, and two little frocks she had saved for her own children, if she should ever have some. She lifted each article, and held it to her mouth. Here also were the few items she had already put by for her trousseau, stockings, petticoats, and bodices. She selected a nightdress. It was made of white cotton, long, with full sleeves, and ribbons with frills at the cuffs and neck. She had made it herself, last winter. Now she put her lips against the tiny pleats of smocking on the bodice. This would be her wedding garment. She undressed with trembling hands. She must hurry, he might not wait. Surely, though, he would. He'd promised her.

She rose to her feet, and stood, like that, completely still. If Robert wanted to keep in with Manstone, he would have to do what was right by her. If Mr. Manstone trusted him enough to send him off to America, with a good job, and money, then she could trust him too. Now, she would give him what he wanted. Perhaps too, when he came back, she would be free to marry, properly, in church. Gertie stifled this thought as soon as she had it. That would mean, her mother would be gone.

Dressed only in her nightdress, her hair on her shoulders, and the candle in her hand, she tiptoed down the stairs.

Robert was waiting for her, his back to the fire. He came towards her, and held her at arm's length for a moment. She still held the candle, high above her. Her breasts were just visible, round pale orbs, pressing against the thin material of the nightdress. She caught his hand, and pulled him towards the table. She put the candle down, and bent over the huge Bible. She laid his hand on top of it, and then her own.

"Will you be my husband, Robert Willoughby, to have and to hold, for better or worse, through sickness and health, till death do us part? " Her voice was firm, but low.

"I will," Robert heard himself say.

"Swear it."

"I swear."

"Now you must ask me."

"Will you, Gertie, be my wife, from this day forward, to have and to hold, forsaking all other, till death do us part?"

"I will, I swear it. I will always be here for you, I will always love you." She put her hand on top of his on the Bible. She knew she always would love him, as she did now.

"Then we are man and wife, and you are my bride," he said. He kissed her tenderly, on the mouth, and, seeing her cheeks were wet, he put his thumb under her eyes, and smudged away the tears. "I will make you happy."

She went limp against him, and he felt her breasts, then his hand went down to her round buttocks. He had been there before, with his hand, and Gertie knew what to expect, but now, it was different. She felt faint with longing, she would die for him, she really thought she would. She had nothing to fear. She wanted him, now and always.

"Is there linen in the dresser?" he asked.

"Of course." She dragged open the heavy drawer, and there were the sheets and towels. "She sat back on her haunches, feeling the love fluids, for the first time, wet on her skin.

In a moment they had spread a covering on the hard, narrow couch. Robert put his fingers to his lips, then pinched the candle flame, so that it went out. Only a thin skein of smoke remained

"Don't be afraid," he said. "Come and sit here." He took her on his lap, and spread her legs. She straddled him. He found her lips with his own. While she kissed him, he had found his way into her. She gave just a little gasp, then buried her head in his shoulder. She felt him within, she enfolded him, she was his. She watched him, with half-closed eyes. He seemed in some way, remote, totally involved with what he was doing. It was almost as if he had to do this. It was his work, it was what he was about. She saw the look of rapture come over his face. He had gone away from her, he was in himself, in his own world. She wanted to kiss him, to hold him for ever in her arms, like this. But he wasn't there for her to kiss. Where was he? She loved him so much, but yet, somewhere in her mind, she wondered still, did he love her? Where was he? Was this all it was, she asked herself? It had been so easy, and yet, what was it? She closed her eyes. She wouldn't think. She would just be aware of him, in her arms, at last.

A little later on, Robert lifted her off him, and laid her on the couch. "Rest there," he said. He went to the fire, and made it up, so the flames danced again. In their light, he could see her cheeks, rose-pink, and her hair brushing the floor. He squatted down beside her, his arm across her body. "Thank you, my darling." He was stroking her face, her eyes. "You have made me very happy. Soon, very soon, you will enjoy it as much. We both shall, together. "

"How can that be possible? You are going away. Tomorrow."

"You must be patient. As I shall be. And we still have tonight." His head lay on her breast, and she felt his ear, and tenderly touched his lips, with her own.

"I will wait," she said.

Later on, they made love again. Gertie felt so proud and glad. She knew now, what he wanted the most, and she could give it to him. She told herself he was her man, and she could please him. She would always do exactly as he wanted, so that he would be happy with her. She imagined him far away from her, on the steamer going over, and then in a strange town, or riding over vast distances, or in a train, crossing mountains. Everywhere, wherever he went, he would remember this night, and he would come back to her. She, too, would always remember it, this was her wedding night.

At last, she went to sleep, in his arms. When he realised she had drifted off, Robert suddenly felt cold. His back was aching. Very gently, he extricated himself, and stood up. He could hardly stand up, his legs had been bent beside the couch for so long. Picking up his coat, he moved backwards to the door, watching her all the time. Next moment, he was out in the street.

There was the faint glimmer of dawn in the sky. He would have to hurry, if he was to get his bag from the lodgings, and catch the first train to London.

Like a shadow vanishes when clouds come up, he was gone.

25

Edna was on edge, waiting for a message. She'd been to the wall, and looked desperately in the little damp hole where she'd told Robert to leave any messages. When she pulled the ivy away, wood lice scurried away from the sudden light but there was nothing else. She'd even been up to the byre in the field, hoping by some miracle, that she might find Robert there.

As she walked back to the house, an idea had come into her head, the idea that Robert was indeed going away. She couldn't picture life without him. If he went, how could she go on living? From deep inside her came the realisation that she might have to call on Tilly to help her in the face of a crisis, which now, she began to dread. But why should she fear that Robert would indeed do as Enoch said he would do? He wasn't going to America, she was sure. Yet a little weed of doubt was growing in her mind. Already, she was beginning to think in terms of "what if?" The unimaginable was taking shape, the weed might grow, its roots digging into the heart of her, the tendrils rising to choke her. She must fight it. There was no need to doubt, none at all. Yet the doubt was growing, growing. Why had he not contacted her?

The rest of the day went past so slowly. Tilly kept herself apart. She spent a long time in her room, trying to think about the contents of David Lockyard's letter. But it was impossible to think for more than a moment, without the memory of Mrs. Turner's face, so full of hatred, and the sound of her hoarse scream, 'they rich men, they think they can do anything, anything they please!' Anything, anything! What had she meant by that? Really, she knew what Mavis' mother meant. Tilly was struggling to shut her mind to the fact that the woman must be referring to her father. The woman hated him, for something. What that was, must be unthinkable. Tilly felt stony cold, but she couldn't stir herself to do anything. If only there was someone to comfort her. If only Deaker was still here. Or Ros. Ros, without actually knowing the reason, would be able to help her. Perhaps she could get a letter to her, and she could go and stay for a while, until she had decided what to do with her life. Tilly was struggling with a new reality, like a novice swimmer in boiling surf.

For Edna too, the long day dragged past. Every minute she was waiting for a letter, a telegram, or even, a visit. Every time the dogs barked she imagined that Robert had come to fetch her. All went past slowly, so slowly. She kept looking at clocks, the house seemed to be full of clocks, ticking, ticking, but going no further, all stuck on the same place. She took to her bed. During the night there was no respite in sleep, her mind was racing round all the events of the past few weeks. She remembered every time she had met Robert, right back to the time when he'd been in the office on Tilly's first day. From the first, she was convinced, she'd loved him. Her mind went on churning, churning. Why could she not have what she wanted? Just to have him here, coming to play the piano, that would be enough. To know that he was there, working in his office, speaking every so often to Enoch, even that would be enough. Even if she never saw him she could live on memories, and hope.

But there still was hope. He hadn't gone yet, and soon, certainly, he would somehow get in touch with her. At this thought Edna sprang out of bed, lit the lamp, and went to rummage through her jewel box, which she kept in her dressing table. She spread all her necklaces, bracelets and brooches on the bed, turning them this way and that so that the light made them sparkle. She didn't know how much they were worth, but she was sure they must represent at least a few weeks of Robert's wages. The pair of them could go away, and she would keep him for a while, till he got work.

She selected a gold bracelet from the pile, and a locket, into which she had once put a curl of Tilly's hair. Finding a lace handkerchief, she wrapped them both up and put them under her hand mirror. Then she went to her desk, and wrote on a piece of paper. *MATILDA...FOR YOU...FROM YOUR MOTHER*. She placed this under the mirror too.

She got back into bed, with her writing box on her knee. She had to compose a letter for Enoch. What could she say? What reason could she give for leaving him? But then, what reason could she have for staying? Tilly didn't need her. Deaker had gone, and might never return. Loving Robert had shown her the emptiness of her life with Enoch, the hypocrisy of it. She was getting older. She needed to be loved, before she died. Yet, didn't Enoch love her? Perhaps he did. The truth was, she, herself, needed to love someone, passionately and give everything up for him. She had to, she couldn't help herself. How could she explain that to her husband? She sat for ages, hunched up, with the box on her knee. It was no good. In the end she put the box on the floor, and as the first light was coming through the curtains, she slept.

At that time, Robert was already on the train which had left at six fourteen. He hadn't looked out of the window as the train sped through the grimy streets of town, and then through meadows, where the river meandered, and the canal cut a neat line beside it. He'd bought a Manchester paper at the station, and he was immersed in it when the first stop came, at Epsilon. He was aware of the stop, but he didn't look up. He had banished everything from his mind, which was totally occupied with his new life. He'd left Gertie's at about four o'clock that morning, and hadn't slept since. In the end he hadn't wanted to leave her. She was such a doll, and she'd clung to him, just gasping a moment from that first thrust. But she'd been pleased enough. If ever he came back, he would have her. The return to his lodgings, the packing up of his gear, and the walk down to the station, had ensured that he was too busy to dwell on Gertie. Nor was he about to fug up his mind with thoughts of his master's wife.

Edna slept late, and when Jeannie came with the hot water, she was told that the Master had already gone to the factory. Miss Matilda had gone to see Deaker. It was nearly eleven o'clock.

"Tell Tom I'll be going out. I shall need the carriage."

Edna's mind seemed to have cleared during the few hours she'd been asleep. She would go and find Robert, and confront him with what Enoch had said. One way or another, she had to know, today, what they were going to do. If need be, she would not come back. She washed herself, hastily, wondering where she would be when she undressed again. She put on her grey dress, black coat, and her hat with the veil. Into her reticule, she put various garments of underwear, and her toilet articles. She realised she couldn't carry all the things which she might need, and she became breathless as she kept dashing from drawer to drawer, packing some things, discarding others. There came a knock on the door.

"Wait," Edna hurriedly flung the bed cover over her little bag. She began to make some kind of order in the room, flinging things back higgledy-piggledy into the cupboard. "Come in."

"If you please, Ma'am, Tom wishes to know when to be ready. It wasn't clear."

"As soon as I've had some breakfast. Just make me some toast and a boiled egg. That will be sufficient."

Yes, Ma'am." Jeannie went out, with a slight frown. She'd noticed the disarray in the room. Had Missus lost something? There was no call to create havoc like that. It was all the more work for her, and Lord knows, she'd enough of that already. She proceeded slowly down the stairs. She wasn't going to be put upon like this, with no help. She'd a good mind to keep Missus waiting for her toast. She felt like a little sit down first, before going up those stairs again. Why couldn't she come down for breakfast at the proper time, with the others, like a Christian?

It was lunchtime when Edna finally arrived at the Works, and, as on the previous occasion when she had arrived at lunchtime, Enoch was out, the gate man informed her. That was a blessing. It meant she had every chance of seeing Robert on her own. Huge relief swept over her. It was all going to be all right.

"Fine for the time of year, Ma'am," the gate man said.

"Yes, yes."

"Makes the winter shorter. We could do with this while Christmas."

At that moment a dray pulled into the tunnel, and the driver came to ask for the inner gates to be opened. “Excuse me Ma’am. I have to check this dray. You’ll be well for a minute.”

“I’ll wait up in the office.” She went off, while the gate man was busy.

A few moments later, Enoch came in, after the dray.

“Missus has gone on up, Sir. She wouldn’t wait down here,” the gate man shouted, seeing Enoch.

Enoch raised his cane, and strode across to the wooden staircase. What on earth was Edna doing here? He had enough to do in the office, making arrangements for a new clerk, without gossiping to her, if she couldn’t be bothered to get up and see him off in the morning. When he reached the door, he saw her standing there, fiddling with the door knob. She turned round, her face pale and drawn.

“It’s locked. I don’t leave it open, you know. You should tell me to expect you, if you’ve a mind suddenly to come.” Enoch barked. Then in a slightly gentler voice. “Since you’ve come, you might as well have a warm up.”

She followed him in, peering at Rob’s desk as they went past to the inner office.

Enoch put down his stick, and hung up his hat. “I’m that busy, with no help. Matilda will have to come back soon, I can’t be doing it all alone. It’s more than I can cope with.”

“Where’s Willoughby?”

“He’s gone. Down to London, then he’s getting the boat to New York. I did tell you. Didn’t take long to make up his mind. He knows which side his bread is buttered.”

“Gone...not coming back?”

“He’s left. Passage booked and all. “

Edna stood there, shaking.

“Sit down, sit down.” Enoch said, pointing to the chair by Tilly’s desk. Happen she won’t be needing that today, so make yourself at home.”

Edna heard a strange roaring in her ears, and the world seemed to be getting dark. She turned towards the chair, then there was crash. She had fainted. Enoch had been making the fire up. He dropped the poker, and went towards her. She was so pale.

“Come on,” he shouted. “What’s up?” he took her hand, felt its warmth, and saw a little pulse beating in her neck. “Come, easy now. You’ll be all right, you’ll be all right.”

Edna stirred and her eyelids flickered briefly.

Enoch saw her reticule, propped up against the leg of his desk. “Salts,” he breathed, pulling the bag towards him. Surely she must have some of her medicaments somewhere. What did women do in these circumstances? The bag was full, packed tight, it was difficult to reach the bottom. A low moan from Edna made him panic, and he tipped all the contents onto the floor. A brush, comb, hairpins, and ribbons, handkerchiefs, underwear and blouses and all, fell jumbled up into a heap on the floor. He brought out a lumpy object, which turned out to be a silk scarf, made into a little parcel. This must be what he was searching for. As he untied the knot, all Edna's jewellery fell in a scintillating shower onto the floor. At the same time Edna recovered consciousness.

"What are you doing?" She tried to rise. "Those are my things!"

Enoch stood up. "What do you think? I am looking for your smelling salts."

"I haven't any. I don't need any." She knelt on the floor, aroused to full consciousness in the desperate moment, grovelling to pick up the brooches, bracelets and necklaces.

"There you are, calm yourself." Enoch retrieved a ring from behind the leg of his desk, and another, which had rolled over to the fireplace. His wife, who a few moments before had seemed to be at death's door, was now breathlessly but determinedly, scooping everything up, and flinging it into her bag. "All my things, all my things, on this dirty floor."

Enoch was standing now, with his back to the door. "I would like to know why you're here, and what this is all about."

There was no reply. Edna was kneeling on the floor, holding her bag, and all her things to her breast. She was weeping uncontrollably.

"What is it? What is it? Tell me." He bent down to raise her up, but she shook him off.

"Leave me alone. Don't touch me." she gasped.

Enoch pulled away, gazing down at her, his face suffused with red. "What is it? Tell me, what is up? Is there something the matter? What has happened?"

There was silence. Then, slowly, Edna pulled herself up on the chair, and was on her feet. "It's nothing. I fainted."

"That's evident, woman. Why, is what I'm after?"

Edna said nothing.

"Well, I suppose I can't make you tell me. Were you thinking of having your jewellery valued? If so, it's already been done. I've the certificate for it in my study at home. And what are all these doing in your bag?" He pointed to the various items of clothing.

Edna shook her head. She was blinking rapidly, trying to prevent the tears. Everything outside looked grey, grey grass, grey houses, grey sky. She was grey, Enoch was grey. She swallowed. This was to be her punishment, this sordid enquiry into her actions and motives. This humiliation, and all for what? Robert had gone. He'd deserted her. He'd never loved her, probably. He couldn't have, or he wouldn't have gone, without a word. What a coward! How could she have thought she loved him, allowed herself to be taken in by him? The last time she had worn this dress was the very first time he'd come to make music with her. She'd worn it specially this morning to please him. And now, where was he?

From somewhere, Edna found strength. She sighed and faced Enoch. "Yes. I was going to have my jewels valued. I may give some to Matilda. In fact, I have already, just two pieces of Mother's." The words came out, she didn't know how. "The other things, I was going to give to that poor family, we befriended, the one whose daughter came for a while, as scullery maid. I knew Tilly wanted to help them. She went there to visit. I want her to go to college, if she wishes. We could work it out for her, between us. Let's do it, Enoch. Here!" She held out the scarf with the jewels in it. "Take these, if you wish." Her voice was stronger. "Sell them, I don't need them, and it can go towards her expenses. There is no reason why she shouldn't go."

Enoch looked down at her white face. She wasn't crying. "And what about me? And the office?" As he spoke these words, Enoch realised how futile it all was. The whole of his life seemed to be ashes. Tilly must have found out about Mavis, that maid, if she had been to visit the family. That drunken spree, at Rosalind's wedding, that had cost him everything, everything which he really held dear.

"You can find someone else, soon enough. There's no reason why I shouldn't help you for a time." Edna could hardly believe her ears, that she was saying what she was saying. But as she said it, it seemed right. "If my daughter can do this work, then I'm sure I can."

"Well. I shall see. It may not be appropriate." He could hardly take in what she was saying. "Perhaps for a while."

"I hate to be at home, especially the last few months, when Matilda hasn't been there. And now, Deaker too....It will be so dreary." Her voice trailed off.

Suddenly there was a clatter on the stairs. The door was flung open, and Tilly entered. "Mother," she gasped. "Father," Her face was white, and she was panting.

"Whatever is it? What are you doing here? "Enoch asked.

"What is it, my darling?" Edna flung herself forward.

"It's Deaker. I've just been to her sister's cottage. And she's not there. No-one knows where she is. Her sister says she's been out twice since she left us. On Sunday. Then again, yesterday afternoon. She hasn't come back. I thought she might have gone home, so I went there to look for her, and she wasn't there either. So I came here. I had to come by train, that's why I've only just got here."

"We shall have to send a search party out. Maybe she's been taken ill again. Oh, Enoch." Edna felt the faintness coming over her again.

Enoch turned to the window, raised it, and shouted down to the gate keeper. "Come up here a moment. I want you to send someone to make some enquiries for me." He turned to Tilly. "You've done well. But this needs some thought. Where else does she ever go? Has she other relatives, or friends, from Church or owt?"

Tilly shook her head. Edna was sitting at the desk with her head in her hands. "We don't know. She never talked about anyone else, but her sister, and where she grew up. We don't know anything, Father," Tilly said in a gentle voice. It was true. To her shame, she realised that they were totally ignorant of everything about Deaker, except that she lived in the house with them, and was their servant.

Enoch, still scanning the yard, saw the gate-keeper in the yard, coming towards the stairs. Also, a little behind him, was a police constable.

"I think we'll have the answer in a moment," he said.

There came a knock at the door, and the two men came in, their heavy bodies imposing their presence on the cosy office.

"Mr. Manstone, sir," the constable said, taking off his helmet. "Madam, Miss." he nodded towards Edna and Tilly. "I have to tell you that a person by the name of Mrs. Deaker has been found dead near the canal. I presume this is your servant, sir?"

"Dead! Oh." Edna whispered. Tilly had gone white, and went to put her arm round her mother's shoulders.

"This is a great shock for the ladies. Dear me. Kindly apprise me of the details. She hadn't been well."

"All as we know, sir, is that she was discovered this morning, very early, by a workman, lying on the path which goes down to the canal from Crimea Street. We are not sure if there has been foul play."

"Foul play! By whom? This is terrible news."

"We have reason to believe that she had an altercation last night, with someone, near the very spot where she was found. Voices were raised, there was obviously an argument. On this account, we have come here today, to have a word with your clerk, Robert Willoughby. We have reason to think he may have some information for us about all this. Where is he?"

"He's gone." Tilly said.

"Gone?"

"Yes. My daughter's right. He's left. He is going for me, on business to America."

"Has he actually left? When did he go?"

There was a pause. "I couldn't say, exactly. I gave him the instructions yesterday, and the...." His voice trailed off.

"He hasn't actually sailed yet?"

"Yes, yes. He will have sailed by now. He's going straight to Southampton. You'll be too late."

"Anyway," Tilly said. "Deaker had been ill. She'd gone to see her sister. "

"Has the Doctor examined her? She has been very unwell. That is why she has been away from my house."

"Thank you sir. I will look into that. Has she any relatives, apart from the sister?"

"We know of no-one."

"Very well, Ma'am. I'll let the coroner know, and when the inquest is over, the funeral can proceed." He bowed to the ladies, and saluted Enoch. "If there is anything further, I will be in touch. If we find it necessary to speak to Mr. Willoughby, after what you have told us about Mrs. Deaker, I will follow it up."

"What did he mean by that, Father," Tilly asked, as the policeman's footsteps could be heard, going down the wooden stairs.

"They won't bother their heads about it anymore. All this about an argument, with Willoughby. That's not important. It's very sad, but there it is."

"Father. When did Willoughby leave?"

"I don't know exactly. He left the office lunchtime yesterday."

"But I thought you said, he was going to London for a week?"

"Yes, yes. But I had a telegraph from Goodrich. There was an earlier boat, leaving from Southampton and I answered to put him straight on the train. It was too good an opportunity to miss."

There was silence.

Tilly stood unmoving. She couldn't help doubting the truth of what her father was saying. For some reason he was protecting Robert Willoughby even to the extent of telling lies about exactly when he had left, or indeed, that he had already left the country. Perhaps there was no reason to think that he had had any hand in Deaker's death. But if the policeman had reason to believe that there had been a quarrel between the clerk and the old woman, then that might at least have hastened her death. For some reason, Father did not want the clerk to be back in Saghead. He wanted him out of the way, and now, he was out of the way, and he didn't want him reappearing. That would cause a scandal, especially if anyone found out the nature of the quarrel between Deaker and Willoughby. Surely, by her father behaving this way, he was making it obvious, that he knew all about the affair in which Edna had become embroiled. It suddenly occurred to Tilly that her father had probably known, for many days now, about what had happened between his wife and the clerk. Why was he protecting the man? Perhaps because he was protecting Edna, and himself, from gossip. Any breath of scandal might bring to light what it was that Mrs. Turner meant when she had screamed at her.

By everything that had happened, Tilly realised that they were all responsible for Deaker's death. She herself should have done more, to look after her mother, so that she wouldn't have become entangled with Robert Willoughby, as a consequence of loneliness and boredom. Perhaps, after all, she herself should never have come to work at the Factory. As for Deaker, they had none of them taken any real interest in her as a person. And Father. Well, she would never be able to face the thought of what her father had done. She didn't know how she could possibly have altered anything to do with whatever that was. And now, they all just wanted it to be hushed up, and consigned to oblivion, the whole sorry business of what had happened over the last few months. All this passed through Tilly's mind in the time it took for the policeman to cross the yard, leaving the gate clerk to shut the heavy doors behind them.

"Could we have some tea, Father," she asked. "My mother looks poorly." Edna was still sitting at the desk, her eyes closed, and her face pale. When Tilly spoke, her eyes opened.

Enoch broke the silence. "I'll take you both home. We'll have a rest, and then we have some decisions to make. I'll carry your bag, my dear," he said to Edna, as he led her out, down the wooden steps.

"Please go home by way of the Post Office," Tilly said. Enoch made no objection.

A few days later, Tilly received two letters which she had been waiting for. One was from Octavia Hill, agreeing to meet her at one of the houses she managed in Deptford, South East London. The other was from Ros, now resident at their new town house in Kensington.

From the Signal, that same morning, Enoch learned that the autopsy performed on the body of one spinster, Milly Deaker, lately a servant at Terrilea, the home of Mr. Enoch Manstone and his family, had found that the deceased had died of Natural Causes. The funeral was to be on the following Friday, at the new church of St. Michael's, recently consecrated in Epsilon, thanks wholly to private contributions, the main benefactor being Mr. Manstone himself.

"I will go on my own," Enoch said, having read the newspaper announcement out at the breakfast table. "There is no need for you two to come. In fact I do not wish it. There is no need for a great show."

Tilly laid down her egg spoon, with a sharp clatter. "I beg your pardon, Father. I wish to go to Deaker's funeral. And I am sure my Mama would like to go as well."

"Your father is quite right, Matilda. It is not seemly. Ladies do not go to funerals."

"I think that is nonsense, Mama. Of course we must go. And Jeannie as well. All the household. I loved her very much, and I know you did too. I am definitely going."

"She would not have expected it."

"Mama! I cannot believe you are saying this. Deaker was like a mother to both of us. The very least we can do, is show respect."

"And what about respect to my wishes? I do not wish to have this wrangling about what you will or won't do. If I say I will go alone, that is what I will do," Enoch growled.

Tilly folded her napkin, replaced it in its silver ring, and stood up.

"Please do not speak about respect, father. Some of the things which have happened in this household, do not inspire my respect. I do not wish to speak about them. And I do not suppose you wish me to name them. I think you know what I am talking about." She was standing, gripping the back of her chair, glaring at Enoch. "I am going to the funeral of my friend and nurse, and if I don't go in your carriage I will go by myself, on foot. Take you choice." She swept out of the room closing the door carefully behind her.

There, it was done. She would say goodbye to Deaker, on Friday, and then she would leave this house, perhaps for ever. Tilly sat down at her desk to write to Ros.

It took Edna and Enoch only an hour to accept the new facts of their lives. They only had each other, now. Tilly was going, had gone, in spirit, Robert would probably never be seen again, and Deaker was no more. They must make the best of it.

At St. Michael's Church, there was a good turnout for the funeral. The usual hymns were sung, the oration was made by Enoch himself. Tilly and Edna sat in the front row, both in long black veils, and the coffin was covered in flowers, the biggest wreath, of white, scented lilies, being from the Manstone household.

Afterwards, at the burial, Edna, Enoch and Tilly stood alongside the open grave, and together, they flung handfuls of earth on the coffin. So, it was done, another life over. Tilly put her arms round her mother, who was weeping, and their tears mingled. Things would never again be the same between them. But perhaps, one day, Edna prayed, they might even be better.

An invitation came from Ros, for them all to stay for a few days, at the Kensington hose. It was arranged that Tilly and her parents were all three to travel down to London together. Enoch couldn't be away for longer than the weekend, since the new clerk appointed to take Robert's place, wasn't yet fully capable, while the Master was away.

Edna would return with him. During their short holiday, Ros would show them the sights, and they could go shopping and round the museums.

They went to Saghead, to catch the fast train to London. On the station Enoch bought "The Times."

As the train got up steam, and trundled away from the bleak cityscape, Enoch opened the paper, and turned to the middle page. There were the details of boats which had sailed to New York, South America, India, and so forth. He turned to the passenger list for SS Batavia. He gripped his wife's hand by the wrist.

Out of his waistcoat pocket, he took a piece of paper.

"Read that," he said.

She unfolded it. It was a cheque for a thousand pounds.

"Enoch." she gasped. "What have you done?"

"I sold your jewels, and then put some more towards it. You can do what you like with it. It's yours."

Edna stared at him, then looked away, down to the paper unfolded on his knee. There was the name SS Batavia, and below, the newsprint appearing to glow, with the name of Mr. R. WILLOUGHBY. So he had gone on the Batavia, but not from Southampton. Enoch had misled the police. She held the cheque for a moment. She knew what Enoch was trying to say. He had wanted the clerk out of Saghead, and that meant he must have guessed what had happened between herself and Robert. But now, he was showing he understood her right to have a choice. She could leave him if she wanted. She had the money to go to New York, if she wished. She had never expected this outcome, that Enoch would actually respect her enough to leave her to make the decision herself, whether to stay or leave. She was overwhelmed. Her feelings, which had been swept away in all the despair and confusion of the last two weeks, now suddenly found solid ground on which to take root, and stability, again. Here was a man, who loved her, truly, loved her enough to let her do what she thought was the right thing for her. After all that had happened, he respected her as a real person, with a right to her own choice as to how to live her life. He trusted her. He must love her. She realised that her love for Robert had completely disappeared. Now that feeling was gone was anything in its place, in her heart? A moment before, she would have said there was nothing that she could name, just emptiness, like a muddy hole in the ground where once there had been a shining pool, full of reflections. But now, she realised, there was something there, a stirring of respect for this solid man beside her, a memory of how it had been between them, perhaps even a hope of something to come again.

Tilly was sitting on the far side of the carriage, with her face towards the fleeting landscape. Edna rose, and sat down beside her.

"This is for you, my darling. It's from us both. And with it, is the promise to try and find an arrangement which will settle you in London, for a while, so that you can further your education, or find employment, whatever is best. I know you have plans."

Tilly read the amount on the cheque. "Oh, Mother. It's impossible. I don't deserve it. "

"You do. Of course you do. It's what we want to do. To give you a better chance. I wish you to have it. Please do so."

"Of course I will. Of course. Thank you."

Tilly went over to her father and bent down to kiss his cheek.

"You've been a good girl. When all's said and done. I shall be proud of you. You've got a head on your shoulders. Now, don't let me down. You work hard. Have you decided yet what you are to study?"

"Law, I think, Father. And Politics. I don't know. I'll take advice. Yes, that's what I'll do. Various people, I'll need to see."

"Of course. What will you do after the studying? If you do it? Will it get you a living? "

"I don't know father. That's not why I'm doing it."

The train whistled, and in a moment, they were pounding through the station at Epsilon. A little further on, it ran along the canal bank. Tilly thought of the time she had been walking along there with Deaker, gathering blackberries. A minute later they were out of the town again, and by craning her neck, Tilly could just see, up on the hill, the beech woods round Terrilea. There it was, the house itself, its belvedere shouldering its way above the trees. George would be there, and Tom and the horses. In the garden, Jimmy would be brushing up leaves. But Deaker would not be there. She was gone for ever. And now, she herself was going, starting a new life. When would she return? The person she now was, would never return. She sat down, on the bench opposite to her parents. For once, she saw her father place his hand over her mother's. They were more than just her parents. They were ordinary, frail human beings, trying to make the best of life, in spite of ignorance and mistakes. She would have to be like that, she would have to compromise, and be tolerant, and snatch the occasional moment of happiness wherever she could, if she were to survive.

The door from the carriage onto the corridor, slid back and the steward appeared. "Three hours to Euston. Your orders for lunch, Sir?"

Enoch took the proffered menu. Tilly snapped open the brass clip on her bag. There it was, the letter from Octavia Hill.

"Are you hungry, young lady?" asked Enoch.

"I am, Father, yes," she replied.

Historical Background

In 1879 Lord Hatherton, who had been called in to arbitrate on a pottery dispute, gave an award which reduced the workmen's wages by a penny in the shilling. Another arbitration, this time by Mr. (now Lord) Brassey, also went against the workmen. Both decisions were received with the greatest dissatisfaction by the workers, and a strike followed, which ended without improving their position. This story is a fictional account of how the matter was resolved by the personal intervention of one of the pottery masters who restored the penny.

46813943R00176

Made in the USA
Charleston, SC
26 September 2015